Praise for *The Pet...*

"A densely hallucinogenic work of ... es ... Carroll's typically trippy imagery ...l; his Manhattan is eternally seedy and u... ...slovenly street vagrancies and Billy's trau.... moments are swift, hard-hitting prose. . . . A well-steered, sincere exploration of the art world's secretive inner politics."   —*The Village Voice*

"The novel has its discrete pleasures. It progresses in a series of episodes, some thoughtfully conceived and executed, such as the story of the origin of Billy's sexual dysfunction. . . . Another dead-on portrait is of Max, Billy's cynical art benefactor/father figure. . . . [Carroll] gives artists' block its due, too. . . . Billy and his creator meditate on the nature of art and commerce, love and sex, civilization and the wreck of the human heart."
                                                                 —*San Francisco Chronicle*

"A hot young artist's crisis of faith sets him on a quest for the divine spark necessary for personal resurrection."   —*Vanity Fair*

"With the posthumous publication of *The Petting Zoo*, we see how seriously Carroll took his responsibilities as a poet, the person who translates pain and beauty for the rest of us. . . . As the archaeology of the artist, [the novel] is fascinating."   —*The Portland Oregonian*

"In some ways *The Petting Zoo* is like 'poet's fiction,' like that of Rilke or Nerval—the genre of a poet's shift to prose in passionate, often elegiac, quasi autobiography. . . . [The book is] moving and poignant as insight into its author. You feel the autodidact trying to measure up, to alchemize his hard-earned experience and knowledge into fiction."
                                                                 —*The New York Times Book Review*

"Some reviewers have read *The Petting Zoo* as yet another installment in a Jim Carroll autobiography. . . . My view is that it is Jim Carroll without the bullshit, which is considerably more interesting than Jim Carroll the cult figure or Jim Carroll the heroin addict. . . . This is a novel about the difficulty of creating art, and of balancing the demands of art and life . . . a novel in which the author stares down death—his own as well as that of his main character. This will not appeal to every reader, but it ultimately makes for an emotionally wrenching book. . . . *The Petting Zoo* is the real thing."
                                                                 —The Recalcitrant Scrivener.com

ABOUT THE AUTHOR

Poet, musician, and diarist Jim Carroll was born and grew up in New York City. Talented at both basketball and writing, he attended Trinity High School in Manhattan on a scholarship and was an All-City basketball star, a period in his life vividly described in *The Basketball Diaries*. Carroll's first collection of poetry, *Living at the Movies*, was published in 1973 when he was twenty-two. His other books include a second memoir, *Forced Entries: The Downtown Diaries 1971–1973*, and the poetry collections *The Book of Nods*, *Fear of Dreaming*, and *Void of Course*. As a leader of the Jim Carroll Band, he released three albums for Atlantic records as well as several spoken word recordings. Jim Carroll died in New York City on September 11, 2009.

THE PETTING ZOO

JIM CARROLL

PENGUIN BOOKS

PENGUIN BOOKS

Published by the Penguin Group
Penguin Group (USA) Inc., 375 Hudson Street, New York, New York 10014, U.S.A.
Penguin Group (Canada), 90 Eglinton Avenue East, Suite 700, Toronto,
Ontario, Canada M4P 2Y3 (a division of Pearson Penguin Canada Inc.)
Penguin Books Ltd, 80 Strand, London WC2R 0RL, England
Penguin Ireland, 25 St Stephen's Green, Dublin 2,
Ireland (a division of Penguin Books Ltd)
Penguin Books Australia Ltd, 250 Camberwell Road, Camberwell,
Victoria 3124, Australia (a division of Pearson Australia Group Pty Ltd)
Penguin Books India Pvt Ltd, 11 Community Centre,
Panchsheel Park, New Delhi – 110 017, India
Penguin Group (NZ), 67 Apollo Drive, Rosedale, Auckland 0632,
New Zealand (a division of Pearson New Zealand Ltd)
Penguin Books (South Africa) (Pty) Ltd, 24 Sturdee Avenue,
Rosebank, Johannesburg 2196, South Africa

Penguin Books Ltd, Registered Offices:
80 Strand, London WC2R 0RL, England

First published in the United States of America by Viking Penguin,
a member of Penguin Group (USA) Inc. 2010
Published in Penguin Books 2011

1   3   5   7   9   10   8   6   4   2

Publisher's Note
This is a work of fiction. Names, characters, places, and incidents either are the
product of the author's imagination or are used fictitiously, and any resemblance
to actual persons, living or dead, business establishments, events,
or locales is entirely coincidental.

THE LIBRARY OF CONGRESS HAS CATALOGED THE HARDCOVER EDITION AS FOLLOWS:
Carroll, Jim.
The petting zoo : a novel / Jim Carroll.
p.   cm.
ISBN 978-0-670-02218-2 (hc.)
ISBN 978-0-14-312009-4 (pbk.)
1. Artists—Fiction.   2. New York (N.Y.)—Fiction.   3. Psychological fiction.   I. Title
PS3553.A7644P47 2010
813'.54—dc22
2010022393

Printed in the United States of America
Set in Palatino   Designed by Alissa Amell

A NOTE TO THE READER

In the monastic seclusion of his room, Jim Carroll, with a prescience of his own mortality, reached out and drew this novel—his last work—from the nucleus of his mysticism and remembered experience.

The Petting Zoo unfolds with a series of fated events. The artist Billy Wolfram is so profoundly moved by the paintings of Velázquez that he finds himself irrevocably altered. Stumbling from the Metropolitan Museum of Art into an eddy of avalanching absurdity—a defunct Children's Zoo, the Aztec façade of the Helmsley Building, the bowels of a dysfunctional mental ward—he diagnoses that he is no longer in sync with his former self. His descent and ascent, so candidly observed, are reminiscent of René Daumal's *A Night of Serious Drinking*, as our narrator reels from numbing cocktails to the nakedness of his mischievous soul.

The poet is the aural lamplighter. He projects himself within the labyrinth of Billy's burgeoning consciousness as he seemingly adjusts to the most outrageous turns of fortune. Jim's mythic energy is at once laconic and vibrating; his bouts of meandering humor are punctuated by undeniable common wisdom. Whether the discourse is with a Chinese psychologist, a Hindu driver, or an extremely loquacious raven, these Socratic dialogues slide pole to pole, from uncanny clarity or a realm where digression is an art of the first order, the multifarious zone of the nod.

Jim Carroll died at his desk on September 11, 2009, in the Inwood neighborhood of Manhattan, where he was born and raised. His diamond mind never ceased writing, even as he read, scribbling copious notes in the margins of his books, the references of his life: Frank O'Hara, Saint Francis, Bruno Schulz. He was without guile, disdainful of his beauty, red-gold hair, lanky body, abstract, bareheaded, empty-handed. Yet he was athletic with singular focus, netting his prey, able to pluck from the air with exquisite dexterity a rainbow-winged insect that quivered in his freckled hand, begetting memory.

The catastrophe of loss, the loss of a true poet, is so pure that it might for many pass unnoticed. But the universe knows, and no doubt Jim Carroll was drawn from his labors and the prison of his own infirmities to the distances of the greater freedom.

—Patti Smith, May 2010

A NOTE FROM THE EDITOR

Jim Carroll was putting the finishing touches on *The Petting Zoo* when he passed away on September 11, 2009. He had spent much of the previous years working on, talking about, and memorably reading scenes from the book in public. He had turned in a first draft of the book in early 2008 and had finished revising the first two parts of it by the end of that year. During the summer of 2009 he worked with Cassie Carter, a literary scholar and archivist, on further revisions. Jim's detailed notes enabled Cassie to assemble a draft ready for publication.

When this book was put into production earlier this year, the review of the copyedited manuscript and first-pass pages sadly had to be done without Jim. That work was undertaken by Rosemary Carroll, Jim's former wife and the executor of his estate, by Cassie Carter, and by myself. Our goal was to fiercely channel Jim, staying as close as possible to the way he left the novel at his death but not fearing to make changes (primarily line and word edits) that we believed he would have approved. Thanks must also go in this regard to Lenny Kaye for helping to clarify a few rough spots in the book, and to David Garcia for his invaluable assistance.

The Petting Zoo would not have seen publication but for the efforts of Jim's remarkable agent, Betsy Lerner, who patiently, methodically, and lovingly got the novel off the ground in the first place and continued to shepherd it through till the end.

—Paul Slovak, May 2010

PART ONE

1

All the trouble, of course, began with Velázquez. Billy Wolfram was running recklessly down the wide steps of the Metropolitan Museum of Art. Craning his head backward, he saw the huge banner with the old master's self-portrait hanging from the limestone façade. Billy was certain those cocksure eyes were fixed directly on him. Mocking him. The slick leather soles of his new shoes slid beneath him, but he recovered before falling. He sped up, watching the yellow streaks of cabs passing down Fifth Avenue. Then he turned his eyes upward to the lights swinging over the traffic like hanging torsos, frozen on red. He heard snatches of conversations from men poised on the steps, smoking in tuxedos: "So I told her it looked more like a pie chart." "I don't get these old masters . . . there's something so *Catholic* about them . . ."

He took the last nine steps three at a time, then sped south on Fifth Avenue until he reached the entrance to Central Park. His legs were straining to outrun the images in his brain and find some equilibrium in speed. A doctor friend once told Billy that he was prone to "racing thoughts." He moved slower now on the path beside the dog run, sweating through the seat of his tuxedo trousers. He was thinking about the sound of traffic out of view, and how alien the body seemed, how senseless and capricious. Nauseous, he started shaking so badly he wanted to collapse into the grass and rest, anything to lose the images of Velázquez, every detail in his paintings, every brushstroke now stuck in loops of racing thoughts.

He wondered what kind of man the old master was. Billy knew little about Velázquez in any biographical sense. Staring up at the trees, he resolved to change that, vowing to thoroughly research the maestro's life by the next day.

Billy Wolfram fixed his eyes directly at the sky, which was filmy and disguised by the lights and melancholy of the city. The cause of his outrageous behavior that night wasn't buried in some biographer's footnotes, but in the paintings themselves. It was their spirituality and haunting arrogance that had attacked Billy. The characters in the paintings still shouted out, and the volume grew until their seventeenth century voices sent him dropping to his knees. As if genuflecting in prayer, he remained in the grass and the sound of peasants, cardinals, and children of the aristocracy continued to taunt him now for the shortcomings in his own work and his frivolous life.

Billy raised himself up, returned to the path, and moved on. He had no idea how much time had passed, but despite the knees of his pants being soaked, he felt calmer. Some of the lampposts gave off light, others had been snuffed out by vandals' stones flung through the opaque casing. It was the type of bare, low light that encouraged danger and disguise, but in his present state of mind, rejuvenated by his rest in the grass, Billy walked south on the pathway without qualms or fear.

Moving through one of those semicircular brick underpasses, the ground filled with puddles and the walls with moss no matter what the weather, Billy recognized that, in his circumstances, there was no better place for him to be. In these shadows, this part of the park had no reference to time or place. He passed a homeless old couple sleeping beneath strips of cardboard. They looked up at him, both toothless, the man with a patchy gray beard. They could have been from any era or country . . . the French Revolution, resting after a day among the crowds gathered to watch the guillotine do its work, finding their only entertainment in its simplicity and precision.

He was speeding up, his body finally falling comfortably into place with his mind's delirious, disheveled drive. *It's amazing and terrible*, he thought, *distinguishing the ironies out of control within you, and not being able to do a thing about them.* What he needed was something to take his mind in another direction.

There was a fork in the path; Billy recognized that the turn to the left led to the zoo, remembering for no reason that the Latin word for "left" was "sinister." Within minutes, he was on a hill overlooking the zoo.

This was fate, he thought; this was exactly what he needed. Billy had loved zoos all his life. The Central Park Zoo was antiquated. It hadn't expanded its cages for the spacious simulacra of natural habitats that many modern zoos boasted. Nonetheless, there was a unique sensation walking around its minimal confines. It was the counterpoint of all those wild, exotic creatures existing right alongside the aloof residents of obscenely priced buildings on Fifth Avenue. Creatures strutting with such certainty a few short blocks away from the neurotic and trendy. This was what passed for irony in midtown Manhattan. It was all the irony people wanted in their lives, and it was all they could handle.

Halfway down the path leading into the main zoo's north entrance, Billy was confronted by an orange DayGlo sign, surrounded by a chain-link fence: CLOSED FOR RENOVATIONS.

Billy circumnavigated the barricaded site by following the grass beside the carriage path leading directly to the petting zoo. He picked up a flyer and read that it was still operating despite the reconstruction of the larger zoo. The fact that it would be closed for the night did not bother him in the least. Billy knew that animals would provide the perfect diversion to redirect his obsessed thoughts, and nothing was going to stop him from that necessity. He stopped for a moment and looked down at what remained of the old zoo. The tall spiked fence that once enclosed the polar bear still stood, and the huge centerpiece, the pool for sea lions, was all drained and dry. It wasn't as deep as he had imagined when he watched the seals circling the gray water and diving down until they were out of view. Now there were just two homeless men, barely visible in the moon shadows.

Though most of the lion house had been leveled, some of the cages were still intact. Billy felt the ghostly presence of cheetahs restlessly pacing. Beyond the brick tier of the monkey house, which remained standing, he could see the petting zoo. He moved down the rocks toward it. He could feel the animal spirits diffusing the dilemma of Velázquez, but not completely. The streetlight from Fifth Avenue played on the red and yellow leaves of the trees, and in them he saw the canvases from the museum. If he stood before a painting long enough, Billy had always thought he could reconstruct every moment of its creation. He could tell which were the starting strokes, the defining cuts of a palette knife, the transcendent afterthoughts in the thickness of pigment. It was as if he were standing in the painter's studio with him. Yet, despite the strange, shocking quality that he had seen in the maestro's canvases tonight, recreated now in the trees, he couldn't pull off that feat . . . not with Velázquez. He was blocked. "This is how it should be," he whispered to himself, before stumbling down the hill to the petting zoo.

There was a metal shutter closing off the entrance, secured at the base by a huge padlock. In his current state of mind, this didn't bother Billy. He walked around the side, where his only obstruction to the zoo grounds and the animals was an old black metal fence. Actually, at second glance, it looked rather imposing . . . a row of ten-foot-high rods, sharpened at the top. There was an old elm to Billy's left, however, growing right up against the outside of the fence. It might as well have been a stairway leading to a slide into the zoo. Its limbs were low to the ground, extending outward into the zoo, only about ten feet from the pond, where a duck floated alone in the dazed, diffused moonlight.

He climbed the tree with ease, but once he reached a suitable height to scale the fence, it was somewhat trickier finding a branch that would both carry him into the zoo and support his weight. He tested one, and though it began to bend precariously, he realized it would only take one more step before he could lower himself into the zoo. He took it, and the branch snapped beneath him, quickly and loud. Billy lurched forward, miraculously sidestepping the pond and landing on his feet. His tuxedo was barely wrinkled. It was amazing.

Billy surveyed the place, walking toward the glass-encased pavilion at the entrance. The lampposts offered just enough light for him to see clearly, accentuating the atmosphere of the place. The little zoo was a remnant of a bygone architectural age—the Candy Land school, circa Cold War 1950s. It had a theme, an odd mixture of fairy-tale and biblical references, and abounded with details. There were the "Three Little Piggies," with houses of wood, straw, and brick. Of course, the actual pigs themselves lived in a rusting tin A-frame and were hardly little, but gigantic sows, pushing the 300-pound mark. They were also extremely unattractive, their bodies a bloated pink, with a few bristly clumps of thick hair.

There was a small Noah's ark, cantilevered out over the entrance to the pond. The pond was the centerpiece of the petting zoo, normally filled with ducks and geese. Near that was an exhibit of tropical fish housed within a glass window encased in a huge blue whale. The whale looked like something on top of an Eisenhower-era drive-in restaurant with waitresses on roller skates. Most of the fish were dead or dying. The whale's exterior paint was peeling badly, but its schizophrenic eyes still stared above a lunatic white smile.

The petting zoo rattled Billy's painterly instincts. On the day it opened, everything about it had had a postwar flamboyance, the colors lurid, artificial, and bright. Now, from time and the city's exhaust, they had faded like the decorations on a birthday cake that had sat far too long in a bakery window.

There were ponies in their red stable, locked away for the night, along with a recalcitrant llama that was fond of—and accurate at—spitting on onlookers while standing in his cramped, sorry quarters. The tops of the lampposts were shaped like buttercups. There was a black wrought-iron birdcage crowned with a wire sculpture of a robin swallowing a worm. This cage was fairly large but hardly large enough for the two fully grown birds inside, hunched sullenly on their perches.

Billy didn't have to break into Noah's ark, since there was no door on it. He quietly slouched up the gangplank and entered. There were ten small cages. Eight were empty; the other two held two shaggy rabbits. They looked rabid. "Rabid rabbits," Billy whispered to the cowering bunnies. It was a fairly pathetic attraction. Why did they call it a *petting zoo*? he wondered. Everything was encased; you couldn't pet these rabbits if you wanted to, and it was doubtful anyone would. Still, Billy reached a single finger through the wire mesh as best he could, and one of the furry creatures actually moved closer. With the tip of his pinky, Billy managed to flick off some of the ubiquitous crud caked beneath its left eye. He tried to get to the other eye to clean it as well, but the rabbit withdrew to the back of the cage. That was enough time for Noah's ark, and he headed for the exit.

About to step onto the gangplank, he forgot to duck while moving through the kiddie-sized doorway. Crack! Billy smashed his head just above his eyebrows. He saw brilliant comets emerging and cracking apart from a deep cherry-red background. The red then dissipated and was replaced by spirals of nausea. He almost went out, his legs buckling beneath him as he reached out blindly and grabbed on to the wood casing of an empty cage.

Lowering himself to one knee, Billy waited for his head to clear. He was thankful that the impact had thrown him backward rather than straight ahead. He imagined the embarrassment of tumbling forward down the gangplank of Noah's ark, directly into the pond, flopping and splashing about, not to mention the ancillary pain of being attacked by obstinate geese. He hesitantly checked his forehead as he began to rise, squeamish about confronting the size of the lump. It was large, worse than he expected. Also, there was blood on his hand—lots of it. He could now feel its slow traverse downward into his eyes and past his nose. It was time to leave.

Billy came to a halt near the birdcage. He gave a quick look around and, to his dismay, discovered that he was trapped inside the petting zoo. There were no trees growing from the inside over the fence, so he was not going to be leaving the way he got in. He decided to circle the edges and see what his options were. On the outside edges of the zoo, dozens of trees grew right beside the fence, but there wasn't the scrawniest sapling rising within the zoo to help Billy boost his way over the fence.

He was about five feet past the cage when he first heard the voice: "Quite a whack you got there, eh?" It was a strange-sounding voice, and though it was slightly high-pitched, he knew immediately that it was male. Billy chalked it up to the effects of a mild concussion. Billy heard the voice again, this time infinitely more distinct: "You have to remember where you are, and when to duck. A painter should have a better understanding of scale. By the way, if you're lost for a way out, there's a ladder over there leaning against the ponies' so-called stable."

Billy turned around to face the birdcage only a few feet behind him. It was the only place that the sound could have come from. He circled the structure and found nothing and nobody. He surveyed every direction and there was no hint of any speakers, microphones, or amplifiers. Besides, there was nothing electronic, no matter how sophisticated, about that voice. In the cage were perched a sparrow hawk and a raven, the raven's talons dug so deeply into a wood branch that the bird could have been stuffed. Nonetheless, as Billy looked down, he could have sworn his peripheral vision caught the black bird opening and closing one eye. Quickly turning back, he saw the bird's eyes were once more tightly shut. Now, Billy assumed, he was dealing with visual as well as auditory delusions.

It was all some form of passing insanity, he was about to conclude, but whoever had done the speaking in this elaborate trick was, thankfully, as good as his word. Across the park and in the shadows, Billy saw a large painter's ladder on the side of the red pony stable. He turned and headed for it. As he was dragging the aluminum ladder toward the tree where he had entered, Billy heard the voice one more time: "I'll be seeing you soon. Good luck with your quest."

Billy found a path leading out onto Fifth Avenue. He crossed it and began speeding across 64th Street toward Madison. The voice was right, he thought; he did have a quest before him. Only now he wasn't just seeking equilibrium in speed, but sanity as well. His thoughts were racing, but his legs could no longer keep up with his brain. He was exhausted. He stopped at the traffic island on glittering Park Avenue, looking downtown, the chain of lights there, red, yellow, and all that green, all ending with the golden-lit façade of the huge Helmsley Building. It seemed like an Aztec temple. They offered their heroes and losers to the gods. All the colors kept repeating, mixing with racing thoughts of bloody Aztec sacrifices, crude stone knives, and buttercups in nursery rhyme. It caused a feeling of vertigo and settled in his mouth with nausea. Leaning over the well-tended hedge, he puked onto the flower bed and collapsed to his knees.

Billy's forehead rested on some cool shrubs. He was just beginning to feel his body settle when a twig sprang out of the bush and slapped him in the eyelid. He saw stars . . . literally, stars in black and white clusters scanning galaxies dripping paint, old as the big bang, fresh as the cans of acrylic in his studio. The voices in his mind were giddy. More nursery rhymes. Sharply polished daggers of milky quartz crystal, dripping with blood. Golden rays and human sacrifices in the glowing Helmsley Building. Still on his knees, Billy vomited again and pressed his hand to his face.

He finally opened his eyes and saw nothing but a blank expanse. *Good*, he thought. *I'm blind*.

To Billy Wolfram's immediate regret, sight was returning to his eyes. First he saw an abstract field of colors beneath the bright streetlights, then there was a return to tear-swelled focus. It must have been an optical trauma from the whacking by the shrub branch, or perhaps a hysterical symptom of his racing thoughts. That didn't matter at the moment. As he wiped the fluid blur from his eyes, he realized that he was sitting in the back seat of a police car, speeding uptown with lights and siren on full tilt. Yelling above the spinning red noise, he asked the cop in the passenger seat what was going on. The cop, playing with the foil from a gum wrapper, didn't even move his head to face Billy as he curtly informed him that he had been deemed a danger to himself and to others. This, by law, meant that they were forced to secure him to the nearest psychiatric hospital for evaluation, and they were at that moment on their way to Metropolitan Hospital Center on 97th Street. "You can't be out on the street yelling to every passerby that you're about to sacrifice them in a ritual stabbing," the cop said, still staring forward. "That's known as making threats. Can you grasp what I'm saying, sir?"

"I wasn't doing that," Billy replied. Authority figures scared the hell out of him. "I wasn't threatening anybody. I was making a joke was all it was . . . saying that this is what people were doing in the Helmsley Building. There was no harm intended."

"It wasn't a very funny joke, sir. The doorman who called it in said you had a knife. Now, we looked around and did not find any knife, but that doesn't mean you didn't toss it and we just couldn't come up with it."

"I didn't have any knife." Billy had grown from scared to confused. "Surely you searched me and found no weapons. I was talking about those ancient stone knives that the Aztec Indians of Mexico would use in their sacrifices. That's what I meant was going on in the Helmsley Building. The way it was lit up it reminded me of one of those Aztec temples."

"Forget about the knife." The cop finally turned and spoke to Billy in profile, squinting at him through one eye. "Nobody saw a knife, so we're not going to worry about that. The threats you were shouting—which were substantiated by witnesses—were enough. Anyway, I thought you were blind. You kept yelling you were blind. And what's with the gash on your forehead? Is that where the blood on your frilly white shirt came from?"

"I'm not blind! That was just a temporary thing from getting poked in the eye by a bush . . . and as far as this cut on my forehead, that was another accident, running into a low, uh, tree branch. This whole thing is all a mistake. I was just a little confused and upset, and certainly had no intention of hurting anyone. It was nothing more than a bad moment, a kind of fugue state I guess you'd have to call it. You see, I was having a bad reaction to these paintings I was looking at. I'm an artist and the perspective broke down into an essence I couldn't sustain. They just freaked me out and I began to run and . . . well, that's not important at all. It was all *a bad moment,* man. Really, my head is quite clear now. I don't need to go to any hospital. I'm fine. If you'd just be kind enough to take me back to the Metropolitan Museum of Art, I'm quite certain that my dealer would vouch for me."

"Your *dealer,*" the cop said, perking up. "You're beautiful, pal. I'm sure your dealer would vouch for you. I mean, you must be one of his best-dressed customers. We don't even know who you are for certain. You have no I.D. on you . . . just four thousand in cash. That's serious money, especially for an artist. We got the line on artists, and most would be doing well holding four dollars."

"No, no, no," Billy burst out nervously, seeing this was all taking a truly bad turn. "I mean my *art* dealer. I'm a painter, and he works for me, selling my finished pieces. He owns one of the largest galleries in New York. You guys thought I was referring to some kind of drugs thing? That's ridiculous. I pride myself on never having taken any drugs. I have a lot of friends that abuse various drugs, but I've never touched them. See, this is all really some big screwup. I never carry I.D. on me, but you can call up the Met on your radio and check me out. Please, turn your car around, or just let me out. I'll get a cab and go straight home."

"We can't do that, sir," the driver said, speaking up for the first time as he turned onto 96th Street. "People signed complaints, so at this point you are in the system and we're just doing our job. You can take it all up with the doctors. Don't be upset, now. I'm gonna bet that it's all gonna turn out to be all right. By the way, would you care to give us the names of some of these friends of yours? The ones who take all these drugs?"

The other cop began to shake in silent laughter. Billy saw that his fate was sealed. He was going to be checked out by head doctors in some ratty psycho ward. He sank into the back seat, resigned, wishing that the blindness had lasted longer. "Fucking Velázquez," he whispered.

2

S itting in the lobby with a large orderly hovering over him, Billy was now lucid enough to find irony in the fact that he had started the evening in formal dress at the Metropolitan Museum and was now winding it down in the loony bin at the Metropolitan Hospital. Where was his wallet? Where was his dealer—shouldn't he have been capable of tracking him down by now? And where were his lawyers and all the other art dilettantes now that he needed them? It was really beginning to sink in. If nobody found him soon, he might be in some leaky adjunct of this place for the night, if not longer. The cops had finished up at the front desk, signing off on their paperwork, and gestured good-bye to Billy as they left. The one who had been driving winked. As they passed through the sliding doors, Billy heard the other one say to his partner, "Jesus, I really hate this hole."

After the cops left, a nurse took Billy down the hallway of the ground floor and had him sit on an examination table in a room crammed with people. A few were on similar tables and some already lay in beds. From the frenzied atmosphere, Billy concluded that he was in the emergency room. To his left, a frail old woman with shrunken lips was groaning as nurses inserted I.V. tubes into the back of her hand. The more serious cases were surrounded by curtains, which rustled from the cutting and probing elbows of doctors. Some patients were just old and fragile, lying in their beds, their faces so filled with misery and loneliness that it seemed they would welcome death if it would take away the fear.

Eventually a young intern approached Billy as a nurse cleaned out his wound, a sluggish abrasiveness to her technique. The doctor peered closely at the wound, then called out for a certain-numbered suture. His breath reeked of cheap take-out Italian food. Billy was in such a bewildered state that he barely felt the needle sewing across his forehead. "Should hardly leave a scar," the doctor said in a terse night-shift manner. "I gave you four stitches. No more, no less, all right?" The intern then took a penlight and carefully examined Billy's eyes. "Well, you don't seem to have any signs of concussion. That's good news, right? All the same, take it easy, and next time remember to duck."

After the nurse had bandaged Billy's head with an industrial-strength Band-Aid, an orderly took him by elevator to an upper floor, then steered him through a maze of well-waxed corridors. The beefy escort was holding a model car that he had obviously built himself. It still smelled of wet glue. "It's the same make of car that James Bond drove in his early movies," the large young man informed Billy. "The only thing is, I can't get the license plate on correctly. When it's on right, it's supposed to flip up and a small machine gun pops out. We're almost at the ward; it's just around the corner."

They arrived at a metal door. The orderly realized he had to put down the model car somewhere in order to press the button on the intercom. Hesitantly, he handed the car to Billy. "Be careful, now; it's very fragile." As the orderly pressed the intercom buzzer, Billy tried the wheels of the car in his hand to see if they would spin. As he did so, both wheels and the tiny metal axle fell to the floor. He was on his knees, blabbering apologies and retrieving the pieces, as another huge aide opened the thick door, which swept inches past Billy's head. He looked up sheepishly and handed the car and its broken bits to its owner, who turned and walked away without a word. Billy then felt truly lost. It would have been better if the fellow had expressed the rage he must have been feeling. He knew, however, that the only reason the model maker restrained himself was because he now viewed Billy as another hopeless mental case, incompetent as all the others.

Another orderly looked down at Billy, who remained on one knee. "You're pretty much all registered in, sir," he said softly, as if he were about to hand him a motel key. "We simply need a few signatures from you on some documents. Come this way, please." Billy took a moment before rising, picturing himself as he was . . . kneeling at the threshold of a city-funded abyss.

Billy Wolfram was led into the locked wing of the mental ward. Nobody was waiting for him in the admittance office. Killing time, he pressed his face against the small rectangular glass window on the steel door he'd just entered. It was one of those perfectly square windows made of safety glass with that octagon-shaped wire throughout.

"Hmm . . . minimal art," he whispered, moving his head back to see the window from a different angle. He couldn't help himself. It was the octagons. Wires embedded inside thick glass. The lyrical tension between the two surfaces, and the glass colored in a slightly greenish blue tint.

Moving his face against the window again, he could see across the hall. There was a similar door leading to another, apparently symmetrical wing. Later he discovered that this was the section reserved for the seriously ill and dangerous patients. Many of them were criminals handcuffed to their beds in locked-down rooms, waiting to be evaluated by shrinks for upcoming court cases. "You don't want anything to do with the animals on that side of the building," one of the friendlier attendants would tell him. "Even the workers over there become savages in time. The tales I could tell . . . hideous, mindless violence. Matricide, molesters, cat killers."

Still waiting for the doctor, Billy noticed the only person in sight was an attendant sitting in front of a bank of closed-circuit TV monitors. He swung around in his seat and spoke to Billy, anticipating his questions and seeming slightly annoyed by them. He told the new patient that several well-dressed men, who said they represented Billy's interests, had been downstairs less than an hour earlier, speaking to the hospital authorities on his behalf. However, Dr. Hui, the acting head of the psychiatric ward, had turned them away with polite dispatch. "I know you're a big-shot artist who's got plenty of people with power hanging on your coattails," the slick young man explained, "but all that don't cut ice with Doc Hui. The boss is a Korean glacier, and everything runs strictly by the rule book on his watch. Once you are signed into the system, you are in until you see the doc, or 72 hours, whichever comes first. After that, your outside sources have the option of transferring you to a more upscale institution."

Billy conjured up an image of his dealer, socialite collectors, and a phalanx of quickly plucked lawyers who, after hearing of his frantic departure from the Met, began searching for him on the streets surrounding the museum . . . somehow, however ineptly, winding up at the hospital. Billy wasn't too disappointed at the news of their late arrival. In fact, he'd been expecting it. Even if they had spotted him speeding out of the place, it is a truism of the art scene that dealers can't run. He assumed they'd come back in the morning with more juice, perhaps from one or both of the U.S. senators from New York State who had Billy's work hanging on their walls. Yet for some reason he didn't quite understand, Billy was starting to realize that it might be better if nobody pulled any strings to free him and he used his time in the mental ward to sort out the panic that Velázquez had evoked. He had a solo show coming up and was supposed to deliver the works to the gallery in a bit over two months. He needed to get his mind on the paintings. What better place than these spartan surroundings to be alone and figure out his options?

Billy realized the attendant was still talking to him. "Besides," the attendant continued speedily, as if he had been given free rein to the cabinet containing amphetamines, "you have no idea how many celebrity types we have coming through here, especially on the weekends. Professional athletes . . . you'd never think it, but they lose it more often than you'd imagine, though it seldom lasts longer than a day or two. Amazing, these fellows. They come in looking lobotomized and, within three days, walk out absolutely shipshape. Usually some kind of drug thing, you know what I'm saying? Wink. Wink. Baseball players, especially pitchers, are under the most stress. Left-handed pitchers have always been considered flaky, anyway. Football players are usually admitted for the longest time. They have to monitor them closely to tell if their problem is mental, or the result of their brains getting smashed so hard by some 400-pound Samoan lineman that it sends the *compos mentis* flying right out of them. Then they ship the guy down to neurology.

"I'm sure we've had some painters in here before, but I can't recall anyone specifically. Of course, I couldn't give their names even if I did. Anyway, you're scheduled to meet with the good doctor yourself now. That's his office in the unmarked room behind you. He's really not a bad guy."

The celebrated Dr. Hui was about to begin his session with Billy when loud noises erupted from a distant end of the wing. In a silky voice the doctor put Billy in the charge of another attendant while he went to handle what was apparently a violent incident with one of the patients. The slight Asian man carefully yet hastily loaded up a syringe from a vial inside a small locker on the wall, like a SWAT cop checking the ammo clip on his weapon, then followed behind a hulking attendant, disappearing into a side door at the end of the wing.

Billy sat anxiously in the shrink's office, waiting for his return and his orientation dialogue to begin. Within a few minutes, the attendant came back and informed him that the situation that had called the doctor away was a bit more serious than initially thought. The doctor would be much longer than anticipated. It was decided the best thing to do was to get Billy into a room and allow him a good night's sleep. Billy was not big on procrastination, but he had no problem whatsoever with this plan. His brain had settled into a more lucid state, and he had a lot to think about. The solitude of a bed, even in a mental ward, seemed a fine place to sort out his concerns about the Velázquez incident. As for the voice in the petting zoo, Billy had no choice but to write that off as a symptom of brain trauma from the whack above the eye. It didn't matter that this was contrary to the emergency room doctor's diagnosis that ruled out a concussion. At the moment, any other possibility was simply too much for Billy to contemplate.

When he began to rise from his seat, however, he noticed that the attendant, who finally introduced himself as Bruno, was cautiously filling a syringe with a liquid agent from an interestingly shaped tiny bottle. The shape reminded Billy of a container for designer perfume. "Something to help get you off on a long night's rest," the beefy man in white offered casually. Billy began to protest, but before he could stutter out the words, the needle had penetrated his right bicep and the drug was being pushed into his system. "Just a bit of the old benzodiazepine to warm that chilly frontal lobe."

Unlike practically all his acquaintances on the art scene, Billy was a full-out virgin to drugs, a complete stranger to the spectrum of effects which varying drugs had on consciousness. Even his closest friend, the rock musician Denny MacAbee, himself a world-class drug abuser, could never entice Billy to take a tiny hit off a joint, even when they were teenagers. His entire knowledge of drugs was based on the testimony of friends and various literary sources. Billy was now awaiting a potpourri of everything his friends had raved about over the years. He was waiting for the doors of perception not only to open but to unhinge themselves from their jambs. However, Billy didn't understand that the function of the drug he'd been given was to erect a concrete wall, without doors or windows, to block out any and all perception.

Billy wasn't expecting the physical sensation radiating throughout his entire body. The shot made his legs feel like the veins had been drained of blood and filled with heavy molten lead or, more likely, mercury, the metal of alchemy. He could feel this metallic blood shifting from one leg to the other as he leaned left and right in the chair. It was fun. He just sat there in the chair playing this game with his legs. There was something interesting about this drug thing, after all. It simply wasn't what he was expecting. This wasn't about the mind at all, but rather a sensuous thing. He was expecting something epic, and all he got was a few couplets that didn't scan. He couldn't imagine anyone wanting to walk around in this state on a regular basis, however. Even though drugs allowed one to maintain an initial sense of politeness and surface enthusiasm, Billy was still convinced that they stole from the deeper passions.

Bruno raised him from the chair, grabbing him by the arm and hoisting his entire weight without any assistance from the artist. It took Billy several moments until he realized that he was indeed standing, and just how difficult this was. There was a rush to his head. Everything seemed condensed. In his tranquilized memory, all the events Billy experienced that night were like the *Reader's Digest* condensed novels his mother had received every month and kept in the bookcase in his room. Space itself was also condensed. The hallway didn't seem as wide, but much, much longer. Billy wasn't sure if the mercury in his legs would allow him to make it to his room. He wondered if, had he begun to bleed, it would be bright silver. Once he began moving, however, it didn't seem difficult at all. He barely needed the attendant's crushing grip supporting his elbow, but the aide had no intention of letting go.

Billy's room was about halfway down the long corridor. His hospital clothes and a pair of remarkably cheap slippers were laid out on the fresh sheets of the bed. Bruno stood there as Billy changed into his new duds. It wasn't easy, under the influence of the drug, undoing the tuxedo, and it was only at this moment that Billy realized how idiotic he must have looked as he pranced about in his formal wear. After he deposited the tux and its accessories into a large box, he slipped into the hospital outfit. The clothes were light green, threadbare, with a scratchy granular texture. Bruno took the box and exited the room, securing Billy's things in a locked storage space near the entrance.

Billy followed Bruno into the hallway, but the weight of the drug quickly returned, covering him like a lead cape, and he backtracked into his room. He tried out the bed and it wasn't bad at all. It was still only 10:00 p.m. and most of the inhabitants of the wing were huddled in the group room, taking in the last hour of TV time.

As Billy lay on the bed, he traced the earlier events of his day, looking for the slightest clue to what had led to his freak-out at the Met. He shut his eyes. The drug didn't overwhelm his brain with psychedelic images, or pull a plug, leaving only blank oblivion. Instead, it just slowed down his internal landscape, making it easier to filter out the racing thoughts and slow-flowing detritus of the brain, while leaving him surprisingly lucid. The train of thought just ran on a much slower schedule. So Billy recalled his day before leaving for the museum in crystalline detail.

He had been late getting out for his daily walk. He was, by nature, an early riser, and there were times he was out, "digging the streets," as he referred to it, before 6:00 a.m., in the motionless afterglow of New York's deeper darkness. On this day it was almost 9:30 when he made it to the sidewalks.

Billy had walked purposefully from his loft, across 22nd Street, and uptown to the Empire State Building. A gray day and gray buildings, all the faces he passed with eyes shaped like flint arrowheads. He wanted to see the city from a great height. It was nothing more than a whim that had come to him as he'd showered an hour earlier.

Like many native New Yorkers, he had never been to the observatory of the great building. The film *King Kong*: that was, of course, what he thought of when he saw the building. He remembered watching it when he was seven and eight years old, sitting on the living room floor before the large television console with the very small screen. It played at least twice a year on *Million Dollar Movie*, a nightly program on a local New York station. *Million Dollar Movie* ran the same movie every night for an entire week, and Billy would usually watch the same film all seven times. Eight times, actually, with the Saturday matinee. The giant ape, Fay Wray, and the Empire State Building were one in his mind. There were the newer skyscrapers, but not one of them ever had the great Kong shimmying up its side with such adroitness and determination. None of them had those huge arms, one hanging on to the tower while the other swiped down puny aircraft with their sorry machine guns. There would be taller buildings, but none of them could touch the majesty, the history, the prophecies within limestone, of the Empire State.

It felt good walking; his legs pumping gave him some sense—some small sense, at least—of purpose. So when he entered the lobby, he thought for a moment of actually taking the stairs to the top. Just to keep on moving. But, opening the door leading to the stairway, he was overcome with a wave of anxiety. The stairs seemed so small, so dank for a building of such size and splendor. They didn't seem fit for the task, and there was suddenly something Dante-esque about the whole idea.

So he packed into the elevator with the mob of tourists and took it to the top. It was an ordeal getting to the observatory deck: a few changes of elevators and, finally, a couple of flights of stairs to climb, even more narrow than those in the lobby. When he finally reached the open air, so high above his city, he didn't even notice the view. Instead, his attention was immediately drawn to two wallet-sized photographs left leaning against the wall beneath the rail. The photo on the left depicted a man and woman in their early twenties, their bodies tightly entwined and faces sharp with careless love. It seemed as if it was the first snapshot taken of the couple together. The one on the right appeared to have been shot about ten years after the first. The color quality was so much sharper. The same couple stood together, older and sullen. Their bodies were no longer tightly entwined, just two fingers from each of their hands brushing against each other, equivocal, forced. And the look in their eyes: his with defiance, hers with indifference.

Who were they? Did one of them leave the pictures, and why there? He looked closer at the shots, so close that he was down on his knees. He was afraid to touch them. They seemed sanctified, lying there. He didn't want to disturb them; to pick them up would be an act of profanity. His eyes were now just inches away, trying desperately to see the background and find some clue as to where they had been taken. It was an indistinct small-town street, surely not New York City. Perhaps upstate in the country, which made him think of apples.

When he was very young, he saw apples on the branch for the first time. It was on a family vacation before his parents' separation, riding upstate in the back seat of his father's black Mercury. His father had stopped the car and he and his brother each picked an apple and ate it on a crumbling stone wall that looked like it had been built during the Revolution. Billy also picked one for his dad, but his father just left it on the dashboard, sitting there like a magnetic Jesus or Saint Christopher.

Maybe the photos were shot somewhere in the Midwest. How long had they been lying there? Didn't they clean away these types of mementos each evening? The two pictures lay there, like weeds that grew overnight, less than a foot apart from each other. The beginning and the end. If the time in between had, indeed, been ten years, Billy wondered if it had been a slow ascent, then a fast falling-away . . . or a long, steady decline? Matters of the heart so high above the megalopolis. It wrenched Billy's brain, there on his knees. It suddenly occurred to him: he was actually *on his knees*. Huddled low, staring at two small pictures on an observation deck whose astounding panorama attracted sightseers from all over the world, and he was kneeling . . . staring at a concrete wall.

He'd had enough about the course of love between two strangers. These thoughts were as dizzying as the view, which Billy finally began to scan, having walked to the opposite side of the deck, 180 degrees from the photographs. Billy finally had a sense of how high up he was. He was glad there were high safety fences. The height created a magnetic charge that stirred in his body, giving him a sense that some force of nature was about to pull him off the deck. The closer he got to the edge, the more intensely he felt it. He remembered a teacher speaking of this phenomenon. It was called, in French, *l'appel du vide*, "the call of the void." He recalled this phrase because he liked the sound of it.

It wasn't a good day to be looking out from the heights. Haze enveloped the city. Still, Billy could make out the bridges leading into the outer boroughs, could see jets landing at LaGuardia. He wondered if one really could see as far as Connecticut under perfect conditions, as he'd once read. He felt in his pocket for some change, and was surprised to find two quarters. He usually never carried loose change. It was an idiotic maxim of Denny's, which he of course followed. "It ruins the cut of a pair of pants," Denny would offer, "and discombobulates your package, sexually speaking." He insisted that there was nothing worse than a rocker onstage with coins and hotel keys bulging out of his trousers. "It ruins your seamlessness." When Billy replied that he was not a rocker and was never onstage, Denny shot back, "You're always onstage in this city, man."

He put the quarters in the slot of a tourist telescope perched on the rail. After swinging it 90 degrees toward New Jersey and winding up on the dim marshlands near Secaucus, he aimed the device straight uptown, hoping to catch a view of his old neighborhood. Through the overcast, he could barely make out the tower in Highbridge Park. Trying to adjust the focus dial, Billy's hands slipped from the telescope. When he looked back through the lens, it was aimed straight into an office building about 15 blocks uptown. There was a man sitting on his desk in a very exorbitant suite. Billy could have sworn that it was John Garfield, the movie star, but he knew that Garfield had died, under shadowy circumstances, in a whorehouse in France almost 40 years earlier. A bird suddenly landed on the ledge of the office, and the John Garfield look-alike went over to the window and, for some reason, seemed to be making gestures at the bird. It looked like either a crow or a raven. Then a large-breasted blond woman entered with a small green box. It was uncanny. She was a dead ringer for the B-movie starlet Jayne Mansfield. But Jayne Mansfield was also dead, horribly decapitated in a bizarre car accident on a foggy Louisiana highway in the late sixties. She handed the box—it seemed oriental by its design and green-lacquered glaze—to the man. She caressed his hair as he opened it, but just as he undid the clasp and raised the lid, the lenses of the telescope went black.

Billy walked out of the Empire State Building disappointed. He had thought that the soaring vista would scatter the demons from his head, but now he felt worse. The gloomy weather had obliterated the cathartic view, and all he had left from his trip up high were the haunting images of two photographs. Not to mention John Garfield, the bird, the Jayne Mansfield look-alike, and the green box, its contents forever remaining a mystery. The falling shutters of the telescope had made certain of that. *This is what the world does to you when you pay attention too closely,* he thought. *The shutter slams down before the final clues appear, before the chain is connected and the fine details are resolved. And there are never enough quarters.*

As he walked north, the skyscrapers seemed to be leaning forward. He felt their weight, a kind of looming interrogation. His usual casual dialogue with the streets was all out of phase. It was as if someone had brushed up against him like a pickpocket and stolen his innate sense of the city, as important as sight, or hearing.

Some mornings there was nothing so wonderful as a walk through the crowds on Fifth Avenue; some mornings there was nothing more miserable. But on this particular morning, Billy didn't know which it was. He felt like Lazarus, back from the dead, but somehow incomplete. Something was different; he couldn't find his walking rhythm. Normally, no matter what direction his walk took him, he would fall into a Zen-like zone, allowing him to weave thoughtlessly through the late morning pedestrian traffic.

But on the morning in question, he felt a clumsy interaction with the shoppers and tourists. Fifth Avenue was not a good street for casual strolling. The executive types walked abrasively with purpose and money, the women swung large shopping bags from opulent department stores.

A few blocks north, he passed the Museum of Modern Art. Some days he could hardly remember which of his own pieces were hanging from its walls, or what they looked like. Then there were times he recalled every brushstroke. This morning it was neither . . . he just passed by the institution without giving it a thought.

Still, he was looking forward to the opening of the Velázquez exhibition that night. Even the idea of hiking into his tuxedo had a certain appeal.

As much as he would believe differently, sometimes Billy enjoyed allowing himself to indulge in the paraphernalia of fame.

On a whim he stopped and bought a watch from a sidewalk vendor. Normally, Billy could not abide keeping time, especially when it was attached to one's body. Time was like a relentlessly needy lapdog one had to haul around. It barked too much and had no sense of loyalty. A sharp, sudden intuition, however, convinced him that a wristwatch would somehow come in handy in the near future. It was supposed to be a Gucci but was surely a cheap knockoff. It would last somewhere between six days and six months, and that seemed just long enough for him.

With his new watch stuffed into his coat pocket, Billy walked briskly back down Fifth to his loft in Chelsea. It was a fairly depressing walk, and the trip up the Empire State had been a sullen letdown, but that's how it goes on these morning walks in Manhattan. You take the good with the bad. It's a sensation, peculiar to New York, that even a native like Billy can momentarily feel lost, and that around the next corner waits the throbbing possibility that anything can happen.

Now, in hindsight, the only thing that resonated from the day for Billy, lying on a coarse blanket in the locked wing, was the bird he had seen through the Empire State's telescope, the one that seemed to be talking to the John Garfield double. Billy now viewed that as curiously prescient of his strange run-in with the raven at the petting zoo.

He continued taking inventory of the day. Back in the loft, he had spent the afternoon unsuccessfully working on a few of his own canvases, but concluded he couldn't concentrate while anxiously anticipating the usual media frenzy, witless socialites, and other detritus he'd soon be facing. Under siege by the invincible threat in his assistant Marta's stare, Billy eventually got dressed for the festivities at the Met. All of it now seemed so long ago.

He remained lying there in his bed in a trancelike state until snapped out of it by a series of loud female yelps from the corridor, not far from his door. It was 15 minutes before lights-out. He stepped into the corridor and saw a vision of a young girl coming from the direction of the television room. She was a beautiful blonde who appeared too young to be kept in this wing. Without speaking a single word, she started flirting so brashly with Billy that, despite his own brain drain, even he recognized that she didn't understand the implication of her gestures. She only knew that they had a very powerful effect. He stood there, his lead-filled legs churning silver as she approached him. He returned her smile. The small, still-functioning section of his brain told him how ridiculous this situation was, but he was nailed to where he stood.

She came closer, as did Bruno, anticipating trouble.

"What is she here for; she's so young."

"She's one of those privileged oblivion-seeker kids," the attendant explained. "She came in about two weeks ago, in a 'K hole' for the first day and a half. Her brain's been fried by the stuff. Her parents think it's best for her to clean out in here. As you can see, her progress is not outstanding."

"What's a 'K hole'?" Billy inquired.

"Ketamine, man. You know, 'Special K,' they call it. It's an animal tranquilizer that puts you into a zombielike state. They call it the *hole* or the *zone*. She may look like an angel," Bruno said, "but you best be careful around her. They call her 'the llama.'"

Billy turned to Bruno for clarification on this cryptic designation, but Bruno was already gone, popping in and out of rooms for bed check.

The young blonde was smiling at Billy, coming straight toward him, eyes overloaded with mascara and lubricity. The purpose of her smile was so obvious that even Billy wasn't fazed when she circled her tongue around her lips. It was done so transparently, with a captivating trace of awkwardness. Billy realized that such ludicrous moves were probably fabricated from movies and romance novels, seen through precocious, and grievously neurotic, eyes.

Through his drug-insulated sentiments, ranging from longing to pity, he continued to make eye contact with the girl. She continued toward him until they were less than five feet from each other. There she stopped, her smile as wide and lascivious as before, though her tongue had receded safely out of sight. Billy thought her sudden halt was part of some dance of seduction, also plucked from the romance genre. He played along, also standing motionless, and continuing to mimic her clumsy smile. Suddenly the girl made a retching sound that reverberated from below her lungs. At the same moment, she bent her knees and, like a shot putter using all his leg strength, bounded upward and hurled one of the largest wads of phlegm imaginable directly at Billy. He was hit full force in the forehead, just left of the bandaged wound.

The projectile possessed such a consistency and mass that it remained in place, defying the laws of physics by refusing to drop. An onlooking attendant quickly tossed Billy a towel and he was able to wipe away the hideous glob in two thorough passes. He ran his face under a water fountain and wiped several times more. He checked his scalp with the aid of Bruno, who had now hurried back. "Actually, you got off lucky," he said, cautiously inspecting Billy's bangs with rubber gloves. "There was a new guy last week and, after she flirted her way into striking distance, she jumped and straddled him with her thighs like a rhesus monkey, then bit into his face like it was a candy apple. She was put into isolation for 24 hours and came out quite docile. Now she's back to her original habit of flirt and spit. I told you they called her 'the llama.'"

"Yes, you did," Billy answered in a weary tone of voice, trying to convey how tired he was with the entire subject, "but you failed to mention why."

Bruno shook his head and gave him a look of pity.

The young girl, whom Billy had only wanted to bond and talk with, was laughing in hysterics. At the same time, she was fighting off the attendants trying to restrain her. At Dr. Hui's insistence, Bruno boomed out the order that all patients should return to their rooms immediately for lights-out.

Back in his room, Billy fell onto the bed. He was so fully exhausted by the fatigue and madness of the night's events that his eyes, once shut, seemed locked. He fell onto the thin city-issued pillow with filmy last thoughts grasping upward from his brain.

3

Everyone was awakened to piped-in sounds of soothing quasi-new-age music at 7:00 a.m. Billy noticed a thin paperback, *A Light in the Forest*, on the table beside the bed. He remembered reading it years ago in grade school. If he recalled correctly, the story was about an Indian in . . . well, a forest. He didn't recall seeing the book last night, but with the drugs and darkness of the room, it wasn't likely that he would have. He didn't even remember the night table.

The main remnant of the drug was similar to the dreadful languor that comes after you've finished swimming in the ocean in heavy surf, when the pounding of waves against you and the acerbic crawl of salt over the skin combine to leave your body numb, aching, and transcendentally exhausted. His first thought was to just toss the sheet over his head and go back to sleep.

Billy rallied, pulling on the curled canvas slippers they had provided him. He walked out into the corridor, noticing the blood in his legs no longer had that leaden weight. It took him about 20 cautious steps before his body fell back into sync with gravity.

Daylight against the institutional-colored paint on the walls was harsh; it renewed the tide of fear in his body. The racing thoughts from last night's incident had subsided, but Billy didn't know if he was depressed or bemused. He knew that he was confused, and the only thing holding his anxiety in freeze-frame was the residue of last night's drugs. His brain was hobbled. What was it about Velázquez?

He was, in the most brutal sense of the phrase, in a state totally void of ambition. He felt like a small bomb had obliterated something immeasurably important inside him, but the explosion had occurred so flawlessly that Billy never felt it happen. Could the simple act of viewing a few masterpieces do this? What happened? Yesterday he had woken in his own bed at the studio, feeling fine, secure enough in his finances and privacy and health to keep clear of quotidian life's big changes, he'd thought. He hated the big changes. He'd had enough of those in his youth. Also, as an artist, he hated wasting energy that could be put to more important things. He always felt that if the art was truly good, the divine emerged, but Velázquez had changed all that last night.

Now nothing was secure and the important things were no longer certain. Now he wondered, was it, after all, the artist's burden to inject an aspect of spirituality into his art? Or was it something onlookers needed to evoke by their open hearts and minds? Billy had thought he had an intrinsic understanding of these basic questions since he had first devoted himself to making art. Now he just didn't know the answers, innately or intellectually. The real problem, he realized, was that on the one hand he was obsessed, and on the other he was becoming indifferent.

Billy still had to talk with Dr. Hui. Billy was a person who did not like to explain his actions to others and he didn't know if this was because of a shallow sense of privilege or a genuine belief in his moral center. If it was the former, then he was no different than any of the other smaller bits of flotsam passing by on the river of celebrity worship, which kept growing wider as the speed of information and media increased. It was a horrible perception to Billy, and this wasn't the first time he had felt it, in one form or another. He ate a breakfast that was better than expected and went off down the hall for the showdown with the shrink.

"So, Mr. Wolfram, how are you feeling today? Better, I hope." Dr. Hui spoke softly, with no trace of an accent. His voice reminded Billy of a friend he had gone to high school with. The guy was a communist. Though rather plump, he was also a ferocious womanizer. Billy recalled the time he walked into the game room of a mutual friend's basement, and the portly Trotskyite was playing nude Ping-Pong with a girl. They didn't even wear sneakers.

"I'm feeling better today, Doctor, thank you," Billy answered with a slight vocal quaver, unable to get rid of the image of naked communist Ping-Pong.

"One small thing to clear up before we begin our talk about the incident that brought you to us." The doctor leaned forward. "On the chart that you filled out, you mentioned you had been hospitalized once before, but you failed to mention what the reason was and when this occurred. Can you tell me now so I can fill this in?"

"Oh, I'm sorry," Billy rushed in, already certain that this was going to be one of the worst experiences of his life. "That was an oversight. It was a hernia operation. I was seven years old and got a knee to the groin while playing touch football. Ouch, eh, Doc?"

"Well, that clears that up." The soft voice floated upward as he made a note on the chart. "Was it an all right experience in the hospital at that time, or unpleasant? I ask strictly out of my own curiosity."

"I really don't recall much about it, aside from my friend sneaking in pistachio ice cream. It was green." The doctor did not appear satisfied, so Billy tried another tack. "Back then I was bound to my bed, tethered to machines and I.V. drips. I couldn't move, you know? That's difficult when you're seven years old. Here I'm unfettered and that's certainly more pleasant. There's a sense of structured community here that is also rather agreeable."

"I see." Dr. Hui loudly put down the chart and swiveled forward in his chair. "So now why don't you explain what happened last night? Just tell me as if you were speaking informally to a close acquaintance. Try to be as detailed as possible, no matter how frivolous it may seem."

Billy, wishing that he too had a chair that swiveled, ran down his experience at the Met to the doctor, beginning with the moment he arrived. Actually, it was just before he arrived. Billy tried to make eye contact as he spoke to the doctor, but just couldn't. He always had trouble with eye contact. Frequently, women thought Billy was staring at their breasts as he chatted with them, but the truth was that he was simply lowering his eyes to avoid any direct visual connection, and their breasts just happened to be there. This was actually the type of personal quirk that Billy would truly like to speak to the doctor about in detail. Find out what it might signify and where its origins might be traced . . . things like that. People so often took it as a sign of aloofness in the young artist and, really, he felt it conveyed quite the opposite. He didn't want to go off on a lavish discourse, however, so he put his curiosity aside and let it lie, reminding himself that the less said in one of these exams, the better. A single phrase taken the wrong way might lead to shackles and three more days.

For Billy, however, telling the story straight and unembellished was not as easy as it might seem. He did not think or speak in anything approaching a linear fashion. He didn't know if it came from crooked synaptic pathways or a childhood rigged by bad luck and a disenfranchised family, but his mind always seemed to go to chapter seven after finishing chapter three.

In as flat a voice as he could muster, Billy began what he hoped would be a straight narrative to the doctor. His hands were squeezing the tubular arms of his chair with such force he was afraid they would bend.

The previous evening began when his art dealer, Tippy Shernoval, picked him up in front of his loft in his Mercedes limousine. Billy had a glass of white wine in the car on the way there; it was the only alcohol he would drink that night. As they entered the museum, it was already three-quarters full. Perfectly timed entrances were Tippy's resolve and talent; he excelled at the subtle, shrewd details of public relations. They stood removing their overcoats and perusing the crowd. All black-tie and flickering gowns. The gowns of the younger, arty women were slit high on the thigh, bare in the back, their necklines swooping with cleavage. The uptown crowd's couture was more contained and definitely more sequined.

Tippy had abandoned Billy before they'd taken five steps into the grand rotunda. The dealer was walking forward in a Frankenstein-like manner, his back straight and arm extended, ready to shake the hand of anyone who mattered . . . the ones who made the art and the ones who bought it. The few photographers allowed inside to document the event swarmed around Billy. They couldn't get enough of him. He was, after all, the golden boy of the New York—indeed, international—art world. Billy was only 38 years old, and his star had risen steadily since his first show at 21. His technique was flawless. Even in the backbiting art world, fellow artists acknowledged his gift, and his hermetic, mysterious lifestyle only kindled the media's interest in him. The fact that he genuinely found the whole scene insuffer-able was of no matter. He was far too polite to expose his own loathing.

He ducked off and checked his overcoat. (As he relayed his story to the doctor, Billy realized that the overcoat must still be hanging in the museum coatroom, the knockoff Gucci watch he'd bought in its pocket. He thought about his tuxedo and wondered if the round plastic coat check was still in one of its pockets. He wondered if he'd ever get the overcoat back. He didn't mention this in his narrative with the doctor, however, assuming the shrink would put it down as an obsessive racing thought. Actually, Billy didn't care too much about fashion, but this coat was so well made and hung so comfortably on his body.)

After he emerged from the coatroom, dodging the cameras, he said hello to a few fellow artists. Billy would have been satisfied to hang out and chat, but his peers kept bringing up Billy's imminent show. It was the last thing that he wanted to talk about. He felt a peculiar stress and continually changed the subject, which just made them more insistent in their prod-ding. Finally, Billy escaped their clutches, insisting that he needed solitude to closely examine the six large canvases by the maestro just up the marble staircase in the first mezzanine gallery. He said he had a bet with a friend that there was a dog in all six of these masterpieces and wanted to confirm if he had won or lost. Billy was not a good liar.

"So, thinking about it in hindsight, I was actually bullied into that gallery and those paintings by trying to get away from everyone," Billy observed to the doctor, who was making copious notes with a ballpoint, "and not say another word nor think another thought about my show.

"You must understand, Doctor, that nobody at one of these black-tie openings, particularly at the Met, spends any time looking at the paintings, aside from the faintest perusals. These premieres are social events, their only purpose is to see and be seen, talk business, and whine about the most ludicrous matters. One gentleman kept complaining that the museum's scotch was woefully inferior to what they usually served. Everyone is there to make connections, to schmooze. What is that hideous term the movers and shakers use?"

"Networking?" offered the doctor, raising his eyebrow.

"That's the word." Billy grimaced. "I truly detest that expression. It's like 'interface,' another word I hate. In this fancy produce emporium where I sometimes shop, I once asked a young girl working there whether she liked her job. She told me that she did, because she loved 'interfacing with fruits and vegetables.'"

"So, you were saying that nobody looks at the artwork at these openings"—the shrink tried to steer Billy back on track—"but you, I have a sense, did examine them quite closely last night."

"I'm sorry I keep going off on a tangent, Doctor," Billy said defensively, "but don't take that as being anything aberrant because of these immediate circumstances. I've always done that. I start with a terse response on a subject during an interview, for example, and before I know it, it's circumlocution in nine directions. I always manage to get back to the original subject, however. Some people find it charming; it drives other folks crazy. You are correct regarding the maestro's paintings. I did look at those huge canvases . . . with each one I looked closer and deeper. The first two simply filled me with awe, but certainly I've experienced that before. By the third one, however, the work lost its wholeness. I watched it break down into its separate elements. The canvas was reduced to its flux, flow, and vibration, and the movement was too fast, leaving me in this swirling haze. I felt nauseous, and stood back a few steps in case I heaved.

"Naturally, I admire those paintings that are considered, for various reasons, masterpieces. It doesn't matter if an artist did them in the fifteenth century or the past hundred years. However, I normally never compare my own and someone else's work; I only evaluate new pieces against older ones from different periods from my past. I don't have control over what someone else does, so I learn from the patterns of progression I find within my own work over various periods. Because of this, I've always avoided petty jealousies and the resentment of other artists. However, when I found myself facing Velázquez's *Saint Anthony Abbot and Saint Paul the Hermit*, I felt an envy that literally hurt. I had to admit I resented his unprecedented facility for creating light and space that rose up the mountain's craggy façade and intersected with the sky's twilit shadows. He made it look seamless, yet I could see the difficulty he must have had linking together all the chaotic connections within that sprawling landscape. In the distances, I could look downward at winding roads on the flatlands, surrounded by more stony buttes. Still, the focus remained on the two hermits at the forefront of the harsh and varied landscape. Both saints were sitting on stones, their old bodies, particularly their hands, gesturing with expressions that had endless interpretations. Above the recluse's cave, a raven swooped downward, carrying bread in its beak to feed Saint Paul.

"The Spaniard was 23 years old when he received the commission and painted this large, complicated piece.

"Then I came upon two faces in two flanking portraits. In one, the condescending curl in the lips of a dwarf, whose eyes were focused on me, filled with conflicting emotions . . . tension, defiance, sorrow, and fear. They were so intense that my skin felt like it was blistering from sunburn. Then, to my left, was the compellingly portrayed *Infanta Margarita*, who possessed a natural charm absent from other members of the Spanish royalty in that era. To offset the commotion of the brush across her ornate court attire, he inserted a lyrical release of delicate roses, irises, and daisies. At most other times, Doctor, I believe this painting could have calmed me down. Instead, the allure in the characters' faces turned into scorn, and those brilliant colors assailed me like lasers, leaving me overwhelmed and drained.

"That's when I first began having the racing thoughts and a dire need to get out into the night air. There wasn't only a profound spirituality in those paintings, Doctor. They were filled with arrogance, as well . . . a *spiritual* arrogance. We always think of arrogance as a reproachful characteristic but, for an artist, that's not always the case. If used by one of the very few who have possessed the genius to back it up, this sort of arrogance can, of course, be better described as an extreme form of confidence. I hadn't thought of these matters in my art for quite a while, but all the dizzying insights that this genius initiated forced me to recognize how completely I'd sealed myself off from any concept of the divine. It was like I'd fortified myself to live under siege, safe from the disturbing and frustrating questions that true artists, sooner or later, must ask.

"You know, I just now realized that this might have been a moment of great epiphany if I weren't a painter myself. However, the fact that *this is what I do* made it impossible to take in the experience without foolishly comparing my style to the master's, and—with a colossal understatement— further magnifying my shortcomings.

"My best friend is a musician, and he's told me that it's difficult for him to attend another band's concert. He says he can never again watch a show as a fan, filled with awe, like he did before his own success. He feels a sense of loss because of this, knowing art shouldn't be seen as a competition.

"When I walked into that opening as, I dare say, the wunderkind of the art world, the only thing I had on my mind was getting back to my studio and working on the pieces for my own show in the morning. I felt so completely in control of the new pieces I was producing. Less than an hour had passed at the Met, and a lot more than the plans for my next day had changed.

"From the little reading I've done on the subject, I felt most of the symptoms for what you would term an 'anxiety attack.' By the time I reached the third and fourth Velázquez canvases, the paintings started breaking apart into their own ethereal flow. Some details, usually the skies, floated off and disappeared. The hills and valleys reassembled in various shapes, all of which made perfect sense. The smaller portraits had a greater effect on me. The sheer technical genius of the way certain characters were depicted in such a fearsome manner that they appeared set to dive from their gilded frames and pin my wrists to the ground, keeping me restrained for as long as they saw fit.

"When I came to my senses, I felt so small, and trembled with fear. The young giant of the scene? What a joke. At that moment, I didn't even think of myself as an artist. My desire to get back to my own work became a ludicrous, private joke. I wondered if I could ever paint again."

Billy took a short break to recall the thread of his narrative, and noticed the doctor leaning closer toward him, as if he were about to begin firing questions. Billy was not comfortable with that possibility whatsoever. Not knowing or caring if it was relevant or not, he quickly began recounting the first thing that came to mind.

"Oh, I didn't tell you about the blister on my foot! As I was moving from one painting to the next, and all these conflicting feelings overwhelmed me, I felt this soreness on my foot like a huge blister. I don't know if it was a blood or water blister, but I remember it felt like it was getting larger and larger . . . I could only explain it as some psychosomatic manifestation of all the internal conflict I was dealing with. I was limping as I began running out of the museum. The thing is that, on Fifth Avenue, I felt the blister break open. There was a vast squishing of fluids—either blood or water, I did not know. My shoe and sock were soaked, and I felt a great relief from the pain, but I also recall worrying about infection setting in. After the police brought me here, one of the first things I did as they were checking me in was to remove my shoe and sock, cringing at the horrible sight I expected to see. But there was nothing there. The socks were clean and dry, aside from the sweat from all that running, of course. I looked at my bare left foot and there was not a mark. No blood, no water, Doctor. It was all an illusion. How do you explain a painting so overwhelming that it manifests itself in a blister? A blister that pains, breaks, then squishes like snow in your shoe, and turns out to not even exist?

"I'm sorry, Doctor . . . another digression. I thought it was worth mentioning. I'll return to the effect of Velázquez. This sort of thing, seeing paintings break down into nothing but their own indescribable essence, has happened before. Those other times, however, were rare and always preludes to something wonderful and not, I dare say, horrific. I'm thinking of those eyes again. It's never happened so quickly either. It's so difficult, finding a way to explain this properly.

"You see, getting to the heart of great art is like washing with a brand-new bar of soap. The first few times, it just doesn't wash. That outer layer is useless for a decent lather. Depending on the soap (and the art), it takes about three or four showers before this layer is broken down and you begin to get some adhesion. *Adhesion*, Doctor . . . that's the proper descriptive word. The same thing with a painting: looking at it, a time must pass before it adheres. Then you feel cleansed and inspired. With Velázquez, it just came on me so fast. Maybe it was the patina or the mastery of his brushstrokes, but all that's just technique and this was somehow far above and beyond any of that in the same incongruous way it emanated from it. Bypassing the irony, and continuing my earlier analogy, the soap was already half used when I first looked up, and the adhesion was immediate. Too immediate. The effect was like I somehow consumed a parasite filled with racing thoughts.

"I'll tell you another thought I've had, Doctor, for what it's worth: I truly don't think what happened to me last night could have taken place if the opening was in the afternoon . . . in daylight, that is. The minute I exited the museum, that darkness made *anything* capable of happening. For example, there is nothing worse than seeing a man die from, perhaps, a heart attack on the streets in bright sunlight." Billy was hoping his analogy was not sounding ghoulish or crazy. "I have seen a few dead bodies at night, and none had the same effect on me as a man hit by a taxi last month who lay dying for nearly an hour in the morning light. I guess we accept, or at least expect, horror in the darkness. Maybe the verbs should be reversed in that sentence, I'm not sure.

"Even the air seems different in the night, as if it's been infused with some new chemical. Something more rarefied that makes you feel fragile. In darkness we are all prey, in every sense. You're cornered; you draw out more of the animal within. If you're not prey, then you're predator. That chemical I spoke of—this undiscovered element of night—opens up the senses to their most base, perverse fullness, as it tightens the valve of rational barriers. In past centuries, the church bells would ring out before dawn in tones and sequences that were calculated to placate the bloodthirsty. Did you know that? That very phrase, 'To placate the bloodthirsty,' was etched in Latin into each bell. Now most churches don't even have bells. If anything, they have those horrible mechanical chimes that sound like a merry-go-round."

Billy cut off his blathering, realizing he was not in a conversation at a cocktail party but defending his sanity to a psychiatrist in a mental ward with locked doors. "Normally, I don't think about such things as the so-called animal within. I am isolated from it by my nature and circumstance." Billy was revealing a truth to the doctor that he had no intention of elaborating on. Thankfully, the doctor let it pass, not realizing the extent of the truth and pain behind what he had just said.

"I see," the doctor said. Billy thought he could detect a slight smile, though what that smile—if it was a smile—meant, Billy had no idea, and at this point didn't want to know. "And what about your incident on Park Avenue? The police report indicated that you were shouting about stone knives and thought the Helmsley Building was an Aztec temple."

"Certainly the mention of stone knives had nothing to do with weapons or hurting anyone. Actually, the key word in the phrase was *stone* rather than *knives*."

"So you understood, during your incident on Park Avenue, that you were only speaking about knives in an abstract sense, as they related to the building's light and an ancient civilization?"

"Absolutely," Billy replied, crossing his legs. "Then the nausea overtook me, and I dropped to my knees, took the twig in the eye, and I thought I was blind."

"The police said something interesting in their report." The doctor moved closer. "A witness told them that you let out an exclamation of joy at the prospect of being blind. Is this true?"

"Well"—Billy stretched out the word—"I might have slipped out some silly remark at the moment considering how blindness—which I knew full well was temporary—would have been an answer to the dilemma I was facing regarding the maestro's painting and my own work. Of course, the prime despair came from the realization that my work was totally bereft of the ethereal, or what I call the 'inner register,' that ambiguous quality that enables the viewer to approach the painting more from the heart than the intellect. That's a lot to absorb in one minor—and harmless—psychiatric episode. But I was joking regarding the blindness, Doc . . . just trying to be clever. It's a habit of mine to use self-deprecating humor in embarrassing situations." Billy was saying what he thought the doctor wanted to hear, hopeful the doctor wasn't picking up the truth through his body language, or the slight rise in the pitch of his voice.

Billy decided to take a leap. "That having been explained, the next thing I was aware of was my sight returning, thank God, and the police arriving. Next thing I know I'm being ushered into your little domain here. So there you have it. End of story."

Billy wondered if his ad-libbed levity with the doctor had worked.

"I do not know if it is the end of anything, Mr. Wolfram," the doctor said, turning serious, "but, for my criteria, you seem to pose no harm to anyone, including yourself. I must tell you that I am only speaking about harm in the physical and not the psychological sense. In that area I can only recommend that you find someone to speak to on a professional basis. Often artists are afraid to seek out psychiatric help, imagining a creative intangible will be snatched from them by therapy. You, however, are in search of something. Consider it.

"I will tell you something else, not as a doctor, but as a lover of art. I think that there is a great amount of spirituality in your paintings and sculpture. The most minimal art can be filled with the sacrosanct, if you will, as long as it is done well and touches the emotions and intelligence of the onlooker. Perhaps what you seek is missing from somewhere else in your life, other than your work. I beg you not to allow your art to be the victim of last night's episode.

"If this were not a city hospital, I would release you right away. Unfortunately, there is nothing I can do to cut through the so-called red tape. While your paperwork is being processed, you can simply consider this a time to rest up until you get out of here tomorrow, sir, so have a good time in my 'little domain,' as you call it."

"Thank you, Doctor," Billy said, "I appreciate your kind words concerning my work. I wonder if I may ask you three quick questions. First, is there a phone I can use to make arrangements for my return home tomorrow? The second concerns the police. Was being taken here a form of arrest? Thirdly, the aide said that, after our meeting, I must report to the window across the hall for my morning medication. Certainly this isn't necessary, is it?"

Dr. Hui assured Billy that he would have no further dealings with the police, since they had found no weapons or illicit drugs on him. A police report would be filed, but it would be sealed as a medical matter, ending any further involvement with the police or the courts. Medication, however, was another matter. "I am prescribing you a very mild sedative," the doctor answered with calm erudition. "I assure you it really does no more harm than an aspirin and will do you good. And as for the phone call, you may use the phone down the hall. Just ask the attendant to help you."

Billy made his phone call and then the orderly directed him to a window where a nurse was dispensing medications. She had Billy's pills all prepared in a paper cup with his name written on it. She shook the two pills into his anxious hand and offered him another cup filled with something Billy surmised as a grape-flavored Kool-Aid, which gave the entire procedure a kind of Jonestown vibe. He heaved the pills into his mouth and began to move away. The nurse, in an urgent corvine voice, summoned him back.

"It's a state law that you must say something to me after you've taken your meds and finished your drink," the nurse, all smiles now, informed him. "That's to make certain that you have truly swallowed and ingested your medication."

"I'm sorry," Billy apologized, as he adhered to the state mandate for gulping sedatives, "I didn't know the procedure."

"That's perfectly all right," the nurse reassured him. "By the way, I saw one of your sculptures at the Whitney last week. It was just breathtaking."

"Well, it's lovely to meet you, then," Billy said, trying to mask his sarcasm as he moved away.

Billy wandered down to the end of the corridor, stopping at the window and staring out over to the East River. This drug was much milder; it didn't turn his blood into mercury like the shot last night. These pills created a trancelike effect. He realized this as he craned his neck downtown, his eyes resting on the small boats and the various shapes of their wakes.

4

B reakfast was now finished and patients were gathering in the hall. Billy's attention switched to the morning light on the tree-tops. He was trying to gauge their height from his viewpoint. Normally, he would be scrutinizing the trees like an artist, but something—probably the drug—silenced the constant intrusion of the painter's vocabulary in his internal dialogue, allowing him to just take in things as they were. He had no thoughts of context, perspective, space, or any other basic laws to impede him. At that moment, Billy was as close to being in the park below as the people he watched passing thoughtlessly through it.

He turned from the window, surveying closely the faces of the other patients. The experience with the llama last night had served notice to his instincts. He was on guard, but a fascination remained with this sluggish assortment of the bent and pained, together in confinement. Surrounded by so much suffering, he thought, there must be some wisdom to be found.

Billy approached a man with a red plastic radio pressed closely to his ear. It was one of those old, cheap transistor radios, popular in the fifties and sixties. It reminded Billy of those Cold War years when he was very young. Too young to understand what was happening in the world, but old enough to be hideously scared. During those years there was a manic pro-liferation, particularly in the suburbs, of fallout shelters, and radios like this curious man's, along with boxes of batteries, were standard issue for such places. When civilization was blown to radiated slivers of meat and stumps outside, and the last bomb had fallen, these little red transistors would relay the voice of someone somewhere somehow pronouncing that it was safe to come out and greet the brave new world.

The man was probably in his early thirties but seemed much older by the clothes he wore and his stooped posture. He had noticed Billy momentarily staring at him and was now giving him the paranoid evil eye in return. Whatever its cause, Billy figured he could mollify the fellow's animosity with a few well-chosen words.

"What are you listening to there, pal?" Billy asked, cautiously closing the distance between them.

"It's the big game," the man replied, "I always listen to the big game. I'm amazed that you aren't listening."

Billy wondered what game this guy could be listening to. It was barely 10:00 a.m. and even Billy, never a sports aficionado, knew that games of any sort simply just didn't begin that early. Also, Billy had gotten close enough to the radio to realize that the man was listening to pure static, the speaker shoved right against his ear, the volume deafening. Still, Billy calmly lobbed another question at the man: "What game are you speaking of? I've been busy lately and haven't been in touch."

"The *big* game, sir, as I have already told you," the man answered. "I don't know any other way to put it."

"Well, then," Billy went on, frustrated, "what is the score?"

The man's voice rose to a scream. "Chaos is the score, and we are losing by more and more every day."

Billy resolved not to engage with any more patients, yet he was drawn to them. He noticed a woman, very old, signaling him into her room, where she sat at the end of her bed arranging cards on a movable table. He entered hesitantly, mainly to disappear from the radio man's sight, and pulled up a chair on the other side of the table. She informed him that she was a fortune-teller, reading the cards to tell others' innermost secrets.

"Tell me something about myself," Billy said to the old woman. Maybe she had the answers. She had a charming, tiny smile on her face and a look of long-lived despondency in her eyes.

She took the deck and gave Billy the cards to cut. She then shuffled them a number of times and proceeded to randomly toss them on the table. For a long time she pondered over them. The few words she spoke were in an Eastern European accent.

"You like cooked food," she finally declared, raising her head with the histrionic air of one divulging a great revelation. Billy almost began to laugh, and although he didn't, by the changes in her lips he could see she seemed to ascertain what was on his mind. They clearly began to quiver with what appeared to be bitterness or gloom. In this sense, she proved to be a mind reader, after all. An aide appeared at the door, informing Billy the woman was not allowed to be alone with visitors in her room. He raised himself politely from his chair and slid noiselessly out the door.

In the hall was another man, speaking in a thick Yiddish accent. He was fighting off two orderlies who were trying to coax him into the line for his medication. He was, apparently, afraid to sleep. Looking at Billy, he began to address no one in particular in a panicky scream as the orderlies kept him in line. He yelled, "That's when the Liliths come and steal my vital fluids. They squeeze me very tightly in the masterful way of their perverse act, and it shoots out of my eye sockets. In the morning the ceiling above my bed is covered with spiral-shaped lines of my vital fluids. It's silver like the trail of a snail or, what do they call them, a slug, yes, a slug, that's it." He pointed at Billy. "You, a goyim, obviously, what with the green eyes and all . . . correct me if I'm wrong, you would call her the succubus, if you are a literate man . . . I make no judgment saying this. Please, I ask you . . . help me. I cannot sleep, I cannot have any more of my sacred fluids purloined by the wretched one . . . the night creature in my bathroom, waiting on the shower rod like a dead branch, ready to pounce."

Billy did a quick about-face and headed back toward his room. As fascinating as the characters were with whom he shared this locked ward, he needed to ponder what to do about the exhibit he had coming up. There was no way he was going to hand over the pieces he had recently been finishing up. He was anxious to see them again, but already he knew that they would not meet his inchoate criteria. One thing he was certain of: his dealer, Tippy, was going to make any postponement or cancellation very difficult.

He was midway to his room when Billy saw a frenzied Bruno running toward him. "The doctors want everyone back in their rooms. Basically, it's lockdown time."

"Fine, Bruno," Billy answered.

"Yeah, have a lie-down." Bruno placed his hand on Billy's shoulder, his voice returning to its cooler, outer-borough pitch. "You can always choke the chicken, you know? A little midday relief, you know? I got to hustle now. I hate these situations."

Bruno was off, flinging open doors and barking, "Lockdown time." This phrase was a bit melodramatic, of course, since in this particular wing there were no locks on any patients' doors. That was, at least, what they would have you believe. Billy suspected that, if need be, they could seal everyone in their rooms with the flick of a switch in the main office.

Bruno's invocation of the 354th euphemism for masturbation rever- berated in Billy's mind and called forth a particular autumn day in 1963 when he was 12 years of age, his precocious mind and body aching with the hairpin turns of puberty. He could remember every detail of that day's color and texture. It was cool in late fall and the playground was filled with twisted, crunchy leaves, brown like grocery bags. He had a particularly vivid recollection of a truck delivering coal to his building as he came home that day. He had to duck under the metal chute from the truck as he entered the courtyard to the lobby doors. The chute was filled with quickly sliding layers of coal being transferred from the huge truck through a basement window into the bin room. The coal glittered in the chute, and as it landed in the basement, a black cloud of filth rose from the window and settled on young Billy, from hair to sneakers. As he opened the door of his apartment, he looked like some kid from a Kentucky coal town after bringing his dad a pail of lunch at the mine.

He thought of this day so often that the memory of it had taken on a ghostly presence. Now, once again, in this forced isolation it encroached itself upon him, kicking down the door to his mind with all its trivial fears. Lying there on the hospital bed, he began losing all sense of time and place. He felt smaller, and the ceiling seemed higher. The painting on the wall reminded him of those paint-by-numbers kits his mother worked on at night, watching detective shows on TV and smoking too much for her frail Irish lungs. She convinced herself it was all right because she had switched to a filtered menthol brand. He remembered her period of religious paintings best: Christ standing in a fishing boat, calming the sea, or . . . praying against a dim gray rock in the garden of Gethsemane. When his mother had tried to get him involved with her hobby, Billy had never shown any interest. It seemed silly. However, he was enormously fond of the paint's sharp smell. Later, whenever he worked, that smell would conjure a fleeting memory of his mother lying on the carpet, meticulously working on her paintings.

Billy still felt the details of the day, more than 25 years ago, falling over him with a frightening clarity. On that afternoon, after washing the coal dust off his face and hands, Billy was lying on the couch in the living room of his mother's apartment, uneasily wishing he'd succeeded in stealing a porno magazine. His mother was out working at the church rectory up the street—shopping first, then cooking for the priests. She'd be gone for the rest of the afternoon. He realized this was a providential opportunity to try following Marco's masturbation instructions again and achieve his mythic first climax, the virgin spurt.

Marco was a 16-year-old greaser who—to hear him tell it—had gotten more female ass than a toilet seat. He acted as self-appointed consultant regarding all matters sexual to his younger brother, Cosmo, and his schoolmates Denny and Billy. Marco was "on the dark side of beyond," as he used to say. He did paintings on his fingernails of the nuns who taught and often punished him in Catholic school. Therefore, he believed he was desecrating these nuns' images every time he finger-fucked one of his girls. Some of this seemed so blasphemous to Billy's adolescent sensibility that he tried, unsuccessfully, to turn a deaf ear to it.

From a technical standpoint, however, he admired these miniature portraits. Marco possessed stunning abilities as a draftsman. The precision of such minute work rivaled the tiny Flemish wood carvings and microdepictions of the Last Supper or the Crucifixion that adorned the reliquaries and rosary containers at the Cloisters. Marco showed Billy the brush that he used on his debauched-digits series. It was the first time Billy had seen a real paintbrush. The tip was so thin, consisting of six strands of camel hair wound tightly together. Marco was proud of his tiny portraits. Above all, he was proud of the multitude of girls into whom he had inserted those bedecked fingers.

As Denny and Billy sat listening to Marco's sexual instruction and escapades, he made them feel that they were being initiated into a cult of supreme righteousness, marching off to do battle in the Holy Land. Billy was waiting for a sword to appear in Marco's hand so he could drop to his knees and be knighted. Thinking about it, he realized it *was* a kind of ritual of knighthood for guys.

"The first thing you need is a porno rag to get your tiny imaginations going. Then, once it gets hard—and if it don't get hard within due time, there is nothing I can do for you . . . just wait a year or so and try again—you've got to start pulling. Now, listen good, because the biggest mistake that most of you tykes make is assuming that it only takes ten tugs or so and you're ready to spurt. *That is bullshit.* Masturbation takes a lot of work, especially the first time. Depending on the hotness of your porno material, you may have to yank your little chubbies for as long as half an hour, or more. If you're not up to the task, please leave now. I promise that no one here will think the less of you. It's hard work, and don't let anyone tell you different. The treasures to be found when you reach the end, however, are priceless. So, let me get into the exotic specifics. Who can tell me the best way to fake the feeling of a woman's vag while jerking off?" This was a snatch, so to speak, of a typical exegesis by Marco, delivered to a horny, attentive young audience. These secret seminars were usually held in the boiler room of the building where Marco's father was superintendent. The heat was unbearable in that basement. One was literally taught by fire.

Billy and Denny decided to raid the tobacco and newspaper store on Broadway to get some decent erotic material for the endeavor. The two thieves had a pathetically inept plan, however. Stuffing their baggy pants beyond capacity with serious skin magazines, Billy and Denny tried to use the rush-hour commuters, buying their *Times* and *Wall Street Journals*, as interference, blending in behind them and calmly sliding out the door. Unfortunately, they walked more like pregnant teenage girls. And at the exit, the old Jew who owned the place was waiting to snag them, retrieving the bonanza of porno they'd overloaded down their pants.

The debacle was made even worse by the fact that Augie, the owner, with a half-finished cigar perpetually hanging from his mouth, had known Billy and his mother since Billy was about four years old. Mrs. Wolfram, with her youngest child clutching her hand, would enter the shop each afternoon to buy her pack of Pall Malls, the evening paper, and some licorice twisters for Billy and his brother, Brian. Surely, Billy thought, she would hear all about her son's pornographic pilfering.

Embarrassed and without visual aid, Billy gave up on the idea of getting stirred up by pictures of naked women on glossy paper, but his determination had not completely waned. He hunted around his living room figuring there must be something—perhaps an old Sears catalogue with a section on the latest in bargain-priced underwear. That would do; they must have *something* in black. He reached over to the stack of magazines piled on the footstool and began flipping through issues. A recent one caught Billy's eye: the cover story about the new luminary of Broadway theater, Barbra Streisand. He had seen her picture before: the counterpoint of conventional beauty with her pouty large lips, which lay desirous beneath that prominent nose. Large noses turned Billy on. There was something comforting about them, as well as a sense of defiance. Also, large noses, for some perverse reason he could neither explain nor understand, connoted outright sluttiness to him. It was his first youthful fetish. He liked the idea of having a fetish; it seemed a very adult thing. Also, he enjoyed the sound of the word *fetish*. It made him think of some exotic food . . . like *hummus* or *knish*.

As he thumbed through the magazine, he was hit by the youthful equivalent of irony in the fact that the best jerk-off material he could find was in a national newsmagazine. He couldn't believe his fortune. Within the educative, glossy pages was a picture—a small insert, really—of Barbra in a terrifying bikini, her hair up in a regal bun, the eyes surrounded in black kohl, as thick as an Egyptian goddess's.

She was emerging from the water, perched on the shoulders of her husband, Elliot Gould, her thighs wrapped with dripping wet security around his neck. Her breasts, also covered by droplets, were just mind-numbingly vast in the sparse beaded top. And the expression on those large lips . . . she seemed to be speaking the exact words that Billy wanted to hear. Yes, she was talking on and on and Billy was just lying there listening, shifting the angle of the picture. As far as Billy was concerned, Elliot Gould had disappeared. In painterly terms, he'd been relegated to negative space. Barbra's legs could be wrapped around anyone's shoulders now.

"A good porno snap is like a battery," Marco had told him. "It gets the thing started, then keeps it up and running." With this in mind, Billy took the magazine and went into the bathroom. It would be at least another two hours before his mom was supposed to be home, but there was no sense in taking any chances. He wanted to feel totally safe from intrusion.

Then, in a flash, came the finishing touch. In another of the sex ed lessons in his basement homeroom, Marco had theorized that the closest thing to the feeling of real pussy was a fillet of veal wrapped around the cock, preferably warmed, though room temperature was acceptable. Years later, Billy had learned that, concerning this pubescent ritual, there seemed to be variations along ethnic lines when it came to the choice of meat. Jews preferred liver, apparently, and it was proffered that many South American youths favored the ample fat of mutton. In the black community, very thinly sliced chicken most often facilitated the endeavor. There was but one common factor among all creeds, countries, and colors: no matter what the meat, the cut was always a thin, malleable fillet.

Billy tossed the magazine on the tile floor and roamed into the kitchen. The perfect picture, the perfect time. As Billy opened the refrigerator, he could only hope that his luck would hold.

It held, all right; he could barely believe his eyes. There in the meat bin was a pack of veal fillets from the A&P, tightly wrapped in white butcher paper and sealed with tape. It really wasn't as much of a coincidence as it might have seemed. Billy knew that veal parmigiana was one of his mother's favorite dishes to prepare, and it was usually on the menu about one night a week. There were four thin cutlets inside, and now the problem was removing one, performing the wraparound ceremony, and leaving it in decent enough shape so it could be replaced without arousing suspicion to the casual glance. The key was unwrapping the package deftly, *sans* any detectable rips or creases. He peeled the tape slowly and with patience.

The problem was his hands, which were shaking with the anticipation of the Streisand image. They were twitching without control, much like the wholesomely rigid organ in his pants, which had, for the first time, taken total command of his body. He took deep breaths to slow his nerves, hands, and motor functions.

In time, the package was unwrapped, satisfactorily undamaged, and he slipped out one of the slimy raw cutlets. He threw it on a plate, letting it settle to room temperature (following Marco's advice to the letter, though heating it slightly in boiling water was simply out of the question). Less than a minute later, Billy decided the meat was as close to room temperature as his crotch was willing to wait. He picked up the plate and carried it into the bathroom with the care of a master chef personally delivering an elaborate entrée. He laid it on the floor of the bathtub and folded the magazine on the page with the bikini shot, his starter battery. God, the expression on her face: the plump lips, the please-give-me-all-of-it expression in the lash-laden eyes. Then there were those breasts, which he respected so fully that his inner voice could not debase them with cheap euphemisms like *titties* or *knockers*. What was the nature of his nose fetish? This was something Billy would have pondered if he were capable of it, but at the moment his brain was functioning only in conjunction with the dire dictates of his penis. He took a peek at it in his jockey shorts. It was an urgent shade of blue that he had never witnessed before. It gave him a bit of a fright. This fright and an innate pulse of necessity told him it was time to get down to business.

Billy eased off his underwear. It did seem as if his penis was truly battery-enriched. Unleashed from the harnessing effect of the jockey shorts, it began to twitch randomly. He wrapped the veal around it and, for a moment, slowly slid it up and down. It felt wet . . . lubricant wet, and inhuman. Billy couldn't imagine it possible, but the feel of the veal made his cock grow even longer. The head slid out of the meat wrap. The cutlet couldn't contain it (and there was enough veal there to feed two people . . . if one factored in the cheese and breading).

He looked at the picture of Barbra, the magazine leaning now, precariously, on the porcelain edge of the bathtub beside the toilet seat.

Just as his body's biological functions were reaching uncharted territory, Billy heard the front door locks turning. It was his mother, returning home hours earlier than she usually did. He could tell by the dragging of her heavy footsteps across the carpet that she was loaded down with bags of groceries. The priests must have sent her out shopping for their food and allowed her to leave a couple of hours early. She always had the delivery boys drive the fathers' huge amount of food directly to the rectory, and carried a couple of bags for Billy and herself while she was at it. He could hear oranges spilling out of their red net bag onto the kitchen floor and rolling across it. He knew the sound, oranges on linoleum. Every time she put away oranges, the pretty red net bag would break open and the dozen pieces of fruit would spill onto the floor in a series of thumps. Invariably, one or two would roll under a piece of furniture out of her reach and she would call Billy to come and crawl down to fetch them, wash them off, and put them in with the others. Rolling oranges were a part of Billy's growing-up.

"Billy, dear, where are you? I got home early, dear, how are you?" his mother shouted, barely loud enough to break his trancelike state, but he heard her and had to reply.

"I'm in the bathroom, Mother," he snapped back, almost too quickly, he realized the moment the words left his mouth. He purposely made his voice quaver weakly. "I'm feeling a little sick."

"Do you want some Pepto?" she asked.

"No, nothing. Really. I'll be great in awhile. Give me some time is all," he continued. "Just relax and watch your shows. I'll be fine." All through the gibberish that he was spewing, his eyes remained locked on Barbra and his hand was sliding the veal. His mind was split in two directions. He was not going to be denied. He had crossed a line.

There was a tingling in his spine and a fluttering from inside his asshole—the anxiety of his prostate, an organ that Billy did not even know existed, but it felt like a moth with sticky wings. He had never reached this point before. Hearing the faint sounds of the TV swept away any fears that his mom would be pestering him with chitchat through the bathroom door. He knew she would be consumed by a soap opera or, more likely, a game show. She was much more partial to game shows than afternoon dramas, which she thought rather vulgar. She actually seemed to get a vicarious thrill for the winners on game shows. *The Price Is Right* was her favorite. She had even submitted an answer to a home viewers contest.

She would be cheering on some housewife spinning a wheel for a new dishwasher and, meanwhile, he could concentrate on his task at hand, so to speak, without care. The sheer concentration was bringing on a righteous sweat, and it was bearing fruit. He could feel the changes within him stirring from a previously untapped source. The knees in his brain were beginning to buckle, and there was a Frankenstein-movie-like arc of blue electricity running from his crotch, up his spine, and out the top of his head. The feeling was so intense that he didn't know if it was something good or bad, if it was sexual or a prelude to death. It was a sensation that went beyond his brain and directly into his spine. This was it, he thought . . . this was what he felt: a snake, a small beautiful snake wrapped tightly around his spine and slowly ascending. He didn't care whether the snake was poisonous or not. He was beyond that, beyond the meaning. A transition was taking place within his body and his being. The pleasure of one stroke to the next now multiplied in implausible increments. He couldn't imagine that the actual climax could be better than this moment . . . wait . . . there's Barbra, Arabia painted around her eyes. "Ten measures of lust were given unto the world, one went to the other nations, and nine went to Arabia." Where had he read that? He didn't care. It was true. Arabia, land of lust, mystery, the three magi, and heavy eye makeup.

The veal-encased hard-on in his hand was taking on its own analogies. It was like a rigid cornered reptile, baring its teeth and ready to strike. Every peek down at the Barbra photo as his hand quickened its pace brought a bluer shade to the head, which was reaching proportions hitherto unknown. The blood-blue head was taking on a scary darker shade, like the fingers of a guy that Billy once saw dead from a drug overdose. Oh, Barbra . . . oh, beautiful Barbra, drenched in tiny droplets . . . it was just a matter of time now. Just hold that pose. Please. Please. Please.

Billy's head filled with an intractable desire to ravage anything female. Dark and violent sexual fantasies cascaded from his brain throughout his entire body. Weird things that he had never read of or seen in the most outrageous porno he had gotten his hands on. He kept one hand beating in the established, steady rhythm to his cock, but with his free hand he pinched onto his tiny pink nipple and squeezed it to a point of phenomenal pain. Then, guided by nothing but an instinct that seemed part of the smell's intoxication, he wet his forefingers generously with his tongue and ran circles around it, now stiff, harsh red, and almost unbearable with pleasure. His eyes returned to Barbra, and she was returning the stare with an effectively contrived aloofness.

Billy realized that Marco was right about one thing: the first time was harder work than he'd ever expected. The veal was becoming frayed from the punishment. He thought a moment about whether his mother would notice the difference when he stuck it back into the pack with the other fillets. At this point, however, Billy didn't care. Damn the veal. Let it be shredded for lust's sake! He could always blame the butcher at the A&P for pawning off shoddy meat.

Billy was in a zone with the nasty angels. It was just a matter of time until the sticky globs of lust spurted out. Then he heard a strange glottal sound from the living room and the volume of the television suddenly shot up. Heavy footsteps and other unfathomable sounds. They appeared to be coming from his mother, but he'd never heard her produce anything close to these noises. They were like honking gasps. He wrote it off to some exciting game show and kept on sliding the veal. It was so close now. The snake he had felt before in his spine was now at his navel, nipping to get out.

He was too far along, too near the big first time to allow his mother's unexpected presence to abort the mission. He could hear her footsteps retreat and the sound of the television return to normal, and that was a comfort. It meant she would be settling in and relaxing, watching the tube with her legs raised on the footstool, her support stockings pulled down to her ankles.

He had managed to split his consciousness: 10 percent on his mother's movements and the other 90 on the virgin breakthrough soon to come. A bead of sweat fell on the magazine, landing on Elliott Gould's swimsuit. He was so close. His wrist was cramping. He tried it with his other hand, but it was flailing, way off the beat. He had to switch back to his mojo hand.

He recalled Marco repeatedly advocating the importance of holding it in as long as possible before one let go. "The decisive squeeze," he called it. "Suppress it . . . you got to suppress it." No matter what the urges of the body dictated, the secret was to continue hanging on once that point of no return had passed. It was like holding back a tidal wave. Actually, holding it in was the better choice of prepositions.

There was a second snake now, curling into the lower back brain. He could feel the widened fangs release something forceful, milky, and tingling. That's when he heard his mother's sudden loud gasp from the living room, followed by her shouting to an otherwise empty room, "My Lord in heaven . . . no . . . no!"

He knew something was wrong. He had never heard his mother speak with anywhere near that volume and urgency. His brain and instincts, however, were currently overwhelmed by an inexorable sensation and expectation. In short, his cock, straining farther and farther out of the wrapper, had taken charge. Nothing short of gunshots would snap him out of it. Nothing would unlock his gaze from Barbra, nothing would undermine the timing of his stroke. More milk from the snake's fangs blasting against his frontal lobe, and there was now a clear, sticky substance clinging to the opening of his cock. It was the precursor of the abundant load to follow. He had almost forgotten Marco mentioning it in his discourse. He had reached *pre-cum*. The time was near.

He heard footsteps in the hallway, and they were heading toward him. The steps sounded very quick, like someone running. His mother never ran. Never had Billy seen his mother run. Still, he could tell it was her . . . not only by the simple fact that there was no one else in the apartment, but by the clomping of her house-worn mukluks. In any other state of mind, Billy would have done something about his prescient feelings, but he just froze in place. A blue haze enveloped his mind, the violent maroon shade of blue like the sky before a typhoon.

The bathroom door flew open. The frail hook-and-eye lock offered no resistance whatsoever against her mounting acceleration. With wild eyes, Billy's mother proclaimed in a breathless rasping voice, "The president was shot. John Kennedy is dead. He was riding in a car in—" She broke off the bulletin there, and finally focused down on her son, sitting illicitly on the toilet. All Billy could think at that moment was why he didn't let the veal drop into the water below. Instead, the milk-fed meat remained where it was, as did everything else. Frozen, with parted lips, the veal around his tumescent adolescent cock, his hand still gripping both, and the magazine opened to the bikini shot of the new darling of the Broadway stage.

His mother leaned all her weight on her right hand against the porcelain sink, breathing loudly and with difficulty. Billy had genuine fears that she was about to have a heart attack. Her mouth was still open from the last words reporting the president's death. "My God in heaven," she softly exclaimed, "what kind of sick . . . perversion . . . what are you doing? Lord, what is that there . . . right there in your hand, young man? Is that my veal for tomorrow night's parmigiana?" Billy momentarily broke loose from his altered state and let the cutlet drop into the toilet, followed by a quick flush.

He had to sit in humiliation until she concluded what she had to say. She signaled that she was finished by lowering her head. He just walked out past her in a trance into his room. He was sitting on the edge of his mattress, squeezing the pillow in his arms. He knew she'd be back to finish her diatribe. Waiting for her, he tried to come up with a reasonable explanation. He could always go with science . . . the biological imperatives of puberty and all that crap. He just wanted to get it over with.

She finally came in and gave Billy a longer look than he could ever remember coming from her.

"You know, son"—she spoke in a voice about three octaves higher than normal—"God, our Father in heaven, looks down over everyone and protects us all. That is because He is omnipresent and omnipotent. Today, however, I cannot help but think that the Almighty was so utterly shocked by the outright perversion of your sin that His attention was momentarily halted. Thus, in the moment that the Lord should have been protecting our president from that insane hoodlum in Dallas, I believe He was so overwhelmed by your demon-induced act that, just for a moment, He took His all-encompassing eye off of that motorcade. Do you understand what I am telling you? I want you to contemplate that in your room tonight. You shall have no dinner and I implore you to fortify yourself against any more sordid acts."

Billy sat on the bed perplexed. Of course he had dismissed—at least in his precocious, conscious mind—all of his mother's ranting about sin and the connection with the president's death. Still, he felt base . . . tainted. All the tingling sensations of sex were gone, and the only thing he felt down there, rubbing against his jockey shorts, was the pain of raw flesh from friction burn, like a skinned elbow after a fall. For Billy, the consequences of sex were assassinated heads of state, the loss of filial piety, and a penis that felt as if it had been whacked for hours with one of those dimpled meat tenderizers. Sex was ruin; the locks that keep it safe are cheap and never hold.

He tried to reason that the circumstances had to be totally aberrant to anyone else's first onanistic undertaking, but that didn't bring any solace. What were the odds, he reasoned, that the president of the United States—a particularly beloved and charismatic president, at that—would be assassinated in the midst of his first full-on masturbatory experience? Not to mention the fact that his mother would return home hours earlier than expected and happen to catch it on the television set, causing her to actually run for the first time in Billy's memory, gathering enough force to break open the flimsy door lock. What were the odds?

So, in coffee shops and cocktail parties, when people asked one another where they were the day that JFK was shot, Billy had always had to slink away and remember the fact that he was caught by his mother jerking off for the first time, with a piece of veal wrapped around his penis and staring at a picture of a bikini-clad Barbra Streisand. If it was the loss of innocence for America that day, then it was certainly a more personal, yet no less powerful, loss of innocence for Billy. He had never been able to perform a sexual act, either by himself or with another, since that deeply inscribed day.

5

L
ater in his life, Billy still saw it as *either* the worst *or* best day of his life, depending on how, why, and where he looked at it. Most often, he attributed his artistic edge to this sexual forfeiture. Even when he acknowledged it was a specious assumption, he needed the artifice in order to cope.

He was not, however, going to start reevaluating those theories now. All the details of that day more than 25 years earlier, along with the medication the nurse had given him that morning, made him tired. He slept. Usually he didn't like taking naps in the day. He had terrible, scary dreams sleeping in sunlight, but he was too wiped out.

He would have slept longer, but the sounds of patients on their way to the latter of two lunches woke him within a couple of hours. He could tell from the voices that "lockdown" mode was over. He entered the hall and, as if he had never left, was immediately confronted by another discursive inmate. It was as if these types were drawn to him for some reason. A well-groomed man with a fixation combining religion and language approached. He was finishing up an orotund discourse on the etymology of the word *siren*, insisting that it came from Simon of Cyrene, the man reputed to have helped Christ carry His cross on the way to His crucifixion. "He must have cried out from the misery and weight of the cross," the man said, "and thus the word *Cyrene* was afterward associated with a sound of extended wailing, like Simon's on that glorious and miserable day. 'We shall call such wailing sounds the *Cyrene*, for that is the home city of this fellow,' the Romans must have decreed."

Of course, Billy knew that this man's remarks were so far off base that they seemed laughable. Anyone who read Homer knew that the phenomenal Greek wrote about sirens well before the New Testament was conceived. But he'd already learned that you don't laugh at the patients in this wing. Better still, you don't react in any manner whatsoever. If addressed, you silently walk away, avoiding the slightest eye contact, and never let your guard down for a moment, acting as if you were on the outside.

Billy then understood that the crazed ranting had nothing to do with being right or wrong. These disturbed people, with their endless stories, inane theories, and continual provocations, were becoming tiresome. After less than a day in the locked wing, Billy found dealing with mental illness from his insider view to be an insipid, sad, and fatiguing ordeal, not at all like the charmingly surreal and entertaining ways these places were always portrayed in films. He could not imagine what it must be like for those who were so afflicted by madness that they could not, even for a moment, neutralize its power and examine it from the outside. How was it that he could walk back into sanity after his Park Avenue episode as easily as if he were exiting a movie in daylight, while others never make it out of that crippling cineplex? Or was it that he wasn't leaving either, but simply going from one film to another, in different theaters one flight higher, surrounded by varying audiences, while others were stranded in their seats seeing the same film over and over?

It was clear to Billy that, for many of these patients, their madness, in its varying magnitudes, was a large source of their energy, passion, and drive. Then again, so many others seemed numb and indolent, drained of all resources. They could barely raise their heads up to life, and the only activities that mattered were television, medication, and sleep. In some, this occurred despite the effects of the drugs, while with others, it happened because of them. Science would contend it all has to do with the proper balance of brain chemistry. Billy didn't doubt the validity of that but, in some sense, he knew it had to do with the spirit as well . . . both as a cause and as an effect.

Billy wondered what went on in their bent minds when the lights were forced off each night and they lay alone in the vagrant darkness. Once they fell asleep, did their dreams relieve them from the distress, or just transfer it to a different landscape? Some of them, no doubt, barely slept, but instead spent the night focusing all their attention on the ceiling's shadows. While returning from a quick trip to the bathroom the night before, Billy mistakenly had opened the wrong door. A man lay in bed, awake and staring upward. He casually mentioned to Billy that the shadows in this place were all wrong, and he had reckoned why. He insisted these shadows were not even American, but either from Bolivia or Colombia. He couldn't be certain, but they were definitely South American shadows.

Billy looked down and noticed a copy of a very small hardcover book lying on the hallway floor. Nobody had made an effort to pick it up or sidestep it, but had kicked it thoughtlessly from one spot to another across the linoleum like a hockey puck. Billy reached down and retrieved it. The book was well bound in leather, probably a gift left for one of the patients by a wealthy visitor. On the spine, in gold leaf, was the title, *The Marriage of Heaven and Hell* by William Blake. It was an annotated volume with beautiful miniature reproductions of Blake's illustrations. Billy loved Blake's poems, and Blake's paintings always left him with an abstrusely pure joy. How had the book wound up in the middle of the floor?

He had become conscious of something else since the incident at the Met. His ambition, in both its basic and artistically imperative sense, no longer played any part in this equation. When any thought about the progress of the pieces for his approaching show came to mind, he simply put it off as a headache and began thinking about something else. He couldn't have done this before. It wouldn't have been possible. Nearly a year and a half earlier, Billy had had to get his passport renewed, and a series of bureaucratic snafus kept him at the agency hours beyond the usual wait. When he returned home, Marta had informed him he needed to shower and dress quickly in order to meet Tippy's car out front. Billy had forgotten that he'd promised to accompany his dealer for dinner at a collector's home in Tribeca. When he recognized that joining Tippy meant that he'd have to let an entire day pass without working in his studio, the overwrought Billy became physically ill, running desperately to the bathroom, seized by nausea. His routine was so powerfully ingrained within him that he had vomited for half an hour as Tippy's car idled in wait downstairs.

In the mental ward, the medication's effect made him exempt from exactly such obsessive behavior. It was the one aspect of the drug that he allowed himself to indulge. He wondered why he'd been treating his painting with such a regimented attitude, especially since his art was always based on instinct, which should call for more spontaneity. Still, Billy had seen the dangers of addiction among neighborhood friends, and he swore that he wouldn't touch drugs again after finishing his stay in the locked wing.

An idea had been gestating in his mind since he'd entered last night. While in a place like this, if you are either forced by external circumstance or simply allow yourself to take one single day off from being a human being, you may never recover. If you cease being part of the human universe in all its aspects, abandoning your responsibilities to yourself and others, you'll never recover what was lost in that single day. It doesn't matter how hard you try, or how fast you run, you're lost to one degree or another.

There was a movie in the TV room that night. It was about submarines and a close call with a third world war. It didn't seem all that appropriate to Billy, but perhaps there was some therapeutic subplot. What did he know? What did he care? His newfound affinity with drugs had him dog-tired and it was only 8:00 p.m. He lay on the bed and, for the first time, read the line of graffiti that someone had carved deeply into the side of the night table. *In the same way that you cannot get out*, it read, *you can't get in.*

6

B illy woke early on his final day in the locked wing. His neck hurt from the tiny pillow they'd given him, which felt like a beanbag.

He read a little of the book on his night table. He hadn't read much lately at home and had forgotten how much pleasure it brought him. He resolved to get a number of books to read when he got out.

He rose from bed and showered for the first time since he'd arrived. His experience with the commonplace pleasures and deprivations of the ward opened his captive insight that, despite his best efforts, he had grown slightly spoiled over the years. Spoiled, always on the move, and out of touch with people like the aide who had led him to the wing from the lobby that first night. What a wonderful thing it was, he thought, that a man who saw so much anguish and unpredictability day after day in his job here could go home at night and build model cars out of kits. It didn't matter that the workmanship was shoddy; it was simply the fact that he could conceive of such a thing, and put so much enthusiasm into it. Billy felt even worse now for breaking the little sports car's axle than he had at the moment it happened.

He got in line for his final day of meds. He thought about asking the doctor if he could forgo the last day's dose but decided there was no sense rocking the boat. Besides, the anticipation of returning home to his loft was certain to be a large ordeal. Having a bit of this pharmaceutical backup, so to speak, couldn't hurt in the least. Through the small rectangular slot in the

Lucite window, the nurse slid him the same pills that she had the day before. He remembered to drink it down in front of the nurse and, afterward, offer her a few words to prove that he had swallowed the stuff. He thanked her and she said good-bye to him, knowing he was leaving this day. Billy was disarmed by the sincerity in her voice. Though his hand barely fit through the slot, he managed to offer her a contorted shake with three fingers.

Billy went to the cafeteria to eat his final meal behind the locked door. He had an appetite for the first time since he'd arrived, and had seconds on scrambled eggs and home-fried potatoes. The potatoes were prepared as he favored them, streaked thickly with the strange freckling of paprika. It was the way his mom had made them for him and his brother along with fried bologna and eggs on Sundays after church. He didn't actually know if he liked the taste of paprika, only that he loved that color. An old orange, soft yet steep, the shaded brilliance of something exotic carried in leather bags on the backs of camels across long desert sands. Volcano sweat.

Billy was doing sit-ups in his room, anxiously anticipating the doctor's final orders for his release. As he bobbed up and down, he noticed a man standing at the door of his room, staring in. He had a rumpled posture and remarkably clear eyes. Their color was either blue or green, you couldn't tell exactly which, only that they were blazing in the hallway light, that strange amalgam of light where neon above bounces off linoleum below.

The man was holding three large stalks of corn. Not like corn from the grocery store where a few leaves cover a yellow ear, but whole stalks, dangling with roots and all. They were huge. "As high as an elephant's eye." Straight from being picked from a farm upstate, perhaps, or New Jersey.

"I know these are a rather odd gift," the man said, "but I had some visitors and just saw them off a few moments ago down at the big door. I never know if I should call it the exit door or the entrance. They were relatives along with an old friend from my hometown in Pennsylvania and, the truth be told, they brought me these stalks of corn at my request. I was kidding when I made the suggestion, but though they are lovely people my family has no sense of irony. They feel more comfortable taking everything literally, whether it's passages from the Bible or corn."

"And are you glad now that they brought them?" Billy asked, really wanting to know, for some reason.

"I am glad," answered the man quickly. "I will tell you the reasons why I'm happy that they took me so literally . . . if I'm not being intrusive, that is."

"Not at all," Billy answered. Rising up from the floor, he signaled the man to come in and take a seat. "I'm intrigued." The man entered the room with tiny steps, dragging the corn behind him. There were still clumps of Pennsylvania dirt dropping off the roots.

"Oh, these are relatively small, to tell you the truth," the man said, suddenly seeming much more at ease, sitting cross-legged in a chair. He was less rumpled-looking when sitting down, with an elegance in the way he intertwined his hands that made Billy think of Sherlock Holmes. "You know, I really only wanted to stop and tell you face-to-face how much genuine enjoyment your art has provided my wife and me over the years. I heard that you were leaving today and I really wanted to take the opportunity. I didn't mean to burden you with my produce."

"Please"—Billy held up a hand and realized he was making serious eye contact with the man—"don't apologize another moment, and I thank you for the compliment, I truly do. So tell me why you were so glad to get the corn today. Does it remind you of back home? Do you live on a farm?"

"I grew up on a farm, the one in Pennsylvania where this corn grew. The place is still in the family. My brother, who was one of my visitors, continued the farming tradition in the family. He actually added more land to the place, buying up the adjacent farm when it went belly-up. In a tough time for farmers, my brother thrives with an almost Faustian success. He's got the grower's touch, something that I never had. Don't get me wrong, I love the farm. I still spend time there, maybe one or two weekends a month, in the old house where I grew up. Years ago my brother and his wife built a fancy new place for his family. My wife and I never had children. She passed away a few days shy of six months ago. It's still a difficult issue for me and, in some way, I'm sure, part of the reason that I'm here. I don't want to talk about that. The only thing to say is that I loved her very much.

"If you don't mind a bit of a mess in your room, I'm going to shuck this one ear here as we talk. You'll have a nice piece of corn, fresh from the soil, to cook up at home since you're being released soon. These large green husks are just yanked off easily. They are very large, as you can see, and act as the plant's first line of protection. They are also shaped in a manner to steer rain directly to the ear and, from there, the roots. I'll stick them in that waste-basket there if you'll be kind enough to pass it closer. These roots are tough, as thin as they are. I can't believe that he left them on. They're like veins, you know? Do you know the so-called rules of the Emerald Tablet?" Billy did not.

The man continued, "The primary occult laws of the universe written by Hermes Trismegistus? The first law is that what is above is identical to what is below, or the workings of the universe out there are no different than those of the earth. This was later vindicated scientifically by Newton's third law of motion, but that's another matter, and one on which I may be wrong . . . physics was never my strong suit. This idea of Hermes, however, can extend or reduce itself beyond the universe and the planet, or within it. For example, the roots of this plant being like the vessels in our bod-ies where blood flows, or the way the connecting flow of rivers is like the body's arteries. Size doesn't matter, only the correspondences. The waters passing through rivers irrigating the land, the blood flowing, sustaining our bodies, the moisture seeping from soil through these roots supporting this corn's growth. All these similarities are variations on the isomorphic theory of Hermes. Look at these silky strands I've reached. Tell me that it doesn't look and feel like the most stunning, natural blond hair. Here, feel how soft it is. Run it through your fingers."

The rumpled man ripped a handful of the yellow fibers from the ear and handed them to Billy. It did feel like hair, and Billy could remember thinking, when he was just a child and his mother was readying corn on the cob to boil, how the fibers resembled the hair of a girl named Liz who lived in a third-floor apartment. The man continued cleaning off the final strands and handed the ear to Billy. "Here," the man said, "all ready for you to take home, as I promised."

"Even the rows of kernels resemble teeth," Billy offered, smiling, try-ing to keep with Hermes' ideal, "though the yellow color is a bit of a put-off." They laughed.

"Our lives are, in the most simple sense, not that different than veg-etables'," the man continued, laying the other two stalks on the floor beside his chair. "Both go through a period of protected gestation, they emerge, they grow, reach their peak, then they slowly rot away until they die." A sense of sadness, which the man had not previously shown, permeated this last analogy. Billy assumed he was thinking of his beloved, dead wife. He could tell that any light remaining in the old fellow's eyes was a remnant of her, the brightness of her memory. Billy imagined that she had died a long slow death. Still, he had no intention of asking about her, or the reason that this man was in the locked wing, far from the Pennsylvania countryside.

After lunch, Bruno and a doctor Billy had not previously seen came into his room. Billy was lying on the bed thinking about the wide-ranging insights of the corn man. There was something both wise and, yes, spiritual in his demonstration.

"We're going to release you now, Mr. Wolfram." The doctor spoke in an even, matter-of-fact tone. "Bruno will get you your clothing; you can get dressed and sign out at the desk up front."

"I can call you a car service if you like," Bruno added, "and I'll take you down to the car myself so there's no mix-up." As he was talking, Bruno was cautiously unfolding Billy's tuxedo from its box and laying it out neatly on the bed. "Jesus, look at the shine on these skimpy shoes. I can actually use them as a mirror."

Bruno brushed back his hair while staring into the shoes, and then he laid them on the floor along with the socks.

"We'll give you your privacy now to get dressed," the doctor said, poking Bruno softly in the ribs. "You'll be met by your escort here when you're ready."

Those terse sentences by the doctor, telling him he could get dressed and go, had a cutting effect on Billy, and it wasn't because they had caught him so off guard, though they had. He knew he would be leaving sometime that day, but when the actual official words were spoken, he was overcome with a sense of deflation he hadn't expected. This controlled environment had given him a chance to shut down, for the most part at least, and focus on the problems in his work, and the quest he had set for himself. He wasn't concerned about ever repeating anything like the incident that had landed him in here. He couldn't even recall where to line up the dominoes, never mind making them fall in sequence. It had only been a short time, but from what he'd learned from his solitude and the wide variety of suffering among the patients, he wasn't sure if he was ready to be out there in that real world again, flooded with its inconsistencies, rage, and buried emotions. He quickly glanced down at the corn and understood he'd had it so easy that, after one spill, he'd hesitated getting back on the horse. Billy was acting foolish and knew nothing could have changed all that much, especially in his world. He had to get back onto the horse, the ten-speed English racing bike, or the Town Car . . . whichever pulled up first.

He realized he would be exiting the mental ward in formal wear. He checked himself out in the mirror above the sink. Aside from his unshaven face and the fact that he had crammed his tie into his pocket and left his top button undone, he looked pretty much like he had when he'd arrived. His stay had seemed longer than it was.

Billy emerged from his room and found Bruno waving him down to the desk at the entrance door, now the exit. Billy stared again through the window with the green tint and the octagonal wires. He liked it, though he found it disturbing that he was at the door to his ostensive freedom and was already seeing art in the quotidian. Billy didn't know if he was ready for this; he just wanted to keep his painter's instincts shut down for a while longer.

Bruno handed him a large manila envelope. Billy lifted the two tin prongs and unsealed it. Inside were his "personal items," thousands of dollars in cash secured by a thick rubber band, and his key chain. Shifting the arc of his body, he stuck the keys in his jacket and shoved the cash deeply into the pants. The larger bills always in his right pocket clustered in sets of rising denomination . . . fives, tens, twenties, and fifties. Hundreds were strictly avoided, since Denny had mentioned, "Hundreds are for assholes and drug dealers." In the left pants pocket were singles and change. Billy liked having coins in his pockets despite Denny's dictum against it. In an age of credit cards and ATMs, the coin was an emblem of antiquity, providing a connection with times and events long before the Common Era. Lincoln's face might just as well be Caesar's or Herod's. Besides, Billy liked the feel of a single coin between his fingers. Again, it was a connection to the past. The past of his youth, when the touch of a dime anticipated a vanilla Coke, or two bags of red licorice sticks.

Billy didn't count the money. The thought never occurred to him. The wad felt about the same thickness as when he was checked in. Besides, though he recalled the cop's offhanded remarks that it was a large amount, he didn't have a clue as to the exact sum.

With one last, halfhearted gesture, he turned the envelope upside down and shook it, hoping the chip from the museum's coat-check room might tumble out. Though he was for the most part vehemently anti-fashion, Billy was admittedly fond of the cashmere overcoat that was left behind. He'd never forgotten that night, years before, when a stunning woman approached him and, with wanton deliberation, began to run her hands freely across the lush material. Leaning so close that Billy still recalled the anisette on her breath, she whispered, "This coat is the *most exquisite basic* I could ever imagine."

He signed the stack of papers that Bruno handed him. Then it came, the inevitable moment. Bruno handed Billy a piece of scratch paper and asked him if he might favor him with a quick, abstract drawing . . . signed, of course. Billy looked at the window in the door and penciled in an octagon within a rectangle, then signed it and passed it back over.

Bruno selected a key from his large key ring and opened the door of the locked wing. Billy followed him to the elevator bank, and outside to the waiting Town Car. With each step, he felt the speed of New York City accelerate, and the outside world taking on more substance. The unexpected apprehension about his medically sanctioned freedom made him rush into the back seat of the car and slam the door shut. Billy tapped the window and signaled, with five flailing fingers, a sincere good-bye to Bruno as the car peeled out, taking him home to what he had to do.

7

The car took off, turning left onto Second Avenue, then 96th Street, and onto the ramp to the downtown side of the FDR Drive. Billy looked down at the freshly detailed back seat of the Lincoln Town Car. Faux-leather nets were attached to the backs of the driver and front passenger seats, like those on airplanes, holding an array of newsmagazines.

The standard artificial pinewood scent wafted through the Town Car, but it was mixed with something pungent that made him feel slightly claustrophobic. For the first time, Billy looked up at the driver. He had a dark complexion and shiny black hair that, from behind, seemed like one of those "duck's ass" styles from the fifties—greasily fashioned with Brylcreem or Vaseline. One of Billy's few memories of his father was the container of Brylcreem that he kept on the bathroom sink. It came in a red and white tube the same size and color as the family's favorite toothpaste. Billy heeded the distinction cautiously, but wondered how often groggy, well-groomed men mistakenly brushed their teeth with this unctuous salve in the morning. Another look at the driver's head brought the TV ad's theme song for Brylcreem surging into Billy's mind. A male group sang in barbershop quartet style:

Brylcreem, a little dab'll do yer.
You'll feel it in your hair, like a millionaire.

The day before, after seeing Dr. Hui, Billy had called Marta. Now, reaching for the car phone cradled between the seats, Billy called again to inform her that he was on his way home. With the sedan veering into the fast lane, Billy pondered, one last time, how capriciously a person's capacity could be labeled "diminished," and, in turn, how—with the signing of some papers and the turning of a key—that same person was suddenly reinitiated back into the status of upstanding citizen.

In yesterday's hasty call, Billy had asked Marta to have the other assistants and apprentices out of the loft by the time he got there the next day. He had instructed her to pay them off—with a generous six-month severance. "Just tell them that I'm dealing with some personal ordeal, and I wouldn't do it if it were not absolutely essential," he had told her in a quavering voice. "Actually, you'd better make that 'some personal bullshit.' 'Ordeal' sounds too much like Tolstoy, and I don't want them to think I'm that bad off." He had assured her that her own employment was secure, and that, no doubt, he would be in need of her help more than ever.

Marta had known where he was calling from but said nothing about it. She had tried to sound businesslike, but there had been an undertow of dismay and solace in her voice. Still, she'd taken care of her uncomfortable assignment and now assured Billy that all the assistants were "more than understanding" regarding his "unanticipated needs" and that the loft was, at the moment, "so quiet it's really kind of scary." He told her that the car seemed to be making good time and that he would be seeing her soon. After hanging up, Billy gradually began to acknowledge the deep concern in Marta's voice.

The driver, from all appearances, was from India. He focused intently on the road. In his incisive brown eyes, however, Billy felt he could see a convergence of deep passions. Perhaps the longing for his wife's familiar body, or the repetition of a single word in Urdu, he didn't know.

Billy felt his thoughts beginning to race and concentrated on the creamy color of the back seat.

If I could only find the doctor who could tell me where the pause button is, he thought. His attempt to slow the process through humorous dialogue with himself failed miserably. He felt like one of those magicians locking together endless metal rings. He closed his eyes for a few moments and things slowed up. The rings ceased flying his way. When he opened his eyes he noticed the driver staring intently at him through the rearview mirror. Billy smiled, his forehead resting on the right side window. For the first time, he felt liberated from the regimen of the locked wing. He was back in that outside world of turmoil and illusion, and it wasn't overwhelming him in the slightest. *Not for now, at least.* He repeated that phrase to himself. He didn't want those words becoming a mantra for him.

Out on the East River, the wind was kicking up and green coasting foam rose in the wake of a sailboat. Moving across the seat to the left window, he fixed on the whitecaps stirring in the wake of a yacht motoring north. He could see the water's gravel-gray tint momentarily turn an inhibited blue as the small waves folded over and spun downward. As it weakened, the backwash formed a pattern, a quivering alliance, out of the initial chaos. This, for Billy, was the unlatched world where art lurked like sin and fear, and the quest still remained.

Billy felt much older. It was as if he'd been sequestered for years, rather than days. Everything was happening much too suddenly. Billy wasn't used to this manic pace. One moment he felt fully recovered from his ordeal, then, suddenly, he was hamstrung by another emergence of the dread racing thoughts. It was a rebound effect in reaction to his sudden freedom. The effect was not unlike the overbearing zealousness of a man newly converted to a religious faith, or a recovering alcoholic. The ephemeral splendor of his marine reflections put Billy close to overload. Ordinary things can seem extraordinary when you're encased in a pseudo-elegant metal box, traveling at 60 miles per hour.

He turned from the river, directing his thoughts to the car's freshly detailed interior. The nets holding the magazines reminded Billy of the red net sacks of oranges his mother had brought home year-round. They were her favorite fruit. A few years back, when offered a commission for a public space, Billy considered a large painted sculpture of one of these net bags. He quickly eschewed the notion; the idea seemed derivative, its reference too limited and personal.

To Billy, if you were given the privilege—and paid abundantly well—to express your vision in a propitious space, whether it be a city park or a corporate building's plaza, there was one requisite. The piece must evoke commonplace joys and sorrows, defy the status quo, or expose the illusory fear in the hearts of whoever passes by. Still, he loved the color of those nets, and could only imagine those dazzling strands at a suitably large scale against the New York sky, particularly at sunrise.

Billy slid back over to the spot where he had been sitting. After hesitating awhile, cautiously framing the words, he spoke up to the driver. The question came out louder than he had wanted. In most cases, people with mental problems seem to speak in a consistently loud voice, and Billy realized that he had adopted this mannerism. He needed to be vigilant of his modulation. "Excuse me, driver." He was now on the cusp of a whisper. "Can I ask you a question?"

The driver seemed slightly surprised. Aside from demands to run a red light or to take a different route to the airport, customers probably rarely addressed him. "Yes, sir." The driver spoke in very fine English, with a fading colonial accent. "I hope the answer is what you seek." His face lit up with a tiny smile through the rearview mirror.

"You are from India?" Billy asked, satisfied with his intonation.

"Yes, from the Punjab region." The man spoke fast, but sweetly.

"Are you a Hindu?" Billy asked, as matter-of-factly as possible, wondering if the man might find such a question unseemly. The ability to take chances and speak with rash spontaneity, he realized, was one more repercussion of the mental ward.

"I am Hindu, yes," he answered. "Is there something that interests you about my religion? I am by no means a scholar."

"A man who professed to study your religion recently told me about how we are in the 'Kali Yuga,' or 'Age of Darkness.' He said that the Kali Yuga is the final age, which is destined to come to an end within the next dozen years. When this takes place, he warned—much like the Christian myth of the Four Horsemen of the Apocalypse, described in the final book of the New Testament—the demon Kali will ride on a white horse with a terrible sword and destroy everything in existence. I had heard others speak about our being trapped in the 'Kali Yuga age' many times before, and I've always been very intrigued by this concept. What I really want to ask you is, when will it end? I mean, is there any specific time or date when all we know will simply cease to be? Could it happen as quickly as this man has postulated? Also, can't mankind somehow redeem itself, and allow a new age to begin? I know these are very likely naïve and foolish questions to you, but how much longer will this age of darkness last?"

The man listened with serious, polite attention. Billy was watching his face in the rearview, hoping the driver didn't notice. Now the beatific smile returned. "And as for you, sir"—the dark man spoke in a curiously mellifluous voice, his eyes still intently on the highway—"are you of the Christian faith?"

"I was raised a Roman Catholic," Billy answered, not including the fact that he had fallen from the faith. That little caveat had become so dominant among Catholics of his generation that it had developed into a cliché. Billy wanted no place with that lot. They had grown too lazy to devote time to any spiritual demands. Though he loathed the politics and hierarchical structure of the church, he still remembered its rituals, the mysterious Latin mass, and the wisdom of Christ's parables, which provided an essential comfort to his youth.

"As I imagined," the driver responded. Billy could see that he raised his eyes now and then to the rearview mirror, creating some sense of contact. "Yes, I am a Hindu. There is my god there, just to my left."

He made a very slight gesture in that direction with his head. His words and gesture took Billy's attention back to the river. The water was still raging. *This is the metaphorical answer of a wise man of great faith in an elemental Eastern religion,* Billy concluded. Most Westerners would not understand the intensity of his subtle analogy. Looking onto the waters, the artist recalled the famous axiom of Heraclites: "You never step in the same river twice." Billy concluded that the driver was symbolically describing his Hindu gods, not in our impulsively anthropomorphic manner, but in the flow of the water.

"Ahhh . . . yes, I see." Billy drew out the words, shaking his head at the simple depth of the man's sagacious illustration. He was amazed how effortlessly this seemingly down-to-earth driver had snatched up the metaphor of the river to represent his elemental gods. The entire complex cosmology of Hinduism boiled down to one of the four ancient elements. "I see and comprehend!"

"You see and comprehend what?" the driver inquired, obviously perplexed. In the back seat, Billy remained oblivious to the Indian's tone. He continued nodding his head, a hazy smile on his face.

"The river, of course," Billy said. "How you speak figuratively of the river as your god."

"What? I made no reference to any river." The man was still perplexed, but there was now a restrained annoyance in his voice. "I was gesturing to this small picture taped to the dashboard, just to the left of the speedometer." He hastily removed his left hand from the steering wheel and tapped the picture with his index finger. It was a brightly colored representation of Shiva on what appeared to be the front of a postcard. Billy felt like an idiot for not spotting the picture of Shiva. He wanted to disappear. He couldn't see the goddess for the river.

The driver had a smirk on his face. Billy only hoped that he hadn't offended the man's religious beliefs in some way, and that the shape of subdued derision on his dark lips was solely from the need to drive this white imbecile around awhile longer. Billy had a lot of Buddhist friends and he knew that it was nearly impossible to offend them. He wasn't as certain about Hindus, but it wasn't going to do anyone any good to just shut up and disengage. Billy had a need to see things resolved. He loathed the onslaught of passive aggression that he noticed evolving at an alarming rate among his younger friends.

"I'm terribly sorry." Billy raised his voice, forgetting his modulation. "When you said 'to the left,' I just assumed you meant the river. I didn't see the image of Shiva, truly. I thought you were offering a cryptic and wise metaphor, using the river. I know it sounds rather foolish, but I've had a bad weekend."

"I understand," the driver said. "I find the entire misunderstanding quite funny, actually.

"With all due respect, sir, at times the mind tends to accelerate beyond its own rationale's limits, like those cars across from us, speeding by in the uptown lanes. Like everything in this city, in fact. This comes from a hurried and unbalanced process of breathing, which you have somehow acquired and which I noticed from the first time you spoke. It immediately drew my attention, and reminded me of the awkward breathing of a man that I knew in India, who suffered a terrible trauma when he was young.

"In his case, it was meningitis, and the anxiety and torment of the painful and exhausting medical procedures, which in time gave him back his health. However, both the disease and the cure affected his breathing to dangerous extents. Like him, you must practice the correct way of breathing, and your mind will flow—like your breath—slowly, with power and certainty.

"But, returning to your question, your friend is wrong. We have, at the least, another two hundred thousand years before the Kali Yuga age comes to an end. Not before then will Kali come, as you say, with his avenging sword. The fact is I don't know of any real scholar who would hazard to name an exact date. Estimates vary widely, and one would be foolish to postulate one specific time . . . whether a day or a year."

"And there is no chance we can save ourselves and turn the process around to be redeemed?" Billy had regained the naïve enthusiasm in his voice and was overjoyed to learn that mankind had considerably more time left to live than his friend had calculated.

"There is nothing to do. We control nothing." The driver was now fully engaged. "A new cycle will begin. Kali will descend on his white horse and—with a stroke of his sword—all will be destroyed. In this age of darkness the only thing we can do is offer ourselves in adoration to the goodness of the Almighty. We do not ask for redemption. That's all past. It is the time to surrender.

"I must say that I have always liked the idea of the feminine principle in your Catholic religion—the Cult of the Virgin. Don't they have a ritual called the adoration of the Sacred Heart of Mary? It is like that—to adore without expectation or petition."

"They do have such a rite. It's called a novena. There is also the adoration of the Sacred Heart of Jesus." Billy was amazed by what the man had said. The female aspect contained within the Virgin cult was one of the few remnants of his religion that he still revered. "Thank you for your information. Let me impose on you one more time, however. You did say we had two hundred thousand more years, correct? There is no validity to this paltry twelve years?"

"At least two hundred thousand, and that is a very conservative number," the driver told Billy with a smile. "Truly, you must learn to breathe. You let too many circumstances worry you."

The traffic was very slow for a Sunday afternoon. Twenty minutes had passed and they were only as far downtown as 52nd Street. The cars on the uptown side of the Drive were just breezing along. Billy and the driver concluded it was either an accident or some kind of weekend-only construction project.

"Perhaps we should get off at the next exit and take the avenues downtown," the driver suggested into the mirror. "I think that would be the faster route."

"That's fine with me," Billy said. "Let's get off at 42nd Street and go down Second. It only seems to be getting worse." That was an understatement. The sedan was now at a complete standstill, as was all the traffic ahead of them. Rising up and craning his head outside the window, Billy could see the line of cars winding before them. As he stretched higher to various vantage points, the sun reflected off the metallic painted rooftops of the endless vehicles. If Manhattan was the kingdom, this traffic jam was the dragon, idling in line, like a single gigantic snake, spewing carbon monoxide and smoke into the low autumn skies.

"This would be a good time for you to practice your breathing," said the sapient chauffeur, finally turning and facing Billy. It might have been the bottled-up excess of stimulation, but Billy could swear there was a nimbuslike glow to the man. Maybe it was his astonishingly white teeth in contrast with his brown features. "Inhale and exhale through your nose, thinking of the air as water streaming back and forth, slowly and evenly."

Billy shut his eyes and gave it a shot. Over the years, an array of people—from athletic coaches to a poet friend who practiced Buddhist meditation—had told him that he really did have a peculiar, and likely detrimental, method of breathing. It carried over to his speaking voice, which contained a sort of quiver. Friends would call Billy at times—it was worse before noon, for some reason—and ask him if something devastating had happened. They inquired if there had been a death in the family, telling him it sounded like he was about to break into tears at any moment. It was very disconcerting for Billy, who was oblivious to this quirk. Even Denny had told him that he could have a decent singing voice if he only learned a more economic method of taking in air.

Now, stranded on FDR Drive, he sat with his backbone straight, trying to control the stream of air flowing in and out of his nose. He had a voice somewhere in his brain assuring him that it was only a matter of time before he screwed up and returned to the labored, awkward technique that he had spent years perfecting. The car crept forward about eight feet before coming to another dead stop.

"Do you know why an infant invariably cries the moment it comes out of his mother?" Now it was the driver asking the question. A strange question.

"I don't know the reason, no." Billy struggled to get the words out while continuing his exercise. "Why do they cry?"

"I will tell you." The man spoke more softly, the sweetness returning to his voice. "But first I must explain what it is like before we are born. Many contemplate, and consume themselves worrying about, what will happen when their life ends. However, we rarely think of what occurs *before* we are born. I must explain this to you before I answer why the infant cries at birth."

The traffic was so locked now that men were out of their vehicles, standing on the sloped pavement of the Drive, trying to ascertain what was holding everything up. It was only six blocks to the 42nd Street exit, but Billy and his driver knew they were going nowhere. They were in no rush. Billy was relaxed, breathing correctly on Corinthian leather. He knew his gridlocked guru was unfazed by the big stall. This was either because of the Eastern factor, enabling him to shift—in the worst of delays—into balmy meditation, or because of the Western factor—that he was getting paid by the air-conditioned hour.

The driver—still facing him—continued his narrative.

"I will try to be brief, but I must be thorough. To begin, you must understand that a child—or the life spirit of a child—chooses the moment that he or she will be born."

"That means he must choose his parents," Billy interrupted, immediately realizing it was a mistake by the slight smirk on the narrator's face.

"Yes, choosing one's parents is essential in selecting the moment of one's birth." The man continued after exhaling his frustration. "The biological mechanics, such as the fertilizing of the egg and other mundane fundamental requirements, occur and, in time, the fetus is formed and infused with this spirit.

"While the child is within his mother on the gross material plane, however, this spirit still maintains all its attributes from the higher plane. This nascent spirit knows all. It has unmediated knowledge to answer every question ever asked by the wisest men on earth. It can transcend time and space. Most importantly of all, it is as one—in complete, harmonious love and understanding—with the Almighty. But the moment that it gives its final consent to the Almighty and is born into this world, it loses all this knowledge, power, and love. No longer is the spirit directly connected to God.

"So, the child waits throughout the pregnancy with all its knowledge and power still intact. Actually, you cannot truly say that the spirit 'waits,' because on the higher planes, which he still straddles from the womb, there is no such thing as time.

"In those timeless moments before the spirit is born into this world, the Almighty speaks to it, asking a series of questions. You and I can only imagine the feeling of absolute love between the two. 'Why do you want to be part of such a world?' God questions the unborn spirit. 'You can remain with me in Paradise, but you choose to enter a world filled with terror and fear. You will yourself become a practitioner of its brutalities.'

"The spirit answers the Almighty, 'Oh, no, my Father . . . I will never become like those brutal beings. I understand too well how they give in to the moment—to their lusts and their fears. I will know how to abate such things and discover my true essence in the world. It is the path I must take.'

"'But you forget that you will not retain this knowledge you are now blessed with,' the Almighty warns. 'You have seen the horrific pain and death mankind has inflicted on the creatures of the earth and seas, which I have created. Will you—absent the wisdom you now possess—perform such vile acts on my beloved creatures? Will the hand you possess on the material plane pick the pomegranate from the tree as you now imagine, or will it tear brutally at the flesh of my creatures?'

" 'No, my Father. I will treat Your creatures with the love and respect that they deserve. I look forward to experiencing the feel of an animal's willing touch. They too are filled with the divine *prana*. How could I ever harm one of Your creations?' "

As the driver paused shortly, images of throwing a tortoise from a cliff when he was a child passed through Billy with disturbing lucidity. The sound of its shell as it shattered on the rocks below. Fortunately, the cruel reverie evaporated as the driver continued. Billy pressed his toes against the inside of his shoes, rising forward in attention.

"Again the Almighty speaks: 'I see men and women in the material world who practice vivisection on their fellow human beings. There was a time that this took place in war and because of economic inequities. That is horrid enough. Soon, however, many will do this for the sheer pleasure they gain from it. Others, who follow the way of the dark lodges, take away life ritually to procure power. These acts will signal the age that cannot be escaped. Would you do harm to another man or woman? Would you kill?'

" 'My beloved Father, the words You speak cause me a trembling with sadness,' the spirit once again replies. 'It would never be possible to kill a higher being, knowing that You as well would suffer. I want to bring comfort to other men and women. I want to unveil to them the truth within them, the sacred connection we all share. I could never hurt another. I know these things will not be as easy as they seem to me in this current form, but I somehow am certain that my path is to enter the material world and devote myself to the goodness of mankind.'

"The Almighty knows that the time of birth is near and asks another question. 'And what of Me? Will you love Me, as you now love Me, once you pass into the world of men and women? The world of dualities and chaos that you insist is your path?'

"Though the spirit of life still has no form, it feels a sensation of impalpable tears flowing from its eyes. It is a manifestation of anticipation and sublimity. 'Oh, my Father, how could this sensation ever subside? I am what I am as Your dream. I will always love You, through the cycles without end. I love—'

"The last words of the spirit of life go unfinished. Suddenly it is pierced by a furious vortex of sound and a dim but growing light at a point that seems to begin or end . . . it does not know. The spirit thinks it hears—or, rather, feels—some final words of love from the Almighty. It can't be sure, however. The connection with the higher planes is fading. It is, however, allowed one final remembrance—like a last breath before submerging into the deep waters of ignorance. It recalls—in a time both so short and so complete it is immeasurable—all it had known as spirit, and all the promises made.

"Then everything goes dark and cold. The child begins to cry as the doctor's hands pull the infant's head out of the womb, into a blinding light."

Billy was sitting on the edge of his seat. The Indian man had told the story—or the allegory or parable, whatever it was—with such melodious conviction in his voice and minimal yet poignant expressions on his dark face.

Billy was mesmerized and wanted the man to go on, but the driver continued to just stare at him with a resolute smile. "My breathing," Billy mumbled as best he could, aware that he was hyperventilating.

"That was not my reason for stopping," the man finally spoke again. "I was simply clearing my throat, and moving my foot, which had, as you say, 'fallen asleep.' But I am glad you are still aware of the awkwardness of your breathing. It must be quite unbearable for you. With all due respect, sir, I can only imagine that early in life you faced a terrible trauma—a death or an intolerable choice—that you have never resolved. Whatever the cause, it has manifested itself upon you physically through a very notable ineptitude in your breathing. It is amazing to me that Western doctors do not notice such things."

"I have never suffered from any real health problems," Billy said, offering this up to the driver without a hint of defensiveness.

"It is strange, then, that my dispatcher told me to wait for you at a hospital. That, however, is not my business. Allow me to continue with the story. You, meanwhile, can discipline your breathing."

The traffic had abruptly burst open, and they were moving down the 42nd Street exit ramp as the man continued his narrative. "To conclude, then—those brilliant lights in the maternity ward, and the touch of the doctor, are the first sensations this child—who happens to be a male—sees and feels on this gross material plane. Just seconds have passed since that moment, as he is exiting the womb, when the spirit relinquished all that the Divine Creator offered and, with such certainty, assured the Almighty that it would never depart from His will. It is then that the child begins to cry."

"But *why* does he cry?" Billy asked, realizing the man was simply reiterating the same ending. "You said the story clarifies the reason a child cries at birth."

"Once again, I thought I would first allow you an opportunity to answer now that you have heard the story, sir."

"Oh, I see," Billy replied politely. "I am afraid that would be impossible. You see—selfish as it sounds—I have embraced every detail of your fascinating and heartfelt story, but from the luxury of total passivity. Its beauty held me spellbound, and I have not begun to interpret its deeper meanings."

"'Action and repose,'" the driver said, "to properly balance these two things is to understand life."

"You know, I believe I've read that somewhere," replied Billy, unable to remember where.

"Fine." The bright smile returned to the dark man's face in the rearview mirror. "Western doctors will tell you it is because of the trauma of the bright lights. But in this era, even in this country, couples have midwives deliver their infants at home, often in total darkness. Still, the child cries the moment he or she is taken from the womb. Lights or pats on the newborn's bottom have nothing to do with it.

"This is the reason. The child weeps because, as its spirit passes into the world from the higher planes, there is that one very incalculably short moment—less than one could measure in time—when it remembers everything. The newborn recalls the absolute knowledge that it possessed and willingly forfeited . . . that it had been a part of the inviolable state of perfect being. Then it thinly recalls a fading shadow of sadness in the Almighty's voice, when He questioned this spirit's insistent appeal to enter this world in human form. The echoes of those last words are with us always throughout our lives.

"However, it is not the memory and loss of its omniscience that causes it to cry, nor even being so suddenly torn away from its relationship with the Almighty.

"No, they are not tears of regret for what it has *given up*.

"The child cries because—in that moment of remembrance—it realizes the depth of the promises it made in answer to the Almighty's questions. Now it is a fully formed infant on this material plane, and it suddenly senses the weight of gravity, and the strange linear movement of time in the voices around it. And in this new and unfamiliar place, it realizes that *it will never be able to fulfill the promises that it made* to the Almighty. It might try, but it will inevitably fail. Already it can feel the tugging of dualities, passions, and perceptions that the spirit had never anticipated. So the child cries for its futility. It cries for the future betrayal of its own promises, to the Absolute and to itself."

The driver had finished his story and, now in the spare traffic of New York on a Sunday afternoon, said nothing else to Billy. There was a moment—lasting about two city blocks—when Billy sat there, breathing correctly and feeling a radiant peace passing through his body. This was some type of metaphysical folktale, not passages from the Vedas, he thought, and, again, it was the sincerity in the man's voice that neutralized any excess of sentimentality. *Sentimentality* was a dirty word in the art scene. It was anachronistic. Besides, as Max, his first dealer, had once told him, *sentiment* was defined entirely differently in America than it was in Europe.

Then, without reason, this serenity was broken, and Billy was again riddled with racing thoughts. His breathing was totally out of whack and his legs were all akimbo, splayed across the back seat. He knew they were nearing his building, so he pulled a pen from the inner pocket of his tuxedo and on a subscription form he grabbed out of the magazine pocket hastily wrote the words, *Learn to breathe*.

They were turning the corner on Sixth Avenue onto 22nd Street. Billy was so disoriented by the driver and his curiously salient narrative that he could not recognize the storefronts surrounding his own building. The upholstery refinisher, which had a sign hanging on the door reading, WE RESERVE THE RIGHT TO TURN AWAY FURNITURE THAT WE FIND DISTRESSING, UGLY, OR BOTH. The seldom-open office supply store. The old sandwich shop with black-and-white tile floors, which had been on the verge of closing for the last 15 years. The Russian Orthodox church, whose cupola was nearly parallel with Billy's east windows, and its pastor, the ever-present Father Mishkin, unlocking the iron gates for evening services, his robe sweeping aside everything in his path.

Normally, these worn façades beckoned. Billy felt the encroachment of the quick and familiar, the inference of being home again. Now he was oblivious to it all. Once more the racing thoughts were summoned by the anxiety of the familiar, of facing his assistant Marta any minute, and being thrust into such close proximity with his paintings, sculpture, and work in progress. The upcoming show and a barrage of phone calls. The days in the hospital were behind him, and his quest—with its constantly vacillating purpose—lay before him. Billy didn't really want the ride to end. He just sat there, sunk in the leather, staring and breathing, his foot tapping on the rubber mat.

Finally the driver, who was waiting for Billy to tell him exactly where to pull over, stopped the car and, seeing his passenger was in a quasi-fugue state, sitting slack with an unhinged jaw, checked the address from his trip sheet. Craning his neck at the storefronts to his right, across the transom in peeling gold paint, he saw the number of Billy's buiding.

They were right in front of it.

PART TWO

1

Aside from anecdotal information—some accurate, some wildly erroneous—there is not much known about Billy's early years, and even less about his father, Joseph Wolfram—especially before Billy and his brother, Brian, were born. Their mother, Emma, married Joseph when she was only 18, eight years younger than her husband. After serving in World War Two, he remained in some shadowy intelligence branch of the military and was away for long intervals, sometimes up to a year.

He was an abusive man; it was a time when most women had no recourse but to accept such behavior—and she imagined having children would somehow ameliorate this situation. They tried getting pregnant and had no success; finally their doctor—a friend of the father's who smoked French cigarettes and weighed a remarkable 480 pounds—advised them that it probably was just not meant to be. The rotund G.P. offered no medical explanation for this diagnosis but, predictably, the husband blamed his wife. According to the fertility specialist that Emma had secretly consulted a few days later, she was caught within an ironic, vicious cycle. The doctor told her quite explicitly that her spouse's brutal episodes only served to exacerbate her strained nerves, causing fatigue, weight loss, and a weakened immune system. To this younger, impartial obstetrician, the effects of all the stress and turmoil imposed by her marriage to a callous, abusive man clearly explained her inability to conceive. He gave her some sedatives and advised her, more like a friend than a doctor, that she had taken a pitiless husband who had robbed her of the youthful hopes and aspirations of a second-generation immigrant.

Slowly a cocoon of indifference encased her and, inside her body, the clock ticked with an increasingly deafening volume. Then, at 33 years of age, when the couple had given up any hope, Emma became pregnant with Brian. When Billy was later conceived, there were so many difficulties in both the pregnancy and delivery that she was unable to bear any more children. This didn't matter to Mrs. Wolfram; she had her two baby boys and they brought life back to her and the apartment in Washington Heights where she had spent so much time alone during her husband's long absences. She doted on her boys, and through this new sense of purpose came determination and energy. She reassembled the bruised fragments of her former life. Motherhood also revived her long-dormant relationship with her Catholic upbringing. "It was your brother and you who led me back to the Church . . . to the Blessed Mother and our Savior, Jesus Christ Himself," she told Billy years later.

It was also the children and her fears for their future that gave her a renewed courage to stand up to her husband's brutality. By all reports, however, the father continued with his drinking and violent ways. Eventually, on the advice of her priest confessor, who guaranteed a swift annulment, she filed for divorce.

A solemn elderly jurist granted the divorce. There was nothing unusual about the actual decree—she kept the apartment in upper Manhattan and the father planned to begin a new life in the woodsy environs of Washington State. He was offered a transfer, and Joseph figured that his bipolarized brain and its unending schemes could prosper in the rugged inland of the Northwest. The unusual aspect—especially for the late 1950s—of the jurist's decree involved the custody of the two children. Brian was eight at the time, and Billy six. Instead of the routine placement of the two boys with their mother as primary caregiver, the aged judge—after years on duty at night court, obsessively fantasizing about living alone in a stand of redwoods—embraced a bizarre and, indeed, biblical tact. He split the boys between the two parents, arguing that this was the only way to ensure equality in the children's upbringing since the parents had agreed to live a continent apart and had limited finances for travel. Emma was spared the angst of having to choose between her two boys. As she later discovered, Joseph's entire willingness to grant a divorce hinged on his desire to have Brian, who was always his favorite, accompany him to the West.

Emma saw it, correctly, as another of Joseph's harebrained schemes cribbed straight from Solomon. She knew that he would favor Brian; Billy was much too sensitive and cerebral for his father. From that time on, it was she and Billy, with the exception of Brian's infrequent and often petulant visits.

Brian moved to Washington State quite willingly with his father. He was more a father's son . . . more interested in athletics and the outdoors than in reading books and drawing pictures. The irony was that Billy was a better natural athlete than Brian. He was thin, yet taut with muscle, and could outrun anyone in the playground in a short dash or long-distance run. Billy simply had no desire to compete.

On the other hand, Brian became progressively more ambitious as he grew older. Ferocious and ruthless, he would do anything necessary to win when it involved contact sports, including bending rules, cheating, and using cheap illegal hits designed to inflict serious injuries on opposing players.

To supplement his football prowess, he took up bodybuilding during the off-season in high school. There, falling in with a select crowd of iron-pumping maniacs, he eagerly joined them in consuming excessive amounts of steroids to enhance his strength. He didn't anticipate the side effects of depression and rage that developed from this "safe" dope.

The two brothers were polar opposites. Billy lived inside his mind and his receptive heart, giving the body its due through its innate dictates. Brian was attached so completely to his material body that his only feeling, aside from varying degrees of physical pain, was a stagnant blur of aimless narcissism.

Billy felt the sorrow and confusion of any young boy having his family cleaved into two halves. After all the decisions had been made, he was relieved he would be staying with his mother in New York. For one thing, late one night a year before the divorce, stumbling from bed to use the bathroom, he had witnessed his father slapping her. It was a full-on swing that cuffed the hollow of his mom's ear so powerfully it created an echo. This abuse had grown worse over time. At such a late hour, the parents never suspected the younger boy had seen it all through the dreamlike haze of his shallow, watery eyes. He never wanted to experience such a terrifying episode again but, through his precocious insight, knew he would.

There was another, more abstruse reason that young Billy didn't want to leave his mother or New York City. Even as a six-year-old whose reasoning was too vague to communicate, he believed himself blessed to be born in what he considered the greatest city in the world. He took that blessing seriously and felt an obligation to fulfill whatever its demands might be. He knew all the possibilities of his life were intertwined with this city. He felt attached to New York like it was an appendage of his body. If he, rather than his brother, had been chosen to go to Washington State with his dad, he would have run away—over and over until they realized he meant it. He believed that someone had bequeathed New York to him as a solemn trust. He didn't know if their motives were good or bad, nor if he was heir to success or failure.

Within a few months after the split with her husband, Emma had accumulated a folder of correspondence from Brian—in his misspelled block letters—informing her that his dad and he were doing well together, and how he preferred living in the country rather than the city. She trusted these assurances as genuine despite her maternal instincts and certain awkward phrases in his communications that could only have been written with his dad's coercion. The crude, sweet messages made Brian's absence easier for her to deal with. Still, Billy could detect gradations of sadness for her absent son—despite her attempts to keep them to herself. Even at his age, Billy understood her sorrow. He also found himself longing for his suddenly absent brother. He missed his father as well, but to a much lesser extent. It wasn't actually *his* father he missed, but the idea of a father. The sound of the man's open hand still vibrated in his memory.

Billy remembered vivid fragments about the day the parting took place. It was the first time he had been to an airport. He would never forget the overwhelming sounds and awesome size of the planes, but it was the look in the eyes of the other three that remained forever locked within him. His father's vacuous, disheveled stare—a confirmation of his undiagnosed bipolar condition—and the longing and will in his mother's gaze that mingled with the drops flowing down her face, as if she were mixing the alchemical aqua vitae within her tears to lure her son back. Brian stared at Billy with a confused array of emotions. There was sadness, there was fear, and there was some feigned devotion to his father, who finally took his hand and dragged him down the runway onto the plane. Before they disappeared from sight, the boy turned back to his mother and pulled loose from his father's grasp. Joseph cuffed Brian swiftly on the side of his head and jerked him back by his checkered shirt. Emma tried to run toward her son, who screamed while suppressing his tears, head lowered submissively. An airline worker who had witnessed the skirmish stepped in front of Emma and blocked her with his wide frame. "I'm sorry, miss," he said gently, "but I can't allow you down there. We can't have an incident. Please, now . . ."

Billy had watched it all. His head swerved side to side, but his feet remained in place a few yards behind her. Emma turned and ran so quickly for Billy that he was frightened at first. She collapsed to her knees and embraced the son that remained. Billy saw the eyes of people in the terminal on the two of them, which impulsively made his small hands grasp his mother tighter. His mother had told him earlier that morning that they would be taking the bus back to Manhattan, but after the commotion at the gate she decided on a cab. Billy pointed at every jet taking off, asking if that was the one with his brother, Brian, on it. Emma looked at him each time and stifled her tears long enough to say, "Yes, my little man, that's the one your brother is on." She never spoke of that day again.

Billy simply couldn't bear to see his mother in any kind of pain, particularly if he was unable to alleviate it. He was quite a brilliant boy when he entered the first grade of Catholic school, and an overly sensitive one, at that. Denny forever teased him about his first-grade theory on the burdens of life. It was Billy's contention that a woman's burden in life was having babies. That was perceptive enough, of course. When it came to a man's burden in life, however, Billy espoused that it was his hardship to have to awaken every day and speculate in the stock market. If he shirked this duty, a man was immediately arrested and prosecuted. "Have you ever tried to figure out the stock market?" he would query his school friends at the 10:00 a.m. milk and cookies break. "It's impossible. It's like having to go into that underground place, you know, the maze with that monster, the Minotaur, each morning." Neither Denny nor Billy himself could remember the genesis of this bizarre theory, particularly the notion that it was mandated by law that every American male over the age of 18 years must play the stock market.

It was about eight months after the divorce that Mrs. Wolfram found consolation working for the priests in the parish rectory. Though Billy's own fountain of belief was rapidly running dry by the time he was 13 years old, he saw his mother's faith as a gift, and envied her for the solace she derived from having rekindled it. Even if his skewed, undeveloped thinking could have formed a persuasive argument, he would never have tried to dissuade his mother or any of the other pious women in black kerchiefs shuffling to mass each morning of the efficacy of their sacraments. To Billy, it would be the most sinful form of thievery. He couldn't imagine deterring these faithful women from the sweet intent of their convictions.

In his intellect if not his heart, Billy had only the barest modicum of faith remaining by the age of 15 or so—that spectral scrap which *all* Catholics sustain until death, despite their most vehement protestations. One of the last straws for Billy was the loss of the Latin mass. He continued to be captivated by the rituals of the mass and the sacraments, but his gut told him that a satisfactory ritual required a mystery language. He had already felt that deep, undefined surge when the priest turned at the altar, addressing him with the phrase, *"Dominus vobiscum,"* and the exhilaration and breathless quickening of his pulse when he replied, *"Et cum spiritu tuo."*

He loved the Stations of the Cross, and the feminine aspect of the church through the Cult of the Virgin. The intuitive compulsion, which Billy relied on throughout his youth and its changes, told him that the female was essential to any religion, to any spiritual wholeness. For Billy, this had a deeper, disconcerting meaning. Because of his continuing impotency, the unworldly female might offer the only means of fulfilling his suppressed longing for women, and the mystery they implied. Unfortunately, for Billy Wolfram blind faith was no different than sex. Though he scoured himself for any means, he couldn't trick the thing into happening.

Also, for purely artistic reasons, he remained intrigued by the symmetry of the altar, and the dance between the altar boys and the priest. It was the feel of Latin as a child at mass, however—hearing it and responding in those obscure words, filled with such smooth vowels—that took him out of time, confusion, and the Cold War.

He did not believe himself, but he believed in his mother's belief. As Denny retorted to friends who castigated Billy and him for skipping mass on Sundays, "I don't believe in God, but I'm pretty sure that Mary was His mother."

In his later teens, his mother struggled with various illnesses, but she refused Billy's coaxing to see a doctor. She loathed doctors. Billy even enlisted the priests at the rectory to intercede in this matter, but she continued to procrastinate through excuses and broken promises. She was adamant: she felt fine and there was no reason to see any doctors. Of course, Billy knew this was out of apprehension for what the most perfunctory examination would uncover. When he looked in his mom's sweet blue-gray eyes during these confrontations, Billy realized there was more than fright inside them; it was knowledge. She didn't know exactly what the medical condition was, but she had an uncanny sense of her own body and she was certain it was terminal. Billy finally stopped prodding her. He didn't have the courage to arouse either her dread or her certainty.

One's senses obviously adapt more acutely to familiar places than to the world outside. The longer you live in an apartment, for example, the more you are infused with its smells, drafts, colors, and, naturally, the people who inhabit it. You know where the shadows fall coolly on sweltering summer days, and when the radiator's heat first rises on winter mornings. It is the *spiritus loci*.

When his mother's health began to fail, and Billy gave up on the doctor, he measured the stages of her worsening condition through those characteristics so peculiar to her and the apartment he had known as home since birth.

First, the rooms were losing the scrupulous care of her cleaning. There was the mess and eventual stench of unwashed dishes. That, at least, was something Billy could take care of. There was nothing to be done about the still-subtle scent of illness. To Billy, it reeked like rancid butter.

His few friends who stopped over could not pick up on these changes, but he could. He swiped mounds of dust off tables and shelves. It seemed unimaginable. The paint was cracking and chips were falling across the floor in the hallways and kitchen. This would have been intolerable just a couple of months before. Billy began to vacuum the apartment despite her protests that "cleaning floors is not a man's work." There were whole clumps of her hair in the carpets. His mom's beautiful hair, unfashionably long for a woman her age—not out of vanity, but because she thought it ludicrous to waste time and money at the beauty parlor. Its color, within less than a year and a half, had turned from its original gingerroot-brown to gray to an unsettling white.

Also, whenever he returned home in the late afternoon, the apartment was no longer filled with the tranquilizing aroma of home-cooked meals. Instead of cooking from scratch as she had always done, it was all frozen TV dinners heated up in a toaster oven, which the priests handed down to her when the archdiocese sent the rectory a new one. Then came the change in the sound of her slippers on the carpet—from firm steps to weak shuffling. Eventually, there were barely any sounds from her movements. She would lie on the sofa or on the living room rug watching TV.

The apartment was no longer filled with the dizzying fragrance of oils from her paint-by-numbers kits or the mayonnaise jars of kerosene to clean brushes. She had no energy for the brushstrokes, no patience for the precision required. Of all the adjustments Billy had to make, the loss of that heady scent was the most painful. He couldn't keep down any food. His stomach was already filled with friction. His mother was accelerating toward her demise faster than he could handle, but he kept fighting to slow it all down.

Her last finished painting, *Christ in the Garden of Gethsemane*, still lay against the wall on the floor beneath the living room table. It had been left there propped upright on some yellowing newspaper since she'd finished it over a year earlier, covered with the hair and dust that affixed to the oils before it had dried. When Billy tried to store it with the other paintings in the closet, she ordered him to leave it there. "I like to look at it right where it is." She knew it was the last "painting" she would do. She prided herself on remaining within the numbered lines, recognizing the weakness of her fingers and how badly her hands trembled.

Through it all, one thing remained unchanged. That was Emma's smoking, her Irish lungs lined thick with layers of tar, like creosote in a chimney. With each of her labored breaths, a shrill whistling emerged from her larynx. He'd noticed a similar, fainter wheeze every now and then for years, but it now screeched persistently like an old steam engine.

As he considered throwing away the smokes, Billy recognized how dire the situation had become. He didn't want to take away her only pleasure as she lay dying, despite knowing they were the cause of her illness. What difference did it make now?

Even the sunlight, which washed across the floorboards of his room every morning around 11:30, seemed weaker, hesitant to enter, as if it no longer had a place or function in this home. The color of Emma's moist skin had now turned a brittle gray that Billy tried to restore through the tenderness of his kisses. For 11 years, the sounds and scents peculiar to the home she'd made for the two of them had been a comforting presence. As each of these familiar senses ceased, he understood she'd taken another step closer to death.

After nearly a year of being completely confined to bed—even the priests were unable to convince her to go to a hospital—she just seemed to give up. Billy saw it in her eyes; there was a desertion there. He took to staying in his room, his head stuck far out the window, escaping this intruding smell of finality that coursed through the entire apartment like another tenant. He wondered how he recognized it, since he'd never been around the process of death before. Animals sense it. Billy recalled Denny's cat crawling off to die in a concealed place. They finally found it on the floor of his parents' closet, in a box of broken Christmas ornaments. It didn't matter how the fat feline knew; it just did.

Eventually, his mother's condition became worse, and Billy needed longer breaks from it. He would climb out the window and sit on the fire escape steps, sucking in lungsful of city life straining through the air.

His mother was AWOL to her surroundings, to this entire gross material plane. Two weeks later, when he arrived home and found her rolling on the floor, with Ironside, the handicapped detective, loudly solving a crime on the television, Billy called for an ambulance. Emma Wolfram was struggling to breathe.

The ambulance workers arrived quickly, and as they began lifting her off the floor, Billy hurried into her room and grabbed a bag of essential articles she had hesitantly prepared for such an occasion. As she was being strapped into the gurney, he reached to turn the TV off, but through that pale wheeze, his mother insisted that it remain on. She watched the flickering images until they lifted her out of its line of sight. She then began clutching her rosary beads and mouthing the Hail Mary. Billy followed the paramedics out of the apartment, but quickly turned and purposefully fumbled as he locked the door. He couldn't bear to watch them carry her frail body down the stairway, knowing she'd never return. After wiping his face with a handkerchief, he hurried outside and jumped into the ambulance.

She died in the intensive care ward the next morning, as Billy was soothing her parched lips with tiny shavings of lemon-flavored ice. A priest dozed in a chair aside the bed, his purple neck shawl slipped to the floor. The doctor told Billy that his mother had been diagnosed with at least nine problems that could have been fatal. For the death certificate, they settled on emphysema.

2

B illy greeted Marta with an awkward hug. By now she could read
him so well that she knew he needed time to himself. She made
it easy, saying, "Why don't you go in your room and chill out?"
It still made Billy smile to hear her use vernacular phrases like
"chill out" in what was left of her Argentinian accent.

Billy did just that, crashing down into the unbearably comfortable
overstuffed armchair in his room, his feet up on the antique footstool. Both
items were among the most used of the furnishings that his beloved dealer,
Max, had given him. Billy spent more time reading and reflecting in this
chair—his feet propped up on the regal velvet stool—than he did in bed.
For Billy, of course, that fact could be interpreted in unique, unsettling ways
having nothing to do with interior design.

The rest of the décor of the room was a hodgepodge of exquisite
antiques and pieces he'd found discarded on the street. The walls were
empty except for an icon that Max, as an impetuous young man, had can-
nily smuggled out of the Soviet Union. The windows looking out on 22nd
Street were old and huge—three large mazes of glass squares in their original casings, so in the late afternoon the sun plunged sharply through, covering the floor with a checkered grid.

Beside the door, tacked to a corkboard, were numerous scraps of paper
listing phone numbers and things to get done. The most recent additions
were the scribbled notations from the Town Car: "Learn to breathe," and

"Reread Schiller's *On Naïve and Sentimental Poetry*." He was trying to get started on the former, but the chair was so comfortable in a well-worn, old-country way that it was impossible to concentrate on his breathing. Though his racing thoughts had slowed down considerably, Billy still couldn't keep up with them.

After mulling over the peculiar ride home and the driver's eerily germane tale, his thoughts drifted back, with the coming of twilight, to his weekend in the asylum. The "locked wing" with its determinedly secluded location, and the slyly placed window views, which faced only onto the East River's russet flow. Why do mental wards, Billy wondered, usually occupy the higher floors of a hospital? The answer seemed enormously apparent now.

Billy recognized that the asylum, with its systems, structure, and mind-altering drugs, all of which gave the illusion of comfort, functioned so efficiently only because it was filled with such fragile and sick inhabitants. While entrenched in the wing itself, none of this had occurred to him. There is something about a psychiatric ward—aside from the drugs—that suppresses the most basic analytical thought. There is a palpable atmosphere that simply demands we shut down.

Billy had spent so much of his life struggling to collate reality and illusion. It was understandable that he would be seduced by the uniformity of the hospital's regimen. He found it almost monastic, and the fact that the rooms were small and spartan was no problem. Lowering himself into the chair, he factored the reason why.

Billy possessed a strange idiosyncrasy. He traced it back to the time he spent a weekend at a friend's house in the country, when the Cold War was heating up. It was one of his few forays into the bucolic as a youth, and the trip had a large impact on him.

In the basement, his friend's father had built such an attractive fallout shelter that Billy asked if they could sleep there for the night. It was well stocked with canned food, flashlights, candles, and classic books. The door was steel and as thick as the walls of an armored car. Billy never slept better. He felt so safe in that tiny concrete room. For one night, he was assured that nobody was going to be breaking in.

For years after that experience, Billy found traces of that comfort in the least likely moments. He would be walking the streets, and suddenly stare, as if in a trance, through the darkened windows of a parked VW bus, its back seat folded down to create a large cargo area. "Give me some foam rubber and a sleeping bag and I could live in this thing," he would tell his friends. At the movies, he'd point out a barren little line shack in a western: "I could live there," he'd whisper. "I'd love it." Once he and Denny were checking out a large wooden packing crate on the sidewalk, empty and waiting to be hauled off. "I could live in there," Billy muttered nonchalantly. The phrase became something of a running joke between the two of them. Billy spoke about these small places with the same glazed eyes one would have when speaking of a seductive woman. Denny once told him that this penchant for tight, cozy places was an analogy he unknowingly created to simulate being inside a woman. Billy dismissed this, but admitted its theoretical soundness.

"That idea is valid but not relevant," he told Denny. "Or maybe it's relevant but not valid. I'm not sure." The two always played with these two phrases when they wanted to drop a subject. It was like an Abbott and Costello routine.

"It's not valid for you to determine what I subjectively believe as relevant," Denny retorted, a sense of satisfaction on his face.

"Oh, fuck you," Billy invariably concluded.

In the locked wing, he had found himself looking backward more and more. His greatest mistakes were in the distant past, and though he had devised methods to avoid their effects, his nature always pulled Billy back to his worst misjudgments. There is a fascination about them for some, or even a sense of pride, but Billy had never allowed himself to examine his past indiscretions. Besides, in the psych ward, where time was governed by mindless distraction, there was no way to trick out any answers.

Billy felt, as his mother would say, "off-kilter." There was something happening that was essential and undefined. All his instincts, however, told him that his dilemma was not irresolvable. It meant change, which he hated. It meant study—which he loved. Nothing made him feel more alive than cross-referencing information.

Then, in turn, he needed to transform this elusive knowledge into some semblance of wisdom and tolerance, assembling the learned trivia into meaning and at least the illusion of truth. He felt as if he were about to run some gauntlet of savages with heavy and sharp weapons. And it meant facing "The Memory." He knew that he couldn't make any kind of art until he had some slight understanding of what the disturbance at the Met was all about. Was it the lack of the spiritual in his work, as he first believed? He didn't know. In his current state of procrastination, he'd have to wait and consider all possibilities.

There was an irony to all this. Normally, when Billy had a problem or was feeling the anchor of depression holding him in place, he would find clues and solutions in the process of work, whether it was painting, carving wood or stone, or welding steel. Now the problem was the work itself, and obviously it could play no part in the solution. For all he knew, he might never create art again.

Billy's arrested development, however, made him incapable of dealing with certain problems, causing him to postpone these dilemmas and simply shut down. His immaturity was obviously some self-preservation device, and it was bolstered by the comfort and congruity of his recent confinement. He was finally sensing that his juvenile behavior and other aspects of his character were skewed and twisted, and that he couldn't select specific difficulties, solving some and ignoring others. Sitting up with spine straight, he made an attempt at the breathing exercises, thinking back to the Hindu driver. *He should have written out step-by-step instructions*, Billy thought. Was the odd man's tale really a wise allegory, he wondered, or what his mother would have called "a bunch of malarkey"? How does one's certainty disappear?

In the evening, Billy emerged from his comfortable chair, all his thoughts unresolved, and joined Marta at the large dining table beside the kitchen. She had prepared a small meal for the two of them. It was the last meal that they would be eating together for a while. Billy had earlier informed Marta that he would be eating in his room from then on, and they ate in silence, bewildered and uncomfortable.

"The doctor gave me this prescription for pills," Billy muttered, emptying his pockets and producing the scrip. He sniggered while he spoke to

Marta, trying and failing to cover his embarrassment. "I really don't think it's necessary to fill it. I think that any sort of tranquilizer will just impede certain reevaluations about my life and work. You know, stuff I thought about in the hospital. I need some time alone, not pills."

"Did they give you pills when you were in the hospital?" Marta asked with a soft caution in her voice.

"Yeah, they did. The first night they gave me something pretty strong, then they gave me something much lighter the next two mornings. I think those are what the prescription is for."

"Were they unpleasant? Can you still feel the ones that they gave you today?" Marta spoke more assertively now. She knew that, to a small extent, she was taking on new duties: not exactly a nurse, but more a caring observer.

"Actually, I guess I do still feel this morning's meds. Somehow, however, I was beginning to think that I got out of there yesterday. I don't know why, but I feel like I've been killing time being driven around for a day in the trunk of a car, or something. To think that it's only been about six hours ago that I was saying my good-byes to Bruno and the man with the corn. I'll explain about them later. The corn man, especially, is worth hearing about. To answer your question, the pills were not that bad. You begin to think in a whole new way. It's like, without the pills we think retail, but with them everything's wholesale. I know that's an oddly mercenary analogy for me to use, and not very informative, but it's the best I can do off the top of my head."

Billy laughed a little, but this time it was genuine, the laugh Marta was used to. It made her feel good to hear him as his old self, even for just a moment. She didn't like it when he sniggered. It made her a little nervous. Marta, after so many years of being around him, was still unable—or, more likely, afraid—to define her exact feelings for Billy. She only knew how strong they were, and that these changes in him were very difficult to bear. It was difficult enough, she thought, to deal with changes in another when your emotions were a constant. When feelings were uncertain, change was frightening, and seemed impossible.

"Well, I think I'll fill the prescription anyway," she said. "We might as well have them around in case you want to think wholesale. Anyway, you don't have to take them unless you feel like it." She picked up the paper he had tossed on the table next to the ear of corn and jammed it into her shoulder bag on the floor beside her.

"I guess you're right"—Billy was sniggering slightly again—"just to have them available. I'll tell you, though, Mar, my one concern is if these things are addictive. I never asked anyone at the hospital if they were or not, and since everything's been turned around since the other night I don't know which of my previous strengths I can trust. That includes my will-power. I know I'm being overly cautious, but is there any way we can find out before you get it filled? Denny would know. He's got this big medical book at his place with complete information about every drug on the market. But he's on the road and won't be back until sometime next week. Why don't you call the pharmacy around the corner and ask them?"

"I'd give Elsa a ring, but she doesn't need to know your business," Marta said. "She could have written that book of Denny's."

"Is that right?"

"Oh, absolutely. Between you and me, she's got a bag of pills with more colors than her palette."

"God, you think you know somebody." Billy's voice lowered, as if he were pulling the words back into his own thoughts.

"Exactly." Now Marta was the one who sniggered.

She called the pharmacy as Billy went off to the large bathroom in the corridor between the living space and the work studio, drawing the scrip out of her bag and deciphering the doctor's writing. It turned out that the pills were Librium, and the woman from the drugstore told her they were probably the mildest tranquilizers available. She asked Marta if she could make out the number the doctor had ordered. It was 30. For a shrink, the doctor had an admirable cursive.

"Just bring it in anytime, honey, and I'll have it waiting here for you," the woman advised Marta. "I'm counting them out as we speak."

Billy returned and she informed him that the drugstore woman assured her that the pills were, strengthwise, on the bottom rung as far as tranquilizers went. "I'll go over there in an hour or so and pick them up. Is there anything else you need?"

"I guess I could go for one of those half gallons of fresh orange juice from the place around the corner," Billy answered. "Oh, and I wanted to ask you something. Do we have a spare television around this place? Did Darrin have one in his room?" Darrin was one of the assistants that Billy had let go. He had his own place in Brooklyn, but maintained a room at the loft for nights when they worked late.

"He does, actually." Marta was baffled by Billy's strange request. He never watched television, except for the night that *King Kong* was playing on the late show, and they had watched it together on Marta's large set in the living room area. She'd made popcorn, and they sat together on the sofa, balancing the bowl on their thighs. Toward the end of the movie, however, when the promoters were crudely displaying the giant, shackled ape to an upscale audience in a New York ballroom, Billy lost out to the late hour and fell asleep. His head involuntarily slipped onto Marta's shoulder. She missed all but the very end of *King Kong*, when the beast fell, bouncing off various layers jutting out of the great edifice. Before that, she watched Billy sleep, fixed on the length of his eyelashes, feeling the tempo of his breathing against her body.

"There's a portable in his room, I think. Why?" Marta answered, continuing to reminisce on her dizzying feelings that night.

"I saw the news on the TV one night at the hospital." Billy's voice was trailing off as he disappeared into Darrin's room and emerged with the set. "I don't know why, but there was something about it that was interesting. Actually, it was disturbing. I decided I should check it out. Well, I'm going to set this thing up in my room now, Mar. I probably won't see you until tomorrow morning. Do you need any money or anything?"

"I'm fine," she answered in a tone of voice he had never heard from her before. "Just do what you have to do and let me know if you need anything."

"Fine. Thanks." Billy wanted to tell her he was sorry for dragging her into his problems, but he couldn't stand there holding all that weight any longer. And the weight had nothing to do with the television set he was carrying. He turned and entered his sanctuary.

Gently closing the door behind him, Billy removed some books from a small, low table and placed the TV on it. Since there was a paucity of electric outlets in Darrin's room—and the loft in general—the assistant had attached its wire to a long extension cord. With the plug in his hand, he got down on his knees and crawled about on the hardwood floor, searching for an outlet. Billy finally found a socket behind the edge of his dresser. Still on his knees, he turtled back to the set and turned the knob to see if it worked. It flickered on and, after a slight adjusting of the rabbit-ear antennas, Billy was surprised by the quality of the reception. He attributed this to the loft's proximity to the Empire State Building. He didn't know that all but a couple of New York stations had switched their transmitters to the top of the World Trade Center years before. Satisfied with the television's performance, Billy switched it off, undressed, and climbed into his bed. He hadn't appreciated how comfortable it had been in his antique brass bed until the previous nights spent in the hospital.

Billy lay in the city darkness and fell into another reverie of the past. It didn't really matter, past or present or what was to come.

He wondered why this particular reminiscence hadn't occurred to him sooner, since he was so obsessed with the notion of fulfilling a *quest*. This memory was built on a well-known myth that had originated during a time when the *quest* was not simply proof of a knight's courage, but of all the essential aspects—from piousness to self-sacrifice and compassion—comprising the character of his noble position. For that matter, it also marked the creation of Billy's first completed work of art. He still couldn't decide if it was a ready-made, a sculpture, or a conceptual assemblage, but, for all he knew, it may have still existed in a back alley uptown.

Billy was about seven years old when he first read a version of the Arthurian tales. In those days, his library card was placed more securely in his pocket than his weekly lunch money. Every Tuesday he'd return three books from the week before, and spend hours in both the children's and adult sections. The tales of Arthur, Camelot, and its knights occupied him for months. They snared his imagination like a steel trap (he'd already read the *Golden Book of Fur Trade in the Old West*). Sometimes he would read the children's edition of, say, *The Green Knight* simultaneously with the adult version. On most Tuesdays he'd find himself having to cough up 15 cents in late fees because he'd kept the books an extra week. As he forked over those nickels to the librarian, Billy learned the price of knowledge.

It was the tale of Excalibur, however, that changed the stories from myth into ritual. In his mind, young Billy amalgamated the Lady of the Lake and the sword in the rock into the same landscape of imagination. The transcendentally beautiful woman hovered in mist over the stone rising from the shallow turquoise water. Years later, when Billy first saw Jackson Pollock's gravestone out at the small cemetery at Springs in the Hamptons, he realized that it was nearly the exact same shape and size as the rock holding the sword in his childhood memory.

No matter how many times he read the tale, evoking the scene in his precocious imagination, Billy's fingers would cause the book to quiver as Arthur placed his unlikely hand around the awaiting grip. He could see the half-parted lips and stunned certainty in the future king's eyes as he raised the blade out of the stone and into the mist.

One afternoon, with school out for Easter and his mother at work, he was reading the Excalibur legend when he heard the building's superintendent yelling to his son to fetch a small trowel from his tool closet. The super in Billy's building was capable of handling any job that arose, from plumbing to laying concrete, as long as he was on the wagon. The man had a wicked affinity for the bottle. One time, sloshed, he broke his wrist falling from a ladder while patching a crack in the ceiling of Billy's room.

The Latino man had taken a liking to the boy in Apartment 4C. A few years earlier, he'd let Billy hang out in the basement on boring winter afternoons. Sometimes he'd let Billy shovel coal into the furnace and explain in detail how the boiler worked. "You never know when you might have to fix one of these things," the man explained in his Peruvian accent. "They're *muy* powerful . . . can be very dangerous."

Billy went to the back window and, looking down, saw the superintendent was replacing a square of concrete, mangled by winter's snow, with a fresh, smooth layer. The job was almost finished, the super leveling the edges with short, sure swipes of the trowel. With the myth still looping through his mind, Billy ran into the living room and opened a bottom cabinet on the breakfront. The breakfront had been passed down to Billy's mother by her own folks, and was, by any standard of working-class décor, the centerpiece of the house. From the cabinet he removed a heavy rosewood box.

He had never actually been told not to open it, but he knew from the queasiness in his belly that he was breaking some sort of trust or rule. He

carefully raised the lid. Before him lay the complete selection of formal sil-
verware which his mother would scrupulously polish once a year, despite
the fact that she had never once used them. The set was another gift left to
her by Billy's maternal grandparents on their death. The silver was bright as
a knight's armor. He reached in and pulled out a knife.

Myth, ritual, and Billy Wolfram's reality were now merging, and he
surmised that this was the beginning of his quest. He went into his room
and grabbed a T-shirt. He wrapped the silver object in the shirt to keep it
from smudging, but before doing this he raised it again up to the light. The
blade had a dull point, and was hardly the size of a sword, but the fact that
it had always been hidden away in a latched chest of polished wood gave
it an ageless fascination. It would suffice for the undertaking . . . the quest
that he had planned. The only thing left was to stash it in his closet and
wait for the cover of night. He had no idea how long the super's newly laid
cement would take to harden, but his knightly hopes depended on at least
four hours.

His mother returned a little before 6:00 p.m., bringing Billy—as she
did nightly—his dinner on a large silver tray covered by a silver dome. She
prepared his dinner while she was cooking for the priests in the rectory,
always starting on Billy's a little early. This way she could shuttle it over to
the boy while the clergymen's meals were in the oven. The silver tray and
its dome belonged to the rectory, which was directly across the street from
their apartment. She was never late getting back and, thus, never burned
the meal of 14 hungry Jesuits. However, she always cringed a little as she
left, sad at the sight of her son stoically eating his dinner alone. "I'll be back
in an hour and a half at the most," she would say, "so you make sure you
get to your homework after you finish meal." It was a strange verbal idiosyncrasy of Billy's mother, to leave out salient words in sentences . . . like,
"finish meal" instead of "finish *your* meal." Billy liked this affectation and
never questioned his mother about it. It had the sound of Neanderthals—or
Ingrid Bergman speaking in the movies.

There'll be no working on homework tonight, for a fair quest awaits this
knight-errant, Billy thought to himself as he wolfed down the chicken, rice,
and vegetables she had left him. Years later, as Billy first heard the hippie
bromide "You are what you eat," he was struck by the fact that for close to

ten years he ate the exact same dinners as the men of the cloth across the street. He shuddered to think that—by that dictum—he was part Jesuit?

He threw the empty plate in the sink, ran some water over it, and sped into the back room. Darkness had arrived, and there was no sign of the super or his family in the back yard. There was always the chance that the handyman could be working in his basement shop, however, so Billy wore a dark jacket and laced up his sneakers for quiet stealth.

He grabbed the silver knife from the closet, keeping it in its T-shirt sheath, and stuck his key in his pocket. He eagerly made it down the stairs unseen, taking the wooden steps beside the mailboxes down to the back yard. Passing the rows of overflowing garbage pails, the smell of boiled cabbage overwhelming all other rotting food groups, Billy gingerly approached the freshly laid square. He had arrived with little time to spare; the cement was setting fast. He laid the T-shirt beside him as he knelt reverently and removed the blade. Excalibur shone in the moon and window light as he raised it up. He wondered if there would be consequences for this reversal of myth . . . inserting the sword rather than removing it. Somewhere in the adult versions of this tale, he thought, this question of how the sword was first placed in the rock might have been answered. Myths do not often bother with causal details, however. Things just seemed to happen, and this explained Billy's fascination with them.

With both hands, Billy drove his mother's fine silver place knife into the hardening substance. It went as deep as he had hoped, the blade disappearing into the concrete and myth in his mind. A mist enveloped the suddenly lacustrine landscape of Billy's back alley. The handle was all that remained visible. By morning, only the worthy one would be able to remove it.

Billy's mother never noticed the purloined knife on their yearly days of silver polishing, or perhaps she did and just never chose to mention it. She even got to utilize the fine silver—though only two settings of it—when a pair of her Jesuit employers came to dinner one night. Billy was happy she finally got to make use of it, despite the small scale of the occasion. One of the priests chose the occasion to offer Billy an exegesis on the life of Ignatius of Loyola. He spoke in a stentorian voice, treating the boy like a child, which is something no child enjoys.

For the next 11 years, at the least, whenever he dropped off the garbage in the back of the building, Billy checked on the knife handle to see if the superintendent or—no matter how unlikely—some other aficionado of Arthurian tales that lived in the building had removed the ersatz Excalibur. No one had, or perhaps, as he liked to think, nobody could. The handle remained there rising from the cement, covered by snow and frozen in ice through harsh winters and shrouded by leaves in fall. Billy himself never attempted to pull out the knife; the thought never even entered his mind. The last time he looked was the day he moved out of the walk-up after his mother had died. He was moving downtown into an apartment with Denny. After loading the car with his last box, he took a final walk around back before heading to the East Village, and for the last time surveyed the only window view he had ever known.

Excalibur had lasted through almost a dozen city winters, and the concrete slab around it remained inviolate. At first Billy thought he would return and check on it from time to time, but, walking away, he knew he was moving to a place where promises were harder to keep, and best not made.

Billy's first serious show was a three-artist exhibit in 1972 in a large but run-down gallery in Soho. In the room assigned to Billy, the floor was so badly slanted that when he placed a round pencil at his feet, it hit the far wall with such momentum that the point broke off. The young artist was so glad to have any place exhibiting his work that he didn't care. Nonetheless, though he'd spent weeks working their sequence out on paper, Billy hastily rearranged the placement of his pieces within the space to best utilize the optical effect of the gradient.

Billy showed a work titled *Quaternion*, a series involving the number four, inspired by his recent reading of Jung. There was the *4 Elements* installation, a series of small, partly kinetic sculptures demonstrating the alchemical belief that all substances consisted, in varying degrees, of each of the prime elements. For example, kerosene is water, containing an excess of fire. Also, there were eight paintings of misshapen spheres with the four cardinal points displaced in various ways . . . south was north, west was south, and so on. In one, all directions were marked "North."

The Holy Trinity was included, painted in miniature and referencing

Billy's days at the Cloisters spent in study and wonder. In one painting, however, Satan was added to complete the essential fourth. In another, it was the Virgin Mother, and in another, the Magdalene. There was a fourth, of course, in the series, and though the tiny face was smudged, it was clearly the artist himself with the Father, Son, and Holy Spirit.

Only a handful of critics, working for magazines from the fringes of the art world, reviewed the show, and they raved—with some befuddled hesitance—in their assessments of Billy's work. Few mentioned Billy's ideas; they were more impressed with his draftsmanship, perspective, the unfathomable sense of movement in the work—especially with the near-3-D dimpled effects of the spheres, and his use of odd materials such as self-made granular pastels. Overall, they saw the show as a technical triumph, citing Billy's ability to make dry pigment appear so wet as a feat bordering on *trompe l'oeil*.

When Denny showed Billy these reviews, the painter's first inclination was to crush the papers into his fist, but his eyes were peripherally drawn to a single phrase, "screeching pigments evoked . . ." Billy focused in to find the context of that expression, and relinquished himself to the praise, reveling in the boldness his name assumed in print. He glanced up at Denny, feigning indifference, then cautiously smiled and muttered, "I'm relevant, my man."

However, what captivated the legendary retired dealer, Max Beerbaum, at that show was a single large canvas off to the side. It was titled *Trapped in Tidal Pool at Low Tide*. Billy had had to fight with the curators to include this work. They pointed out that this outsized painting simply didn't fit in. However, days before the opening, as the three artists were completing the final details of their individual installations, the curators reconsidered, deciding Billy's painting was simply too impressive to exclude. They justified it as a "transitional" work, and mounted it on a bare wall leading into one of the other artists' rooms.

It was a stunning abstract work highlighting his unconventional palette, whose texture would increase and diminish as he created a subtle swelling though the layers of acrylic. Doubtlessly, some viewers didn't notice this ascent and decline throughout the canvas, since there were sections where the paint's thickness built up almost imperceptibly. This was unfortunate, since it gave the "pool" a swirling motion. On close examination, one could see Billy had composed the painting entirely with wedgelike brushstrokes shaped like small fish scales. The repetition of wedges and the ingenious mixing of his self-made pigments created flecks of color that gave it an iridescent effect, increasing with the viewers' distance from the canvas.

It was sheer kismet that Max was even at this show. He had been planning on meeting a friend at another gallery, but had misplaced the scrap of paper with the address, so he followed some young people into this space on the vague chance it was the assigned place. It was not, but in his 67 years, Max had come to accept the concept of fate on many levels. He had to believe in it. Through all his experience, he knew that things come together—unlikely and random—as surely as the laws of entropy prove that things eventually fall apart.

When Max was a child in Europe, he had watched his mother staring intently at a single fish lying on a bed of ice in a peddler's window.

"What are you looking at in such a way, Mother?" he asked. "It is only a fish."

"What color is it, my precious son?" she asked Max.

"It is brown, brown and black."

"No, it is not. Look again. This time I want you to move your eyes and see the colors on each tiny bit of it, on every scale of the fish, as they are hit by the sun." His mother spoke sweetly but sternly.

Max stared for a while, tilting his head from side to side, dropping his eyes and squinting. Finally, he let out a yell so loud that the fishmonger came running out onto the sidewalk. His mother apologized to the man, who returned inside. "I can see it, Mother." Max tried to lower his voice for his excitement. "I see the greens, and the blues and the strange violets, and even a blue scale that turns red as the sun moves on it. The colors are like there is a lamp inside the fish."

He looked up at his mother and he could see the pride in her eyes. It would be two years until his bar mitzvah, but Max could tell by her look that he had learned something in that fish peddler's window that would change his life as much as any ritual. He walked home in a daze, holding his mother's hand.

From that day on, young Max saw everything differently. He saw the capillaries and halftones of the spectrum in sunsets, Moorish patterns on a tortoise's shell, and, in the clouds, an anxious wren on a branch of ice.

All this came flooding back to Max as he stared at Billy's canvas. He looked at it for close to an hour, from every angle. Even as he tried to concentrate on the other works in the show, he was drawn back to that painting.

Max could not ignore the all-but-forgotten childhood memory that the large work evoked. After all, it was the greatest gift of art to permit the onlooker to make another's work his own and suddenly witness the animation—and clarification—of one's own experiences. He had been going to art exhibits for much of his long life, and expected some semblance of beauty, horror, truth, or innovation in any serious young artist, but found in studying Billy's work that he was innervated by a transcendent vigor that he hadn't experienced—at least to this degree—in many years.

Max recognized the stunning feats of technique that this unknown young artist employed in *Tidal Pool* to achieve his ends. He saw the same elements and capabilities in the artist's other works, as well. His style and his color-coding were still undefined, but this fellow was light-years beyond his age in raw talent. He tried to think of other contemporary painters who were capable of producing a canvas similar to the large abstract. The list he settled on was quite short and the names were luminous. He looked down at the crudely printed "catalogue" for the exhibition, and saw the name Billy Wolfram. In that moment, it imprinted itself on him like a lithograph.

He read the short biographical note, discovering that Billy was only 21 years old and lived in NYC. It mentioned a single year of study at Cooper Union, and Max was surprised at the paucity of his formal training. What mainly interested Max, however, perhaps more so than his young age, was the fact that this Wolfram fellow had been born and lived his entire life in Manhattan. The bio mentioned nothing of the once-mandatory intervals of study abroad. For all Max knew, the farthest the young man had been from Manhattan was the last stop on a subway line. If this was the case, the elderly man thought, what prompted the large work's oddly sad and longing title, *Trapped in Tidal Pool at Low Tide*?

How long had it been since Max had seen such light exploding—at once vividly and insouciantly—on canvas, and by a boy who spent his entire life in New York City? "Pure *finzioni* landscape," Max whispered, unaware he was speaking out loud. This was the art expression—more often involving portraits—for a work that comes entirely from the artist's imagination. Absolutely giddy, Max didn't want to leave the gallery. His eyes went back to the painting, then scanned the young male faces in the room, wondering if one of them was Wolfram.

3

On the first day of what Billy was calling his reclusion, Marta was preparing a breakfast tray that he requested she bring to his room. While cooking, she saw him stealthily appear in the kitchen, wiping sleep from his eyes, and wearing black Japanese slippers, along with a sweat suit that, Marta noticed, actually had a crease in its pants. He went to the coffee machine and poured a cup. "No mate?" Marta asked. "No, thanks," Billy said in that deep first-words-of-the-day voice. "I just need some quick caffeine." Marta nervously twirled at her hair, placing the ceramic mate pot down on the table with excessive care. Billy was dismal in his attempts to read a woman's mood but was fairly sure he'd offended Marta by turning down her offer, and quickly asked—his voice in a higher register—if, on second thought, he could have a bowl of mate. Marta gave him a suspicious smirk, which morphed into a smile. She suspected he'd changed his mind to appease her, and she'd never seen Billy make such an aberrant and sweet gesture.

Mate was the tealike hot drink of choice in Marta's native Argentina. Billy normally loved the stuff, and Marta brewed an old-school authentic cup, using both a recipe and jade-colored bowl handed down through four generations. It was one of the reasons he originally gave her the job, Marta always maintained, seeing her credentials were fairly slim compared to the other applicants.

Billy made his personal and business decisions by relying almost completely on the same instincts that he used when making his art—though it seemed imprudent and even reckless to the few people he told. He never formally questioned Marta regarding her credentials or experience, but instead he relied solely on the few observations she'd made regarding the strengths and weaknesses of some new color-field artists after the two emerged from a gallery's group show. He tried not to compare any of her comments with his own takes on the paintings, since they were only opinions—subjective and not binding. By their first hour together, Billy had sussed out the scope of her capabilities, her honesty and humility.

Apparently, like Billy's, her own needs were spartan, but, in nearly all matters, she had a faultless sense of taste. As far as her will to succeed she had no problem with hard work and was smart as a whip. Though it was far from the season of Lent, that day at the gallery Billy had been taken by the girl's streak of ashen dirt near the middle of her forehead. It looked like she'd just come from a church on Ash Wednesday, carrying the fresh dark smudge that gave her the look of a Dickensian street urchin. Billy had found it endearing: the fact she could disregard her looks in a city that relies too much on them.

He looked at Marta and smiled. Billy told her he would commence his reclusion as soon as he got a volume of Velázquez's work from the bookshelves. He followed the alphabetical order down the hallway, grabbed a heavy folio from the top shelf, then sat down to finish the coffee. Marta went to her desk. It was cluttered with clips of the media fallout regarding Billy's incident at the Met, all of which he'd steadfastly avoided glancing at since he returned from the hospital. One gossip columnist in a tabloid—obviously getting the information secondhand—traced Billy's "hasty, somewhat disoriented disappearance" to a quarrel with a mysterious raven-haired woman which occurred in a secluded area of the Egyptian wing. The article went on to say that such impulsive behavior by the normally aloof young artist seemed stunningly out of character. The woman could not be traced, and neither the artist nor any of his reps were returning phone calls.

Other articles on the opening, including one in the *Times*, made no mention of Billy's departure, although he was listed as one of the art world luminaries whose presence graced the show. The fact was that the whole affair happened so quickly, among people lost in booze and networking, that it was unlikely anyone noticed the artist's exit. Tippy probably fed the gossip item to the tabloid as a preemptive maneuver in case one of the paparazzi had noticed Billy's dash down the stairs. The deflecting phrase "raven-haired mystery woman" had the dealer's slick P.R. DNA all over it.

Later that same day, Marta knocked gently on Billy's door and informed him that Denny was calling from California. Billy was sitting on the edge of his bed, glaring ahead in sorrow and bewilderment, looking like some general on a distant hill watching his troops being slaughtered in the battle below, realizing their poor fates were caused by his hubris and faulty tactics. He should have known he had left his flanks wide open.

Marta's voice shook Billy loose from this reverie. He could not abide self-pity, even by metaphor.

Billy had been anxious to speak to Denny since being locked in the hospital, but now he felt a peculiar hesitancy in taking the call. If he was going to find answers through reclusion, he might as well take it all the way. He told Marta—at first speaking through the door until he recognized how silly this seemed and opened it in midsentence—that he was having second thoughts about speaking to Denny after all.

Thinking he just needed some encouragement, Marta first took the phone in her hand and jabbed it at Billy, hoping her teasing would make him realize the foolishness of postponing the inevitable. From the adamant and sad expression on his face, however, she quickly realized how serious he was and left the room without another word, still grasping the receiver. In the kitchen, Marta asked Denny if he could wait a few moments, and placed the phone down out of earshot. She rushed back and pleaded with Billy to discuss the incident with his oldest friend, assuring him that Denny would understand anything that might possibly have taken place. "He's still waiting on the line, but you have to decide quickly. God, you really need to talk to someone about this, and who else can you really open up to except him?" As she spoke, Marta seemed like she was angry, but lacking any ability to discern a woman's emotions, Billy apologized for acting so childishly and not listening to her, assuring her she was right, but he genuinely didn't feel up to talking to anyone about it at that moment. He then smiled and asked if she'd get the phone. She handed it to him and left the room, noting, sotto voce, that his putting off Denny had more to do with "some pissy, male embarrassment" on Billy's part.

After shutting the door, he couldn't help but smile at another of her charmingly half-ass uses of American vernacularisms. He finally picked up the phone, which seemed to weigh 20 pounds, and, in a voice that probably seemed as pissy as Marta had stated, asked Denny if he was still there.

Denny sounded cautious as the two began to talk, as if he were not sure to what extent Billy had gone off his rocker. Billy didn't hesitate to reassure Denny that he felt fine, that the entire mess was a misunderstanding. Denny then proceeded to gently castigate Billy on how ridiculous this notion of his work being devoid of spirituality was. "What's with this spiritual arrogance crap? If that's what you're after, maybe it's not too late to become a cardinal."

Billy replied that painting gives a different meaning to the term *arrogance*. "Arrogance has nothing to do with my purpose," he told Denny. "We both know there's a certain attitude that's necessary to create art, no matter what the medium. Call it arrogance if you want. You've referred to a sense of 'cockiness' essential to performing rock and roll. That's an internal thing that's required to drive you on in your work. I guess you could just as well label it *certainty*. It's not to be confused with that external sort of arrogance, which is a character trait, invariably accompanied by rudeness."

"Still," Denny countered, "there are good and essential forms of arrogance for painters as well as musicians. Before we get immersed in one of our tirades on semantics, let me clarify. I know the sort of arrogance to which you're referring, of course, and most people probably think that's the word's only connotation. I also agree that, by this definition, it is a destructive character trait, used mainly to heap abuse on other individuals and institutions for our own aggrandizement. But I'm speaking of turning your arrogance onto yourself, so that you're not setting up a me-against-them-situation paradigm, but challenging yourself. Perhaps I should just call it ambition, but there's another word that your peers quickly construe into something shifty. We all need to compete, but only against ourselves. We've had this talk before. It's no different than in that interview Max had you do years ago, when you had that show at the Whitney that put you on a whole other level. They asked you to compare yourself to that young

Spanish painter. You told them you don't ever compare yourself to others. It's useless because you have no control over the competition."

Billy had told the interviewer, "I compare myself to only myself; besides, what you're really trying to ask me is not if I would compare myself and my art *to* this other fellow, but if I'd compare myself *against* him. That's a cheap trick to provoke me into denigrating him, spewing out a bunch of vapid invectives that would still be no more than totally subjective and not binding. The one thing you'd avoid is a serious, long, and boring analysis of our respective styles. You guys want only to incite divisions among peers, and it's amazing how many fall for it when they're first experiencing a bit of notoriety."

"To bring my theory to an end, Billy," Denny concluded, "whether you call it arrogance or ambition, the young artists that produce sincere and motivating work invariably possess this characteristic. Also, you must admit that—to my admittedly underfed opinion—they are the rare and notable exceptions in comparison to most painters on the scene, whose boring, derivative canvases hang from the walls of an incessant expansion of new galleries throughout the city."

"I know you feel that way, and in my current state of mind I can't disagree," admitted Billy. "It's not like that with the old guys."

"The old guys are always great," Denny agreed. "So listen, I got to go to the sound check. I've been blowing off so many lately that the band is getting pissed."

"Treat your brother musicians well, Denny."

"Of course I will. I'm fucking stellar. But that means I have to give you the brush in your time of mental illness. I'll call you back later . . . or if not, tomorrow. Then we can talk about all this spiritual crisis shit going on with you that I've been uncomfortably trying to avoid. Also, I'm just dying to hear your assessment of the pills the doctor gave you. Welcome to a better world through chemicals, brother. I love you, Billy."

"Me too." Billy drew out his response. It was a long time since Denny had used the phrase with him. He must have sounded worse than he thought he was letting on.

It was the spiritual, in all its aspects, that always drove Billy Wolfram and had now vanished from his work. Or so he believed. He was no longer certain of anything. He knew he wasn't—as Denny and the hospital doctor had conjectured—confusing spirit with religion. Religion, in any institutionalized sense, could not possibly function as either impetus or subject for art in these times. Its strictures demanded exclusion. Its preconceptions and the weight of its own dogma allowed for no aesthetic action, unless it was proscribed. It was a closed system, which is the year-round residence of entropy. Art must remain an open system—like a salt marsh, an infant, or an array of spiderwebs—unrestrained by the passivity of formal "beliefs." It was only then that art could liberate.

Maybe he'd lost that divine spark, the *scintilla vitae*, or anamnesis, which propelled him with such ease to clarity in his intuition. His greatest fear was losing the inner register, which had served him so well. Billy also had to wonder whether the problem was not in his work, but in the jaded cultural atmosphere in which he lived, where the cult of celebrity stripped the artist's work of all dignity and put him or her on the same aesthetic level as a fashion model. Perhaps the trauma roused by Velázquez's work at the Met was a curtain raised on society itself. It was just as likely that it was not Billy and his peers, but this society and this age, with its impenetrable, superficial ideologies, that was deprived of the spiritual. Perhaps the upheaval of these very thoughts—always there, but suppressed—was what now was paralyzing him.

He thought back and grimly wished he were standing on some lonely beach, testing if he could still feel the earth rotating beneath his feet. Billy had never understood Denny when he had spoken of his success seeming like a prolonged dream that could all abruptly disappear at any inconsequential moment. Now Billy fully grasped that everything had changed, and he was being led through a dim, murky forest, filled with curled leaves and fallen trees, where the sure path was all but lost.

As the days of his quarantine clicked away, Billy was in an almost constant state of dread and confusion regarding what to do about his upcoming show. Tippy's badgering was becoming both distracting and annoying. Though it had been less than a week, Tippy grew so desperate that he eventually tried to get Billy's attention by sending a strippergram to the loft. A very young girl, depressed and clearly doing this job out of economic desperation, awkwardly shimmied out of a police uniform while butchering her recital of Tippy's message. Billy understood the gist, which reprimanded him for hiding behind Marta's skirts and tried to provoke him into acting like a man by answering the phone himself. Such a disparaging remark concerning his masculinity had no effect whatever on Billy. If Tippy thought this pathetic display would provoke its recipient to sprint into the studio and promptly knock off a couple of sofa-sized canvases, he was mistaken. Billy, of course, had long since become inured to such crude sexual denigration, and Tippy had no chance of provoking him into childish games of retaliation.

This sense of defiance was his usual reaction, but as time passed in the artist's current state of confusion, there was a chance that Tippy's foolish gesture would backfire on him. It could push Billy beyond defiance, into a state of total noncompliance. If this was the case, and he'd lost all respect for the dealer, Billy could rationalize not making his upcoming deadline, and not feel either guilt or consequence. It was exactly the justification he needed, and, ironically, Tippy himself had handed it to him.

Instead, with each passing hour, the cruel stunt distressed Billy in the worst possible way and forced him to deal with the one issue he'd successfully sidestepped for so long that he'd thought it no longer affected him. In that sense, the predicament grew so overwhelming that—for varying intervals—it just disappeared beneath its own weight. During these interludes, Billy's deeper, suppressed fears took shape. They were like weeds waiting for pavement to crack, providing a place to rise. Tonight, he questioned whether his art had been feeding all this time on his sexual annulment. What if this abstinence truly was the source of his artistic instincts? Were the perfect shadowing that viewers saw on the finished canvas or the gravity-defying feats of his sculpture an expression of his own flesh's forfeiture?

Of course, he had wondered if a nexus existed between his artistic skills and his sexual impotence, but he had always dismissed the idea. Now Billy saw that this rejection was an arrogant concession to his success. Things had been gliding smoothly along and, while he was in that zone, spirituality was *in the creative process itself*. It was almost shamanistic. Subject and object became one. Without looking, his hand would lower the brush's tight bristles into the palette, thoughtlessly filling the tip with an unmeasured, yet exact, amount of paint. Like a Zen archer, Billy was intuitively in sync with the precise touch, the proper pressure and blending, of each stroke. He instinctively *felt* each step of the process passing through him like an electromagnetic current. This was, Billy believed, his true gift. He simply followed a series of inherent links, which literally connected him to the canvas.

Now Velázquez and seclusion had put him on notice. To phrase it crudely—giving a personal turn to Malcolm X's quote—the sexual chickens of J.F.K.'s death had come home to roost. The joy, turmoil, illumination, and heartbreak elicited by his work had come at the price of his carnal deprivation. This bargain had always seemed worthwhile. In its simplest terms, the pain of his suppression was—until now—worth the pleasure and inspiration the viewer took from his work. Billy now recognized that sex—no matter the moral or aesthetic reasoning that tries to circumvent it—was also part of the human spirit.

Billy had lost track of how many days he'd been sequestered in his room with his brain thrashing around for answers. Except for the coming and going of the sun, there was no way to gauge the beginning or end of each day. It was all becoming a blur, and he was aching to check out the streets. He felt an overwhelming pressure bearing down on him in this confined space, as if he were a deep-sea diver who emerged too quickly from the ocean floor, winding up with the bends.

He made some green tea on the hot plate Marta had bought him. Having the hot plate facilitated Billy's isolation, allowing him to avoid meeting up with her in the kitchen each morning.

He wondered if he should mark the days off on a wall, like in a prison movie, but it was too late for that. He had no calendar in the room, but it seemed like weeks had passed since returning from the hospital.

At least he'd slept well the night before. Since this ascetic phase began, it was the first time that he hadn't woken up numerous times throughout the night. These awakenings were not pleasant at all. It was something Denny had often described, and Billy feared terribly, yet had never experienced. He was facing insomnia, each night in larger gradations. Deprived of so much more than others in his waking state, Billy had more invested in his sleep life. It was strange, because, when really consumed by work, he could easily stay awake for days, completely unaware of time. Then again, there were other periods when he had to replenish himself, or simply disappear.

In the first days of his quarantine, Billy had found himself rousted from sleep into quick firm consciousness. That had been a very unnerving ordeal for him. Since he was cut off from working or walking, sleep was his only form of escape. He would stare at the ceiling for a few shredded minutes, which seemed like hours, until finally throwing off the covers and turning on the TV. One escape had betrayed him, so he opted for the other. These were the times that Billy would reach for the bottle of pills that Marta had insisted the pharmacist should fill.

The insomniac nights led to another problem. Those interrupted sleeps revivified the longing that he thought he had learned to suppress. These were the nights Billy's buoyant imagination was set loose. He'd rise to the ceiling and look down on himself in bed, wondering painfully what it would be like to have a partner to sleep beside him. Some woman to lay a hand against lightly, allowing a single finger to trace the alphabet of her spine. He became convinced this contact—feeling the rhythm of a woman's body breathing—would have returned him to the sanctuary of dreams. Lover or just friend, it didn't matter.

One night he had a strange dream—stranger than others in a sleep jammed with dreams. Billy was very astute at handling dreams. He could induce lucid dreaming, and, if necessary, avoid returning to an interrupted nightmare. The only dreams he could not control were those that occurred within the actual room where he slept. Stripping him of the ability to distinguish his surroundings, they were invariably frightening. His strange dream belonged to this category, which gave each distressing detail the luminescent authority of real time.

A raven landed on the ledge of his large window. Everything was the same in his room as the moment he'd turned out the reading lamp. The fluorescent lights were on in the offices across the street, and Billy could even make out his favorite sweatshirt, as he'd left it, crumpled up on the footstool. The black bird hopped about a bit on the ledge. It was old, Billy intuited—its beak mangled and wings frayed. Then it began speaking. The voice was familiar to Billy, but he couldn't place it. "You have to retrace your steps and see how you got to where you are," the bird said sarcastically, "which, I might add, is a pretty pathetic situation."

"Get away from here," Billy said casually to the bird, which had ceased hopping and stood in place, thrusting its beak through the open window and into the room.

"Listen, this can be easy or difficult, but I don't come and go at your bidding. It's quite the opposite, in fact." The sarcasm gone, the raven now had erudition in its tone.

"What do you want?" Billy asked. The dialogue in his dreams was always very terse.

"I think you know that, but I'm perfectly willing to spell it out if it helps you with your dilemma." The raven was beginning to slowly raise its wings, as if it were planning to leave when it finished speaking. "The problem is simple. The sacrifices and evasions and repressions have taken their toll. They manifested themselves that night at the Metropolitan Museum, when you saw something in Velázquez that a few select painters have recognized. His paintings possessed such a flawless technique that he created a religion out of his art. You too have tried to reach God through art.

"If you had confided in Max what happened the day Kennedy was killed, he might have helped you. Now that task has fallen on me. And believe me, I am old, tired, and not eager to undertake this chore. When I return I'll explain myself. For now, do what I said. Retrace your memories. It can be easy or very difficult. Don't be a rationalist and make me take you by the hand through every step. Open your heart. I know that phrase is a cliché, but it wasn't when it was first used."

"When was that?" Billy inquired. "And who said it first?"

"You have no idea how long ago." The raven's voice lingered as the bird flew off. "Besides, why do you assume that it wasn't me?"

Still in bed, Billy raised his head and called out for the raven. For all his usual proficiency at manipulating sleep, Billy had never experienced such a unique, vibrant dreamscape, which he perceived with startling and unprecedented clarity. He was also extremely perplexed, and the sheets in the bed were drenched in sweat. Though the confrontation with the bird had occurred in his own bed, during real time, Billy felt no fear that the scraggly creature intended to harm him. At first the black bird only seemed an annoying intruder—like an unwanted visitor during dinner. Now the thought that it wouldn't return was unbearable. Billy ran to the window, screaming for the raven to explain what it had said in the dream—if, indeed, it had been a dream. After all, the room hadn't changed, and there were no frayed, tiny feathers or other signs of its presence on the ledge. Still, the vibrant and unique light remained, as Billy continued calling out, but the bird was gone.

4

After the previous night's distressing dream, Billy looked for solace by reminiscing about Max. He soon felt like a boy diving for pearls. The deeper he plunged into the recollections of his departed mentor, the clearer were the details of the memories he brought to the surface. By the time he'd finished diving, however, Billy was exhausted by the onslaught of so many vacillating emotions, from sincere elation to grief and regret.

Finishing his juice, he stood looking out the window, at a large innocuous cloud hovering over the Empire State Building, remembering random occasions from Max's life. Billy decided not to force it and grabbed each of the memories as they darted at their own pace through his addled brain.

In his final year, nearing 82, Max would forget to ring for the elevator when visiting Billy's loft and foolishly walk up the stairs. The tiny figure would invariably have his right hand raised in the face of whomever opened the door, breathlessly repeating the same phrase, "Was dumb . . . know now . . . don't scold old man." As he spoke, Max lurched his hunched body toward the large chair nearest the door. He leaned over its back, sucking for enough breath to take a few more steps and collapse into the cracked leather upholstery. There was nothing funny about a man of that age taking such chances, but whenever he visited, he'd repeat each step of this imprudent routine with such remarkable similarity it became comical. Max would make the same dismissive motion of his hand and pant that identical plea.

After the desperate lunge for the chair, he'd have a short brandy and recover in about five minutes. Eventually, Billy had one of Max's housekeepers call ahead whenever Max was on his way to the loft. He'd then dispatch an assistant downstairs to intercept Max on the sidewalk.

Whenever they visited a museum together, Billy recalled, Max's normally soft voice would rise markedly in enthusiasm if they happened upon an unexpected masterpiece. At an art institute in the Midwest, Max was so enthralled by a Vermeer he'd suddenly encountered that his volume began to ascend strikingly. Eventually, a group of elderly day-trippers approached the dealer and made sibilant "shushing" sounds at him. On such occasions, Max delighted in pretending he was deaf and, staring obliviously at the crowd, he told them he had trouble ascertaining his tone in enclosed spaces. They eventually approached him with profuse apologies and two security guards softly whisked him off to an amazed and bemused young curator's tiny office.

Another time, he bluntly told a pack of philistine tourists that his outburst came from sheer enthusiasm and exuberance, and he did not intend to upset anyone inadvertently. Billy couldn't be sure, but he believed that— for the only time—he detected a hint of anger, or perhaps a deep sadness, in Max's demeanor, as the small figure informed them that if they could only see these masterpieces through his eyes, then they would speak as stridently as he.

Max was arguably the premiere authority on pre–World War Two modern art and was sought by all manner of institutions and universities to speak for large honorariums, which he always turned down. Once he relented and agreed to a lecture at a Bay Area museum, debunking an art historian's recent book on the Surrealists, who were enjoying an increasing vogue among the academics. Max knew from personal experience the book was simply another unoriginal heap of conjecture about this artistic movement, riddled with half-truths and outright lies.

During a Q&A at the end, Max became outraged when an audience member asked Max about certain lubricious incidents that the author had erroneously attributed to two of Max's friends in the book. They were all dead, and he was prepared to be one voice in their defense. Disturbed, but trying not to lose his temper as he addressed the irascible man, Max forgot to speak into the microphone, and answered the question at a very low volume.

"Could you please speak up, Mr. Beerbaum?" the fool interrupted Max, who was in the middle of a salient point. "You are talking at a very low volume." Max paused and retorted with raw sarcasm: "Perhaps you, sir, would do well to listen louder."

Max took pleasure in charming women young enough to be his grand-daughters. He explained once to Billy that, with each passing year of his so-called old-age, he was able to flirt in the most overt and outrageous manner. "When I turned 70, they all believed I had become an innocu-ous old man, unable to follow through on my alluring little innuendos. I became harmless, and it allowed me to harmlessly indulge myself with innocent delight. Lately, a few lovely young women assume I've lapsed into complete senility and tend to my every need. They bring me food, feed me like a child, and always clutch a large napkin in case I drool. I could make the most explicit sexual proposal, and they would dismiss it as a symptom of my senile dementia. I say whatever I wish with total impunity." He con-cluded by informing Billy that, after two bodies fumble about making love, they seldom remember any of the mechanical actions, but, instead, recall the words of love and lust that have passed between them.

Billy heard Marta go out about 8:00 p.m. He was tired from spending almost an entire day reflecting on the past. It had been a more arduous task than he'd imagined, but, aside from some heartrending moments, it had succeeded in relaxing him. He took the most pleasure recalling his early encounters with Max. It was as if Max were still there, sitting in the easy chair as Billy lay back on the bed, hands cupped behind his head. Memories may not have been as complete an escape as sleep, but in the waking hours they were pretty much all he had. Memories and television.

With Marta gone, he took the opportunity to have a long shower and scanned the bookshelves for some new reading. Billy had never considered reading as escapism. Even fiction invariably led him to cross-referencing, which amounted to work. All his life he had avoided looking back. Now he was making up for lost time. What was it that the raven had told him in his peculiar dream—"Retrace your steps"? Billy was following the advice of a disheveled bird in a dream.

He randomly snatched three biographies from a stack of paperbacks and quickly returned to his room. After noticing the top book in his hand was on the life of Saint Francis Assisi, Billy tossed it onto the top of the unmade bed. Laying the other two on a chair, he straightened the rumpled sheets, slid onto the mattress, and began the book on the well-known saint. However, by the time he switched on the reading lamp, with its funnel of concentrated light, an exhausted Billy could already feel his eyes struggling to stay open long enough to complete the next sentence. Before long, with the light still on and the book facedown on his chest, he surrendered to a deep sleep.

The next thing he knew, the bird was back.

"What the hell is going on here?" Billy asked, not knowing if he was awake or still flat asleep in the bed. "Who are you?"

"You met me before," the bird replied, feigning hurt feelings. "Am I so easy to forget?"

"It was at the zoo on the night of the Velázquez show. God, I remember that scratchy voice now." Billy was baffled. "I was asleep, for god's sake. Seriously, are you a dream? It's either that or you're some very clever talking bird. If you are real, are you a crow or a raven? I thought only parrots could speak so well."

"I am a raven, and there is a difference. People confuse the crow and the raven, but I haven't time to go into the distinctions that separate the two. You see, my talon is badly hurt."

Billy looked at the bird's trifurcated foot. There was pus oozing from between the tiny cracks. It was a pretty disgusting sight.

"What's wrong with you, bird?" Billy said, trusting his senses for a moment and speaking back to the strange apparition. He didn't care if it was fantasy or dream or reality. He couldn't tell the difference anymore. "That sore should be attended to. I can put you in a cardboard box and run you uptown to the animal hospital. The place has some of the best vets in the world, according to the woman on the third floor. You want to take a trip? I'm willing to use any excuse to get out of this place. I don't want a dead raven on my windowsill. I don't even want a dead figment of my imagination on the windowsill. Tell me what's ailing you."

"Well, you finally spoke the right words. Now we can continue." The raven's tone changed again. There was a slight satisfaction in its voice, and the talon suddenly ceased oozing. The creature was completely healed, and its coloring changed. A moment before, it had seemed old, its sticky black feathers frayed. Now there was a bluish iridescent sheen on its wings. The ulceration had healed right before Billy's eyes, as if he were watching time-lapse photography on a PBS nature documentary. The cure's speed and thoroughness were beyond any reasoning.

"Come on . . . are you real?" Billy still didn't trust what was happening, but what did he have to lose? Exhaustion had set in from doing nothing for so long and had undoubtedly affected the condition of his sleep. On the other hand, he was so starved for company that talking to a raven might be entertaining. "Besides, so what if you really are a raven? Ravens have been spotted in this city before. It's rare, but it happens. I still think you're a figment . . . a flimsy, fucking figment."

"*Figment* is a funny word," the bird snickered. Aside from the constant shifting of pitch and inflections, it sometimes produced an irritating hiss by sucking air through its beak when it spoke.

The entire experience was becoming aggravating. Each day since the start of his reclusion, he was having more and more trouble distinguishing dream from reality. There was no contact with anyone, aside from Marta and phone calls with Denny. There was no possible way it could be Marta's voice he was hearing.

Billy suddenly felt terribly lonely. He usually enjoyed his time by himself, but he understood the need for friends. Unfortunately, though Billy genuinely cared about people in an idealistic, or archetypal, sense, he had awful difficulty dealing with most of them as individuals. With every day of his reclusion, he'd been weighing the difference between an artist working within a necessary solitude as opposed to shutting himself off from everyone and brooding away the time in isolation, bitter with anger and fear. Most of his really close friends understood his predilection for holing up in his loft for long stretches of time, trusting in Marta to handle all outside contact. However, there were some who took it personally, and it led to hurt feelings, apologies, and a number who just fell away. He'd had enough of that. If this stunt had done nothing else, it proved to Billy that he had to get out more. If he didn't, he was going to slip into a chasm of isolation, or worse. He was already talking to birds at his window.

He shut his eyes for about 30 seconds and checked again. The raven was still there, strutting slowly back and forth, its head raised up. At first Billy thought it looked regal, but when his eyes adjusted to the darkness, it just seemed old and weary.

It was surely a dream, but this winged apparition was blurring the lines, and he was beginning to, once more, sweat into the sheets. Billy sat up and stared at the ledge, straining to hear a few more words. It was so vivid, its left eye fixed on him like a surveyor's laser.

"You know who I am." The black bird pumped out its chest, and it now sounded like a dusted-over professor lecturing at Oxford. For the first time, however, Billy detected a distinct sincerity growing in its voice. "I am the first raven and the last raven. I am every raven you've ever seen.

"I am the raven from the great flood as recorded in Genesis. When the skies darkened in the valleys of Mesopotamia, and a man named Noah began to load the ark that he'd built with his sons, filling its four deep decks with two specimens of every living creature extant on earth, I was chosen to represent my species."

By nothing more than sheer luck the raven was seized and caged with a suitably random female that morning while feeding on discarded scraps of bread in the shadow of the great ark. "I always liked the scent of acacia wood," the raven mentioned offhandedly. "That must have been what drew me there, the smell of the trees being stripped and hewn permeating the valley where I roosted in the cliffs."

There was little reason in recollecting these antediluvian accounts, the raven mentioned, since Billy was surely well aware of the flood myths. Having said this, however, the hunched bird proceeded to describe the first day of the deluge, adding personal insights and anecdotes that varied from those in Genesis. In the excitement of declaring his version, the bird sometimes referred to Noah by his Sumerian name, *Utnapishtim*.

The raven told how all the panicking nonbelievers, who tried to storm the ark as the waters rose, almost killed Noah's second son, Ham, with a fusillade of stones as he shook them from the gangplank. How quickly the rain fell, the bird recalled, lifting up the ship to float away. "You could hear the delirious screams of men and women drowning, pounding logs against the side of the ship, irrationally trying to gain entrance or, perhaps, sink it out of vengeance. Then the waters swallowed the screams. Noah was in tears but unyielding, and he ordered them to repent. His sons knelt together around him, but I could not hear what they were saying. I didn't care, frankly. I knew what I had to do. All the animals that came did. I can't explain that. I'm just a mimic."

The rain continued, and by the seventh day they were far from the valley and any landmarks that they could identify. Earlier, on the third day, Noah's first son, Shem, and his wife freed the birds from their cages and allowed them to fly about the lower three decks. The raven estimated that about 14 to 15 days had passed before all land was totally submerged. "The downpour was so heavy that it was more like constant night, a blackened rain, like oil." The ark held, however. The timbers groaned, predatory animals snarled, as the vessel rolled about on mounting seas, withstanding indomitably pounding waves. "It was a supernal feat of engineering," the raven uttered in a low voice. Noah and his family worked tirelessly, feeding the animals, cleaning the slop. They never opened the doors to the main deck. Those doors were sealed with pitch and nails and to break that seal would have soon flooded everything within. The only light was from a few candles that burnt inconsistently. For the bird, this sense of constant enclosure—*claustrophobia* we would call it now—was the most terrifying part of the trip.

"This was the reason that Noah and his sons imbibed themselves with wine. They could see nothing, but, without speaking the words, were now certain the world they had known was gone. Actually, all these drunken stories of Noah were overblown. The man saved the world, for god's sake. Would you deny him and his sons a drink at the end of a hard day?

"I have witnessed, over the course of my life, the extinction of thousands of species, and the coming forth and changing of others. At this point, though I am getting ahead of my narrative, I should set straight another falsehood regarding the account in Genesis: the flood did not take place five thousand years ago as the holy books would have us reckon. Nine thousand years is more accurate a figure."

"Wait a minute," Billy interrupted for the first time. "Are you telling me that you, some raggedy bird perched in front of me, are—"

"I told you that I was getting ahead of myself," the raven retorted, peevishly cutting Billy off. "I am telling you the whole story here. Let me get on with it. I digress too much as it is. Questions come later . . . perhaps.

"Noah and his crew's eyes finally adjusted to the sunlight that came through the windows. Looking out, there was no land in any direction.

"'Then he sent out a raven, which kept going to and fro until the waters of the earth had dried up.' That's the quote from Genesis 8:7, and that is all you hear about the raven. There's nothing else about the black bird in the entire remaining Old Testament." According to the bird at the window, it was like a cliffhanger from some old movie serial, except here the bird is sent out and flies off at the end of one episode, but you never hear about it again. "That's not right. The *dove* . . . well, there's a whole different story. There was plenty written about the dove.

"According to Genesis, the dove was sent out three times. The first time it returned empty-handed. The verse goes on to report the dove's return to the ark . . . not only that, but actually contends how Noah himself let out his hand for the tired bird, and presses him against his bosom to rest. Then another week passes, and Noah sends the dove out again. This time the damn dove comes back with the famous olive branch in its beak, and everyone rejoices that the wonderful dove has found some proof of land." The raven paused in its tale and preened its old feathers. For a moment, Billy thought it was done.

"And it wasn't even a branch, you know." The raven flapped its wings menacingly. "It was no more than some paltry little sliver of leaf from a drenched little olive tree."

As the raven spoke about the dove, its beak twitched in anger. "The dove with the olive branch in its bill; that's the image that you see everywhere. It's carved in marble all over the world . . . a symbol for the offering of peace. The entire thing is a sham. Allow me to straighten you out about what went down once Noah opened the window.

"I, the raven, was sent out the day that the windows were opened," the bird reiterated. "After that, however, you hear nothing more about me. The fact is that I found land within three or four days. I saw plenty of olive trees; I rested on their branches and chewed a few leaves for sustenance. The idea of returning to the ark with some raggedy old bit of olive branch, however, never even occurred to me. I thought this to be a momentous occasion. It was literally the start of a new epoch on earth. No, this was not the time for olive branches, nor any of the other commonplace plants or trees of the new planet. To usher in this era I decided that I must continue flying on, not satisfied until I found something suitably magnificent to bring back to Noah. You see, all that time he was cuddling his precious dove to his breast, I was out there searching for, and finally finding, the most rare of orchids. It was so violet in the renewed sunlight that it irradiated the air around it. Surely this exotic flower was a mythological necessity to welcome this new age. An olive branch," the raven spat out venomously, "that's exactly what one would expect from some damn pigeon." It squawked loudly, reverting to Raven in its state of rage.

The agitated creature continued telling Billy of his search for the orchid, and how very far it had taken him from the ark. The black bird had lost its bearings and was unable to find any reliable landmarks since the new plains and mountains were constantly changing as the waters receded.

Weeks later, when the ship finally landed on Mount Ararat and Noah and his family threw open the huge door and unloaded the beasts and the birds, setting all free with the divine fiat, "Go forth and multiply," the raven, flying desperately with the rare flower, had still not returned.

Fortunately, the innate mating drive compelled the female raven, which Shem had earlier let loose, to fly off and eventually find her disoriented mate, the unscathed orchid clamped in its talon. After a prolonged aerial interlude, the reinvigorated female led him back to the ark.

"That's another bothersome detail concerning my inconsequential flight, as written in that single verse of Genesis 8:7," the raven said. "It makes it seem that I simply flew off and never returned. So the obvious conclusion any reader would make is clearly that the poor, inept bird never found land in time, ran out of wing (as we birds like to say), and dropped dead of exhaustion, vanishing into the waters. This, of course, defies all logic . . . Since the modern skies are filled with ravens, it is clear that the species exists. If I had died in the flood days, plunging into the tumultuous waters and drowning, there would have been no male left to mate with the surviving female and, thus, that would have meant the denouement of existence for ravens. So any fool would realize that, even in what is regarded as Holy Scripture, there was an editorial oversight or something was concealed and covered up. Yet have you ever heard a theologian question this basic incongruity? No, the entire incident was simply passed over without any further explanation. I'll clarify the reason for all this in a moment."

The raven went on to explain how a week had passed before the pair of ravens returned to the ark; the great sea vessel lay dry-docked in the muddy hillside of Ararat. When the two landed, Noah, his sons, and their wives were still unloading the larger animals from the lower decks. Still, the unexpected return of the raven, sent out three weeks ago now and given up for dead, did not go unnoticed.

When notified that the long-flying bird had returned—clasping a strange, rather magnificent flower in its beak—Noah himself put aside his other tasks and—employing strange words that the others could not comprehend—summoned the creature to his extended arms. The raven complied, and Noah walked some distance, cradling the bird until finding a rock to sit on. He took the flower from its beak and commented on its exquisiteness, then informed the raven he accepted this beautiful offering and now understood the black bird's true intentions regarding the gift. "What you must understand, my dear, tired creature," Noah said, "is that the rituals that endure come most often from the commonplace, and not the exotic. For example, an olive branch often serves one's needs more effectively than an orchid."

Noah, however, realized that the raven would be shortchanged and deserved better than a single verse in Genesis. There was nothing he could do to change the Holy Scriptures, decreed, as they were, by the Almighty, but he still had the power to strike a deal.

So Noah, speaking for the Almighty, made the bargain. Because of this divine editorial oversight that would both deny the raven's proper credit in the Scriptures and allow the dove to usurp its place as the new symbol for peace, Noah proposed the exhausted creature be compensated with the gift of immortality. The patriarch also awarded the raven other, more exotic powers.

For the time being, the bird refused to elaborate on these powers to Billy. Obviously, one of them was the power of speech and, apparently, some sort of mind-reading ability was another.

Billy was stunned. He was now beginning to believe that the raven was exactly who it claimed to be.

"In every myth, you will find me there," bragged the raven. "I was recorded in the Sumerian tablets of Ur, telling the tale of Gilgamesh. You'll locate me in every culture around the world. Even in Siberia, legends persist of a great deluge. The nomadic people of that region referred to Noah as Nama.

"I am a harbinger, a sign or symbol in the consciousness of man in every nation on the planet. It depends on the tellers of the tale and their tribal cultures, whether I stand for good or evil. I don't understand either of these polarities. I just bring the news, and others decide such things. Nothing changes for me. I'm tired and, at this point, all I care about is contacting people who excite my attention, which, at the moment, is you.

"I fed Elijah in the desert. What are the odds of finding the same raven in all these scenes from the Holy Book? And I did it with the same beak you're looking at this very moment, though it's turned brittle and gathered growths over the millennia. I carried him bits of unleavened bread, which I soaked in the water of a nearby spring. He would have died that day if not for me . . . a great man and true prophet. You've read his work, I assume. If you haven't, then I believe now would be the time.

"Did it ever occur to you that, through Noah's faith and perseverance, God saved the ravens, who were considered worthless scavengers? Why did the Almighty do this? If you've read your Scriptures, then the answer is simple: it was our destiny to feed Elijah. We were outcasts that the law considered unfit to sacrifice, yet I was chosen to feed the prophet. This was because the people of Israel abandoned him in the same manner that we ravens were abandoned and despised. They were scavengers as well, who broke the covenant with the Lord and were cast out by their prophet from the Holy Land. Ravens generally stay to themselves, you know. We look after one another. So, in feeding Elijah at God's behest, I did a very unusual thing. When God does something aberrant, it is time that you pay close attention and learn from it. Perhaps some of the people back in those times did. I do not know. You understand the state of things in this world that we live in as well as I. It is abhorrent. Things moved slower back then, and there was time to redeem oneself. I don't believe that you human beings have the luxury of time now. The information overwhelms you, and the earth has grown small. I do not know what will happen. I am only a raven . . . a mimic who is old and wants to die. I have no answers, but none of that matters now.

"I also brought food to Elisha, another prophet. Again, I dipped bread in clear water, providing him with enough sustenance to recuperate. These men were patriarchs in the line of Abraham, Noah, and Moses. Later, in the fullness of time, came the warrior and king David. By the way, Moses carried about a feather of mine. It was fixed by rawhide to his staff, as he walked the desert and ascended Mount Horeb. That very same staff, along with my dark plumage, was passed on to his brother Aaron. Some of this is recorded in the Old Testament; some is not. All of this is duly recorded in the apocryphal Book of Enoch.

"Yes, I gave sustenance to two of the great prophets of the Bible. Still, I am considered a pariah in the very same book. I am portrayed as a filthy carrion-eater that should not be consumed. Do you see the irony in that? I am not fit to be eaten, and I myself have fed the prophets. Not that I am in any rush to be roasted on a spit in the desert, the meal of some caravan of nomads. I would think I have a right to be bitter and recalcitrant in my old age. Strangely, I am not in the least bothered by any of it.

"What was it that Christ spoke of in Matthew's gospel, some allusion to 'wolves in sheep's clothing'? If you keep reading, it goes on to say they are *ravenous*. Even the etymologists conspire against me. I have suffered from the most banal of men's words, not only the divinely inspired, which I have discussed at length. My kind—a proud, essential part of the ecosystem—has been besmirched by such expressions, as well as similar fables and myths. I am either a god or a villain. I seem to bring either wonder or death."

The bird's voice was now coarse from his long tale. It actually stepped down from the windowsill into the room, perching on top of a bookcase, beside an alabaster bear carved by a Zuni Indian. "If you seriously want to know more about who and what I am, I will be quite glad to inform you. As to whether you believe it or not, that's your decision. It makes absolutely no difference to me. As you used to sing when you were young, 'Jimmy crack corn and I don't care.'

"I am the trickster who waits at the crossroads, signifying Toth, Mercury, and Hermes. In the hyperborean lands, I was known as Luki, and in Africa, as Exu Eligibar. I am the inventor of alphabets and the messenger of the gods. I sat on the Emerald Tablet as it was written.

"Look at that book there, beside you. You know something of Saint Francis Assisi? Were you aware that his real name was Giovanni Bernardone, the son of a wealthy garment merchant? He was not only a towering saint, but also a devotee of the troubadours, and composer of the 'Canticle to the Sun.' On one Sunday, Francis was ignored and turned away by the wealthy nobles and landowners as he tried addressing them while exiting mass. He yielded graciously, however, and delivered the sermon to the birds, instead. I was there . . . one of the birds in the graveyard at the edge of that town. Yes, his entire homily took place in the cemetery, and the congregation consisted of the lowest of winged creatures, both God-forsaken and forsaking of God. Everyone reads this tale believing that Francis addressed only the delicate sparrows and hummingbirds. It is always portrayed as him and the spry, attractive birds beside a flowing fountain, basking in the sunlight of a cobblestoned square. Instead, he gave the wisdom of his words to the outcast birds, the scavengers and predators. And none of it happened in sunlight, but during a cold sticky rain . . . my talons washed by dread and floating bits of bones as I listened in that cemetery of shallow graves. There were no *doves* there that terrible, splendid day, I can assure you!"

"You often tend to get very wet, don't you?" Billy asked facetiously. He had mastered lucid dreaming, but this was something strange and new, talking to a dream character.

"And I flew with the other birds to find the Simurgh, in the eponymous poem by Attar, a great and unheralded Persian poet." The creature kept on flapping that well-worn beak, completely ignoring the bewildered painter's wisecrack. The dream's clarity had become frightening. It wasn't making the usual transitions through the dull haze that differentiates sleep and reality. Billy felt his shirt starting to grow wet. Despite the slight draft coming from the open window, sweat was beading and moving down his chest.

"Do you know this epic of Islamic verse? It was based on a real event. Thirty-six of us succeeded. Many other birds began the journey, but dropped away for various reasons. The hummingbird missed sniffing his precious flowers, and the parrot longed to be caged. Again, the scavengers prevailed. By the end of our arduous flight, we had passed over the Valley of Bewilderment, and finally reached the Hills of Annihilation. You must seek for yourself the mysteries we uncovered at the finish of our voyage.

"I certainly do go on, don't I? Then again, it is my right to go on. It is, literally, my God-given right. Do you think I flit about babbling to any fool that happens by? I choose one person in a generation to speak to, and I've been doing it for over 9,000 years."

"What is it you want?" Billy asked, now exhausted and confused. It was the only question possible. If it was a dream, he couldn't jar himself awake, and it seemed certain that the raven wasn't going anywhere. Billy figured the only course left was to play along. He had already accepted the fact that if he bought into this bird's far-fetched claims, he was also starting to validate his own form of insanity.

"It's quite simple really," it replied. "I have come to fill you with sublime terror. I will leave you in bliss or in madness, but it is time you moved on to another level. You are stagnating, in both your life and work."

Billy didn't have any idea how to proceed from here. What if he accepted the complete squirrelly story at face value, with all its immense implications? That led to a very large question, which was twisting around Billy's mind like a wet towel. If this bird was for real, was it coming from the darkness or the light? At this point, Billy was so freaked that—for the first time in many years—he was thinking about concepts like good and evil, even heaven and hell.

"You look like you're getting a bit nervous, Mr. Wolfram." The bird must have sniffed his burgeoning fear, and its voice became very matter-of-fact. It reminded Billy of the incidental tones of Nazi officers in films, right before they shoot the man under interrogation. "You're really quite the cynic for an artist, aren't you? You're impotent, lost, talented, rich, famous, and cynical, as well as a nerve-wracked skeptic. You have convinced yourself of so many lies that you believe them, but that's completely normal in these times.

"Should I perform some silly magic trick to convince you? Oh, ye of little faith! Do you really need a hokey stunt to see that I am not a dream? Perhaps I can offer some proof by relating some of your personal memories. I'm talking about the short time you spent in the country at summer camp when you were a child. You were seven or eight years old. I'm not certain because neither are you. That summer you were at Boys' Club camp upstate, and you killed a small bird. It was a fledgling sparrow with an injured wing, abandoned by its mother. It was lying in the road, barely moving. You were at an age when boys apparently enjoy seeing a living thing die, particularly if it's helpless. You used a slingshot made from a wire coat hanger, loaded with a handful of gravel. You still think about that, don't you? It was a nasty thing to do. You wonder how it was possible that you were so cruel to one of God's tiny beings. These were the same creatures Jesus spoke of in parables, and that Assisi gathered for his famous, aforementioned sermon, which I was fortunate enough to attend. The fact is I have seen the same brutality throughout time. What I have witnessed in my immortality would make you really weld shut the doors to this fake fortification in which you've isolated yourself."

"I remember that. The poor bird was so feeble and helpless. God, what a terrible thing to do," Billy spoke, or thought he spoke. He no longer knew. "What would cause me to do such a thing?"

"That's your problem, pal. It's sure not the reason I came here tonight. Also, as I've said already, I'm just a bird who happens to be quite a good mimic."

"Then why did you come?" Enough was enough. Billy decided to give it one more shot. "I still maintain that you're some form of dream. I'm asleep or in a prolonged hypnagogic state, but either way you're nothing more than a fantasy or illusion. I'm not certain, but you are not real, crow."

"Now who's playing games? What do you think, that was some fortuitous guess?" the bird sneered. "Fine . . . if that's the way you want to play it, then allow me to show you how this so-called dream can poke around within the tiniest recesses of your memory. It's all there. I can tap into everything you revel in and all you've managed to suppress. I'll confirm who I am by unveiling who you once were. That kills two birds with one stone, if you'll pardon the pun. I should warn you, however, that it might get a bit unpleasant.

"So, let's continue where we left off. The subject was cruelty. What about the other incident at that same camp? What were you thinking when you killed that wretched old tortoise you spotted crossing some dirt road? You loved finding that reptile . . . it fascinated you, wondering how old it might be, and how it reminded you of a dinosaur. Then, with some trepidation, you grabbed it up from the road. You didn't want the creature, which seemed so ancient to you, to be squashed by a car. You reached out your hand to feel the rubberlike creases of skin on its head, but the cautious reptile instantly withdrew into its shell. This creature was ageless and harmless. There was such beauty in the mottled yellow lines on its leathery underbelly. You knocked the shell with your thumb to hear the solidity of the sound, then drummed across it with your fingers. You thought you'd forgotten that experience, didn't you? Let me tell you something: we forget nothing. We let it disappear or we trick it into changing, but your brain retains every experience since you left the womb.

"But I digress. That clay-colored shell seemed impenetrable, and that was what piqued your darker impulses. It was your need to understand. If I might coin a phrase, curiosity killed the tortoise. I've seen the shape of continents change in my lifetime, but one thing that has never changed is mankind's drive to comprehend, and constantly experiment and test. Unlike birds and animals, they're never content with what is, but must uncover what is not. Everything must be tried out, and pushed to its limits. It's especially true with children, and it can be infuriating.

"Afterwards, you just go on your way. You turn your attention somewhere else, leaving behind you ruins and death. It's your kind that sustains carrion-eaters like me, but I'm the one they portray as abhorrent. Do you get the irony here?"

"We're made to be curious. It's *human nature*, and if you're as wise as you allege, you know that." Billy tried to squeeze in this remark, but the raven just kept talking.

"You think everything is excused by the phrase 'human nature.' That day you stood at the cliff, which seemed so high. The fact is it was only about 15 feet above the bottom, the remains of a slate quarry used by locals since your Revolution.

"Anyway, it was the cliff that tempted you. You had to test the limits of that shell's strength, as if you were calculating stress factors for a piece of steel sculpture. You just held it over that parapet and dropped it, shell facing down. It landed with the sound of a giant egg cracking. The shell was so fragile that, after rushing down the stone face, you cried as you reached it. It was the same reptile you'd saved less than three hours earlier, and now it was shattered and dead. You killed it to test its limitations, just as you killed the bird to test your own limitations. You shouldn't feel guilt for doing this, though I see that you do. You are experiencing it this moment. But it is the way of all children. It is the way of mankind . . . what they have done throughout history."

"What's happening? Were you there when I did those things? Are you reading my mind? Get away from here." Billy wanted the bird to shut up and get to the point. As far as he was concerned, it was whatever it was. But what did this supernal creature really want? This caused his greatest stress and a terrible sense of foreboding. He was worn down by his own lack of sleep, and felt trapped within some loop of madness that had no end in sight, save for the flight of a bird. He was at its mercy and he still questioned whether this creature emanated from the light or the darkness. Had he reached a point where demons could simulate forms as he slept in bed with his own fears and loneliness? Then again, perhaps the raven was the portent of great secrets. Billy wanted the answers.

But now, with two large beats of its wings, the creature flew from the ledge. It had a wide span for a raven. It dipped down and rose back up into the light from the office window across the street. Billy leaped out of bed and strained his head out the window, watching it head toward Broadway. From there, the raven turned uptown, and Billy lost sight of it. It left without responding to Billy's last questions. He wondered if it was returning to the zoo in Central Park.

Billy again tried convincing himself that it was all some fantasy and a waste of time. He thought he didn't care if he ever saw the spectral figure again. He just wanted to get back to sleep.

The fact was Billy did care. He cared too much and was now bearing the brunt of all he had suppressed. He considered the possibility that he was still the child who wanted to believe. Maybe it was time that he anted up to Pascal's "wager." He was getting a lesson in the spiritual, all right, but it had nothing to do with his painting. He wanted to find a path to the faith he'd seen, clear as quartz, in old Father Mishkin's eyes. He remembered a few months earlier, stopping in the church down the street to study the stained-glass windows, imported from an old Spanish church shelled in the war. He wound up just standing there watching a young woman. She was clutching both her child and her rosary beads with the same intensity, meditating on the Stations of the Cross. He wanted the peace he had seen in his own mother's face as she stared at him across the dinner table all those years ago.

He couldn't imagine ever thinking this way, but something was going on. His early fame had left him in a state of perpetual adolescence. He climbed back into bed and stared at the ceiling. Whatever the raven was about, Billy wanted to see it again, and his instincts told him that he would.

5

At 16 years of age, a desperate Billy decided to take another crack at reviving his comatose libido. He caved in to confusion and inner-city peer pressure and added the token teenage dalliance with homosexuality to his list of failed sexual experiences. With all other recourses exhausted, he figured it would be pure discrimination not to give it a shot. The fact that men had never appeared in his most far-flung and imaginative fantasies made no difference. It was time to throw common sense—not to mention the instinct he relied on so deeply—to the wind.

Experience certainly turned out to be the word for it. Billy, of course, could never summon the nerve or know how to maneuver these uncharted waters without an accomplice, preferably someone who had already endured its rough channels. He wanted an experienced seaman navigating the way. At the same time, the associate needed to be a discreet type that Billy didn't know very well, even if that meant choosing someone he normally wouldn't have anything to do with. In fact, that was preferable, and the reasons were all quite clear. The boys in Billy's neighborhood, no matter how homophobic, had no qualms about allowing some wealthy fag gentleman to exercise his jaw on their rigid Johnsons . . . as long as the motive was strictly mercenary. However, there was always a fear that one of the boys might detect some small, imagined sign that the other was exhibiting pleasure beyond animal relief. Even worse was the possible misinterpretation of affection for the john. It could be the thoughtless movement of one's fingers through the guy's hair as he labored on his knees below, or a boy's fragile tongue running across his own lips a bit too tenderly as he watched the other two. If one of the kids picked up on one of these vibes—no matter how misconstrued—he would never again look at his cohort in the same way. Even when the john himself dismissed any putative reciprocation by the accused, and it turned out to be a very lucrative transaction for both boys, he might find himself assaulted after the fact—maybe the next morning, or perhaps as long as a week later—from vestiges of Catholic guilt.

Either way, any accomplice in this tiresome sex for pay would be sharing a secret that—for a boy of Billy's age—could do nothing but harm. You would first see it the moment the two of you got on the subway back to your neighborhood: neither could make eye contact with the other, and barely a word would be spoken.

So, for such a dubious undertaking, it was simple foresight to choose as an associate someone you knew you could—on the drop of a dime—never speak to again and not feel or think twice about it.

Keeping this in mind, Billy chose Lester Foucault. Word around the neighborhood was that Lester was a regular on the gay hustling scene, and apparently quite successful at it. Lester was also known as "the Cable." Billy thought this appellation derived from Lester's penchant for stealing giant spools of insulated cables from the power company's storage lot, melting off the rubber, and selling the strands of pure copper wire for surprisingly good money. He was also an odious person, without any real character, moral or otherwise. He was exactly the type Billy was looking for. With Lester the Cable, he could open the doors to their dark side without concern for any virtuous recrimination, since the Cable did not possess the insight to recognize it. The guy wasn't even Catholic. To the best of Billy's knowledge, he was Lutheran (Missouri Synod). Best of all, Lester had already approached Billy as a possible partner. Billy had turned Les down that time, but that made it easier to make contact with him this time. Lester was delighted and made plans for them to meet at the 181st Street subway station Friday afternoon.

For Billy, this homoerotic endeavor had a motive far more urgent than money. It was now over four years since his mother had burst into the bathroom that day with news of John Kennedy's assassination to find her beloved son on the toilet, masturbating with wild eyes, his bluish red penis bursting out of a raw veal cutlet. Her shock, the fracturing in her eyes, and her subsequent impassioned sermon had fatally deflated Billy's first, and last, full-fledged erection. He had been only a few strokes from ejaculation. Indeed, he had achieved "pre-cum." He could still recall its glutinous clarity rolling between his fingertips.

At night, there had been the occasional and wondrous wet dream to meekly fulfill the physical needs of puberty, but during the day there'd been only momentary twitches, usually without rhyme or reason. Otherwise, his bewildered penis remained flaccid in his waking hours. Any single event of that afternoon in November 1963 would have been hard enough on the psyche of a healthy child on the verge of his first self-inflicted orgasm, but the stress had been compounded by Billy's theft of family meat, the interruption of his mom's unexpected return, the irritating sounds of the TV and her gasps and moans. The otherworldly sensations in his body and the expectations they offered, the unprecedented pounding of maternal footsteps, the chaotic—almost symbolic—breaking of the lock, the magazine open to that photograph of Barbra Streisand, the news of a president's death given to him as he sat on a toilet holding a prominent erection wrapped in expensive veal, and the look on his mother's face, its color wavering from chalk-white to demon-red. Billy couldn't imagine the massive weight of all these links once they were fused into the chain that he seemed destined to wear around his neck.

Though he worked his hardest to override the sexual impulse through puberty and beyond, Billy could not circumvent thousands of years of biological mandates. He had reached a point of desperation. He finally conceded that his problems stemmed from the suspicion that he was—beneath dense strata of repression—secretly gay, and needed only one act of validation to throw open the floodgates of a fulfilling and fulfilled life of gay promiscuity. The fact that he'd never sensed any lustful urge toward another man, Billy carefully reasoned, only served to further verify the depth of his suppression.

What would Billy do if the man did arouse him? With his lack of passion for the same sex, and his overall resignation, he hadn't bothered to ask himself the question. It was the longest of long shots, but if some old man could cause him to get a hard-on that bore any comparison to the one he'd had for Barbra, Billy would certainly find a way to deal with it.

Billy and the Cable took the A train down to 59th Street, then walked over to the East Side. They hardly spoke a word to each other, aside from the Cable assuring Billy that he had already made contact with a semi-regular trick of his, and they'd be meeting up in front of a bar on Third Avenue.

"He's loaded, has a great apartment right nearby, and he's been up my ass, so to speak, to organize a threesome for quite a while." The Cable laid out the details to Billy in his nasally whine of a voice. "You're just his type . . . tall, dark hair, and a thin yet *active* body. I thought I was gonna have to get this spic friend of mine, but when you said you were interested in going over, I called the geezer and told him it's on."

"Is he like really old?" Billy asked.

"Oh, yeah . . . the dude be in his forties, but he ain't fat or gross or anything. He showed me a picture of his ex-wife once, and that bitch was fine. I thought of her face while he was sucking my dick."

"So that's basically all he's going to do with us, right?" Billy asked, revealing his neophyte status.

"It's up to you, my man." The Cable was playing with Billy's apprehension. "If you want to pitch, he'll gladly bend over and catch. Or maybe you're into the bottom, huh? You like the bottom?"

"What are we talking about here, Les, bunk beds?"

"That's a good one. That's funny. You need a sense of humor in this kind of business. Well, it's not really a business to you; I suppose it's more like doing 'piecework' now and then. Seriously, don't worry about a thing; you'll do fine, Wolfran." Lester enjoyed making humorous variants on Billy's last name; apparently, he wasn't the total dolt that Billy had at first assumed. "Just make sure to settle on the price and get the bread first. Actually, I'll take care of that for both of us. By the way, I should tell you that this guy could get a little freaky. There's nothing involving whips, handcuffs, or other S&M paraphernalia, but he enjoys playing tedious games. Did I mention his sandwiches? He makes the greatest sandwich that you have ever had . . . really. Instead of mayonnaise, he uses some soft cheese. It's good. When we're done with the job, don't leave without having one of his sandwiches."

Billy wasn't sure if Lester's sandwich reference was some gay sex jargon or if he was really talking about food, but he wasn't going to ask. Every time he spoke, the Cable reaffirmed his reputation as a world-class slimeball. In that sense, Billy had chosen the perfect partner to undertake this askew adventure. Lester was experienced enough so that Billy could just follow his lead to avoid any embarrassing blunders. Later, after they'd divided up the money, the two of them could split, and if he never saw Lester "the Cable" Foucault again, it would be fine with him.

"What do you mean about playing games?" Billy asked, but it was too late for clarification. There was no backing out now, as Lester motioned to a well-dressed older man standing beneath the veranda of a fancy building. The man had his hand raised, with one finger flicking up and down, as if the two were a taxi he was flagging down.

Lester shook hands with the man, then rotated what Billy just that moment realized was a bizarrely long neck and said, "Mr. Vegin, permit me to introduce you to Billy Foxjam. I think you'll agree that he's everything I said he'd be."

The man lunged for Billy's hand. "All you said and more, Lester, indeed." The man's voice was deep and devoid of any regional accent. He sounded like a D.J. on a classical music station. There was an oily servility to his grip, and his index finger was caressing Billy's palm. "And how are you today, young Billy?"

"I'm fine," Billy replied. He wasn't. The man would not let go of his hand, the finger speeding up its soft circles. *I'm making an enormous mistake,* young Billy thought. Lester was staring at him with an unctuous smile, giving him a thumbs-up behind Mr. Vegin's back. Billy considered making a run for it. The man slowly let the hand go with an adroit sliding motion.

"Billy, you seem a little nervous, no? Is this your first time down here with Lester? There is nothing to be ashamed or afraid of. Are you a virgin to the dark side?"

Mister, you have no idea what I'm a virgin to, Billy thought.

Billy was far too polite to say this out loud. Besides, the line wouldn't come off sarcastic, but purely cryptic. He finally told the john that it was his first time and, yes, he was a little apprehensive.

Mr. Vegin, on first view, seemed fairly well kept for a guy as old as he was. He was tall, slender, and had a full head of curling salt-and-pepper hair. He wore a blue blazer, gray flannel pants, and wine-colored loafers. The look was pretty lame to Billy's spartan taste in dress, but likely considered dapper in his forty-something circles. Now, as the three began to ride upstairs in the building's elevator, Billy noted that the top of the man's scalp was actually a mediocre rug, woven into the real hair remaining on the sides, which was spewing dandruff across the shoulders of his jacket. The man opened the door with two keys and, with some discomforting formal words, signaled his two guests to enter. This was Billy's last chance to bail, but he felt Lester nudging him forward and he numbly relented. The door shut with a deafening permanence.

From that point things speeded up and took on a businesslike air. The Cable got the money for Billy and himself in cash up front. Mr. Vegin offered them a cold beverage, which they both refused, though Billy's throat felt like a gravel quarry. He then disappeared up the upholstered stairway of his duplex. "Everything that the two of you need to wear, you will find laid out on the table in the living room around the corner. Get dressed and I'll be down momentarily. Oh, and flip off the light switch on the wall once you're fully dressed. Remember what I told you, Lester, it's going to be similar to playing the part in a movie or a play. The better the two of you act out your parts, the bigger the tip you'll get when you leave. On top of the table along with the outfits, there's a photo of a boy dressed correctly in this type of clothing. Just refer to that if there's any question about what goes where. Chop-chop, now."

The two looked at each other. Billy looked accusingly into Lester's eyes. "You should have told me about this dressing-up shit, man. This ain't cool."

"I only found out last night on the phone," Les retorted. "It's not going to change anything. He knows it's your first time, and he's crazy about you, bro. He called you an abundant hunk . . . whatever that means. As we already discussed, just don't get rattled, and follow my lead."

"I will not dress up as a pirate, and don't ask me to," Billy said.

"I hear you . . . no pirate." Cable stared at him. "You are one odd dude, Wolfram."

He followed Lester around the corner and into the living room. It actually was a pretty nice place that this Vegin guy had. Billy had always been content with the walk-up tenement apartment that he had grown up in. It was solid, comfortable, and clean. This place, however, was in a whole different league, from the doorman in his uniform to the fact that the man had a stairway leading up to his bedrooms. A staircase within the apartment itself! That was something you only saw in movies with George Sanders and women in seamed stockings, smoking with frighteningly long cigarette holders.

When they turned the corner they descended two more stairs down to the sunken living room. It had a fireplace that—from all appearances—actually worked. "By the way"—Lester lowered his voice—"here's the bread . . . one hundred and eighty dollars. He really thinks you're the bee's knees. There might be more later, but here's your half for now." Billy grabbed the $90 and jammed it into his pocket. He figured that $180 was an unlikely sum, surmising Vegin had probably paid Les $200, and the Cable had pocketed the extra $20. Billy didn't mind. He had other reasons for being here, and besides, it seemed unlikely that he would be earning the money he'd just gotten.

Once they moved down the two sunken steps, however, both of the boys noticed there was a rather large piece of furniture that didn't fit with the room's additional surroundings. In the corner of the room was a meticulously assembled tent. It was no mere pup tent either. It was spaciously sized and stood at least five feet in height . . . big enough to comfortably fit about, well, *three people*. The sofa, tables, and armchairs that had previously occupied that space were pushed up against the wall haphazardly.

Lester reached over and opened the flap of the tent. "There's three sleeping bags on the floor in here, and a couple of kerosene lanterns," he said in a puzzled tone of voice. For the first time, Billy detected that the Cable was losing his matter-of-fact demeanor.

"It's a nice tent, no doubt about it." Billy stared quizzically. Tents always fascinated him. Actually, in the unlikely context of the fancy living room, it seemed like a piece of sculpture. "What the hell is it doing in his living room?"

"We'll find out soon enough, that's for sure." Lester continued examining the tent, fingering the all-weather fabric. "Meanwhile, let's get dressed for this old bastard." He swiped up one of the cardboard boxes and tossed it to Billy.

Billy stood there in trepidation, watching Lester emptying the contents of his box onto the thick green carpet, piece by piece. There was a well-tailored tan shirt, two thick gray knee socks, and, color-coordinated with the shirt, a pair of very skimpy suede shorts. They were adorned with thick rawhide stitching.

"What the hell are these?" Lester queried Billy.

"I think they're called lederhosen," Billy answered hesitantly. "They wear them in the mountains in, like, Germany and Austria."

The outfits, the tent, the sleeping bags and lanterns—these were all the props of an elaborate pedophilic fantasy. Mr. Vegin's fantasy, however, was Billy's reality. He froze, slack-jawed, at the realization that he was an integral prop, as well.

"Well, whatever they're called, we better get these costumes on." Les was already half stripped out of his street clothes. "I told you this guy was a bit freaky. German Boy Scouts . . . heh, heh. That's beautiful."

Billy opened his box and dumped the contents on the floor. The costume was identical to the Cable's. He could hear Mr. Vegin's footsteps in the room above. Billy picked up the lederhosen and realized they were faux-suede, made of a pliable, one-size-tightly-fits-all material. Lester was already naked and pulling on one of the high wool socks. He wasn't wearing underwear, and this instantly clarified a major misunderstanding on Billy's part as to the genesis of his nickname. The appellation "the Cable" did not stem from his theft of copper wiring from those humongous utility-company spools, but from the ungodly gigantic tool hanging between his legs. It was scary, not only for its massive size, but also because it was the first uncircumcised dick that Billy had ever seen. It looked like an infant python in a turtleneck. "Pretty impressive, eh, Wolfbane?" Lester quipped tauntingly. He had, no doubt, noticed Billy checking out the old cable. Billy didn't answer. When he compared himself to his schoolmates in the shower room after gym class, he had never felt shortchanged in that department. *There are always anomalies,* he told himself. He was just glad that Catholic boys of his era were snipped. At least his was *pretty*—no matter its operational problems. Lester was already completely dressed in his outfit. Once inside those clinging pants, the cable was the most offensive thing he'd ever seen, and for the second time, Billy considered bolting out the door. He let it pass, and lethargically slipped out of his street clothes.

Billy had to take off his underwear to get into the remarkably tight faux-leather shorts. "He's gonna love you, Foxtrot," cracked the Cable, who was lying on the deep carpet at the entrance to the tent. There was a huge mirror pushed up against the wall, obviously just moved there in alignment to Mr. Vegin's warped tableau of the tent and the area surrounding it. The man had even spread some potted palms around to enhance the woodsy atmosphere. Billy looked at himself in the full outfit. He could have laughed or cried. As with Lester, the space-age fabric molded the outline of his cock nastily. It looked like an arrow, pointing to the right, as if designating a direction. Surveying the entire Teutonic mountain presentation as the mirror framed it, Billy couldn't help but break out in a suppressed but everescalating fit of laughter. He looked down at Lester, who was now joining him in whatever the joke was. He had no idea that the joke was Billy's realization of what a moronic undertaking this had become, and, man, he would give anything to be somewhere else. That's when Vegin's voice came floating down from the top of the stairs.

"Lester, shut all the curtains in the living room." Vegin's tone made it more a command than a request. "Then light the kerosene lamps I left in the tent, leaving one inside and placing the other at the entrance." The man orchestrated his fantasies with the passion and fine detail of a ballet-master choreographing his small company for an upcoming premiere.

They were now in almost complete darkness, and Billy was nervously wondering if Lester should be trusted with anything as combustible as a kerosene lamp. However, when the Cable squirmed out of the tent and placed the second lamp on the rug, he could see that the "lamp" was an ingenious fake—probably a movie prop—powered by batteries and a bulb that gave off a flickering firelike effect. Vegin was a perv, but he wasn't going to allow some hustler to burn down his duplex for the sake of a fantasy. The tent glowed, and the living room filled with a subdued, glimmering light.

Into this light walked Mr. Vegin. It was shocking. He was dressed in the same outfit as Billy and Lester, the only exception being a forest ranger–like hat designating him as the master scout, or uber-scout . . . whatever.

"It's a clear, fine night, isn't it boys?" He was speaking in character, with a bad German accent. "Yah, we have a hard day tomorrow, and should be getting ready for sleep. Allow your supervisor to sit between you two scouts, so he might help you out of that tight clothing."

Billy was about to snicker at the man's histrionic speech pattern, but fell silent as Mr. Vegin, his so-called supervisor, lowered his body onto the rug between Lester and himself. Billy was certain he would make his first move on the more experienced Cable. But instead he turned toward the new blood, slowly caressing Billy's thigh as he pulled down the high wool stockings. If Billy had been suppressing his gayness, a man stroking his fingers across his thigh in this adroit manner—not to mention the faux-leather pants pressing against his genitals—settled the question.

It was unfortunate, but the answer to Billy's problem was not so simple as lusting for the wrong sex. As he'd expected, his long shot didn't pan out. He might have been impotent, but he was straight and impotent.

Mr. Vegin had another agenda entirely, and was pulling down Billy's lederhosen. He got them as far as the knees when his fingers surrounded Billy's flaccid penis and sensuously squeezed. The pressure of the tight shorts had made the boy's joint deceptively large in its limpness, but the more Vegin worked on it, the more it receded. The scoutmaster was getting increasingly frustrated, and only made matters worse as he removed his own pants, revealing a thin, warped erection. It was bent to the left, and reminded Billy of a puppy's raised leg. If Vegin imagined this sight was going to arouse Billy, he was stunningly mistaken. Lester quickly saw that this was almost certainly leading to an annoyed Vegin demanding a refund, and he was not going to allow such a possibility. He whipped out the cable and stage-whispered to Vegin, "Mr. Supervisor, look what's happening. My big penis is getting all hard, and I'm afraid to sleep if you don't suck me first."

Vegin lunged toward the cable, but he still had his head craned at Billy in disbelief. It was so temptingly well proportioned and the man had tried so hard, yet it remained so soft. Lester coaxed Vegin into the tent to fulfill as much of his fantasy as he could, under the circumstances. Before his head disappeared through the flap, however, Lester turned and signaled Billy to take the opportunity to get dressed and beat it. It was either a charitable act on his part, or perhaps he'd figured that any further participation by Billy would muck up—to an even greater extent—the good thing he had going with Mr. Vegin. Billy saw it as the former, and was awed at how badly he had underestimated old Lester. He whipped on his street clothes and exited the premises as stealthily as he could. He gave one last look back as he opened the door. The bright, phony lamplight within the tent outlined the shadow of Mr. Vegin on all fours. Lester was on his knees behind him, and that twitching cable was on its way to making clear just who the supervisor really was.

Billy was so antsy on the A train home that he couldn't sit, but just paced from one car to the next. It could not have gone worse. It certainly provided no solution for Billy. There was no sexual feeling of love for men. Billy hated Vegin for more reasons than he could number. Billy was angry with the Cable despite his finally coming through (so to speak) and facilitating Billy's exit. Angry with him just for being there. This was not sexuality, nor homosexuality. It was a weak man being dominated by a ludicrous, elaborate fantasy. This farce had served only the most perverse and harmful elements of sex. It was a predatory tableau of pedophilia and ruin.

He should have trusted his initial feeling that he had no attraction for men. Wouldn't he have known by now? He was aware of the irony involved. How most kids his age who desire other males go through hideous ridicule, anguish, and deceit, as they stumble through the same piles of guilt, suppression, and false façades that they will eventually need as barricades to hide behind. Meanwhile, Billy suddenly and ludicrously had convinced himself that this was the answer to all his problems. It wasn't only pathetic; it was pathological.

His obsession had taken him into the realm of foolishness. The only true faith he had was his trust in his own intuition, and his sexual exasperation had caused him to ignore that faith and that trust. He was angry with himself for what he saw as an act of blasphemy—a betrayal of the inner register—and vowed that it would never happen again. His sexual problem, he realized, was a terrible consequence of fortune, but he was getting nowhere but lost trying to find a remedy.

As for the ordeal with the Cable, Billy planned on sharing that debacle with no one, excepting perhaps Denny. He hoped that Lester was worth his word, and would honor the plea Billy had made during their ride downtown, to bury the whole affair, no matter how it went down.

As the train got closer to the Highbridge stop, Billy just glared—in complete stupor—at the tracks from the front car's window, reverting to eight or nine years of age, before any of this came to be. The engineer was a real cowboy, racing through red signal lights at risky speed, particularly on the curved track banking into the 125th Street station.

Whether he was able to pull it off or not, he was adamant about circumventing the entire sexual issue for now. He'd allocate all that excess energy into his recent commitment to art. He had been steadily developing an already uncanny gift for draftsmanship. Each afternoon at the Cloisters, he'd work on exercises that his school's art teacher gave him to expand his burgeoning technique. The results might be glorious; they might be terrible. They could be both, which would be the worst outcome. Billy stared at the tired commuters jostling each other as the train pulled into the 125th Street station, and he broke out laughing at the same instant its doors slid open. He seemed delirious; people looked up at him from their seats. "A tent in the living room," he burst out, "that really cracks me up." He realized people were staring, so he fell silent, turned, and focused back on the tracks.

6

Billy and Denny had been living in the apartment on 1st Street for almost a year when Billy received his first check from the gallery. It was for the sale of the *Tidal Pool* painting. "I don't know the art world," Denny said, "but those seem like some pretty sweet numbers for a first sale. I'd say that some grudging congratulations are in order, you uppity bastard. Can I still be your friend?"

The gallery owner also included a note stating that "a very important collector" had bought the canvas. He also informed Billy that he'd caved under the collector's persistence and given him Billy's phone number. He attached the buyer's glossy card, which had three phone numbers in embossed print. The dealer implored Billy to strike first and get in touch with the man as soon as possible.

The name on the card, Max Beerbaum, did not ring any bells with Billy, and he was hesitant to call the man. At this point, he just wanted to keep pace with the unceasing ideas in his head, as well as the nearly completed canvases that he barely had enough room to store properly. What was the point in meeting such a so-called important man compared to producing the work itself?

"If I wasn't producing anything at the moment, maybe I'd consider calling him," he told Denny. "I just wish I had more damn room."

"That's exactly why you should call this guy," Denny said. "If he's such a big collector, then he's got to have some serious bank. Aside from bread for sculpture, you have to think about a bigger work space of your own. They're not going to let you sneak in to Cooper Union at all hours forever, you know."

"You trying to get rid of me?" Billy laughed.

"Hell, no . . . not with sweet checks like that coming in. Besides, I'm usually spending the night out anyway. I'm just saying that it can't hurt to talk to the guy. I think that you're upset that he was the first person to buy a piece of your art, which in your mind is a precious piece of you, and you don't like that, do you?"

"Jeez, Denny, I don't know how you came up with such a spectacular theory, and the fact that you're correct makes it no less baffling. Am I that transparent?"

"It's as if this star-maker kidnapped one of your children. The irony is that he's paying you the ransom."

Standing with the check in hand, Billy was, of course, slightly curious about anyone who took enough interest in his work to buy that particular painting, and for what appeared to be such a surprisingly high price.

Trying to beat Denny at his own game, he stealthily went in back and grabbed up a reference book on contemporary art, checking the index for the name on the card. As he thumbed through the corresponding pages, Billy felt an elflike breath on the back of his neck. Denny was reading the same tiny print as his friend and began summarizing the section on the buyer, utilizing a sarcastic, histrionic tone. "Jeez, this guy hung out with all of those hot shots in Paris when they still made good art there. It says he owns the largest private collection of Surrealist art, and not just paintings either. He has a vast archive of handwritten manuscripts from poets like Desnos, Éluard, Breton, and Max Jacob.

"Imagine that, Billy. The fellow seems to have some credibility, huh?"

"But it just doesn't seem the time."

"No way you weasel out of this one, pal. You read the names in that book. This person has worked with the best, and he just bought your painting. If you didn't see him, it would seem like a slap in an old man's face. Also, I don't swallow this 'suffering artist' crap. You *do* care. Maybe not about the bread and the fame, but you need to test your work on an audience and see if it flies. It's their opinions that will either validate your abilities or tear them to shreds, and change the entire scope of your intentions.

"Why are you so adamant about this matter, brother? There's nothing wrong with a little ambition, as long as it remains natural and integral to your vision. It's like you're suddenly playing the rebel, and that's not your thing. You're just afraid and trying to hide from the inevitable. You know it's what you want, and I can't believe it's just fear of rejection. You've rolled with worse punches. If you don't make some contacts—especially when this certified legend, in effect, flies right to your window and makes you an offer—then you're going to regret it. Maybe not now, but soon, and for the rest of your life. Man, you don't even have Ingrid Bergman and Paris to fall back on. In fact, you have hardly any memories to compensate for your circumstances and bad judgment.

"Now, if you don't pick up that phone and get in touch with this guy in the next day, I'm not giving you a cent for next month's rent. That's *twenty-four hours,* and"—Denny adjusted his knockoff wristwatch—"it starts . . . now."

It was only a day after this conversation that the phone rang and Denny picked it up. Billy was in the kitchen, and Denny signaled for him.

"It's the kidnapper," he whispered, feigning solemnity. "Try to keep him talking for as long as possible so we can get a trace."

Billy had some trouble finding the right pitch for his voice. He wanted to sound older than his 21 years. Denny began to smile and finally left the room, not so much to give Billy his privacy, but because he was going to lose it if he stayed there another moment watching the expressions on his friend's face.

"Yes, sir, I just received your card in yesterday's mail."

Denny could still hear the conversation—at least Billy's side of it—from the tiny bedroom.

"Dinner? Well . . . sure." Billy's voice had settled on a tone: complete befuddlement in near-falsetto. "Would it be all right if I brought along my roommate?" Hearing this, Denny felt humbled and reentered the room.

"No, it's not a woman. It's just a very close friend. Fine . . . I'm writing the address down as you speak. What's the cross street there?

"Oh, it's right *on* Gramercy Park." Billy looked over at Denny with raised eyebrows. Denny gave the thumbs-up sign.

"One of the brownstones on the west side. Fine . . . Tuesday at eight. Well, thank you. That's really kind of you to say."

"Wait," Denny interrupted. "Ask him if he really gets one of those keys to that park there. You know, you can't get in without one."

Billy, fortunately, had already hung up the phone.

There are seminal memories that somehow retain not just the event, but also the emotions that accompany it. They transport one back to the exact moment, and these remembrances are so potent they carry a vague fragrance. This was true of Billy's first meeting with Max. He was *there*, in all his senses . . . in time and space. He could smell it.

It was winter as they left for dinner at Max's house. It always puzzled Billy that so many of his most fond and formative memories took place in winter. The fact was that he never liked this season, except as a young child when falling white flakes were magical, and the sun on the snow-covered baseball fields in the park was the color of light through quartz. Back then, he could watch winter for hours from his bedroom window. Of those dim years, all he recalled of the outdoors was being bundled into an outrageously overinsulated and unattractive jumpsuit that made him impervious to the frigid air. As he grew older, the season turned gray. The slush and salt soaked his shoes and left white rings caked around his pants legs. The trees were bare and the cold savage. Inside the apartment, loud steam from the radiators cracked open the dry skin on Billy's hands, making it painful to draw. Also, whatever strain of flu was going around each year, Billy invariably caught it. He'd mope around the apartment with ratty slippers, a quilt draped around him like some funky emperor, and soon needed half a glass of orange juice before his swollen, tender larynx could rasp out a single sentence.

Ironically, winter was invariably Billy's most productive time of year, its dim freeze bringing out his drive. The cold clarified his imagination. He would think of it as a kind of camera, which froze his speeding thoughts and held the images in place until he could get them down on canvas, or into his notebooks.

Billy's conflicted attitude toward winter had continued throughout the years and was most likely the one constant in his life. He hated the weather yet thrived on the creative spurts it initiated. So much of his life depended on the seasons. Even the time of day affected him. He remembered being in Vermont in January, watching the shifting rhythm of the sun, and feeling its slow arc pulling at him as it crawled over the earth.

Unless it was very urgent, he rarely worked in warm weather. He felt stalled in summer. He'd read, make notes on future projects, and take endless walks. Summer was a time for repose, and winter a time for action.

That night, as they neared their destination, it was just cold enough for Billy to need his corduroy coat, which he wore over a gray linen suit jacket he'd picked up for 15 bucks at a secondhand store. The label on the inside pocket had the name of some London boutique. Feeling the grainy light texture of the thin lapels, he'd thought of the Beatles and bought it. Tonight was only the second time he had worn it, and he felt glad he'd splurged on it. Billy usually loathed the very concept of fashion, and nothing rubbed him raw like the elitist mob that referred to fashion design as an "art form." Still, he loved linen since he'd read that it was the only fabric Matisse wore.

Denny was more into clothing, but he managed to play it down for the night with a peacoat and dark sweater. He could see how this sudden foray into the upper echelon of the art world was causing his friend apprehension, defiance, and other major grief. Though it went against his character, he was trying his best not to add to it. Entirely in black darker than an unscheduled eclipse, the outfit made him look like a cat burglar. He added a bit of rocker flair by sporting a droopy wool hat. It was unique, resembling something worn by a Tibetan Sherpa—if the Sherpa happened to be a mezzo-soprano in a Wagnerian opera. The two had already agreed they were going to be woefully underdressed for such a fete. Max, however, had been emphatic on the phone, insisting they wear whatever they like.

"We look like the Little Rascals," Billy murmured as they checked themselves out in a store window on Park Avenue South.

"Relax. You're the guest of honor," Denny reassured him. "Anyway, these dudes are rich enough to be beyond fashion."

Now Billy wished that he had worn a scarf. The temperature was dropping and, augmented by an impetuous wind from the East River, its chill was seeping through his corduroy.

Gramercy Park was an amazing sight in the evening, like stepping back into another century. It skewed Billy's senses so sharply that he scanned the sky, believing he would see stars above, but he only quickly glimpsed a patch of diffused light from the Empire State Building. The homes were quaint and sedate, built decades before the city's oldest resident had been born. Aside from a rococo building designed by Stanford White—with its blanched marble façade filigreed and imperious like a royal wedding cake—none of the houses around the park was taller than four flights.

It was the only privately owned park in the city, maintained and used solely by the residents of the surrounding buildings. A wrought-iron fence enclosed the well-tended mix of exotic trees, granite fountains, and green wooden benches.

Billy and Denny crossed the street and scanned the row of houses bordering the park's west side. They hesitated a moment in front of Max's brownstone, then opened a gate in the wrought-iron fence, which led through a small, elegant rock garden. One tried to harness his dreamy anticipation; the other stood, stunned and still, with an expectation of dread. They ascended a stone staircase, and, at the top, Denny pushed a buzzer beside a massive oak door. There were no intercoms or any other visible signs of the security paraphernalia endemic to the homes of wealthy New Yorkers.

"He must have this entire fucking building to himself," Denny said. "This guy is *steeped* in it."

"Just be good," Billy implored.

"Hey . . . you know that gallery guy who put on the show that Max saw you in?" Denny's breath was visible from the cold.

"What about him?" Billy hurried his friend. He heard footsteps approaching.

"Well, he told me on the phone that this Max dude has a small Renoir painting in an upstairs bathroom."

"Don't even think about it, man." Billy was only half kidding. "I will tackle your ass if you go anywhere near a stairway to the second floor."

The brass knob, which both of their eyes had been focused on, began to turn.

A short, balding man in a Savile Row suit opened the door. He had a tender smile and extended his hand. "I'm Max Beerbaum," he said. "Am I shaking the hand of Mr. Billy Wolfram?"

Billy smiled and nodded. He couldn't speak. He was still looking upward at the Roman arch above the door, gauging the enormous pressure form could take on a single keystone. It was Denny, naturally, who spoke up first. He hardly moved his lips, having done this so often over the years. It was almost like a ventriloquist act.

"It is indeed, sir, and I'm his best friend and spokesperson, Dennis MacAbee."

Max gripped the musician's hand, pumped once, and released. He then clutched Billy by the shoulder and squeezed firmly, guiding him out of the cold and into the foyer. Max then heard a voice calling from the kitchen and he moved toward that room, shuffling backward.

"I've got to see about something for you fellows to drink. Just take your coats off and hang them over there." He pointed to his right as he continued to backtrack. His movements were like a little dance. He was very light on his feet.

"Anything's fine for us," Billy finally managed to say, about two octaves higher than normal. There was a quaver in his voice that brought a slight smile to Max's face. They removed their coats.

Tugging off his corduroy, Billy instinctively rummaged through its pockets. They were empty except for a small envelope with a bulge in it. Billy pulled out the tiny package and emptied it into his palm. It was a tooth! It must have been there since he had an impacted wisdom tooth extracted almost a year earlier. Fortunately, no one was around to witness this disgusting oddity. Billy held it up to the track lights. It was much bigger than you'd expect. He then turned it around and saw a rancid hole of decay blasted into the enamel. Looking at the depth of the cavity just revived the pain, so he turned it back around with the roots pointing up. It reminded him of an artifact from some archaeological site. The two long prongs, bifurcating at the top, looked a bit like the thin, pointed ears of a primitive carving of a cat. Perhaps it was a rabbit. Denny was emerging from snooping in a side room, so Billy slid it into the breast of his blazer and decided it was a good omen, having this personal totem close while they ate.

It was at this moment that Billy committed a faux pas still spoken of at art gatherings.

Just inside the door, a rack of darkly stained mahogany was fixed to the wall. It was the work of an expert carpenter, and Billy stared at it in admiration. There were six round pegs fastened at even intervals to a slab of smooth, burnished wood. Above it, there was a shelf. It was the same well-worn wood, and it held six bowler hats. The anachronistic black derbies were laid out delicately, spaced evenly above the corresponding pegs. They were made of fine material. Seeing them, one was transported right back to the 1920s.

The only problem was that Billy did not see the hats. He was so intensely focused on the carpentry work that went into the wood that he didn't look up. He took his coat and hung it on one of the rack's wooden pegs. The peg immediately snapped loose under the weight of Billy's corduroy coat, and both dropped to the floor. The broken round peg rolled away from the coat, finally halting against the young man's shoe.

"Didn't you see the plaque, for god's sake?" Denny said, helping Billy gather up the coat. He tossed it on a chair on top of his own.

"What plaque?" Billy was baffled. "I didn't see anything. I was admiring the craftsmanship."

"With good reason. Look." Denny tapped the wall. "What a bonehead. You were in another grand mal space-out. Get the spool thing and fix it."

Beneath Denny's finger was a smart brass plate designating the assemblage *The Dinner Party*, by Billy's favorite Surrealist, René Magritte. If Billy had only looked up another foot and taken in the bowler hats, everything would have become clear.

Mortified and mumbling, he swooped down and retrieved the peg with his long fingers. Fortunately, when he pressed it back into its hole, it stuck. Denny thought it was hilarious, and the sound he grunted out trying to suppress his laughter just made the situation worse, drawing Max and his guests into the foyer. Max was the only one who could make this right, and, realizing what had happened and the effect it was having on the flustered young man, he did so without hesitation. "That happens all the time, Billy," he said, gesturing his hand in a calming motion. "Don't think twice about it. Just come inside to have a drink."

It was probably that moment that sealed the fate of both the elderly collector and the young artist. There was a bond formed by the connection in their respective eyes, merging in the moment: Billy's awash in embarrassment and dismay, Max's bathed in palpable compassion. There was a nonchalant certainty to Max, an immediate faith in others, that Billy had never experienced before. It took making a fool of himself to appreciate he'd made the right decision in coming there. Following the collector into the other room, he realized that Max was the first person who could actually calm him down just by speaking the words "Calm down."

Everything about the dining room—its size, the décor, and the servants— was beyond anything either of the two young men had experienced. Ordinarily, they felt lucky if they had enough money for a meal at one of the lo mein joints in Chinatown. Max certainly lived up to everything the dealer from the group show had claimed in his letter.

The chairs were antiques with enormously high backs, like something from a sixties English horror movie. Nine people sat at the dinner table, which was large enough to handle twice that number. Denny's slightly glazed eyes were fixed on the huge stone fireplace, which blazed steady with a low aquatic-green flame. On the wall to its left, there was a portrait of Max's dead wife. The painting's lighting and its traditional gilded frame distinguished it from the Surrealist works that comprised the bulk of Max's collection. Even the scent of the room was wealthy, a hybrid of leather and cedar. It smelled like the inside of a Cadillac, still on the showroom floor.

All the other guests were dressed in suit and tie, excepting one South American writer wearing a silk turtleneck. The food arrived in five courses. It was French and very rich, the white sauces heavy with the scent of fresh tarragon. The soup had the consistency of oatmeal. Billy could have made an entire meal out of this porridge, and he tried to pace himself. After the entrée, however, Billy's appetite gave out. It was medallions of veal, drenched in béarnaise. Still, he noticed Denny obliviously shoveling his plate clean through all five courses, and making a loud smacking sound with nearly every bite. Billy was so accustomed to the impulsive noise that he no longer paid attention to it. But the other guests took notice, and repeatedly focused on the garrulous stranger throughout the meal. By the sound, some assumed he was brazenly throwing kisses at them.

The last course was carried in on a silver platter. Billy assumed it was dessert. It appeared to be a thin cheesecake. When asked, he told the woman serving that he'd prefer a large slice. It wasn't very big for such a gathering, he thought. When he bit into the soft substance on the end of his fork, Billy recognized it was not cheesecake. It wasn't any kind of cake, and it certainly wasn't sweet. It had a rather musty taste.

"You enjoying that scrumptious Brie there, chief?" Denny whispered with his clucking grin. "I didn't know you were so big on the foreign cheeses."

He knew exactly what had happened, but Billy was not about to let on. There was no way he was about to repeat the folly of the surreal coatrack.

"Oh, I love the Brie, my man," he answered nonchalantly, clearing the plate. Nobody else suspected his blunder.

Before that night, of course, Billy had never seen, smelled, or ingested any cheese more exotic than Swiss. It was too bad. His only real vice was an insatiable sweet tooth, and midway through the meal, he began to fantasize a finale of very dark chocolate. It was at that point that Max addressed him for the first time since they sat to eat.

"Let me ask you these two things while we are all gathered together." Max tossed his napkin onto the table and faced Billy. "You and I will have a talk in private soon. For now I just want my friends to learn a bit about you. I hope this isn't putting you on the spot, but I'd like to inquire what you hope to be working on in five years."

"That's only one question," Denny said.

"You are absolutely correct, my young friend," Max persevered with a note of sarcasm, eyes remaining on Billy. "I also wanted to know if Billy here thought himself capable of building a bridge."

"Well, I wasn't expecting this, but I'll give it a shot if you'll bear with me," answered Billy after taking a sip of wine. He had prepared himself to talk to this Max person at some point, but not in front of all these strangers. "I try not to get caught up wondering about the future," Billy began. "I don't usually make plans, or even think about things, beyond two weeks. The main reason is that I'm a bit of a fatalist. I don't see how anyone who was born after the atomic bomb could be anything else. Therefore, the first is really an impossible question for me. I usually trust in my instincts and go with them. Of course, I'm excluding any commitments I've made, including shows, or any specific engagements. You also asked if I'd know how to build a bridge. I could probably construct something ornate. I'm sure I could do an arch or tunnel for cars to enter. It would be something basic and minimal, and it would function efficiently. I'd have to see the place where this bridge is being built. That would dictate everything. Maybe a different kind of tollbooth . . . something that was very geometric and without frills. I feel I'm capable of that, and I am including the engineering aspects. Getting all the stress factors and analysis of tensile pressures worked out . . . that sort of thing. An entire bridge, on the other hand, is completely beyond my scope."

Billy looked around the table at the faces of Max and his guests. He thought he had rambled on too long. He wasn't even sure if it was a real or hypothetical bridge. He figured he was being tested through some sophisticated psychological game, and assumed he had failed miserably. One man wiped his glasses with a soft foam green cloth. The younger guy beside him was relighting a large cigar, probably Cuban, which he'd been smoking earlier. Max was totally enthralled. He had mischief in his face, with a radiant smile and eyes blinking in quick, random sequences. The man must have been near 70, but had an energy that Billy appreciated. He was also still willing to take risks.

"Well said, Billy Wolfram . . . well said, indeed," Max finally said. He spoke through an impish smile, clapping his hands slowly and silently together. He apparently relished addressing his protégé by his entire name. He must have used Billy's full name four or five times during that first encounter, and this penchant continued throughout their relationship.

"You need to see where the bridge would be," he continued, repeating Billy's phrase, his tone radiating smoothly outward. "You are as certain of your limitations as of your strong points. That's marvelous . . . wonderful."

Billy didn't know what he had done well. He was thinking that he had never heard a person use the word *marvelous* before. A few of the others at the table smiled as they slyly glanced at Billy. The remainder, Billy concluded, found Max's unrelated queries as puzzling as himself. The man with the cigar put it out once more.

The guests soon passed through two adjacent doors, entering a large room filled with books, small sculptures, and a young woman serving exotic drinks behind a small yet fully stocked bar. Billy noticed Denny standing alone, fanning a deck of cards beside a two-foot-high Giacometti, and trying to bum a cigar. This was the big-money, uptown crowd, and by now everyone was on to Denny's routine. When Denny approached with "You have an extra one of those gigantic smokes, boss?" they just laughed. Eventually, Denny got his cigar. Billy noticed him in the corner with a man wearing dark glasses who was showing Denny the proper way to light a good Havana. Denny inhaled and blew some smoke rings, then smiled widely and flashed a peace sign at his perplexed new pal. Billy had to shake his head. "Unbelievable," he whispered inaudibly, stepping back and taking a seat in a large leather chair. He focused on how evenly the candles on the dining table continued to burn. They were in holders fashioned like golden snakes.

"They're Egyptian," a man whispered. "Quite stunning, aren't they?"

"Definitely," Billy answered without facing the man. "Is that inlay jade?"

"It is unpolished emerald, if I'm not mistaken."

"God." Billy was spaced out and in deep focus on both the craftsmanship and the flame. "That is some very sweet work."

A previously unseen servant approached and informed Billy that Max wanted to speak with him alone in an adjoining room. Billy was anxious, but not about this upcoming interrogation. The butler made him more nervous than the idea of meeting alone with the man who employed him.

Billy followed the stoop-shouldered fellow into a small office. Max was behind a desk, but he shuffled around and ushered Billy into an armchair. The servant was already gone, and Max was pouring two glasses of wine.

The collector sat in a similar chair beside Billy and asked some vague personal questions, which Billy answered as best he could. He wasn't any more uncomfortable than he imagined he'd be, but that wasn't saying much. He'd never been in a place like Max's, and it simply overwhelmed him.

Billy dug his fingernails into the chair's burgundy upholstery. After another half a glass of wine, he began to loosen up and speak a little more freely. This legendary figure seemed genuinely interested in the little that he had to say. Feeling startlingly relaxed, Billy unconsciously put his sneakers up on the ottoman. Having been around so many painters, Max understood that the last thing they wanted to discuss was their own work. The two eventually chatted for half an hour about the movies. There was some common ground there. Billy managed to make it over to the St. Mark's Cinema once a week to catch three reruns for one dollar.

"You can learn a lot about another person by going to the movies with them. This goes for a stranger or an old friend," Max remarked. "Sometimes, talking about it later, you wonder if you saw the same film as the other person."

Max then leaned forward in his chair and leveled his eyes at Billy. His entire demeanor changed. It was drastic. For a moment, Billy expected the old man to ask him to leave his house and never come back.

"Where did you get the idea for that splendid piece that I purchased, and how did you come to call it *Trapped in Tidal Pool at Low Tide*?"

"I saw a photograph of a tide pool in some magazine," Billy explained, relieved at the seemingly innocuous question. With so worldly a fellow as Max, he knew that he should keep his answers short and to the point. "I also saw a documentary on the diminishing of wildlife habitats, and other ecological matters. They had some footage of these guys in high rubber boots rummaging through some tidal pool in California. I think they were collecting algae, or anemones, to bring back to the lab for tests. It was beautiful . . . probably on public television."

"I had a feeling that you hadn't actually seen such an environment for yourself." Max was silently gleeful that he'd been correct in his assessment of Billy's upbringing. "You haven't had the opportunity to travel much, have you?"

"Well, I've been to the ocean." Billy spoke with a slightly defiant tone.

For the first time that night, he perceived an iota of condescension in Max. Billy was not as thick-skinned as Denny, and sometimes had difficulty reading others, especially in such unfamiliar surroundings. He also did not possess his friend's ability to make social transitions. Denny could diminish or expand himself for any situation, whether with street kids or wealthy folks like Max. Billy was totally lacking in this ability, and his over-the-top sensitivity sometimes led others to misinterpret otherwise harmless intentions.

"Oh, my God, no." Max quickly shadowed Billy's defensive words. "That's not what I meant at all. I know you've been to the ocean, I wouldn't doubt it for a second. I was alluding to the fact that you've been blessed with a very strong imagination, and much of your work springs from this gift. Please don't take offense; I was simply paying you a compliment. I believe you're extremely talented, Billy, and believe me, I'm very much on your side."

"Sorry, I'm not at my best around strangers, and you have no idea how far out of my element all this is. Please just accept my apologies."

"There's no need for that." Max tilted his head. "Listen, it's already forgotten. For what I have in mind, it is imperative that I know more about you. Let me just clear up one thing that you made reference to just now. I don't want you to think of me as a stranger. I need us to be open with each other. Are you up for that?"

"I think so." Billy was still hesitant, uncertain of what the retired dealer wanted.

"Experience is sometimes more important than years and years of school," said Max, changing course. "Stay with your instincts for now; they've served you well. I understand that this house and all these surroundings seem like another world to you, but it's your city. As I understand, you were born and raised here. If anything, I should feel the stranger. A bit of trust can remedy whatever rift you feel between us. What I'm after is an understanding of the nature of your talent. It's a natural enough curiosity, stemming from my appreciation for the limited amount of your work I've seen. I was really taken by that painting. I'm anxious to get a look at more.

"Regarding travel, that's insignificant at this point. I only asked because, if you can paint like that utilizing books and instinct, then it proves what a powerful internal landscape you possess. As I said, the visits to Florence and Barcelona and Paris can wait. They'll be there. That's up to you. Believe me, nothing is going on in any European city that can rival the work being produced right now in New York. As far as art is concerned, there's no other place that comes near the energy flowing from this city. You might as well use that energy. This is stuff you already know, I'm sure. It might be your time also, Billy Wolfram."

There was a cursory knock on the door and the servant entered. He informed Max that a certain guest had just arrived. As Max excused himself, he gestured to the bookshelves and walls, inviting Billy to have a look around.

Billy approached a bookshelf and began thumbing through a stack of catalogues from Max's old gallery, each page validating the dealer's reputation. The man had been curator of shows that included the giants of twentieth century painting, and, of course, had added most of those artists to his own collection. It was heady stuff for Billy to imagine his work being connected to such monumental names. He didn't dwell on the thought, however. It was a good bet that Max had purchased the painting for somebody else . . . as a gift, perhaps. Billy was not without a quiet, burning ambition, but he always erred on the side of caution. He was disciplined to a fault, probably something to do with his Catholic upbringing. He wasn't going to make any assumptions until he saw *Tidal Pool* hanging on the wall he now faced, right beside the row of collages by Max Ernst.

His host returned with an apology and the same smile he had worn when he left. Billy did not know if it was the catalogues, the surroundings, or the wine, but his entire attitude had changed. He liked Max, and trusted him. It was, perhaps, the first time he felt this way about an older man.

"Could you answer one more question for me?" Max asked, lowering himself into the leather swivel chair behind the desk. "I'm afraid it's also something you'll find difficult putting into words. I wanted to know the source of your vision."

"I learned that you have to see things through another's eyes." Billy himself was surprised when he said this.

"How do you mean that?" Max seemed both impressed and puzzled.

"The idea is pretty simplistic, actually. I picked it up from conversations with my uncle when I was a kid, only about six or seven years old.

"He was a fireman, and the closest thing I had to a father figure. He would point out different buildings, as we'd walk by, and map out exactly how he would best deal with the place if it were on fire. He'd go into great detail about the unique features of each house, exactly how they'd have to work the hoses and make sure the guys inside were on radio and knew the right exit points . . . all that stuff. He was really obsessed by all this, complaining how dangerous the air shafts in certain tenements were. The flow of oxygen could combust some smoldering newspapers in the basement and spread the blaze upward. In less than ten minutes it's in the upper floors, and by the time they get there it's a complete conflagration.

"Some places could be handled easily, then there were others he made seem impossible. I particularly remember we were passing a commercial building and he was raving about the steel shutters that they used to seal the windows shut. He said the metal was so strong that firemen would waste so much time trying to break them open and get to the flames. I imagine you see what I'm saying here. Everything was based on function. For him, the moment it takes to find beauty was a luxury that could cost a life. He never noticed the brickwork, marble inlay, or the variance in slope between adjacent façades. He had no use for the cornices or gargoyles over the entrances of apartment complexes built in the twenties. My uncle didn't care one bit about the most basic tenets of architecture. He simply saw everything according to how a structure would burn."

"I get what you're saying," Max said, "but how do you put what you're saying to use? Do you try to see things through another's eyes? That's laudable, but it has to be fairly tiring."

"Well, I built on this little theory over the years, and realized that you have to be capable of putting yourself in someone else's place. It's no different than the old adage 'walking a mile in someone else's shoes.' To me, that's the poor man's Golden Rule. It's very similar to 'treating others as you'd have them treat you.' To know how to treat them—or not treat them, as the case may be—you have to understand them. That means walking in their shoes or seeing through their eyes. Anyway, I try my best to scope things out from as many points of view as possible. The whole idea's not very profound, really."

"In its way, it is," Max said. "It just seems it would be hard to stick with it. There are so many bastards out there. You have to wonder if it would be worth the effort. Looking at the world through their eyes might even drive you a little nuts."

"No doubt." Billy was picking at his fingernails. Unlike most guys, he didn't bite them when he was nervous. He would just slowly tear at them. Sometimes, if he was really nervous or excited, he'd keep at it until they bled. He realized what he was doing and quit by tucking his hands into both sides of the chair's cushion. "It can really suck, and it takes a toll. As far as keeping at it, there's the proverbial rub. It takes discipline, which any artist must have, and I'm constantly struggling to sustain it. I don't think you can be a compassionate person until you at least make the effort. The world is so egocentric and solipsistic. Most people don't want to take time to consider what someone else might be thinking. As I said, they have enough trouble thinking about anything on their own. I at least give it a shot. The fact is you can learn a lot by seeing through an asshole's eyes. It keeps you humble, and teaches that reality is a slippery substance to keep in your grip."

"I don't know if you have any interest in physics, but there is that element of the uncertainty principle that states, 'Every time we look at an object, we change the nature of it.' " Max was smiling, but there was no sign of condescension. "Your idea is similar to that."

"Yes, Heisenberg did say that." Billy was excited, but kept his fingers in the velvety fabric. "I don't understand the entire quantum theory, but I always got that aspect of it. I never saw it as an analogy to my idea before, but you're right. My notion is an extremely simple version of that aspect of the quantum. It's sort of amazing that it all stems from a fireman obsessing on how buildings burn."

Again, there was a knock on the door. It was a guest stopping in to say a hasty good night; he apologized to Max for leaving so quickly, then darted his eyes toward Billy.

"I'm quite sorry for the interruption." He spoke with the last vestiges of a southern accent. "Will you be so kind as to let Max here see me out? We have a minor business detail to work out."

Max left the room again, laying a hand on Billy's shoulder as he passed him. The gesture indicated he'd be right back. Max was in and out of the room so often, it seemed, that he was initiating Billy to a rapport of silence.

Billy recognized the smartly dressed visitor. Two of his silkscreens hung directly behind Max's glass desk.

"He'll be back in a flash, I promise." The drawl was gone; the famous painter was now sounding more like Harvard. "By the way, I liked that painting of yours. I wouldn't say that if I didn't mean it. Good luck."

"Hey . . . thanks," Billy replied, but the door was already shut. He felt like an idiot who had blown a chance to converse with one of the few people he could actually refer to as an idol.

Max came back into the room, passing Billy with short steps, flailing his arms about. "Once again, I'm sorry. I knew he'd only be staying for a few minutes, but it was wonderful just to share a few moments together. Really terrific guy . . . I've known him since he first came to New York after college. He lives in Europe about nine months out of the year these days."

"He told me he'd seen my painting." Billy tried to sound nonchalant, but his mouth was cotton-ball dry. "Is that true?"

"Absolutely. I was showing it to him when you first arrived. Actually, he usually hates everything he sees by younger artists. He's a bit neurotic, and he usually doesn't pay attention to work by someone your age. He thinks he's getting old.

"Let's get back to the conversation. I'm fascinated by your idea of seeing through another's eyes, especially how it led you to compassion. It once again struck a personal chord. Like your painting, it reminds me of something from my own youth. I found that compassion too, though it was much later in my life, after I'd gone through some foolish and painful experiences. I was traveling throughout Europe. I'd grown up in the country and I was drawn to the large cities, living a disastrous, self-absorbed life . . . the same directionless life most of the artists and students I fell in with were leading."

Max then numbered the changes he went through when he was Billy's current age. It was mainly general stuff, but he did get into a few specifics, and when he did, a change came over his demeanor. Losing his smile for the first time, Max confessed that the greatest guilt of his youth was his cynicism. He was caught up in prewar Europe's Faustian hunger for cleverness, pursuing knowledge completely devoid of emotion. His eyes were used only to measure the amount remaining in glasses of red house wine, and his ears for listening to an endless flow of specious ideas, which contained neither love nor conviction.

"To be a cynic one must first be a naïve optimist," Max said. "When I first moved to Paris, I was a few years older than you are now. Believe me, I was as adrift as everyone around me, drinking too much and spending the money my parents would send me on whores for my friends and myself. You'd never know it to look at me, but I was quite the scrapper for a fellow my size. I took some bad beatings, and sometimes gave a few out. I know how strange that must seem to you. I was, in a word, a jerk. The so-called Lost Generation was aptly named, young Billy.

"I would go home to visit my parents' estate and recuperate. I'd feel my old self for a while, working around the fields and reading incessantly. Aside from whatever was served with meals, I never touched a drop of wine. Perhaps the sunlight in the country brought me to my senses.

"I would always return to the damn city, however. I had no discipline whatsoever. Did you ever see a worm that has been cut in half, Billy? It will eventually grow back the part that was lost. I believe the biologists call it 'homeostasis.' Well, Billy, I was like that little worm, always returning to the equilibrium of whorehouses and drinking binges in Paris.

"When I was at my lowest point and everything was crashing in on me, seeming hopeless, I stumbled into a conversation with a certain poet. He had been born in Russia, but his family, who I believe were fairly well-off landowners and certainly about to be arrested, escaped after the Revolution. They immigrated to France, and he was raised and schooled in the outskirts of Paris.

"We talked through the night, and he quickly became something of a mentor. He transformed my life, and it was through him that I learned the real importance of Karma and putting others' needs before my own. He also taught me much about literature, particularly his insights into the Russian writers. I thought I knew their works inside out, of course, but it was through his interpretation of their writing, which was based on certain Eastern Orthodox teachings, that I came to understand compassion.

"I don't know if we met by sheer luck or fate. By the way, I believe fate exists. He took me under his wing. I use that expression almost in a literal sense. You see, the fellow had a large, hooked nose that made him look like a bird. All his friends called him 'Peregrine.'

"Sorry, I'm digressing here. I think I might have had a bit too much wine tonight. I don't drink much lately, but someone brought some particularly rare vintages to dinner and I couldn't resist. I'm no wine snob, but I enjoy a good burgundy if it comes my way."

"To tell you the truth, I'm also over my limit." One of Billy's legs slipped as he uncrossed them. The truth was that Billy had never drunk fine wine before, and he'd felt a buzz after his first two sips at dinner.

Max lifted a cigar from a humidor to his left. He rolled it around in his hand, then smelled it through the wrapper. "I've tried to live my life with certain beliefs that are beyond the boundaries of religion. Compassion is a fundamental principle in all of them. That is why I was so struck with your story. It evokes a period in my life when I discovered the same truth. Perhaps I just bought into one more naïve ideal, but at least following this path allows me to look at myself in the mirror when I shave each morning. It's foolish not to see anybody else's point of view. This is true on many levels, even in business. It's certainly true in world affairs. Though I've become an American citizen, I am not generally a very political person. I think in global terms, and I've seen enough to know where the problem lies, and it all boils down to finding a way to deal with the dark side of human nature. There is no better time than the present to examine evil and hold it up to the light, as if with a magnifying glass, for everyone to see. We can't do that by insisting we don't understand it. Our apathy allows all sorts of dictators and brutal regimes to take power whenever we let our guard down. We owe it to the past, as well as the future, to be vigilant. There are hard times ahead, Billy. In the end, I believe that, through compassion, righteousness will triumph. Now you see why my interest in you extends far beyond your talent, no matter how considerable it may be."

Max stood and walked toward the wall with the Ernst collages. As he rose from his chair, there was a loud popping sound from the joints in his knees. "Damn these old legs," he muttered as he bent over to rub them. "Growing old is so damn frustrating. I'm so out of shape. I had a soccer injury in school and it never healed correctly. Then there was all the abuse I heaped on myself in Paris. I don't think I've broken a sweat in close to ten years. The last time I remember sweating was out of fear rather than any strenuous activity. A sculptor I worked with, who drank too much and took too many sleeping pills, dropped a cigarette in his studio and, before he knew better, the fire department was arriving. It was a mess. He lost everything that wasn't stone or bronze. There was clay everywhere. I was on my way to visit him when I saw what had happened, and I don't mind admitting I began to sweat like a pig. I was a mess, but, looking back, I now see that moment as a milestone in my life. I wouldn't want it to be under the same circumstances, but it was a wonderful sensation when my silk shirt was drenched right through to my jacket. If you have enough money you never need perspire after you're 60 years old. It's all the air-conditioning and fancy showers, not to mention my knack for evading any real exercise."

"Did your friend get hurt in the fire?" Billy asked, uncertain where Max was headed.

"With your uncle being a fireman, I should have known you'd ask that question. Well, he was fine. He had already left the studio and gone into the living area when the cigarette fell from a metal table and ignited on some sketches. He just forgot about the thing . . . it was one of those nonfilter brands. By the way, Billy, do you smoke?"

"Is that a question or some sort of test, Max?" Billy was amazed that he was speaking so freely to this art-scene legend.

"No, nothing like that," Max replied. "It's strictly a question. I used to smoke two packs a day when I was your age. Of course, that was in Europe, and light-years before all this surgeon general stuff. Also, I saw your friend Dennis lighting up a cigar after dinner."

"Oh, Denny will smoke anything." Billy smiled. "Actually, he'll do anything . . . at least once, and probably a few times more. He's a madman, but also my oldest friend. We're like brothers, and he really is a dynamite musician. He writes very strange songs. I'm not much of a rock music fan, but Denny's stuff always sticks with me. To answer your question, I never smoke. As I said, I hardly ever drink. That's why this wine is kicking my ass at the moment."

"Well, if you did smoke, it wouldn't really matter. Most artists I know are smokers, I guess. I suppose it comes with the territory. The only point I was trying to make was how quickly and out of nowhere everything can disappear, even if you're cautious. It would be tragic if even a single drawing of yours were lost. As an artist, you have to be very careful, and most of those I've known have been quite the opposite."

For a long moment, they were both lost in their own thoughts.

Then Max smiled. "To get back to the matter at hand, the reason I invited you here tonight is because I want to see your work hanging in this room. I'm certain you have the talent, and our talk tonight has only made me more determined. You see, I've been thinking all week about becoming your dealer, Billy Wolfram. I believe that the two of us could work very well together. If we do this right, there's a good chance we could do incredible things for each other.

"Before we go on, it's quite important you understand that I haven't acted as a dealer for nearly a decade now." Max jabbed his hand at the air as he spoke, signaling that what he was saying was serious and might take awhile. "Aside from managing my own collection, I function solely as a consultant to institutions and a certain few individuals. I also must say that some of my oldest and most trusted friends believe I am a bit insane to rush so precipitously into the offer I am about to propose.

"When I accidentally came upon that three-person show, I saw only a small sampling of your work. I'd like to see more, naturally, but I refuse to believe your large painting was an anomaly. It was, by the way, the first work by an unknown artist that I've purchased in over ten years."

Max rested his arm on the bookcase. "I like you as a person as well. It was obvious that my questions during dinner had a purpose. I was really quite impressed when you said that you understood your limitations. Normally, there is no such beast as unmanageable as an artist of your age. So it was refreshing to hear you speak with such maturity on the subject of limitations. No young man at your point of development knows anything about his own confines. They think they can hurl out a masterwork before breakfast.

"Of course, too much self-reflection and good sense can sometimes be counterproductive, especially at your age. I mean, there is something to be said for indulging youth's blind abandon. It is natural for young artists to feel that the world is theirs to conquer, and that they shall do so with pure energy alone. It doesn't matter how far their ambition exceeds their talent. In your precociousness, I hope you have not lost this attribute. Still, as I've said, the ability to understand one's limitations is a rare gift, and I don't think you're even aware of this. Don't lose it, but I hope you also use the recklessness of your youth. It is the time to go wild and fail. This is also a gift, though very fleeting."

Max set his glass on the table. In a moment he seemed entirely sober.

"Since I closed my gallery a decade ago, I have been out of touch with the so-called hands-on workings of the art world. I realize now that I jumped the gun, as they say, on my retirement. It was a foolish decision that I now regret, but I think it can result in good fortune for both of us. If you do decide to work with me, I can assure you of one thing. When I take on a painter, I go all out. I make certain that he, or she, wants for nothing. I need you to concentrate solely on your artistic endeavors, and it makes no difference whether it is painting or sculpture. I leave the questions of medium and process completely up to you. In return, I can offer you my support and an educated opinion.

"For my part, I will give you a large studio in a building that I am fortunate enough to own. You can live and work there. I can also provide you with enough money to cover the cost of getting by in this city. I am well aware how expensive it can be for a young artist."

It was a staggering proposition that Billy never saw coming. He assumed that the old man was going to toss him some weary words of advice about the dog-eat-dog nature of the art world. He never imagined that some guy with a Magritte in his foyer would be making such an outlandishly generous offer. Most young artists Billy knew would trade over their wives or lovers for such a deal.

Nonetheless, Billy felt a wave of uncertainty. He sat there with his fallback expression for indecision, which was a bemused grin, impossible to read. Billy tried not to think about it, but he still couldn't place his confidence in men who were older or in positions of power over him. This lack of trust was surely a result of his father abandoning him, but it also stemmed from the aborted attempt to prostitute himself with that slimy bastard who lived in the midtown duplex. Billy couldn't even remember the guy's name, only the dandruff on his collar and the silhouette imprint of him on the pup tent as Billy ran out the door. Those images still haunted him. Sooner or later, sex intruded on every aspect of Billy's life. Still, Max was nothing like that creep. His reputation spoke for itself, and Billy never even considered that Max had any such intentions. Besides, Billy was too consumed with astonishment at the moment, sitting there as one of the most famous painters alive casually entered and consulted with a pensive Max. It was Billy's nature to be wary, and you could never be positive about these things. In the end, he relied on his conversation with Max, and tried seeing the world through Max's eyes, putting himself in Max's dapper Gucci loafers. Finally, Billy realized he had to raise himself above all the bullshit and get on with his life. This was serious business, and it could change his entire future.

7

illy laid down his book on hearing the evening thunder, walked to the window, and watched the clouds above—sudden, dark, and jagged. Twilight turned black in an instant, as if the storm had bullied it away. The clouds were so low and loose that the antenna from the Empire State Building penetrated one like a syringe. He retreated to the chair, sinking low and pulling the throw blanket over his body, assuring himself that a quarter inch of crochet would soften the blasts of thunder. He thought about his upcoming show and wondered how it had come to be that he was missing his rapidly approaching deadline. Throughout his entire career Billy had never failed to bring in a show on time, and he knew he should be searching frantically for a way to trick the thing into happening. His work, however, seemed a thousand miles in another direction and, for the first time, he starting doubting that he could pull it off.

Raindrops began to skim loudly off his windows. They seemed thicker and more weighty than usual this evening. It was an intimidating yet lucid rain.

The windowpanes, loosened by wind, rain, and time, made squealing porcine sounds, as if they could be dislodged from their frames at any moment. Billy sat very still and thought of the raven, staring trancelike at the sweeping sheets of water. In his mind he was taking in the shape of this massive rain, which was falling vertically one moment, shifting to diagonal, and then almost horizontal as the wind gusted. At one point the currents of air gathered such force, they actually appeared to reverse the rain, lifting it upward a moment before it surrendered to its descent.

Later, when the storm subsided, the smell of the streets—scraped clean by the pressurized downpour—rose to his rooms, and Billy thought back to the time when the cord was still within him, attached to his mother's piety. Back then, Billy imagined that drops of rain were unanswered prayers falling back to earth.

Billy stepped to the window, crumbs of rotted wood and sealant at his feet. He inhaled deeply and realized what the post-storm smell was really made of. Aside from the musky city filth, it was the smell of exhaustion. He had thought all this time spent sequestered in the room would be a needed respite, but he just felt wiped out.

During a long phone call earlier that morning, Denny asked Billy if he had ever considered the possibility of never painting again. Could he simply start over from scratch? Billy thought he could. He had insisted to Denny and Marta—who had hesitantly joined the conversation from the phone beside the sofa—that he could easily leave art behind. For all his hypothetical conviction, however, Billy thoroughly avoided any specifics about what he might possibly do instead.

Denny was not so confident when he turned the same question on himself. His childhood, with its loveless poverty and varied abuses, was a catalyst for many young vows, mostly involving some way to acquire what he'd always been denied. Though his unworldly side was undeniable to anyone familiar with his songs, Denny kept a constant inventory of what he had gained in his life, and he gripped it tenaciously. He understood the fear of loss better than Billy. The thought that he could lose it all—common to most kids who grew up like Denny—was usually within shouting distance.

This seemed ironic, since Billy was now once again anxious over his unfinished paintings for the impending show. From a strictly financial point of view, Billy was pretty much set for life. Still, he agonized over the need to get the work done, and in his case it had nothing to do with money or childhood vows. It was embedded in him. The fear haunted him that, if he didn't get it together quickly, he might *truly* conclude he'd lost his ability and would never make art again. He knew this was wrong thinking. Creating art was rooted in him like the muscle memory of an aborigine on a walkabout. In the barren wilderness of the Outback, that native *knows* where the water is hidden underground, simply by a sort of tribal anamnesis. Billy always assumed he was thoughtlessly drawn to his work like that man to water, but there was a flaw in the analogy. As his career flourished, he had always assumed his doubts would be resolved, but they only increased. He would settle for a sense of solidity in his work and in his life. His reclusion had only led to more frustration, and, in turn, exhaustion, the smell of which continued wafting through his room.

He inhaled deeply and lowered himself back into the chair. Again, his thoughts turned to the past. In the room, he realized, direction was dictated more by past, present, and future than the cardinal points of north, south, east, and west. Denny's postulations regarding the future were vague and irritating to Billy. The past was the only direction left to him.

Despite—or because of—his young age and seemingly meteoric rise to the heights of the art scene, Billy was always perceived as an outsider, an independent operator who had no interest in taking part in the social functions of the art world unless absolutely necessary. It wasn't a negative appellation, and most fellow artists found Billy quite affable beneath his initial guardedness. There was a small group of cynics who speculated that his shyness and inability to interact socially were cleverly feigned deceptions for controlling others while gaining their sympathy. Most recognized that there was no way Billy could fake his palpable discomfort at a formal affair, especially if it involved the media.

When he moved downtown after his mother's death, he knew it was time to cautiously cash both the modest and exorbitant checks that his vision had already signed. From his earliest memories, he knew that his brain was rigged for artistic and spiritual hunger. He understood the need for intellectual understanding, but he put his deeper trust in the innate. In large and small ways, both his own experience and Max's influence had taught him to trust his heart's intuition. He put his faith in a succinct phrase he had read in a book by Henry Miller, which resonated precisely with his personal aesthetic experience. It defined this knowledge of the heart so tersely and evocatively that it became a key part of Billy's aesthetic vocabulary. Miller called it the "inner register."

Denny had told him a similar thing existed in rock and roll. How, up onstage with his band, he could "feel" the will of the audience, and, though they always began their shows with a "set list" of the order of songs they planned to play, he would invariably alter the list according to the dictates of this sensation. "Sometimes," Denny said, "the list would call for a ballad as the next song, but I could just feel from the audience that they wanted things to speed up. I'd drive the band crazy running from one to the other telling them which song we were going to do instead. It was a very raw and base form of empathy, but it came through the heart. I would literally feel it at times, moving from the crowd and passing through me like a jolt of electricity, a sense that the world had suddenly speeded up even as it slow-motioned, an anticipation and focus that finally rested like a fist squeezing beneath the heart." Billy knew athletes who spoke of this same sense of "touch" and "certainty" either on a pitch or jump shot, or sprinting against others in a dash.

In the few interviews he had done, Billy would speak of this "inner register" in his initial years as an artist. He'd refer to the time spent in his high school library, poring over art books. In a large volume on the Cubists, Billy could see why the works, though technically momentous, failed in their overwrought ambitions. The artists in the movement thought they could one-up the physicists and penetrate the hidden depths of reality, but they had failed in their goal, and finally admitted as much. The best of these paintings were striking in technique and perhaps even essential to the evolution of art into the twentieth century, but they did not pierce any veils. In the end, they only revealed a mirror, which, when obliterated, led to another mirror—on and on until they'd finally encountered a vertiginous void.

On the other hand, Billy recognized, the Fauvists and the Blue Riders were simply having a blast with color. The inner register was at work with them and Billy used almost all his time free from class examining the glossy reproductions of their work. He always proudly made the point that he'd arrived at these teenage critical conclusions purely by scanning those replicas, well before he read the scholarly texts on these movements. When he did finally devour the written histories and essays, he found his nascent theories validated—in suitably pedantic terms. The whole process taught him to trust fully in his artistic intuition, not only regarding dead painters and historic matters, but also as it pertained to his own developing ideas and ambitions. Even in those early years, Billy was completely oblivious to the way other people perceived him.

Though most of his acquaintances thought he was putting them on, Billy insisted that Marco's sacrilegious fingernail portraits were his first great influence in becoming an artist. Though he admitted to admiring their sheer audacity, it was the detailed draftsmanship of these miniatures that truly turned the worm for him. The tiny expressions of horror, awe, and—on Marco's left pinky—pleasure in the faces of these various nuns overwhelmed Billy. That was when Billy began his own drawings. At first, he also worked in miniature, then swiftly progressed to larger scale. He knew right off that he was good; it felt so smooth—the pencil over the page. It was like music. Billy wasn't capable of bullshitting himself. If he felt he had talent, then he did. The rest he put aside. Even then he had a sense that there was no time to waste fooling yourself.

This realization, along with Marco's intricate fingernails, led him to cross Broadway each weekend morning and pass through the wrought-iron gates of the Cloisters for its 10:00 a.m. opening. The Cloisters—in clear view crosstown from Billy's living room window, yet always seeming inaccessibly distant—is an adjunct of the Metropolitan Museum of Art. It is a simulacrum of a medieval monastery, imported stone by stone from Europe, surrounded by beautiful gardens and overlooking the Hudson River. Inside, beneath the orange-tiled roof, it contained most of the museum's medieval art, including the famous Unicorn Tapestries and anonymous statuary from the twelfth to fourteenth centuries. Billy would descend directly to its damp stone bowels. Beside a large chamber with acicular windows, where two effigies of knights lay in relief on marble slabs, was a small triangular room containing minute objects encased in glass. The cases held ornately engraved reliquaries that once housed the relics of saints, crudely hinged wooden globes, arduously decorated and used for storing rosary beads, and rows of what appeared to be pillboxes. All these objects were, to varying extents, done in miniature. They were mainly carved or etched, and sometimes painted with gospel scenes, particularly the Crucifixion and Last Supper. They were stunning, and he couldn't imagine how such detail could have been executed with the tools available in the twelfth century.

Comparing these works to Marco's fingernails, Billy learned the meaning of the sublime in art. For all its admirable technique, Marco's work did not elicit that same feeling of wind moving through young Billy's veins. Later, he would grasp that his sleazy mentor's portraits simply lacked nuance. Marco's crude blending of color caused the nuns to appear stiff; there was no flow or rhythm in their habits. More importantly, they didn't fill Billy with the sense of wild, untamed sorrow and possibility that he felt when he noticed how the veil dripped from the dizzying features of the Magdalene on a Flemish rosary box, which was round and no bigger than a woman's compact. Billy had encountered the distinction between a talented thug and devoted masters. By his fifth or sixth trip to the Cloisters, he knew his purpose in life.

Billy had graduated at the top of his class from one of the city's best high schools. While there, he chose all his elective classes with art in mind. He had also taken a few unlikely courses because of what he sophomorically called "an intrinsic imperative." He simply had a sense that, at some point, he would need to know these things. He enrolled in advanced calculus and trigonometry; despite at first finding them difficult and superfluous, he somehow knew they would become necessary over time.

Billy spent one intense year studying at Cooper Union. There he'd chosen a number of classes in the technicalities of painting, from the basics of mixing different colors to the complexities of perspective. He also took an obligatory course in art history. Mainly, however, Billy focused on sculpture, where he had learned the basic skills needed to work with any medium available to him, from clay and wax to bronze and steel. That and another year apprenticing with one of his teachers from Cooper Union had been the bulk of his formal training.

In school, he had been a loner, with no use for making the scene. He steered clear of the wannabe movers and shakers who schlepped their work from one dealer to the next by day, while networking and partying at gallery openings or clubs through the night. The other students hadn't known what to make of this attractive man-child with the tousled hair, too young to be so focused, and always taking off in the other direction. There was something else about him that nobody could put their finger on, at least for the first four or five months. Finally, a few of the more perceptive students figured it out. He gave off no sexual vibe whatsoever. It had nothing to do with being straight or gay, nor was it a Warhol-like asexuality. The vibration—essential and inviolate to anyone of any sexual orientation at that lubricious age—was simply absent. There were a few who took umbrage at this assessment. Two insightful and stunningly beautiful female students insisted they felt some sexual pulsation radiating hesitantly from his green eyes, but it was disorganized and very, very sad. Billy was oblivious to all of this, and the speculation only added to a popularity which he never laid claim to.

Acknowledging Billy's advanced abilities, his instructor allowed him free time in a basement space, utilizing sophisticated machinery normally off-limits to students. In painting classes, he was overjoyed simply by the access he had to such fine materials. He had never before put acrylic on real canvas and was amazed at the possibilities in its texture and in its sense of depth. He dedicated every moment of those years to editing out the dispensable and soaking up any knowledge that would accommodate and facilitate his vision. Billy was forming the basic code and artistic vocabulary of his work.

His only real friend was Denny, and though they shared an East Village walk-up while he was at college, Denny was out most of the time. He had finally assembled the right musicians for his band and was beginning his ascent in the downtown music scene. Though they'd been inseparable since the age of seven and could finish each other's sentences, Denny's social life was far different from Billy's. He was smoothly gregarious and rabidly indulged his own passions.

The apartment they shared was basically a space to sleep, furnished in a frugally spartan fashion. There was a record player, and at a peculiarly subdued volume, Billy would listen to Mozart, Roy Orbison, and Paul Butterfield. And he read the poetry, biography, and myth suggested by teachers and friends, as well as arcane texts discovered in used bookstores.

He'd sit beside the window devouring pages by low light in a half-upholstered armchair. A single earnest African violet was propped on the windowsill, right where it was left when they moved into the apartment. The lone flower hit Billy like a ghostly sucker punch. Every Mother's Day he had bought his mom a bouquet of decorative cut flowers and a tiny African violet. The bouquet would wilt and die within a week, but the violets, in their little clay pots, inevitably survived for years. There were three still flourishing beside her homemade drapes when she died. Now he sat at the other end of Manhattan, beside another window, another view, and another African violet. It was dead for the winter, just one bare stalk standing up straight before the frosted pane, as if it were giving the finger to the bracing cold beyond the glass. *Give me your hardest winds and deepest freeze,* the plant was saying. *Come spring, you'll be gone and I'll be blooming purple buds.*

Unlike most outsiders, Billy rarely had to deal with the hardships that accompanied talent and resolve. He also avoided the self-abuse and misjudgments that can either cause such hardships or become their by-products. He knew if he expected the least, he'd usually get just enough. He could always find something to eat, and someone's place where he could safely sleep, sheltered from night's elements. He never had to worry about the ravages of drugs or drinking, since he'd already resolved they would only throw him off an already precarious sense of balance. There was also fear of such substances' side effects. Billy dreaded losing control and—even for an instant—severing connections with the human spirit and intuitive consciousness that piloted him. The seeming ease of his creative process sometimes concerned Billy. He never fully trusted his gifts and occasionally began to doubt his own talent. Faced with this fragility that he himself created, Billy was not about to allow drugs to further confuse him. It was also the mathematician in him. After observing many of his neighborhood acquaintances on drugs, and the directions they wound up taking, he just didn't see the odds in it.

During those years with Denny in the cheap run-down apartment, Billy survived with dizzying frugality on a few thousand dollars that were left to him on his mother's death. He lived so much in his mind that some toast and fruit juice would easily sustain his body for days. Focus was another quality that Billy possessed beyond his years. Once his mind had become fixed on a task, he was tenacious in not letting go. That's where his hunger went. Not to his stomach, but to his doubts. He was consumed by his endless array of doubts and suspicions, and each became a task. It was a blessing and a curse to be haunted by such rapacious concentration and so little self-confidence at this young an age. His schoolmates appeared to have everything about their lives—past and future—figured out. It turned Billy into a loner and an enigma, but kept him thin as well.

Later, after he and Denny had made money and garnered fame, they looked back at those days and the methods they developed for stretching a dollar with amazement and a certain giddy pride. Then, though they spurned the ostentation of fresh wealth, the pair could blow more money picking up the tab for dinner and wine at a fine restaurant than they had spent on rent and food for an entire month in that tiny East Village walk-up. It astonished them, as comparisons before and after suddenly fulfilled dreams often do, but it never seemed unreasonable to them. They were young, on their own, tracking their desires, and, most of all, they didn't know any better.

Remarkably, though at the textbook years of peak male virility, Billy seemed less bothered by his sexual demons than at any other time before or since. All his immense energies, naturally and unforced, led in other directions. It was a matter of postponing the inevitable, and he was aware he couldn't avoid these unbidden demands much longer. He would feel his indifference crumbling and the painful yet undeniably wondrous desires rising from their roots. Also, much of this libidinal shutdown had to do with his penchant for walking. He could walk 80 blocks uptown to the various museums, so engrossed by people, traffic, and the cornices of old buildings that he barely noticed the passing of time. Then he'd return, again on foot, to the East Village, measuring the physical energy he'd expended only by examining the amount of rubber lost on the soles of his Converse.

Certainly there were some trying times for Billy. The East Village was not the place for an attractive young man striving to keep his asexuality in the closet. He began going out to clubs with Denny, who had become such a fixture on the music scene that he had no problem bringing back ridiculous numbers of fine-looking, club-crawling ladies to their 1st Street apartment. Never daring to condescend to Billy about "The Memory," Denny engaged his friend in typical male bravado about women, and even cautiously tried to fix Billy up. For his part, Billy would join in on the palaver involving Denny's escapades but couldn't be talked into joining one of these women and her girlfriend for a night out. Billy knew that the women on this scene were often as aggressive as the guys. There was one time that he indulged himself in a long French kiss with a thin, riveting girl who led him backstage to a side room. He was beginning to feel some arousal when the fast-moving young lady began caressing his crotch. That set off a torrent of thoughts, emotions, and apprehensions, all leading inexorably back to *that day*. Billy broke away from her so quickly he knocked over her margarita, which was resting on top of an ice maker. He knew his fate with this person was sealed, so he saved face for both of them by telling her that he found her ecstatically beautiful, but was engaged to another woman. Their wedding would take place in June at an outdoor service in her hometown of Darien, Connecticut. After that experience, Billy sidestepped any of Denny's matchmaking attempts.

It was during this period Billy realized the unique power his stubborn elusiveness had on the opposite sex. The trendy downtown girls considered Denny and him mysterious and physically enticing new blood when they'd first arrived on the scene. They were always together, but their romantic styles couldn't have been further apart. Denny was easy and he made no apologies for it. Billy seemed that much more desirable because of his mysterious sexual aloofness. The two found themselves in the company of the most attractive young women in the big city—models, actresses, and socialites. For all the loving Denny was getting, Billy found himself feeding off the thrill of his power to turn away, especially from those who'd never had it happen to them before. Rejection just increased their pursuit, in progressions that the young artist could almost measure mathematically. Billy was discovering a new power within his sexual annulment. It gave him a sense of some purpose behind all the turmoil and pain the terminus of his libido had caused, and which he constantly needed to elude. Though he still fed vicariously from Denny's tales of actual conquest, Billy could now listen to his roommate's narrations believing he possessed his own manner of conquest, more subtle, more modern, and perhaps more powerful. Of course, Billy knew he was creating a new charade—another ball to juggle above his head—but he figured he was up to the task. Jugglers need to be steady and disciplined, and those were traits Billy was secure in.

Naturally, the allure Denny and Billy held for women—each in his respective way—increased enormously when they became famous. Denny only called Billy on his self-deception once, when he inquired, in a pained and almost jealous frustration, "Don't you ever long to touch the soft skin of a real woman? Don't you feel that yearning?" Fortified by years of denial and compensation, Billy didn't answer, but smirked and retreated into the bathroom, knowing he quickly needed to begin his juggling act before this unexpectedly incisive question caused him to drop and smash his head against the tile floor. During that particular period, Billy's carnal desires had been effectively held in abeyance by the uncharted knowledge that school forced him to confront. Nothing consumed Billy Wolfram like the hunger to understand. It was simply an aspect of his doubt. The facilities available to him in the workshops of those erudite halls were like Solomon's ring.

It was at this time that Billy realized those classes in advanced trigonometry and calculus that he had struggled through with both bewilderment and devotion in high school were an innate, prescient calling of destiny. This mathematical knowledge allowed him to compute scale, stress points, and the vertical pitch of various metals, while most of his fellow students stared at the slide rule like it was minimal sculpture. Billy felt his success validated his reliance on the inner register, and following its dictates, he was able to recognize his most random choices seeming to come together. Chaos, if you followed your instincts and walked on a thin enough edge, could reveal the most unexpected and contradictory insights over time.

He needed this knowledge to comprehend the nature and uses of materials that would benefit the aesthetic goal of creating previously unseen forms that would defy the physical boundaries of the material itself. It didn't seem so arrogant an ambition for a 19-year-old kid undisturbed by the obsessions of sex and the paraphernalia surrounding it.

Billy's only diversion those days was, perhaps twice a month, riding the subway lines. Billy had had a love for the subway system since he was a child. The subways were emblematic for kids born and raised in Manhattan, a rite of passage. He and Denny would race from one car to the next. They'd observe the weak passengers shying away from the strong, and watch as the husks hardened around the few who had already given up hope because of all their fears and losses, and the jobs they despised.

He liked working on sketches while he was in motion, wanting to test the effect this movement would have on the work. He realized, soon enough, it was a harebrained idea, but this was the time to try such things. Unlike most of his peers, Billy recognized that to be a true artist, judgment was as important as talent, at least in the long run, but he vowed not to let it suppress his ambitions. This was the time in an artist's life to defy judgment. It was difficult to balance the two, since talent came naturally and judgment from discipline and experience. Idiotic concepts had their place, if only to be recognized and dismissed as quickly as possible. Sometimes, Billy found, these failures could be neutralized from within and modified into something useful. Billy discovered early that continual assessment was any painter's lifelong companion. Art in all its forms was an obstinate, querulous, and baffling mistress. Some potentially great masters were burnt out early by faulty judgment, and as many were crippled by its excess. Still, judgment emerged necessarily through his thoughts and instincts. For example, if Billy's purpose for sketching on a speeding subway car failed, it was simply another flawed exercise that didn't matter to him whatsoever. He was trying anything possible to turn the baffling mistress on her head.

Most days he made the subway excursions, Billy was able to put aside his drawing materials and allow himself to simply unwind. Usually he took the A train, starting at West 4th Street, then downtown beneath rivers and boroughs out to the last stop at Rockaway Beach, the train eventually rising aboveground, passing over the buses and immigrant mothers pushing baby strollers in the streets below. As the air filled with the scent of salt and tide, Billy turned and watched from the side doors. The Atlantic Ocean crashing lonely onto empty winter beaches. Wind pushing up whitecaps past the horizon. Dim gulls gliding above the cold, gray currents.

8

Billy heard the freight elevator door rattling as it slid open at 9:00 a.m. Marta usually took the stairs when she went out. The steep wooden steps in the old building were good exercise, and if she were just shopping and running errands, he would have instead heard the stairway door's firm thump, followed by the tumbling of double bolt locks. She must have been taking some of the iron rods to Elsa, the woman sculptor who occupied the third floor. Yesterday, as she brought him dinner, she asked Billy if he planned on using them, and if not, could she give them to Elsa. She needed the materials posthaste for an upcoming show. Billy told Marta to help herself to all the rods Elsa needed.

Elsa had become Marta's closest friend. She was a very attractive 28-year-old blonde with a thick Romanian accent, and, according to art world gossip, quite sexual with both women and men. Billy liked Elsa. She respected his penchant for working in solitude and knew never to intrude on him once he'd shut the imposing doors to the studio. He also enjoyed the safe, innocuous way that she flirted with him.

When Elsa had arrived in New York at 21, she was a shy waiflike thing from the countryside outside Bucharest. New York had intoxicated her with that energy that affects young, migrating artists more powerfully than artists who were born and raised here in the city. It doesn't matter whether they arrive from Eastern Europe or Madison, Wisconsin. She and Billy had a long talk about this phenomenon one night when she came upstairs—as she often did—to share dinner with Marta and him.

She expressed her jealousy of Billy being born and raised in New York, having all its speed and excitement available to him through his formative years. Billy, in turn, declared how he envied the glow in her eyes that still appeared at the mention of the city. He admitted that having grown up there caused him to put up certain jaded barricades, take the city's velocity and resources for granted, and distance himself from the scene she found so invigorating. "I'm talking too personally now, and confusing the subject with my own foibles and aberrations," he acknowledged, "but, still, I believe that painters—or, for that matter, musicians, writers, or dancers— who come here at the right time from somewhere else are the artists truly infused with New York's inspiration. They, such as Marta and yourself, are the only ones allowed to drink from the fountain." Marta and Elsa looked at Billy in a way that made clear they knew he was leaving something very significant out of his assertion. Billy could only think back to the way he felt when he was six years old and his parents' divorce suddenly opened the possibility that he might have to leave this city with his father, and his relief when his brother left instead. He recalled how blessed he felt to remain in New York, and the recognition that his fate and this city's were intertwined. What happened? he wondered.

"Keeping all that in mind, however, don't mistake the importance of the relationship between myself and this city," Billy said after a long pause, wanting to lighten up the mood. "Always remember that I too have been to Arcadia."

Elsa had struggled for years showing at group shows in badly lit East Village galleries that would close down after a few months, quickly reopen for a time as stores for handmade jewelry or vintage clothing, and eventually return as galleries, usually with different names and the same owners.

Eventually she holed up in a friend's apartment and produced a series of elongated black-and-white self-portraits, which became her signature works. The body positions on the canvases made the series look like the letters from a strange alphabet. Critics and the Soho royalty suddenly embraced her. Her reputation blossomed.

Those years sleeping on floors in the East Village, with all the partying and clubbing that went with them, had matured Elsa radically from the shy country girl who had arrived in New York from deep behind the Iron Curtain. It had not, however, prepared her for what came next. The first gallery owner to exhibit Elsa's work solo happened to be the infamous Cindy LaBararge. Cindy was a savvy businesswoman, as well as being stunningly attractive, the proud-to-a-fault owner of a capacious rack of bosoms. Her looks belied her age and eye for talent—talent for finding and grooming not only gifted, money-generating artists, but stars of the scene, those ones who never brush against a velvet rope or endure a quizzical stare.

Ms. LaBararge was also notorious as a bisexual predator, and she explained to Elsa that to succeed artistically she must masturbate at least five to seven times a day. The comely dealer claimed her daily regimen of multiple orgasms bolstered the stamina and aesthetic insights of all her artists. In her back office, on a wine-colored velvet divan, Ms. LaBararge personally instructed the wide-eyed girl in novel techniques of self-satisfaction, things never imagined by one raised in a closed, iron-fisted dictatorship.

The dealer had no problem admitting that her notion of success through excessive self-gratification had been plagiarized from Dr. Wilhelm Reich's decades-old speculations. However, though she did believe in the man's controversial theories, she mainly enjoyed simply sitting alone in her office, imagining her stable of attractive young artists from the East Village to Hoboken manipulating their collective genitalia at her bidding. She also mysteriously insisted on Elsa bleaching her chestnut-colored hair a criminal shade of blond.

Elsa, moreover, was a fast and eager apprentice. The dealer and the young artist had quite an open and torrid affair, often involving men, for close to a year. At that point, for reasons no one really knew, the two's affair fell apart, but the dealer—with her usual canny aplomb—continued to represent Elsa's business affairs.

With knowledge of the libidinous Romanian's sexual range, together with the sheer volume of time Marta spent visiting the third floor, Billy fantasized the two best friends could possibly have something salacious going on.

Expecting Marta to be out for some time with Elsa, Billy scanned his bookshelves and searched his desk for a notebook. While opening drawers, he unexpectedly discovered a velvety black manila envelope encircled by a lace ribbon. It lay beneath a batch of notepads on the bottom of the drawer, looking stunning and possessing a strong tactile attraction. He ran his finger across a wine-red wax seal, which was carefully stamped across the opening flap, securing it. He lifted it closer, and noticed the seal depicted a sun and half-moon, separated by three diagonal lines. The image seemed familiar, and he recalled seeing this same motif on a large plaque in Max's study. He realized the soft envelope contained his personally relevant version of Max's will.

Billy's trembling fingers now let it drop to the floor like a cursed ancient artifact. He quickly grabbed two pieces of cardboard and used them to scoop up the untouchable black swath and slide it back into the desk. As if the entire piece of oak furniture were now contaminated, Billy raised his left foot and viciously slammed the bottom drawer shut. Trembling, he ran to the huge kitchen sink and continuously tossed handfuls of cold water across his face. That quick glimpse of the envelope gnawed away at Billy for the entire day, and not only summoned the usual sad thoughts of losing Max, but, for some reason, also served to remind him of his own mortality, and how badly he was failing his deathbed promises to Max. Sometimes he wondered if his late dealer's final display of generosity was worth it.

When Marta returned, a dejected Billy listened as she prepared a fresh pot of mate. The number of meticulous steps she took to prepare the Argentine breakfast drink never failed to astound Billy; the entire procedure reminded him of a ritual, like the elaborate Japanese tea ceremony. However, it was more likely that, over the many years, Marta simply became so adept at making the beverage that she developed the process itself into her own personal ritual. Thoughtlessly, we all try to ritualize life's commonplace tasks, hoping to develop our focus and cause time to dissolve.

As Marta began pouring into the crude clay cups, the phone rang. Holding the receiver to her ear, she appeared at the door to Billy's room, giving their usual signal that Tippy was once again on the line. He answered her by shaking his head with more emphasis than usual, and she began handing the anxious voice another excuse. It was his second call that day. His first attempt had rung out a little before 8:00 a.m., jarring a barely awakened Marta as she stood before the bathroom sink, splashing cold water across her face. Marta didn't consider answering, and turned the ring tone down to the lowest setting. Billy was having a rare night of deep sleep, and she had no intention of disturbing him for another of Tippy's manic calls.

Billy shook his head, completely distraught. He was engulfed by a growing suspicion that his current dealer was simply unable to help his new star resolve his unprecedented problems painting, and, indeed, only worsened the situation. Thanking Marta with a half-formed gesture of his hand, he hastily sought solitude inside his room, sprawling on the bed.

Tippy was a hustler who, indeed, had made large sums of money for his so-called stable. But Billy's main problem was clear-cut: the man wasn't Max and possessed none of the qualities which Max utilized not only by far surpassing Billy's financial expectations, but also by guiding him in becoming a better painter. Max had infused Billy with self-confidence, provided exercises, and convinced him that he was able to keep widening the range of his art. With Max pushing him and restoring his faith, Billy succeeded. On the other hand, Tippy didn't possess either the passion or the acumen relating to the technical aspects of painting.

Despite the enormous discrepancies between the two men, it was Max who first recommended that Tippy should succeed him as Billy's dealer. After his initial astonishment, Billy knew that one reason for this unlikely decision was the aged maestro's mistaken conviction that his protégé possessed the maturity and insight to deal with the vapid trappings and excesses of the art world.

The truth was that, whenever possible, Billy avoided any contact with that incestuous world. Nonetheless, the iconic Max remained blind to his young artist's shortcoming.

Billy was baffled at how easily Max repeatedly ignored his embarrassing lack of social skills. When interacting with strangers, Billy followed his first instinct and simply shut down. For some inexplicable reason, this was never the case with Max. From their initial meetings, he could relate to this unique character with an effortlessness he'd only experienced with Denny.

For his part, Max's misapprehension stemmed from the fact that Billy's entire demeanor was completely different around him. Unlike the other residents of that demimonde, Max had never seen him act in his usual manner . . . shy, awkward, and inept.

Whatever the case, the two were so intertwined in each other's destinies that Max either genuinely didn't notice, or deliberately chose to overlook that, in group situations, this phenomenal talent was like a frightened deer whose first instinct, always, was to flee.

Nonetheless, they each clearly had what the other needed. Aside from all the irrelevant speculation on the nature of their improbable relationship, it was a seduction neither could refuse.

Max had always suspected he'd retired too soon and he'd always kept one eye open for a talented young artist. More than pure talent, however, this person needed a trusting and tolerant disposition. Max had nearly given up, until he took a turn into the wrong gallery and found Billy Wolfram.

Meanwhile, this unprecedented confidence that Billy acquired from Max gave his life a sensation of fluency and cohesion that he'd previously experienced only while painting. He had greater trust in his abilities to deal with others and, for a time, he began attending functions he'd consistently avoided.

They both fed off this mutual catharsis. Billy worked tirelessly on new paintings, while Max examined his earlier sketchbooks and encouraged him to start constructing large sculptures. He paid for the materials and introduced him to the best foundry workers on the East Coast. Meanwhile, he began to carefully plan out the phenomenal talent's career.

After 15 years of both men benefiting from this reciprocal relationship, Max, whose efforts helped establish the young painter's career, implored him to sign with the art scene's most rapacious dealer. If it hadn't been for the distressing circumstances of seeing Max connected to drip tubes and monitors, along with his seeming dementia, Billy couldn't imagine a more improbable transition.

Sitting that night drinking ginger tea, Billy still did not speak to the perplexed Tippy when he called a third time, but sat there like a coward, making even more emphatic gestures to Marta as she lied on his behalf. He stared downward to the floor, knowing how pathetic his behavior must have seemed, and, perhaps as payback for his lack of courage, the troubled artist was again obliged to continue retracing the bizarre sequence of events that led to Tippy's ascendance.

Though painful, this task wasn't difficult. Each detail of the ill-fated transition was burnt into Billy's brain. It had occurred on the night Max lay dying in a hospital bed.

Max's oldest son had made the call to Billy on an April morning nearly two years earlier, confiding that his father had been bedridden for the past four days, barely eating and refusing to see any of his doctors. Billy listened in stunned silence, then, as if he'd been kicked in the groin, slumped into a wicker chair and doubled over in pain.

"Can I come over?" he asked, having caught his breath.

"Well, he took a turn for the worse last night, and was rushed by ambulance to the hospital," the son continued.

"I see." Billy bit down hard onto his index finger, hoping his body would absorb some of the pain. "Please, may I see him? I believe I can help. I implore you." He signaled Marta to get him some scratch paper, hoping to write down a name and address. He couldn't contemplate the possibility they'd deny his request.

"You certainly may. That's the reason I'm calling you. When I first saw my father, he insisted I phone you. He's at New York Hospital. It's a suite on the sixth floor. Do you know what street it's on? I'll be waiting . . . please hurry."

Within the hour, Billy was rushing across the lobby's mosaic floor and entering Max's private room. Marta had accompanied him, but she stood waiting at the door.

Max turned slowly, partly smiling, partly wincing . . . his small body filled with tubes and drugs, lying with his legs raised on the mechanized bed. His skin color was the cloudy gray of dishwater.

Billy removed his sunglasses and pulled up a chair beside the bed. Barely able to speak, his head sunk into the blanket covering Max's ribs, he began to cry. "Hang in there," he finally said, his voice quavering as his fingers cautiously squeezed Max's hand. "You're going to get out of here. Think of this place like a hotel, and you're just having a little rest. They're the best, Max. God, I love you. I've never said it before. I love you, Max."

"It's all right. I love you as well." Though his voice was weak, Max spoke in lucid, if halting phrases. "Billy, your talent . . . and potential . . . revived me. You gave purpose to my life's end . . . a meaning. If we never met when we did, Billy, I would have burnt out from the exasperation. Who knows how low the misery would be?"

"You possess too much elegance for that to ever have happened, Max," Billy said, immediately realizing how exhausting it was for the frail man to speak, and that he shouldn't interrupt him—even for a compliment.

Max's body lightly shook. It was the closest he could come to a laugh. The humor gave him enough strength to speak in full sentences. "You really are so ultimately Catholic. If I understand Pascal well enough, I would have to say that you have given me some of the grace that you possess. Billy, we must talk business immediately. I have taken it on myself to find someone to continue as your dealer. I know you'll disagree at first, but hear me out. I was thinking of Mr. Tippy Shernoval."

Billy couldn't believe what he was hearing. He wondered if his old friend's illness included sudden forays into delirium. As sick as he was, Max sensed his disappointment.

Naturally, Billy was puzzled by Max's suggestion that a man with such a despicable reputation would be the best candidate available to take over as his dealer. He had grown so accustomed to his mentor, with his Old World charm and watertight reliability. Tippy was the polar opposite of the exhausted man before him.

Tippy had arrived in New York with the highest-reaching ladder he could find. He then, over time, carefully tilted it against the façade of the social scene and proceeded to climb. Billy had spoken to a number of acquaintances represented by Tippy and discovered they all agreed that— despite his somewhat gauche demeanor—the man had indeed helped bolster their careers.

Now, recalling their last talks, Billy understood the reasoning behind Max's decision. They both knew all along that when Max inevitably passed, there would be no one who could possibly replace him. Nobody in the younger generation of dealers came close to possessing Max's high standards, or his ability to impart, with a unique passion and ease, life's most crucial lessons. He was the last survivor of a dying generation, the final alumnus remaining from the "old school," and they were both aware of it.

"I have confidence in Mr. Shernoval, but, more importantly, I have faith in your good sense," Max had continued, his breathing raspy and labored. "If I didn't, I would have suggested someone else. In the end, of course, it will be your own decision."

Max knew that—all else aside—Tippy Shernoval was the most canny and aggressive dealer around, and he insisted to Billy that his career had reached the point where this type of dealer was what he needed. He pulled the conflicted young man closer, and spoke in a low voice with clenched teeth. "You need a pushy and assertive goyim to get you all you deserve. That was never my style, and I often regret not acting more dynamically during these last few years.

"In this sense I am asking you to trust in me. I know your apprehensions, Billy, but believe me, I have also heard about this fellow's improprieties and I've scrutinized every facet of him and his background. I will get to that in a minute, and hopefully assuage your fears."

"I would be nowhere without you, Max." Billy wanted to tell the dying man so much, but knew it was essential that Max finish what he needed to say.

"I think you exaggerate to an old man, but I thank you, and the feeling is certainly mutual. You really are an unusual young man. There is something very sui generis about your entire disposition, as well as your work. It amazes me how a young man who treats the rules of painting so defiantly can simultaneously behave as genuinely unaffected and well mannered as you. It's strange how the two qualities don't . . ."

Max had to stop midsentence. He looked so tired. Billy had been holding out some hope for a recovery, but he saw that was out of the question. Max was not going to last much longer, and that was for certain. By this time Marta had stepped into the room. Steadying herself on the arm of Billy's chair, she lowered one knee onto the floor beside the bed, almost like genuflecting, and greeted Max with a quick pat on his elevated leg, which was now covered by a blanket. By this time, Max had come to know Marta well. From their first meeting he had scrutinized her thoroughly and respectfully, and trusted that she was exactly what Billy needed. He was impressed by her "zeal, intelligence, and intractable honesty."

He also found her quite entertaining. Max, even in his latter years, loved the company of smart, attractive women. With the advent of feminism, his views might appear somewhat misogynistic, but his charm always managed to compensate for that. He knew Marta made it possible for Billy to think of nothing but his work. He could also rely on her to keep an eye on Tippy.

"I'm glad you came, dear," Max said, attempting in vain to raise his hand and greet her. "It's very good to see you. I'm sorry, but I was just telling Billy here that we don't have the time to fall into sentiment. It's time that we stick to business."

Marta noted his failed effort, and lowered her hand onto Max's, gently massaging the fingertips. She wanted to assure him she understood the urgency of his talk with Billy. Max beamed at her, and continued.

"Your recent work, Billy, has grown beyond even my expectations. You've reached the point where you no longer need a mentor, but a shark-like dealer, who does his job in your best interests. Aside from business, don't let him impose his judgment on you, except in the most anecdotal sense. Certainly, don't listen to a word he says regarding your own art or, for that matter, anyone else's. The man may be a good negotiator, but is an absolute idiot when it comes to art, which is, after all, the product that he sells.

"I remember the evening you and I first met. You impressed me by acknowledging your limitations at such a young age. Well, a dealer must also understand his limitations and strengths. I came along at an auspicious moment in your career, and, I dare say, we accomplished a good deal together.

"But I must repeat that it is the right time to move on to somebody with a more aggressive style. Even if it were not for my health, you know that I'm telling you the truth. Trust me, Billy, as you have in the past."

Certainly, Billy could never refuse the dying request of his friend and benefactor, despite his sense that any affiliation with Tippy was bound to fail. He looked down at Max and smiled, nodding his head up and down in affirmation. It was a fait accompli, and there was nothing else for the conflicted artist to do.

"Consider what I say," continued Max. "Now you will only have to answer to yourself. Tippy will be little more than a salesman." Max's voice was growing louder. "My research has shown that he is honest as far as his artist's finances. Considering the gossip, that was my biggest concern, but I had a team of . . . well . . . very loyal forensic accountants surreptitiously get hold of his books for a night and check him out thoroughly. Frankly, their findings surprised me, considering his ruthlessness in other areas. Besides, I'm quite close with the CEO of his money management firm, and their operating system would make it impossible for Mr. Shernoval to pull any shenanigans. If he wanted to fleece his clients, he'd hire a shady outfit . . . of which there is no shortage. Anyway, Marta will be there to double-check everything. Won't you, darling?"

"I will, Max. Count on me." Marta, her hand still pressing his, leaned forward until she was whispering into Max's ear. "*Prometo con todo mi corazón.*"

Billy couldn't make out what Marta had whispered but thought it amazingly sweet when her lips pecked Max lightly on each cheek.

"*¿Usted lo ama, no? Lo he visto y . . .*" Max hastily murmured back in Spanish as she quickly straightened upright, but Marta rushed her finger to his lips, cutting him off.

Blushing deeply, she took a furtive peek at Billy, terrified he'd overheard. He was out of earshot and smiling at the gesture of her kisses. Suppressing a sigh of relief, she switched back to English and continued addressing Max's original concerns. "Anyway, don't worry one bit. I'll follow your instructions to the letter. Nobody is going to mess around with this guy here."

"*Gracias*, my dear. I appreciate that. I truly do." Max turned his head and Marta fed him a lick of lemon-flavored ice that the nurse had left on the night table. "Now I'm feeling a little tired. I believe the medication is making me woozy. Billy, there's one more thing. Now that we've gotten these business matters out of the way, it's very important to me that you never forget a few basics of art.

"I'm quite aware that I've told you most of this a thousand times before. You can't ever stop developing your judgment, and not only regarding your artistic abilities, but also your judgment of other people. If you continue in this manner, then you can take your art beyond your own imagining. You are in charge now, and don't hesitate to make that clear to Tippy. Now is the time to abandon all preconceived limitations and criteria. Make art for yourself alone, as if it will never be seen. In fact, keep all the wolves in abeyance. The truth always comes more easily when no one is watching you. That's the time when fear of failure and the expectations of others fall away, and you'll find tears dropping impulsively while you stand working before the canvas."

Max passed away at about 4:00 a.m the next morning. Marta heard the phone ringing, and her hand searched about in the darkness until she found it. She knocked on Billy's door and found him still awake, reading. They both wept openly and exchanged words of commiseration. He got up and embraced her awkwardly. She laid her head on his chest, and he was caught off guard by the scent of her hair, which he cautiously began to pat lightly, and then stroked tenderly. When their bodies parted, he grabbed a paper napkin and wiped the damp tracks from her eyes and cheeks. She laid her hand on his forearm while relaying the details for the service, which would be extremely private and begin early at an old Jewish cemetery in Westchester. As Billy slowly sat on the edge of the bed, continuing his partly suppressed moans, she softly inquired if he'd be all right. She didn't want him to be alone, and almost volunteered to sleep with him, but decided on a less explicit proposal.

"You know, we'll have to be downstairs for the car in less than three hours, anyway. It might be best if we just stayed up until dawn together, killing time on the sofa with the late movies, don't you agree?" she suggested. "I'll put on some fresh coffee while I call the car service."

"I guess." Billy hadn't felt this sort of emptiness since his mother's death. "I have to check the closet and lay out that dark suit, then I'll join you."

The phone rang again at 8:00. It was the limo driver downstairs. The two had fallen asleep on the sofa. Billy was upright, with his legs on the coffee table. Marta had drooped sideways, with her head resting on his left knee. She jumped up and almost tripped trying to get the call. Billy's eyes slowly opened, still moist and red, directly before the TV, which was still playing at a very low volume. As they began to focus, he stared at the flickering image of two bearded Norwegian men crossing a glacier.

Rushing into his room, he changed from his paint-streaked sweats into the black suit.

"The chauffeur says he's waiting out front," Marta yelled into the room. "Could you get down there and ask him to wait? I'm so sorry, but they sent a substitute guy and he's threatening to leave. I swear it'll only take me a minute."

As the car took off, both of them feared they'd be late. Marta kept blaming herself for falling asleep. Billy just sat forward, anxiously rubbing his feet back and forth on the carpet and checking if the driver was heading in the right direction. The cemetery was in a very inaccessible wooded area, and he now worried whether they'd ever find it, much less on time.

Fortunately, the traffic was almost nonexistent that early, and the new driver happened to be Jewish himself. He veered off the highway and took a shortcut down a narrow dirt road and arrived with five minutes to spare. When their destination came into view, Billy was so relieved that he reached over and squeezed Marta on the thigh. The action was purely reflexive, and he pulled away apologetically, but she just smiled, grabbing his hand and squeezing it. After maneuvering her fingers so their palms faced each other, she continued holding Billy's hand as the driver opened the door, escorting them as far as the entrance gate, where they spotted Max's eldest son waving from a plot about 20 feet away. Greeting them both, he handed Billy a yarmulke and introduced him to the others in attendance. There were only eight mourners, mostly elderly family members, sitting stoically in folding chairs. Most were speaking in an amalgam of German and Yiddish.

After prayers and a few words from a young rabbi, a doleful, beautiful chanting rose from a previously unnoticed cantor wearing a toupee. Still clutching hands, Billy and Marta stood behind the chairs, and both began to sob.

As the simple pinewood box was lowered slowly into the ground, Billy watched the eldest son step forward and ceremoniously jab a small new shovel into the pile of russet-colored clay beside the grave. With a turn of his wrist, he filled the back of the shovel's blade with a thin layer of earth and spread it over the casket in the traditional Jewish manner.

As the son carried out this duty, the artist reflected on his face. His features were frozen in a contorted guise as he attempted to suppress his emotions. Billy desperately wanted to be holding that shovel. It was his final chance to compensate Max—if only slightly—for all that this noble gentleman had done for him throughout the years.

Instead, Marta pulled him forward and they followed the other mourners in tossing a handful of earth into the grave. The thicker clumps of clay hit the wood hard, sounding like hail falling on a shed. Billy was deep in thought, obliviously shaking his head from side to side as they returned and stood behind the chairs. Marta quietly asked what was upsetting him.

"Don't worry. I'm really not upset or angry. Besides, Max was a humble guy who couldn't care less." While he reassured her, his hand surprisingly brushed against her arm. "Personally, I only wish I'd been given the honor to drop the first earth over his casket. You know, using the bottom of the shovel symbolizes the difficulty of the task. Max always made my life so easy, and asked for nothing in return. If I were the first to cover him in that horrid crevice, I would certainly have felt the pain, but it would have been the most important moment in my life, providing me with a final chance to express my gratitude to the only man I've ever loved, and publicly acknowledge all he has given me throughout the years.

"In addition, I must admit being disappointed that so few were invited to honor the memory of a true giant, who touched so many lives in so many ways."

A week later, Max's sons, along with three attorneys, arrived unexpectedly at the loft, calling from a car phone downstairs. It was barely nine in the morning, and Billy was out of earshot in the back of the studio, in the process of considering whether to reframe some old canvases.

Marta, who was fixing breakfast, answered the call, and Josh, the brother who had greeted Billy and her at the services, recognized her voice, and politely requested she wait a moment until the others had left the car. After she heard a door slam, he confided that their father had large holdings in real estate, and that, before today, none of them were aware of this particular building, then sheepishly asked how they might get in. With a press of the intercom, Marta let them in through the street-level door, then ran back to fetch Billy. The two greeted them at the elevator and escorted them to the kitchen table.

After Marta had served coffee, the eldest brother casually informed Billy that Max had willed the entire building to him. The thick document, which a young lawyer quickly placed on the table, also included a monthly stipend for anything necessary for the future upkeep of the old structure, including general maintenance, heating oil, garbage disposal, and the part-time superintendent's salary.

Billy and Marta, in stunned silence, turned and looked curiously at each other, but the eldest attorney, his reading glasses fixed on the manuscript before him, continued. Max had also bequeathed his protégé an unspecified trust for his personal use.

At that point, Billy quickly stood and, in an uncharacteristically sharp tone of voice, insisted that the elderly man cease. After immediately apologizing, he softly requested they leave their card, promising he'd make an appointment to meet at the gentleman's law firm sometime within the week. Any further information relevant to him could be divulged at that time.

They shook hands and left. Billy knew it might well be the last time he'd see any of the sons. Unlike their father, none of them was interested in the arts, and never attended any shows he was involved with, so he wasn't likely to run into them at any gallery or museum. The brothers made handsome livings working in real estate and the stock market and, through success in these chosen fields, all three were far wealthier than their father. This meant none of them had any possible intention of contesting the will.

Billy couldn't get his mind around the fact that he was a landlord and couldn't bear to hear one more word concerning Max's generosity. This bewilderment was his main motive for cutting off the lawyer. It wasn't the only reason, however.

Billy had never inherited anything, aside from the hard-earned savings left to him by his mother, which was a family matter. That was his other incentive for sharply halting the old man's monotonic drone. Max seemed so much like family, and had become such a father figure to Billy, that, with his growing critical acclaim, some resentful young painters had spread rumors that Billy was the dealer's illegitimate gentile son.

9

T ippy had called three times inquiring on the show's progress. Marta dutifully screened each call, allowing Billy to chart the way through his dense isolation. Still, he could always hear the faint ring of the phone, marking the passing of time, the only predator in his landscape.

Billy's meteoric success had always haunted him, causing him to keep hidden all sorts of suspicions, failings, and misjudgments. Max had warned him about the dangers of fame, but didn't concern himself much about such matters. The dealer took Billy's inner resources for granted. He made the mistake of equating Billy's emotional assets with his artistic talent and the humility with which he handled that gift.

For his part, Billy went along on the ride, trying to assimilate himself to Max's illusions. It wasn't a deception: it was an effort, but it was flawed, and doomed sooner or later to collapse under its own weight. He respected the man too much to burden him with his failings, and now realized the extent of his mistake. He'd transformed Max into an idealized father figure, but in doing so he found it necessary to idealize himself to Max. The ground had been creaking beneath him from the beginning. Billy needed advice and knew their unhealthy relationship was in danger, but without any paternal experience to gauge it against, he could never bring himself to broach these problems with his mentor. This was at the time when the critics were adopting him as the young darling of the scene. Less than three years after

Max began guiding his career, the 24-year-old Billy's paintings dominated the Whitney Biennial, and he discovered himself on the cover of that week's *New York Times* Sunday magazine. All this attention occurred too fast and soon turned overwhelming. Still, Billy was especially apprehensive whenever writers tagged him "the next big thing."

Billy's analogy for this sort of unspecified praise came from an old Bogart film, *High Sierra*, which he no doubt first saw on *Million Dollar Movie*. In it, Bogart plays Roy "Mad Dog" Earle, a legendary thief just released from prison and conflicted by the outside world. While the aging Bogart character is sick of his reputation and wants out of the criminal life, he needs to make one large last score, enabling him to retire. The opportunity for one easy and lucrative heist quickly arises, but he needs to put together a crew and hasn't time to find any of his companions from the old days. Instead, he must rely on a hastily assembled batch of young unqualified drifters to fill out his four-man team. He also finds a devoted love interest, played by Ida Lupino. Because Earle lacks the time to prepare the brash and incompetent punks, the robbery—at an upscale mountain resort—goes completely awry. One of the nervous kids winds up shooting a security guard, and they scatter in various directions, ordered to "lay low" by the frustrated Earle. He and the woman go into hiding in the Sierras. Two days later, he is filling the car with gas and picks up a newspaper. It seems one of the others has already been caught, and the young hoodlum named Roy Earle as the mastermind and the shooter. The headline of every newspaper reads "F.B.I. Names Mad Dog Number One Most Wanted." The woman, not caring about her own fate, suggests that they turn themselves in and convince the police that he did not shoot the guard. That's when Bogart turns to her, seething and repeating the headline as he points to it. He finally starts the car, takes off higher into the mountains, and delivers the key lines: *"Baby, you don't understand. Once they hang that 'Number One Most Wanted' moniker on you, they shoot first and ask questions later."*

Billy always visualized that movie and heard those lines resonate whenever he was referred to as the new phenomenon of the art scene. It's *High Sierra* all over again, he would say to himself, thinking the media labeling any young artist with the catchphrase "the Next Big Thing" was identical to "Number One Most Wanted." It didn't matter . . . critics or cops, it's only a matter of time before they start shooting. Denny would always back him up on this point. According to him, the rock and roll press, especially in Britain, could take an unknown musician and write him up to the point of apotheosis. Then, just as swiftly, they could tear him to shreds with his next release. "It's as predictable as the swinging of a pendulum," Denny told him, "so it's best not to pay attention to all that paraphernalia—which is all it is—no matter which way it's swinging, or the bullets are flying."

The odd thing was, Billy was an anomaly. Throughout his career and its continuing ascent, the media never fired on him. They asked questions . . . lots of questions, but Billy usually didn't answer. Thinking about it now in his reclusion, he realized his uncertainties and fears didn't arise until a short time after Max's death. In the vacancy that event caused, Billy's self-doubt took root.

He believed in his talent but did not yet have the experience to trust his judgment, the problem that had haunted him since those art school days in the East Village hovel with Denny. That was the first question that Billy would ask himself: should he have stayed longer in school? Perhaps, like so many of his fellow students, he should have weaseled some way to go to Europe, maybe even studied there.

It seemed a catch-22 situation. Billy's accountability to craft was a double-edged sword. He had seen so many talented painters who were never satisfied with the opening lines on a canvas, or had repeatedly mixed two colors for days on their palette, trying without success to reach the perfect tone. Inevitably they fell short, beginning over and over until they just walked away. They were stuck in their intellect, and had shut off the flow. Billy just threw himself into the canvas, trusting, even depending on, his need to reach some conclusion to his *own* impulses. He knew it was an open secret on the art scene that de Kooning never felt even one of his paintings was "done." Billy figured that he had studied the essential painters and mastered beyond the basics. The next step was to follow the flow and trust in your instinctive nerves. It sounds simple, and for Billy, in those early years it was. But for one who relies on gifts beyond his control, there is always an eventual reckoning.

Sometimes, as if a perverse gift from the muse, the misjudgments in a painting could be its most important features. In a similar way, Billy often found that he learned more about pure craft from a mediocre or even "bad" painting than he did from a masterpiece. He had the ability to spot the exact moment and place—no matter how deeply buried in the muddy layers of pigment—where the artist had gone off course, or lost his confidence and vision. It didn't matter. Sometimes, this was due to a lack of talent, but more often Billy attributed it to the artist's loss of faith in his initial impulse. At that point the artist would, in effect, give up and rely on the usual stylistic bag of tricks. Billy would naturally choose the epiphany from a masterpiece rather than a technical revelation from the lesser work. However, he questioned if the same could be said for most ambitious students with a brush. If they were able to choose the secrets of perspective, rather than a moment confronting the divine, they would toss aside the latter and grab for the mastery of craft. And if they put these technical revelations to good use, Billy could not fault them for their choice.

It was probably because of his discovery of art through an intuitive wisdom, but one thing always seemed obvious to Billy. Any true artist needs to go through a transitory stage of at least a few years before he fully realizes his technical vocabulary and stylistic code, and must trust in the axiom that one learns mainly through failure. He had an insatiable need to master every aspect of his craft, but he also possessed an uncanny ability to circumvent any problem that came his way.

He couldn't deny that he enjoyed aspects of the fame, but inside it was eating a part of him up. He also sensed that early fame would lead to arrested development, not only in his work but in his life.

Was it true that the rise from one strata of recognition to another in the art world was essential to evaluate the true power of his paintings? Billy wondered. He concluded that he could only control the struggle getting there on his own terms. It would be foolish for him to allow the "art world," with its politics, artifice, and machinations, to determine the extent of his capabilities or the quality of his work.

Billy was deep in thought when Denny arrived at the loft, unannounced as usual. He apologized, as he had many times previously over the phone, for not coming sooner. He told Billy that he'd been gauging his moods throughout their talks, and concluded that if solitude was what Billy truly needed, then who was he to muck it all up with his shabby, boisterous presence?

Billy stood and hugged his old friend, a shudder of defensiveness in his embrace. After Denny passed on the well wishes of some of their friends, Billy launched into the matters that were earlier on his mind, specifically how those youthful failures and misjudgments as an artist developed both character and the expanse of one's art. "Are spirit and character one and the same?" Billy asked Denny. Denny had heard all this before.

Denny inhaled and replied, "The spiritual is like a very intimidating dance partner. I've embraced her and abandoned her. I bolted right out the side door of the ballroom trying to distance myself from her. You made the mistake of allowing Velázquez to cut in on you."

"That's not bad"—Billy pensively drew out the words—"but the billing made it quite clear that this was his night and his exhibition. When he tapped me on the shoulder, I would have been horribly rude not to defer. It wasn't the night for my lesson."

"There are many dance floors in the Father's ballroom," Denny shot back, his biblical allusion made with surprising solemnity.

Denny continued, "I sometimes wish I'd actually gone to classes at Columbia, instead of using my scholarship as a way out of the draft. But music just dialed me up when it was ready, and I answered the phone. These things don't leave messages on machines; they simply never bother to call back. You and I have an intuitive education, as opposed to the purely academic. Remember when we were kids, and I was so desperately in love with some girl, and the two of us sat up in your room looking for poems to woo her? We weren't expecting it when we ran across that old toe-tapper 'The Ecstasy,' by John Donne, but we were both as moved as the first time we heard Roy Orbison sing. Well . . . almost that moved. We were clueless regarding the poem's metaphysical and literary aspects, but that poem deeply affected both of us at 16 years of age—just two mutts from the streets.

"That's why I think spirit and character may be the same. Art can tap something beyond intellect, but your character determines if you will receive it through your inner register, through the intuitive wisdom of an open heart, through your instincts, nerve, and heart.

"Those instincts made you into the artist and the person you are. That is who chose you and took you to the dance, and that is certainly who you should leave with.

"Check that out . . . now I'm back with the dance metaphor again! It's strange, but if your intentions are right, then these random factors always seem to come together in time. You can dance every other tune with the academics. You can travel, study, and find something new to learn until the day you die. But when you leave the dance, go on the arm of the one who brought you there, that's how you find your strength, the edge in your style. Rely on those instincts! You've now reached the point when your own experience is your best source of judgment. You still learn every time that you paint, or sculpt, or look at the way a leaf attaches itself to a wet stone wall. Seems to me like you're just brooding, man. That's all right now and then, but in time you become comfortable as that person, and your healthy reclusion just ends up as bitter isolation.

"Remember when we first had money and notoriety? We reveled in it. And God looked down at us and said, 'It is good, for these two ratty goyim have earned it.' And we did earn it. We paid our dues in every sense, wrestling the fates to get here, and, as long as we don't turn into absolute arrogant assholes, there's nothing wrong with feeling good about it.

"The point is, my brother, do you really think *we* should brood and retreat into isolation, and let all the money be spent and all the fun be had by these junk-bond, 25-year-old pinheads in red silk ties—who create nothing and get rich from some other sap's losses? Not me, Billy."

Billy just stared, and Denny, turning to open the door, wondered if he'd gone too far. As he raced down the stairs, he concluded that Billy was either on the mend or had turned into a totally hopeless case.

Billy looked out the window, watching Denny weave through the traffic. Why was he hurrying away? His gait reminded Billy of their teenage years, when the pair would sit for hours in his room on the opposite end of Manhattan, mapping out each detail needed to attain their future goals. After his mother called, Denny would hastily depart for home, moving with the same dispassionate swagger across "the back way," as they had referred to it. This shortcut was adjacent to Billy's rear courtyard, the same one where he'd buried his "Excalibur" years before. A cuspidate whitewashed wooden fence separated the courtyard from "the back way," and Billy would look down on Denny as he climbed through some broken slats and cut across 25 feet of stubbly parkland until he connected with a cracked slate pathway.

Twenty-five feet of dead leaves and insect-ridden sod, pocked with clumps of crabgrass and dog crap. There were two old, unkempt trees on the scruffy terrain of "the back way," and both had grown higher than Billy's fourth-floor window.

Those trees terrorized Billy, especially in winter when the haggard old branches were empty and gray. When he was three or four years old he'd had a serious fever and was isolated to the bed in that very room. Brian had to move his things and sleep on the sofa in the living room. The doctors thought it was scarlet fever at first, but it turned out to be something that only mimicked that disease's symptoms. None of the M.D.s ever did put a medical designation on the fever—at least to Billy's knowledge. The recollection of their somewhat innocuous omission made him realize that the answers to all his questions about childhood—no matter how inane or significant—had been lost with his mother's passing.

This idiopathic fever was the most severe illness of his childhood, but it took more of a toll on Billy's psyche than on his body. Billy did not recollect any of the physical pain—the searing chills and cramps—only the fever-fueled nightmares and hallucinations, which all had to do with the trees.

In actuality, the branches, parallel to Billy's room, were no closer than ten feet from his windows, but when the fever dreams flared up, they extended and rested right on his windowsill. This way they formed a jagged bridge, providing entrance for the hideous fever dwarves that lived in the base of the tree trunks. They would enter day or night and Billy, sweat-soaked and terrified in his bed, could see them coming, furtive and unwavering, along the branch, helping to lower one another onto the floor. Less than a foot in height, they were not "dwarves" as defined by medical standards, but at this age Billy had not yet learned of gnomes or other similar fabled beasts. He heard the terrifyingly delicate volume of their quick footsteps making their way to the bedspread, where they would climb up its crocheted fabric as if it were one of those rope ladders used by pirates to board ships. Then they would jab his body with tiny knives, and he couldn't move or yell because he was paralyzed by fright. It still seemed more like something that actually occurred than a dream caused by the fever. When he told his mother about these attacks, she treated them as real and would pull up all the blankets so the creatures no longer had access, then she would lie in bed beside her son's shivering body, dabbing him with chilled water.

These memories of his fever-fed illusions passed through Billy as he watched Denny disappear down 22nd Street.

On the day of his mother's funeral, Billy recalled, he and Denny had sat looking out over "the back way," trying to identify the source of some strange music. As the sound grew louder, neither of them could find its source. Billy had to grab Denny by his belt to secure his friend, who was craning far out the window.

The slate pathway was bordered by a retaining wall. It was about five feet tall, constructed crudely—though in its way quite beautifully—with natural, rough-hewn stones, secured by mortar. The wall was topped with slabs of the same slate as the walk. It looked like something created during the Revolutionary War period. Over the years the mortar had worked loose, and the burrows created between the stones became a popular home for a particularly large species of rats. One of the only memories Billy could recall of his brother, Brian, was kneeling on chairs together to see out the window, watching the rats scurrying about in the rain for wet bread crumbs tossed about by some misguided soul to feed the pigeons and squirrels. Later, when the city Parks Department plugged the spaces in the wall with some space-age polymer, the rats soon disappeared.

Looking at that wall, Billy and Denny were recollecting the rat infestation period.

"I always thought it was a bit cruel, trapping the little vermin inside and burying them alive," Billy said.

"Maybe they had an escape exit up the hill," Denny offered, staring astray in a trance. "Anyway, at least they met their demise burrowing. That's what rats are born to do. It's like a dog fetching itself to death."

"You've got a strange mind, Denny Mac, you know that?"

On the hill above the wall, large shimmering boulders jutted out. For many years, at least one day each semester, young Billy would predictably notice geology professors from Columbia University on field trips, clambering awkwardly up the hillside with their students as they identified these outcroppings of crystalline formations extruding from the hillside. It was called milky quartz, and Billy would listen to the geologist's strident discourse from his window as the students knelt beside the slick streaks of mineral, poking around and, on two occasions, slipping and tumbling entertainingly down the hillside. Apparently, this hillside behind Billy's apartment was the only place in the continental United States where this particular quartz formation was found, and there was no academic consensus why.

Billy always loved the term *milky quartz*, and when he was eight years old, he took a small hammer up the hill and chipped off a few tiny stones, which he laid out on his dresser. And though the silver flecks covering them would shine eagerly beneath the high setting of his reading lamp's bulb, the crystalline samples themselves weren't as impressive to Billy as the sound of the words *milky quartz*.

The uniqueness of these rocks was another justification for Billy's feeling blessed that he was born in New York, and reinforced the sense of fate this city demanded. He still felt liable for a last debt to the megalopolis, which was the unspecified payment due for not being taken west with his father after the divorce.

Those rare, dappled stones were no big deal to the people who took that same old walkway daily on their course to the subway at Broadway and 181st Street, and just referred to them as "the white rocks above the back way." To Billy, their peculiarity paralleled his chosen environment.

And it was on the path—right beneath the large mother-lode boulder to their left—that Billy and Denny spotted the source of the inexplicable noise. They had been tricked by the sound's ricochets and were looking in the wrong direction.

It was a lone man playing a bagpipe. Denny informed Billy that the mysterious figure was basically just warming up, checking all his valves and pipes. It might have been due to bizarre acoustics bouncing off the quartz boulders and up the building's wall, but the exotic instrument was stunningly loud. Heads were popping out of windows beneath them. The stranger began running through melodic chord progressions. "Wow," Denny commented, awed by this fellow musician. "What a tone. I think this guy is really good, and those things are amazingly difficult to play. Do you hear the smoothness of those notes?"

Neither of them had yet commented on the piper's dress. He was attired right out of the Scottish Highlands, wearing a kilt, high wool stockings, and, beneath a plaid vest, a stiff white shirt with large ruffles across the front. He had one of those tartan hats with the tassels dangling from it. To the unknowing eyes of the boys, it seemed like the epitome of Scottish formal wear. He even had one of those traditional embroidered bags hanging from the center of his belt.

That led to the main question. Why was this burly fellow, about 30 years of age, playing the bagpipes by himself in the rain? The ambience of him standing before the ancient-looking gray wall of craggy stones and slate, the alien clothes, and the mournful minor chords made it seem as if they were looking down on a tableau from the eighteenth century.

"What's he all about anyway, you think?" Denny muttered. He didn't realize Billy had already left the room.

Billy checked the daisy-shaped clock over the kitchen sink. It was now half-past nine, and the lone piper out back had suddenly stopped, as if he too had just checked the time. Billy wished the music would keep on as a distraction. He was looking for anything to divert his eyes from locking on to the reality of his mother's death. He unfolded a sheet of paper and focused on a list of people he had called and informed of her wake. It was a very short list. He knew that those invited would call others, and those others would call more. It was a cultural dynamic . . . a reliance on compulsive gossipers.

The one serious problem was not being able to reach his brother. Brian and their father were, no doubt, away for deer-hunting season. Billy just kept calling every evening beginning at 7:00 p.m. Pacific time, with no answer. Now any chance of Brian attending the services had passed.

Billy allowed the parish priests to do most of the planning for the funeral. Aside from the fact that they were paying for the interment, Billy reasoned that no one else knew more about the Catholic way of death and its accompanying rituals. This was how his mom would have wanted it, though she never broached the subject directly, even on her deathbed.

On one point, however, Billy was adamant. He ruled out the traditional two nights' open casket viewing of the body at the funeral parlor next door to the church on Broadway. Despite the priests' passionate entreaties to have his mother "properly laid in rest," for public mourning, Billy refused. He found such displays maudlin and, in ways he felt but could not express, slightly perverse. His intractability on the matter brought out a touch of ire among the fathers—as well as excessive shot glasses of Johnny Walker Black. Perhaps it was his own fear of facing her death so directly, or having to greet people whom he barely knew after they knelt before his dead mother with God only knows what thoughts in their heads. Besides, caskets, with extraneous trappings such as fake pearl inlay and gaudy silk lining, made Billy extremely uncomfortable. He couldn't help visualizing the coffin as it would soon be . . . underground, besieged by insects, dank water, and the pressure of absolute darkness.

The only compromise acceptable to Billy was a "private" viewing of the casket in the funeral parlor's smallest room during the two hours before the mass began. At that point they had to pick up the body and transfer it to the church anyway. It went without saying that the casket would be closed. Billy decided that these hours would accommodate any genuine prayers of petition by the priests. Billy's crooked leap of faith included the efficacy of genuine prayer. He did not comprehend it, but acknowledged it as connected to his notion of the sacred nature of intuition and the wisdom of the heart. He also felt that, for equally unfathomable reasons, prayers by women were more forceful than those by men, but there were exceptions to this. Billy believed that he himself had not yet learned how to pray. He imagined that the closest he got to it was when he was painting, but that seemed like an overly romantic notion. It could have been the exact opposite.

He noticed the parish newsletter facedown on the Formica table. Billy hadn't seen it before, but there was a picture of his mother that took up the entire back page. Beneath the photo it read IN LOVING MEMORY—OUR BELOVED EMMA WOLFRAM. It was a picture from her youth, and she looked beautiful, her hair very long and straight. It was a sweet gesture by the priests, Billy thought.

Seeing the unexpected image of his mom caught Billy off guard, and the tears finally began to flow. He was relieved they had finally materialized; after all, what would he make of himself if he had no tears left for his mother? Now, once the tears began, he wondered when the moment would come that he might be able to stop them.

He took a deep breath and grabbed a paper napkin from the plastic caddy on the table. It was still three-fourths full from when his mom had filled it months ago. He pressed the paper firmly against his eyes as if putting pressure on a laceration. He remained like that awhile, staring off at the ceiling. Then he blew his nose and gathered himself as he went back to explain the presence of the bagpiper in "the back way" to Denny. The music had just started up again.

"I know who he is and why he's there," Billy told Denny, who stood swaying to the notes as if he hadn't budged from the window.

"Well, of course," replied Denny, turning around to give Billy a curious look. "He's playing for Aunt Em."

"Well, sure . . . in a sense." Billy saw there was no irony in his friend's statement. That was Denny, however. He needed neither explanations nor understanding to see omens. Still, Billy took the time to summarize his detective work for him, explaining he had also noted in the church bulletin that the mass preceding his mother's was a requiem for a local policeman killed in the line of duty.

"He's been warming up, I guess, but he'd better get a move on." Billy eyed the small clock on the shelf. "That service begins in about 25 minutes."

"Oh, so he's a *cop piper*," Denny replied without taking his eyes from the musician. "No wonder he's so good. Those guys have to endure a rigorous selection process and consider being chosen to be a serious honor. Well, I still say that *something* drew him to such a secluded spot directly beneath this window. You might say he's been tuning up, but I still insist that what he's playing—here and now—is for your mother. Later at the church, the music will be for this fallen comrade. This is for Emma. By the way, I heard on the radio a couple of nights ago about that detective getting killed, you know. I had no idea he was from this neighborhood, though."

I can't argue with Denny's enchanted logic, Billy thought. He moved close beside him at the window and listened some more to the fragmented, elegiac melodies.

After a few minutes, the man checked his watch. The two boys were dreading the moment, but, as he grabbed a leather attaché case resting on the wet slate and began stuffing pages of sheet music into it, it appeared he was about to leave. Suddenly he decided to rehearse one full tune before heading over to the church. The music was sweet with reverb and almost jazzlike improvisational riffs. It was "Amazing Grace," and his playing, along with the acoustics of the milky quartz, made it sound never so beautiful as at that moment.

Denny began to sing along. Billy sang as well, but he only knew the words to the first verse, and, of course, the chorus. Denny went on flawlessly with the lyrics for all four verses. He had such passion and purpose in his trembling tenor phrasing that Billy had to take a couple of steps backward, providing him more space to dab away the tears with his shirtsleeve. Its beauty aside, Denny's voice was belting out with such volume by the last lines that the piper looked up toward the window, searching and finally fixing eyes on his accompanist. He even seemed to adjust his dynamics to accommodate the vocals.

At that moment, an astonishing thought came to Billy. Does each song, he wondered, have a certain time and place—beyond the subjective aspects of technique and talent—when it is perfectly played by the performer, or perfectly received by the listener? If so, he wondered, what if by some huge cosmic coincidence *both* occurred simultaneously? He felt he had just witnessed such a phenomenon. Could the same process occur with other art forms? It would be different in the case of painting or sculpture, since the work is not performed or viewed in the same moment and place where it is created. That gap of time changes the nature of the process. Perhaps it makes the experience of examining a painting deeper in some sense. The subject and object become one, as do the artist and the audience—or only a single member of that audience. Billy found it unlikely that Denny was affected by the piper's performance in the same way that he was. Billy always recalled this epiphany with a slight guilt, realizing that its genesis was somehow abetted by his mother's death.

After the long, last note dissolved into the quartz, the piper took a step to his left to get a better line of sight at the window. He lifted his head and cocked it slightly, moving his hand in a concise gesture of recognition. He then folded up his pipes and hurried off to the church.

The two boys arrived at the funeral parlor for the last hour of the wake. This was the time that Billy had conceded to the priests, and the casket was laid out in the traditional manner. They took turns, slowly approaching the closed casket, kneeling before it, and saying a short prayer. Against all expectations, Billy felt the urge to lift the wooden lid so he might see her face one last time. He was so bent by this thought that it had a bracing effect. After receiving condolences from the priests and a few of Emma's women friends, Billy took a seat beside Denny and stayed in the room with her body until the casket was carried to the church and the mass began.

10

It was his 13th day in seclusion, and Billy was looking forward to seeing Denny again. At first he wondered if his anxiety, moodiness, and boring rants during last week's visit hadn't scared Denny off, but realized it was a foolish, paranoid idea that denigrated the strength of their friendship. The artist was feeling slightly better, but he couldn't say why. He still had a deluded sense that delicate deliberations holding the answer to his recovery were taking place on a single synapse, thin as a tightrope, directly above his brain's stem. However, he had repressed all thoughts and memories from this particular portion of gray matter, so that he could no longer gain access to the negotiations now taking place there. They simply wavered on that line, swaying precipitously, and he was trying everything possible to upset the balance enough to shake loose an answer.

He had discovered he could suppress all the confusion and contradictions by watching the TV. Ever since he impulsively moved the box into his room on his return from the hospital, it had fascinated him. The second night back from the loony bin, Billy had caught a bit of an old low-budget western and was permeated with calm as hand-cranked cameras panned across a southwestern desert landscape, with its red mesas and rows of mysterious clay obelisks shaped like hieroglyphics. But watching from his supine position, Billy quickly felt far too wasted to focus on the screen and switched the set off. He rearranged the large pillows into one soft mound, and his body plunged into one of the most potent sleeps he'd had in years.

On waking, Billy inadvertently tuned to a small UHF nostalgia station that bombarded him with both the archly contrived and the sentimental memories of his youth. These recollections appeared to continuously follow in seductive sequences from Billy's past, and he spent nearly all of the following nights captivated by that channel, which aired nothing but old B movies and reruns of various TV series from his childhood. He had woken at 2:00 one morning and watched James Cagney starring in *White Heat*. According to the commercials, the same channel played old black-and-white westerns and detective programs from the sixties and seventies throughout the day. It was such a strange feeling for Billy. He hadn't watched television in 20 years, and the same shows were still playing.

He was engrossed by the westerns, but his true favorites were police dramas like *Dragnet* and *Naked City*. When this station went off the air for the day, Billy would kill the volume and let the static continue playing. It gave him a bit of serenity, falling asleep beneath its misty glow.

He had dismissed the notion that his fondness for such shows stemmed from pure maternal affection, but after a few nights, he brushed aside his own denial and indulged himself in the black-and-white comforts of those same shows he would watch with his mom. He would lie on the green carpet, and she on the sofa, a throw pillow bracing her neck and a cigarette burning in the heavy glass ashtray. Watching many of these programs now was a sort of study for Billy, an attempt—futile and foolish as it was—to see through her eyes these portions of their common past, preserved by technology.

However, aside from the succor of nostalgia, Billy still maintained that the older shows were better than the majority of present network offerings. Just hearing the theme songs sent him into a frenzy of melancholic recollections. The old western *Branded*, starring Chuck Connors, had just ended, and Billy caught himself singing softly along with the lyrics, which came into his head with the reflex of muscle memory:

> Branded, marked by the coward's shame
> What do you do when you're branded?
> Will you fight for your name?

The irony delighted him. It made him feel that, for once and for a little while, at least, time had been outwitted. Max had always told him that in *Parsifal*—one of the dealer's favorite operas—a character postulates that time could be transformed into space. In Billy's warped way of seeing things, maybe that's what the TV was doing, changing time into the illusionary space of the television screen.

Billy was fascinated by the television. At its most basic level, it occupied his time and shut out the demons of isolation. This was another irony because, for so long, he had shunned the tube for a similar purpose—to prevent it from bombarding his brain with demons of banality. However, each time he turned the machine on, he began to discover a world of assorted delights, as well as gain insight into the insidious manner in which this medium was shaping the mass psyche. If nothing else, he learned there was nothing innocuous about it.

He even enjoyed the normally irksome task of fiddling with the rabbit-ear antennae for better reception. They were so much sleeker now than in the old days. You couldn't even correctly refer to this particular configuration as "rabbit ears." It was more a metallic circle within a circle with appendages jutting horizontally out of each side. Sometimes he just stared at the way the aerial was positioned. It was minimal sculpture.

Denny arrived late in the afternoon. Billy heard him speaking in hushed tones to Marta and then heard the knock on the door. His old friend smiled and entered, giving a quizzical glance at the TV, which was left on with the sound muted. Billy could see through the exaggerated smile and sensed how ill at ease Denny was, certainly much more than he had seemed during his last visit. Billy suddenly worried more for Denny's condition than his own.

Denny was fed up with Billy's sulking around the loft feeling sorry for himself and couldn't bear to hear another word about the meltdown at the museum or more horror stories from the mental ward. He sometimes had a sneaking suspicion that his pal was indulging himself, using his troubling changes in circumstance as an excuse to evade his work. After their last meeting, Denny reasoned that he wasn't helping Billy by acting as if these shifts in Billy's personality hadn't changed their relationship. As he finished climbing the stairs, he decided that he would no longer treat Billy in the same old way he had before the incident at the Met. He decided before he entered that he would, at least at first, try to engage Billy as he always had, but do the right thing as his closest friend.

Billy asked how the current tour was going. Denny shrugged it off. "Same old same old, night after night," he murmured, then—despite his intentions—his voice began to rise. "Actually, it's going fairly well. The opening band is surprisingly good and quite unusual. They've got a hit single and an androgynous lead singer who used to be a gymnast. This short kid does backflips as he's singing . . . can you imagine? The crowd eats it up."

If this was how Denny decided to approach things, Billy was going to play along. "I've seen that guy. He wears those skintight leotards, and looks like he's no more than 14 years old. What's his real age?"

"Oh, man . . . there lies a strange tale. In regards to his sexual predilections, that is." Denny sounded genuinely at ease for the first time since he had entered. "First of all, he's actually about 24 years old, though he really does look like he's 17—at the very most. But this kid is a certified freak. One of his roadies verified a rumor I'd heard before the tour.

"It seems he is a sexual narcissist in the extreme, with a most bizarre fetish, and he retains a separate truck just to carry the equipment for it. The band is pretty furious at the way this eats into their expenses. It costs a lot of money to rent out an extra rig, especially when it's hauling nothing but the implements of one guy's sexual gratification.

"According to my informant, he gets the largest room available in each hotel they stay at. The roadies empty out all the furnishings and set up these intense video installations. When they're done, there is a circle of television sets with VCRs projecting seven life-sized and startlingly real images of this guy sitting in a breakfast chair, totally naked, and masturbating. That's when he kicks the roadies out and enters. He gets in a real chair in the center and goes for hours sitting with seven virtual selves that play with his favorite erogenous zones, some basic, others unique, perplexing, and even amusing. The eyes and the lips stare longingly and wantonly at the actual kid sitting at the center of it all. Now, that is one strange young dude."

"God, it sounds so elaborate." Billy had heard a lot of outrageous sex tales from Denny over the years. They mainly involved Denny's own escapades, but he had, at times, divulged the bizarre predilections of other illustrious rockers. This new technologically enhanced exploit now topped the freak list.

"I wonder if he ever has sex with other people," Denny wondered aloud. "I mean *real* people—be they female or male."

Billy didn't answer. For him, the story had hit a wall and could go no farther. His brain was welded in place to the image of the young singer in the center of the videos. A shuddering realization struck Billy, his thin frame collapsing backward on the bed. For all his impoverished narcissism and virtual sex, this unctuous rocker was no different than Billy himself. Hadn't he constructed—guardedly and precisely over time—his own series of emotional holograms? Hadn't he—ever since that day in 1963—sidestepped the joys and pains of true sex with rows of self-deceptions and virtual assemblages, which he used to shield not only himself from his true feelings, but everyone else?

There were the conquests through omission in the East Village club scene, the power experienced by rejecting women who'd never faced rejection before. For Billy, it was a form of taking their virginity. He could shamelessly flirt and tease, assured he would never have to deal with the complexities of *bringing it on*. There was the rancid satisfaction he allowed himself to consume in the stares of female admirers at parties or openings. Throughout these conceits, he was convinced that his ego was empowered by his art, not his ersatz sexual conquests. In that sense, Billy deluded even himself that his sexual forfeiture was evidence of a higher moral character. Then there was the teenage hubris that he could somehow will himself into turning homosexual in the debacle with Lester and that sad pervert with the tent, not even allowing himself the foolish youthful curiosity to fake his way through the consequence of his folly. Worse than any of this was the growing suspicion that his annulment of sex as the source of his artistic edge and aesthetic purity was itself—whether it be true or false—one more deceptive, emotive structure of light, gas, and mirrors.

Billy looked up at Denny, who had a concerned expression on his face. He wanted to come clean about all these distressing matters. If not with

Denny, who else? After all, Denny was the only person alive who knew the source of his sexual dysfunction. Billy wanted him to clarify the deception behind it all. He suspected that Denny had seen through it all along anyway. He surely had sussed out aspects of it back in their days at the East Village apartment. Billy suspected that Denny could see it this moment in the clarity and shock of his addled expression, in its pathos and supplication. Nonetheless, he could not find the words. He'd been deprived of serious conversation for two weeks now, and the analogous insight had left him inarticulate.

It was true. Billy had now come to terms with how similar he and the video-obsessed rock star were. His fetishes were simply lacking the high technology. Over the years, Billy had surrounded himself with his own sexual totems, but it was more like a wagon train forming a circle to protect itself in one of his rediscovered TV westerns. For years, he'd been strategically circling the wagons, defending himself from all kinds of fantasized renegades. He did it for his art, or that's what he'd told himself.

Denny could see the effect of his anecdote on his friend, but had no idea of its depth. He wasn't going to push. Instead, he rose from the footstool and made a small, silent circle, stopping in front of the television.

"By the way, what in God's name is *this* doing in here?" Denny laid his hand on top of the television set. "You despise the tube."

"I love that thing, Denny." Billy's voice jumped with enthusiasm. It had been turned off and gone unnoticed during Denny's last visit. "I don't know what I could have been thinking all these years. I found a station that plays all the programs that you and I used to watch like *Wanted: Dead or Alive, Wagon Train,* and all those great cop shows. Imagine . . . checking them out again together. Actually, I believe what I've mostly enjoyed was staring into those stations with nothing but interference . . . you know?"

"You mean nothing except snow?" Denny was not really surprised.

"Yeah. That's what they call it, don't they? You know, I read up about what causes interference. Most people think it's just stray electromagnetic waves, or the excesses of other TV and radio signals. Well, that does account for some of this 'snow,' but only an infinitesimal amount. Most of it, they've discovered, is a visual residue of new stars being formed and dead stars collapsing. That interference has been traveling here at the speed of light for nobody knows how long. It could go back to the big bang itself . . . a remnant of the universe taking shape. I can watch it for hours. It's amazing."

"Maybe that's what God looked like to Moses on the mountaintop." Denny spoke sarcastically, not able to stop himself. "It wasn't fire coming from the bush, but snow."

"You're goofing now." Billy stared at Denny. "But there's some sort of *information* in that stuff."

Denny didn't want to deflate Billy's enthusiasm by informing him that his ideas were not very original, and that the entire SETI array of enormous satellite dishes were constantly monitoring the stars for a coherent signal from space. The odd thing was that Billy was making all this out to be some big discovery, but these vague theories, which he clearly hoped would make an impression on Denny, were standard arcane trivia that Billy *already knew*. Denny was certain of it. In fact, they had discussed these same sidereal matters within the past two years. Billy appeared to be the victim of partial amnesia.

Denny saw there was some sort of change in Billy. Billy had always been enthusiastic about new knowledge, but there was something about his sense of perspective and priority that seemed all screwed up. It was a classic case of not seeing the forest for the trees . . . or bypassing real knowledge for gadgetry and entertainment. Billy's brain had misplaced its ability to cross-reference the most mundane trivia until it led to something universally evocative and, thus, artistically useful. Otherwise such information was neutralized from within itself, and he disposed of it out of hand. If there was one thing that bothered Billy no end, it was the plethora of information now made possible by technology. Information without any true meaning was one of Billy's major peeves, and here he was raving about *television*. Three weeks ago, Denny thought, Billy would have tossed the set into a bathtub of gasoline and set it ablaze.

"Have you been watching any actual shows, or are you just into trancing out on snow?" Denny asked.

"Of course I've been watching shows," Billy answered, "and most of the new ones are terrible. I like this detective show *Columbo*, but that's only on Sunday afternoons in reruns. Best of all, I found a channel on UHF that shows all the old shows that we used to watch as kids."

"Sure, channel 24. Mondays they have westerns, on Tuesday police shows . . ."

"That's the station, but it's channel 41, not 24." Billy seemed upset. "I told you, it's on the UHF band."

"It's the same station." Denny spoke softly. "I get it on a different number because I have cable. You're operating old school, man."

"I see." Billy dragged the words out as if this were another huge revelation. "That's right. The stations have different numbers on cable. You get an astounding amount of stations too, don't you?"

"I think you should forget about cable. There's no *snow* on cable."

"I agree. Besides, I like playing with the antenna. Do you ever watch *Bonanza* on that channel?" Billy asked. "They have some great old movies at night too."

"Ever see the *really* early detective shows?" Denny phrased this very carefully, recalling that Billy's mother died while watching a detective show. "I'm talking about ones from the fifties, like *Naked City*."

"That was when the police cars in NYC were green," Billy told Denny. "In the TV series *Naked City* and, for that matter, the movie that it was based on."

" 'There are eight million stories in the naked city . . . this has been one of them,' " Denny quoted. "That was on before my folks even had a TV set. That was the line that opened and ended every show, though, remember?"

"Sure," Billy came back. "One of the great lines of TV history. It makes me think of the line 'There are many rooms in my father's mansion.' They both have the same meter or something. But remember in *Naked City*, the old police cars? They only had a single red light on the roof. Not as rococo as those overloaded racks on the top of the blue cars today. They were minimal and functional."

"Yeah. Sleek, and the sirens sounded different back then. It was a rising and fading oscillation. More subtle."

"It was a more classical siren sound, and there was more *information* in it. They were *green*, for god's sake. You probably know this too, Denny, but there are hundreds of young artists I've met who have moved to New York from some other state or country, and they don't believe me when I tell them that the police cars were once green."

"I think they have a couple on display at some museum of police history or something," Denny concluded, locking eyes with Billy. "When you break reclusion, we'll check it out and see the green police cars."

"You're talking to me as if we were at the fucking circus and I was a kid who wanted a balloon." Billy was more perplexed than angry. "But a postcard of a green cop car *would* be valuable. We could show it to these new arrivers who think you're putting them on when you talk about the police cars being green."

"In L.A. they're black and white."

"Yeah, like those cookies."

"I love those cookies."

"Me too," Billy agreed. "You should bring a few the next time you come over. Seriously."

"Doesn't this hermetic quarantine, or whatever you're calling your self-imprisonment, include a fasting?" Denny could see this inane banter could go on endlessly and he'd had enough.

"Fuck, no. I haven't eaten much, but I eat what I want," Billy replied, ignoring Denny's disdain. "Actually, a fast would be something my body could use, no question. Marta would know all about that sort of stuff. I'll mull it over. *Mull* is a great word, isn't it? But for now there's an amazing bakery on 20th and Eighth Avenue. So, next time you come, just bring the fucking cookies."

"Go fuck yourself," Denny said, walking out the door.

Billy paced back and forth. When he was young, he always loved going to the zoo and watching the large, graceful cats pacing in their cages, but his stride at the moment had nothing to do with that. It was awkward, with no rhythm. He looked at the television, wondering if he had thrown himself too deeply into its blurred promises.

Of course, anyone familiar with Billy knew that, during his early years, he had changed from a lonely kid, utterly obsessed with the magic that flowed from the ten-inch screen on the console in his living room, to a young man with a passionate contempt for the box. Billy had been unable to bear television since the day the paramedics took his mother to the hospital. As they had lifted her frail body onto the gurney and carried her out of the apartment, the TV had flickered in the background, through her delirious protests and weak dry coughing, playing an episode from a series about a handicapped detective.

Billy could never really figure why he impulsively borrowed his assistant's bulky portable television that first day home. Perhaps he snatched up the TV hoping that, after many years, a renewed relationship with it could provide an effective way to relax, if he maintained control and moderation.

Waking on the 16th morning of this TV marathon, Billy fixed his eyes on the same shimmering rectangle that had been running an episode of *The Twilight Zone* when he'd fallen asleep the night before. Something was wrong, however. The old screen was now filled with nothing but crackling shards of impenetrable interference. When he turned up the sound, it vacillated from a deep, steady hum to indecipherable fractures and squeals. After rushing groggily into the kitchen and snatching up a full quart of juice, he knelt before the flashing box and began rotating its tuning dials, with the precision and diligence of a thief picking a safe's lock. After readjusting the antennae and turning plastic knobs until his wrist throbbed, he saw that all the other channels had also completely lost reception in a dense blizzard of black-and-white static. Billy decided to leave the frustrating old machine as it was. He now recognized it as just another intercession of fate. After lowering the volume, he kept the set on.

Billy sat at the kitchen table, puzzled by the TV clunking out overnight. Marta, who was making eggs that Billy would most likely refuse, reminded him that it was a very old model. She had learned that when he didn't have a viable reason for complaining about a problem, no matter how large or small, it was best to just speak to him in broad, and often moronic, generalizations.

Perhaps the tolerable reception from the old rabbit-ear antennae over those first nights was a fluke, he thought, and the antiquated apparatus could simply no longer sustain it. They were surrounded on all sides by tall buildings filled with complex electronic devices that snatch up the signals other stations transmit. The fact was Billy had no idea what had caused the change. It could have been anything from an influx of solar winds to some highly charged gadget that the kinetic sculptor was testing three flights above him.

Over the next few days, he walked thoughtlessly past the bulky contraption, barely noticing the shards of bad reception with his peripheral vision. On only one occasion, he stopped and studied the thick black-and-white static that silently snapped on the screen. It was like he was staring intently through a window and watching a dense blizzard steal all the visibility outside. Billy found this image particularly unnerving. He decided he wouldn't be wasting any more time staring at the broken TV. He considered turning it off, but forgot about it when Marta yelled out, asking if he cared for a cup of the mate that she was preparing.

One afternoon he knocked against the antennae and the images immediately turned clear. Astounded, he turned up the volume and dejectedly realized he'd chanced onto nearly perfect sound and picture just in time for the world championship of pocket billiards. The idea of watching two minuscule men playing pool on TV didn't thrill Billy. He had hoped, if the television set had again begun to operate, it would be during a western or police movie, or some other mindless entertainment. Billy's eyes, however, were surprisingly drawn to the screen to see this event, and as he lay back on the bed watching the two players, a strange sensation began moving through him. It wasn't painful, but pleasing, as if his body were being softly rocked by his heartbeat's steady thump.

The main camera view looked directly down at the table, as if the lens were embedded in the light fixture above. It was odd to watch the TV from this unique, descending perspective. Billy was watching from, literally, a bird's-eye view, and he felt the pleasant throbbing grow as he remained glued to the screen until the show had finished.

Billy's eyes were fixed on the tiny men battling each other, and from time to time he parted his lips with a sly grin of satisfaction, as if recalling an inside joke. When the championship was decided, he immediately felt deflated and depressed that it hadn't gone on longer. He could have watched for another two hours, and finally leaped off the bed, with that smile widening on his face.

Of course, Billy hadn't forgotten that Denny and he had spent much of the winters during their early teens hanging out at the neighborhood poolroom, Mister Eightball, but until he saw the fluidity and grace of the competitors striking the cue ball, he'd failed to remember one of the most salient events from those days.

This winter refuge was in the basement of a small building beside the subway station on 181st Street. The entrance was at the bottom of a long flight of stairs, giving the place the seedy, subterranean quality required of all successful poolrooms.

Without question, Billy's most distinct memory of Mister Eightball took place the night a professional player came to give an exhibition. The shaggily dressed man sashayed from one shot to the next with nonchalant intensity, using English that caused the cue ball to move in ways that defied the laws of physics. The teenage boys sat captivated, watching the man move seamlessly around the table, oozing with complete control.

The two competitors shooting on the television undoubtedly possessed amazing skills, but Billy's memory of being in the presence of the balding man that night, feeling his quiet, pulsating confidence, made a far greater impact than the flickering images on the screen.

Aside from his remarkable talent, the disheveled figure with the checkered jacket understood the full extent of his capabilities and limitations. The cue stick seemed to become an extension of his arm. He was one with the table, so involved with the game that there was no room for other bothersome realities to intrude.

Walking home that winter night, young Billy had also recognized the grueling years of work it must have taken the visiting pro to attain that level of expertise. The dazzled teen was convinced that if he could adapt the confidence and dedication of this pool player to his own work with art, he could have a shot at success.

Billy hadn't thought about Mister Eightball, or even this particular experience, for years. Apparently, that exhibition had imprinted Billy so powerfully that its consequences lay dormant deep within him until they'd finally surfaced that afternoon.

The next day he called a well-known billiard supply house in Brooklyn. "I believe I'll soon have a rather large order for you," he assured the man on the other line, who smoked a cigar with such passion that Billy could sense it on the phone. Finally, he gave him the necessary information and requested the man rush him a copy of their catalogue with all due haste.

11

A week later, the phone rang. Marta moved to pick it up but was stunned when Billy, gesturing and waving his arms manically, rushed over to the extension beside the sofa and snatched up the receiver. It was the first time she had seen him answer the phone in years.

The manager from Monarch Billiards Company informed Billy that his pool table would be ready for delivery that afternoon. Billy checked to be sure the gravelly-voiced man had the correct address and asked him to send out the truck as quickly as possible. He dressed and fidgeted as he straightened the place up and made preparations. He realized that taking the freight elevator and letting in the workmen meant skirting the strict parameters of his reclusion, but Billy no longer cared. Still, he had to explain this dilemma to Marta.

She listened with a puzzled look, then, with a strange smile forming on her lips, quickly answered that he should do whatever he thought best. She also assured him that this period of solitude had served a purpose, though it might take time before he understood it fully. Marta didn't hold any of this against Billy. She understood his anguish and hoped this fascination with pool could help Billy return to the painter she once knew. Otherwise, Marta was simply growing tired of all these strange, foolish changes, and had her own issues to deal with. They had been kept buried long enough.

Billy had looked, on and off for the past three days, to find the ideal location for the table. He'd made up a list with a variety of requirements, and eventually found the most suitable space in the front of the loft, beside his own bedroom. He marked some measurements in chalk and stood in the center, scanning it through his painter's eyes. Billy realized that, after all these years, his artistic perspective had become an inescapable reflex action, and he understood it would always be as if some doctor were thumping his knee with a tiny rubber mallet.

Jotting some more numbers in his leather notebook, he sat at the large kitchen table, picking at a muffin. Billy waited two more hours before the bell rang. He took the freight elevator down, then jumped into the truck's cab and guided them to the elevator entrance. Within minutes, the driver parked, pressed a button, and the doors to the rear of the truck slowly lifted. Five burly men, who had been riding in back, immediately lowered the table on a motorized platform. Using a minuscule forklift and brute strength, they cautiously transported the hefty object from the sidewalk to the freight elevator. The workers didn't view the rickety wooden lift with confidence, but Billy stepped in and gave them a smirk tinged with enough sarcasm to question their manhood. They had to accept the challenge of this puny painter and rolled the lift onto the thick, knotted floorboards. Billy transformed the smirk into a reassuring smile, and the heavy load rose with a slow but smooth resolve.

Seeing they would have to pass through a doorway, the workers hoisted Billy's precious cargo onto its side and held it secure as the hand-operated lift moved across the wood floor. As they rolled through the studio door, he guided them down the hallway, around the kitchen table, and into the front section. He'd already placed four chalk marks on the floor where the table's legs should be set.

When deciding on this optimal location, Billy took a number of factors into account. Obviously, he needed enough room on all sides for his longest cue sticks to shoot unimpeded from any position.

Billy had also spent nearly an hour scurrying around on his knees, measuring the inevitable gradients in the floorboards with a level while jotting down the results on the back of an envelope. No floor is perfectly flat, especially in a building as old as this one, but he was surprised at the minimal amount of incline, which meant the job of correctly balancing the table would take much less time than expected.

After the movers had aligned the object with his tiny chalk circles, Billy squatted beside one of the legs and began to fiddle with the leveling apparatus that he'd read about. The driver of the truck, younger and much smaller than the others, leaned in and whispered to Billy that he happened to be the technician who usually performed this task, and would gladly offer some advice. There was no anger or envy in his voice, but instead he sounded bewildered and slightly amused that this stranger could do his job with such precision and speed. Confounded, the technician rambled on, explaining that most of the company's clientele were older people swimming in wealth, who probably purchased their product strictly as status symbols for the pleasure of their guests.

As the fellow spoke, Billy never offered a word in return, continuing to tweak knobs as he checked his level, now placed in the center of the forest-green felt. Each of the legs had a clever device built into it that could regulate its height, utilizing the same pneumatic principle as a jack for changing a car's tire. Since Billy had calculated the differentials fairly accurately beforehand, he finished the process in less than half an hour.

The billiard company's mechanic peered at the level, whistled in astonishment, and told his men to gather up their equipment. They loaded everything back onto the elevator and Billy ran them downstairs. Back at the truck, the movers stood with their gear, waiting for the truck's mechanical platform to lower. A suddenly ebullient Billy took the opportunity to shake their hands, handing each a $50 bill. They wished him luck and ascended to the back of the truck, where Billy noticed them lounge into two deep sofas facing each other in the back. At the door to the cab, the young technician stood staring at this unique customer, showering him with compliments on his ability to set up a billiard table. He told Billy the balance of its surface would meet the standards of any professional tournament.

"Coming from an expert like yourself, I appreciate that," Billy replied, his eyes clanging like bells. "It would be disgraceful to possess your establishment's excellent table if the balls didn't roll true, without the slightest variant. Lately, I've had a vague feeling I am on the verge of a significant personal project. If my suspicion turns out to be correct, I owe a great debt to your company, which was an immense help in getting it under way." The truck pulled out with the driver shaking his head.

Back upstairs, Billy immediately unpacked the boxes that accompanied the table, stacked against the wall by the crew. They held every accessory required to play the game properly. Every piece of equipment painstakingly chosen by Billy from the Monarch's thick catalogue looked as good as it had in the glossy pictures . . . all top-of-the-line. The first box included three sets of perfectly balanced balls, wood racks in assorted shapes, and a satin bag filled with cubes of chalk. The other box contained a movable storage cabinet, over five feet tall with locking wheels. Its glass door sealed tightly, protecting the enclosed pool sticks from the elements. Opening it, Billy found his two-piece Balabushka, the Stradivarius of cue sticks. Billy laid the top of the grip on his open palm to check the balance, and it felt as if he'd gone to the showroom for a personal fitting.

Having transformed the front of the loft into a private billiards parlor, Billy gradually escaped deeper into the soothing complexities of pocket billiards. The game provided the ideal state of calm he needed after each day of not working in the studio. He grew mesmerized by the sharp solidity in the sound of the balls colliding against each other. Eventually, the noise built into an overwhelming surge that echoed through his head, as if he were playing within a canyon. He kept discovering new facets to the game and its appeal steadily continued to escalate.

One evening Marta found him crumpled over the pool table, his body trembling.

"The slightest thought of facing a canvas right now makes my stomach cramp up," he murmured. "I've never missed a deadline, and the thought of actually failing . . . "

"We can work it out . . . no matter what the problem is," Marta offered softly. For the first time in years, her internal dialogue switched to her native language. She even began uttering soothing words in Spanish.

"God, I've been so stripped down. It feels like, instead of skin, my body is covered with cheap latex that I could peel off, layer by layer . . . right down to the bone. I'm lost, empty, and alone, Marta. How can I work, feeling this way? How can a mess like me paint again?"

Billy's voice was getting louder and thinner with every sentence, and his phrasing was strange. He would speak in bursts of three or four words, then awkwardly take in breaths, making what he said sound less like a bold confession than a series of quavering fragments without cadence or emphasis. When he finished speaking, his body slid clumsily downward until he was sitting on the floor with his arms wrapped around his knees, his forehead pressing against interlaced knuckles. He began to cry steadily, but suppressed his tears. His chest heaved and he made a peculiar grunting sound in his attempt to keep everything in.

Marta was on her knees facing him. "Calm down. Relax. Breathe slowly and let yourself relax." Marta herself let out a sigh. She couldn't bear to see Billy in such a state. The pain was so much deeper than she'd ever imagined; it felt like a thin wire was tightening within her, strangling her heart. At the same time, she was afraid. He was so complex and vulnerable—especially at this moment—that she feared saying the wrong thing. She wanted to call someone, but she knew that was out of the question. She would simply have to follow her heart's direction.

Marta took his wrist, stroking it caringly. He was blathering indecipherable words, which sounded like the bleating of sheep. It sounded like he was being whacked in the stomach by a baseball bat. She could feel his pain by the weight of the sounds.

"I lost it," he said; there was a trace of growing anger in his voice, and to her there was something exciting about seeing him in a state of rage. "I lost it, babe . . . the passion, the edge, the instinct. Just lost it. *I am lost.*"

He winced from a sharp pressure in his empty stomach. Marta just wanted to get him to his bed and let him lie down and sleep. She slipped her arm around his back to support Billy's weight and hoisted him up with her hand beneath his armpit. She was surprised by the ease in her strength. His legs moved like those on an extremely drunk marionette.

"You just need to rest now," she whispered as she guided him to his bed. "Everything that had to be done is taken care of. I do understand you. How can I have ever misunderstood you? Now your body must rest."

"Marta, I'm so sorry that you had to be part of this. I didn't want you to see me like this," Billy said, lowering his head and turning it toward her.

It was another look she could not read. But there was a devastating intensity in his stare.

"Don't be silly, now." She was choosing her words with caution. "You . . . who have treated me so well. We all get upset. Would you not do the same for me? Now lie down . . . easy."

Billy was supine and lay on top of his rumpled dark green sheets. Exhausted and trying to check his shuddering, he looked up at her. He had on a robe, which had opened to reveal his long jean shorts and T-shirt. He had lost weight. She kept her eyes on him and knelt down with one leg on the bed, accidentally brushing across him while trying to pull up the top sheet. He uneasily reached out for her hand and held it firmly.

Marta put his hand to her cheek, then walked to the door and hit the light switch. The tired radiance drained from the single bright lamp, and the room was black, save for the living room light bending at the door. Billy let out a tiny moan.

"What is it?" she asked. "Are you all right?" She moved a step closer to the bed.

"I just got bit by the darkness," Billy said. "It stunned me. I feel funny, Marta. I'm a wreck. Will you stay?"

"Oh, my poor sweet." Marta had never used that term with him before. It just burst out by default from her tired, besieged feelings. They had developed one of those relationships where they both felt too close to rely solely on names, but were afraid to use pet names or endearments. She moved with quick tiny steps, as if avoiding broken glass on the floor, and slid into the bed beside him.

She was on her side, gazing with concern at him. She was wearing a peasant blouse, whose neckline had already fallen beneath one shoulder. He hesitantly turned to face Marta and she smiled, saying, "You are comfortable now." It was a statement, not a question.

Imperceptibly, Marta's upper body curved, like a bow, closer to Billy. He first felt her thick hair sweeping across his shoulders, then her mouth damply came to rest against his ear. "Now I too am comfortable," she whispered.

The wedge of light from the door shone on the couple like disturbed moonlight. He inhaled her unique female fragrance as his eyes moved across the supplicating arc of her body. The entire room seemed wet and enveloping in his dark fatigue, encased by this aroma he'd never experienced.

Marta took pleasure in the meticulous curiosity of his eyes as he scanned her body. She could only think of all the time wasted and how this was what he needed now. This was surely what he wanted from her . . . it was in the measure of his stare. She straddled his body. Her green eyes pressed down rapaciously on Billy and she flicked her tongue with total abandon along her lips and into the air. Her hands were on his nipples, squeezing tightly, then her thumb receded and her forefinger circled them at varying speeds. Billy was nailed in place. He didn't know if it was the day, the exhausted vulnerability, or the exquisiteness of her tongue unfettered to the air. This was what D. H. Lawrence was referring to when he wrote the phrase "going to the dark gods."

Marta slipped off her blouse and shorts. Then, before he could protest, she unsnapped his pants and withdrew his cock. It was no different than Billy, half bewildered, half aroused. Wet, and hissing through clenched teeth, Marta straddled him again, and in one deft move, squeezed her fingernails into its base while insistently shoving the engorged head of his miraculous hard-on inside her. Billy had no idea what had happened, but suddenly felt a staggering contraction, as her inhalations grew louder.

Marta squeezed his cock harder, then moved in slow, steady gyrations, intermingling her lips and tongue with his, caressing his testicles with supple fingers. She let out two unrestrained moans, her legs quivering with preternatural speed. Billy felt the same snake moving up his spine as the day in his bathroom so many years before. There were no interruptions this time, however, and Billy lost all passivity to the moment and his masculine instincts. Grabbing Marta's classically rounded hips, he slammed her up and down on his perfect erection until he began to shudder in orgasm. Billy released with such force, he feared it would hurt her. Marta finally collapsed off his body, her hand remaining beneath his shirt, digging the razor-sharp nails into his chest one last time. From a painfully deep place, Billy let out an extended groan, purging his body of all the exhaustion, anger, and exasperation from that distressing day. The sound was like a long, random fusion of feline sighs, fluctuating from the satisfied purr of a house cat to a mountain lion's ominous growl. In time, Billy's eerie, uncontrollable exhalations ceased their frightening vacillations, and morphed into the equally odd, yet soothing cooing of a dove. This sound continued as Marta, who was facing his back, thrust her breasts with such force against each side of his spine that he could feel the pressure of her taut nipples. She then wrapped one arm around his waist and playfully lowered her hand down to Billy's testicles, clutching them gently and securely until they both had fallen asleep.

He woke very early the next morning in a bizarre collision of desire and trepidation. Mostly there was regret. He had wasted so much time overcoming the curse uttered in his mother's doctrinal ignorance. Now he had fulfilled what he'd assumed was unattainable. He had validated his masculinity and awoken a part of his humanity he had thought dormant. He was a man. He had been with a woman. He could intuit the resonance of its mystery and command . . . the dominance and submission, the tender, indelible wonder of her female scent.

He had made an enormous trade-off. He felt hollowed out. Yesterday he was disorientated and perplexed about not being able to paint, but it seemed something ephemeral, a phase essential to his growth. He had not lost his *hope*. Now he had bargained that away, and it seemed a drastic mistake. He still defined himself by his art. It was all he knew.

She had slit his tendon, he thought. The sensations of her female gifts—the warmth, the motion, the moistness, and the mystery—had kept him blindfolded as his locks were being indifferently shorn away.

He watched the steady breathing of her body beside him; the rhythmic rise and fall of her breasts. He lingered on the sharp arc beneath her ass, the abrupt curve of her richly colored flesh returning to her thigh. He was tripped by ambivalence, and felt his puzzled bitterness vacillate into rage. Everything had changed and it was all too quick to filter. His instinct had nothing to offer.

He looked down and saw his penis, now stealthily, defiantly erect. He marveled as it twitched rowdily by its own volition, making its own unprecedented demands. With this uncomfortable hunger, he knew the dark gods had returned. He was now overcome with another, baser aspect of his revivified masculinity.

Marta woke and smiled at him, eyes glowing and her lips moist with satisfaction, desire, and a complete ignorance to it all. Sleepily, she began to reach up at him with her hand. Without a word, he seized her wrist and pinned both hands against the green sheets. Her skin was so smooth, her arms thin as a sapling's branches against a green sky.

"You've been sleeping with Denny, haven't you?" Billy stared down accusingly. "Tell the truth."

 PART THREE

1

The opening was star-studded. Billy found himself desperately clutching the sleeve of Denny's jacket as they moved through the gallery. A loud hum was rising from the circular clumps of chattering parvenus. Through these dense clusters, Billy could see fleeting bits and pieces of his paintings on the wall. Concentrating low and to his left, he caught a strip of dark red, and five feet upward, he glimpsed two ends of a thin blue arc. One end curved out of the breast of a slender woman wearing a metallic dress, then converged with the shoulder of a man's cashmere jacket. This chance connection of two objects with a stroke of paint finally focused the star's attention, replacing his dread with a momentary calm. Within half a minute, however, a burly member of some German film crew carelessly shoved the wheels of a large spotlight into the back of Billy's legs. Billy quickly turned around, disoriented and beginning to panic. His arm instinctively reached out and felt for Denny, searching the space around him like a blind man.

The musician had already slipped off to greet an old friend he'd spotted on a sofa in the next room. With a panicky Billy stranded and shuffling in place, three overly perfumed young socialites saw their opportunity, swooping in and assaulting him with cautiously worded but pointless questions. In response, Billy's hands made a futile array of gestures as the puzzling phrase "I don't think ready to lose . . . and then can't say" shivered out of his cotton mouth.

Though it was barely half an hour into the ordeal, Billy was beginning to feel woozy and he seriously thought about bolting. Alone once again, he found himself staring directly at a familiar sight that always evoked a shiver of suspicion. It was the ubiquitous coterie of "true believers."

These small, dense groups of die-hard aficionados were in attendance wherever Billy Wolfram's art was shown. It made no difference whether a multinational corporation was unveiling a large sculpture in front of its midtown headquarters, or a small Massachusetts museum was displaying two early collages recently donated by a private collector. They would gather around each new piece, invariably standing in the same semicircular shape, gawking.

It would appear ungrateful, if not altogether incongruous, for any artist to hold his most dedicated fans in such contempt, but Billy couldn't help himself. To make matters worse, they consistently acted with politeness and respect. During the countless times he had seen them over the years, not one had ever tried to approach him. They were either so shy from awe, or intent not to intrude on their idol's *privacy*, that they barely made eye contact.

Billy had come to believe that he somehow owed them for their unwavering devotion. Yet at the same time, he felt none of these sycophants had the slightest notion of the struggle and tension an artist must endure to produce even a single piece of work. None of them could know of the descent he'd undergone to finish those neat rows of luminous squares that hung on the wall. They had no concept of the recent transformation his personal life had taken. He himself had no idea if he could possibly ever recover from these changes.

Billy realized he had never felt a single moment of pleasure as he stood before any of his finished pieces. The actual process of creating—taking the journey from the first to final brushstroke—provided a genuine sense of purpose, but he was unable to relax and find the release and contentment that his contemporaries seemed to experience in their completed work. Billy only noted the flaws. These feelings were particularly bitter tonight because of the turmoil he had endured while putting together this show.

Though it was impossible, Billy tried to avoid the people staring at his work. Most of those invited were heading immediately for the bar anyway. Many were business executives who didn't get out of the office until 6:30, and who, with two quick martinis, drained away the workday, then mingled through the crowd, checking out the skirts. Others planted themselves and continued getting sloshed on the free drinks. Every straight man in the room was well aware that art events were a mecca for picking up women, and all gay men in the room knew that art events were a mecca for picking up other men, usually with far greater success.

Billy glimpsed a particularly captious critic passing straight ahead. The bulbous little man was covered with an uncanny shadow that somehow accompanied his every step. It had to be some trick in the new lighting system installed for the show. These nights were filled with every element of the art world's psychological paraphernalia that Billy detested. As he saw it, attending openings was the nadir of an artist's career. Only tonight was worse.

After the opening, about 90 collectors, critics, and general luminaries of the art world gathered for a sit-down dinner at a hotel down the street from the gallery. Tippy had reserved the elegant ballroom for the night. Billy thought it a little ostentatious, but the affair was his last chance at finding Marta. He couldn't believe she would miss it.

Billy plowed hesitantly through the side aisle, searching for his table, and a hand reached out from the crowd gathered around the bar and snatched the sleeve of his jacket. It was Franz Kubiac, a Swiss minimalist who had been living in New York since the sixties, now ensconced on a stool, sipping a martini. His work was also handled by Tippy. He congratulated Billy on his show and offered a few anecdotes concerning their mutual dealer. Franz's voice slurred and it was clear that he was already drunk, but Billy always liked the guy and wanted to hear what he had to say about Mr. Shernoval.

"Let me just relate one anecdote about Tippy," Franz confided in his effeminate whine. "It speaks volumes, believe me. I was still a fairly young painter, just beginning to get some recognition. I was part of a group show at my first gallery and finally seeing some red dots beside my name—I don't know about you, but I find those horrible red circles so tacky. They remind me of elementary school. If you wrote some hideous memory of summer or whatever—and your handwriting was decent—then the teacher would stick a gold star to the top of the page. The dots are just more gold stars to me.

"Anyway, Francesco and I were in the kitchen at Tippy's place down in the Village after some maudlin reception," he continued. "Tippy'd kept calling all night and pestering me to come over to his new apartment. Eventually I relented and we took a cab uptown with some friends.

"I knew he wanted to sell me on showing at his new gallery. The idea was out of the question. I was doing fine where I was, and I've never been big on change. Unfortunately, Tippy, as you well know, can be so damn charming. We had smoked some reefer—this was in the late sixties and everything was *Sgt. Pepper's*, you know?

"By now everyone else had left, and four or five of us sat around, stoned and carrying on. I remember we got real hungry, but the fridge was bare except for three brown eggs. Everyone had brown eggs back then. Meanwhile, Tippy is cursing out his housekeeper because she never shops. I know now that, at that time, he had no housekeeper. We searched through the kitchen. Aside from the eggs, there was nothing to eat. I finally spotted a box of gourmet pasta on a high shelf of the cabinets. Now we had the pasta, but no sauce.

"That's when I got my first glimpse at Tippy's true character. It might have been the grass. Who knows? He's at the stove, boiling water and tossing in the pasta. Then he's over a bowl, casually separating the yolks from the brown eggs. Before I know it, he's dumping a colander of pasta onto two fine china dishes. I'm wondering what the hell this idiot is doing. The floor of the kitchen is a mess of noodles and sticky egg white. He whisks the yolk with a whirlwind wrist motion, and pours this raw glop over the pasta. I thought it was disgusting, but watched as the eggs began to cook from the heat of the freshly boiled pasta. I have to admit that I wolfed it down and was quickly filled. It tasted like rubber bands topped by some chalky flaky stuff, you know? It was the ingenious idea that was impressive. You had to admire the quickness with which he sprung into action, and the outlandish quirkiness of his ersatz recipe. I realized that it was all attitude and fast hands. There was nothing to the resulting meal. It really sucked."

"Exactly," Francesco, Franz's longtime lover, chimed in. "I felt the same thing. See, he dazzled us with the motions, the flash, and the ingenious concept. It was all very impressive. To my untrained taste buds, it seemed pretty good. However, the truth is that it was the culinary equivalent of smoke and mirrors. All style and flash, with no substance. It really had the texture and flavor of rubber bands. That's the way everything is with Tippy."

"Why have you stayed with him all these years if that's the case?" Billy asked.

"Simple . . . I got a contract saying my accountant handles all financial matters. He can't cook my books or doctor the numbers with charm or diversion. I let him do his hype thing, which is what he does best. He can shovel the shit and give the media the old razzle-dazzle. There's no denying that."

"No question," the lover added. "When it comes to connections and hype, there is nobody better. Just keep him from your money. A word to the wise."

This was a disturbing allegation. Billy didn't deal with sudden complications well. The racing thoughts turned faster and darker.

Franz went on, "I was young and naïve when I first reached an agreement with Tippy. That man knew how to stroke my ego until I felt like the planets revolved around me, always making clear that he plotted their orbits and kept the machinery running. Anyway, around that time, Francesco and I were attending some big charity fund-raising banquet. It had nothing to do with art, and we're sitting there with six strangers, but guess who was holding court at the adjoining table? I swear . . . it was the legendary Grannie Vonsawitch, who was *at least* 101 years of age at the time. You know she actually slept on Gertrude Stein's sofa at the age of 14, after running away from home in Louisiana. I once got to hear the tale from her. Gertrude and Alice found this very disheveled, yet striking, urchin in Washington Square Park during their Sunday morning stroll. The tiny fugitive was dancing to a plaintive dirge by a lone Italian fiddler. They fixed her up and sent her on her way back home within a week.

"Anyway, within ten minutes, who arrives and casually takes the seat beside Granny? Tippy! Granny's asked him to be her escort. Apparently, the two were very close friends.

"When he finally noticed us sitting across from him, Tippy rushed over and stood behind me, massaging my neck as he began to loudly hype me with his famous wit and humor."

"Well, Tippy *is* funny. I'll give the idiot that much," Francesco joined in. He'd looked as if he were going to sleep on the bar.

"I agree, babe. He always manages to make me laugh. The problem is he never knows when to stop. That night he followed every compliment with some stupid, but funny, personal crack. I felt so uncomfortable about all these strangers staring at me as he raved on as if I were invisible. I mean, the man was pimping me out to this wealthy gay crowd like I was some new bathhouse.

"He then crossed the line and started to ridicule Francesco here, who was very young at the time. He made crass remarks about his small stature, then started on regarding his age, and in effect called me a pedophile."

"I was 23, and new to this culture," Francesco said, again rising from his bar nap. "I did not think such things were proper to speak of, and certainly not in public."

"Francesco tossed his drink all over Tippy's body . . . ice cubes, lime twist, and all. People were speechless . . . even Tippy, who retreated to his chair. The only emotion on his face was confusion. He looked like a man who had shocked himself while trying to fix a toaster.

"At the intermission, Tippy came over to apologize. Surprisingly, Francesco, my little firecracker here, accepted graciously and told Tippy he would pay for his shirt to be cleaned. Tippy looked up at him and casually replied, 'Don't worry about it. I'm leaving now to take home Granny and then going straight to my place. I'll just pour some sparkling water on it. That stuff gets out any stain. I swear . . . everything will wash right out.' He took the bewildered Granny's arm and walked away, laughing deliriously."

"As I told you, the man is funny," Francesco echoed. "You've got to give him that much."

Excusing himself and finding Denny waving at a table beneath a strange bluish light, Billy had no idea how he had made it through the opening.

This dinner party was going to be insufferable. He sat on a thinly cush-ioned chair and clutched Denny's arm like a frightened first date.

"You'll make it," Denny whispered emphatically. "They love you. Look at it from their point of view. You always used to babble on about the need to put yourself in someone else's shoes if you really want to care about them. How that's the workingman's version of the Golden Rule, right? Well, I never knew what the hell you were saying when we were kids, but I get it now. Look around, my man. These idiots love you. You have control. Seize it, man. Now that you're certifiable—and I mean *really* certifiable, as corroborated by the New York City Department of Mental Health—you have to listen to the madder voices in your head. Just say whatever you want. Hey, tonight you are the man. It's your party, and you can fucking cry if you want to."

Halfway through the meal, Denny sauntered over to chat up a model at a nearby table. Billy looked hesitantly around at the seven other com-panions they'd chosen haphazardly to join him for dinner. He didn't rec-ognize any of the names on the place cards. A rotund woman, wearing a black beaded bustier with a brooch the size of an anvil, suddenly launched into a discourse on Billy's recently installed sculpture across the plaza from City Hall. It was quite large and had taken six months to finish, but he still hadn't been down there to check it out.

"Your art is important to the public good," she stated bluntly.

"I appreciate that," Billy replied hesitantly, "but your statement leads me to a question. Does such a thing as a 'public good' exist?"

Billy quickly scanned the table. Fourteen eyes locked on him, jaws dropped. He felt as if he were being sunburned beneath the assembled gaze of the red-silk-tie crowd. They were stunned that Billy had spoken with such authority. He knew at that instant that Denny was right. Now was the time to either make the point for once in his life, or just sit silently and sink into the quicksand of the *Bardo*. He'd reached the end of his proverbial rope.

"I meant 'public good' in the sense that art can be a means to some end," the brooch woman, whose breasts were resting on the linen table-cloth, answered. "It depends on what the viewer brings to the work."

"Maybe . . . but perhaps there's no end point for the means to reach." Billy had made his choice. He sat upright in his chair, as if about to stand at any moment. "Everything and everyone is in a continuous flux. That's an old and valid concept, but this contemporary flux is so enhanced by artificial means that we have lost control of the changes. In fact, they control us. The airlines decide when we'll arrive and the media decides what we will feel. The city—for that matter the entire world—imprisons us with speed. Very few people have time to waste on art."

"We're here tonight, aren't we?" The woman's husband, a balding man with a tie that looked stained from teardrops, feebly leaped to her aid.

"I see that and I appreciate it. I really do." Billy pushed both hands on the linen and stood up. The entire room focused their attention on him. "I'm only saying it's possible that there is no finality. If there were, we'd never bother to do anything, because it's the learning and execution that make it all worthwhile. It's the journey that matters, not reaching some obscure destination. There's no need to rush simply because taxicabs and tall, stunning women in six-inch heels are coming at you from every direction. That's one of the problems with living in this damn city. If everything's available to you 24 hours a day, then you're lost. All this speed and convenience only desensitizes you.

"Then a problem arises and people don't know what to do. They've become so used to having the solution handed to them that most of the public have become a bunch of automatons, banging over and over into a wall, pretending it's not there. When you reach an obstacle, all you have to do is step back far enough and look. There's always a way around it.

"Returning to the topic, which, if memory serves, was 'public good,' I must ask again: does it exist, and, if it does, then how can it be served? I think the first question is the only question. It will *always* be served because there is always mediocrity available to serve it. You'll get something in a space that is *called* art. That's simply politics as usual . . . a function essential to the bureaucracy and the need for the government to fool themselves and the public they serve. There's one irony. Naturally, there will always be avaricious artists willing to do it.

"I don't know why everyone seems so surprised. I'm asking a very basic question and you are looking at me like I'm responsible for the catering of this morbid affair. Is there such a thing as public good? That's all I'm asking.

"I mean, is your good the same as my good? I doubt that seriously. So, if we do not agree on a common sense of *good*, then how can there be any larger public good? I ask these questions with complete conviction.

"What about some homeless person who sleeps on a heat grating down the street from that sculpture? Does he feel the public good when he stares up at this excessive interplay of metallic shapes? More likely he interprets this art through the way its form and function are relevant to his life, making this piece fairly useless. Such a lost soul's aesthetic viewpoint is overridden by the terms of his subsistence. Maybe he feels frustrated and hopeless that a behemoth made almost entirely of metal contains no surfaces large enough that he could use as shelter from rain or snow. Seeing the abstract metaphors, analogies, and conclusions that they invoke, or just laughing at the artist's pretense or the corrupt visions, which are particularly rife as this century comes to an end, requires taking your bank account for granted. That's a fine luxury for those with places to sleep and clothes that are clean."

The people around his table were listening and sat silent, astonished that the shy Billy Wolfram was speaking so passionately. It was so out of character. Billy understood this. His eyes were scanning the faces of the onlookers when he felt Denny's hand grip his elbow. Denny had returned to the table when he saw Billy flapping away and was now trying to lend some moral support to his friend.

The fact was, even Denny had no idea what had brought on this outburst, but he was feeling quite good about it. *The worm has turned for little Billy*, he thought.

"There will be some small segment within the public aesthetic that will need art," Billy continued after two large sips from his wine, "but that has nothing to do with goodness. I don't think so, at least. Those who are in favor of it will provide a dialogue and, within this debate between the many individual tastes, they might find some common ground. These commissioned works will inspire the most fortunate to rediscover the imaginations of their childhood. That's good, but is it public good?

"A painter can't worry about what anybody viewing his work thinks, and that includes the critics. The equivalent would be a writer writing a book with one eye fixed on Hollywood. You have to just do it, and later hope someone can lock into it, finding something that hits a nerve.

"It would be fine by me if we all could be *locked in*. That's the phrase my friend and I use to define a state of free flow between artist and audience, whether you're alone and painting at the canvas or fronting a band before fifteen thousand raving fans. The medium is irrelevant. For example, my friend, who I believe you know, likes to sing into a gooseneck microphone. For some reason, I love the sound of *gooseneck*. It's a very evocative term, and a wonderful example of the power of words.

"Even now, when I say *gooseneck*, I 'lock in,' and my imagination soars. It's because the image it evokes grabs me by the collar and elevates me into the sky. All of a sudden I am flying south for winter with thousands of Canadian geese. Each flock is in a V-shaped formation, like the head of an old spear. I feel like I'm with them up in the sky, as their wings flap lazily through the dawn.

"You'll have to pardon me. I am not much of a speaker. Also, I am, as you all can tell, I'm sure . . . very nervous. As you know, my work is confined to the studio and I am more comfortable in that solitude. See . . . I've once again gone off on a tangent, and it's best if I return to the matter concerning the existence of a public good . . . and, if it exists, how art can figure into it.

"I believe nothing is provided by the art itself. Instead, the public debate over the *quality* of art might serve some kind of function. I'll admit that art does provide a service. Whether these benefits have anything to do with good, I can't say. That's completely subjective, and therefore not binding in our discussion.

"Since I've already gone on longer than I could have imagined, there's one more point I feel compelled to make. I think it's germane to the topic. One thing's for sure, there will be no meeting of minds if our elected officials continue to slash funding for public art—mainly because of their own antiquated tastes and moral codes. There will certainly be no 'locking in,' as I've explained it, because the aesthetics will be proscribed. The overwhelming majority of Americans will dismiss anything but the most rigid, conventional art, and quit paying attention to anything but their solipsistic lives. That's when the real trouble will begin, and existing in a nation of philistines will be the least of our problems.

"Of course, I'm sure you are all aware that such a state already exists to varying extents. Dealers and the cognoscenti now groom artists to their own manageable standards. I won't mention any names, but many contemporary artists have paid too much attention to the trends, and hobnobbed much too closely with the media, the collectors, and the dealers, who ostensibly work for the artists themselves. In doing so, the artists have let them consume their passion, edge, defiance, and their souls. All they have remaining is technique, without passion or the courage to carry it out.

"Gone are the so-called good old days of the Cedar Bar crowd, when rugged, alcohol-chugging giants of the fifties would sweat over a painting for days, or, using welding torches and rivet guns, construct sculpture the size of dinosaurs out of scrap iron and I-beams.

"They're all dead now, and their legacy seems light-years away from contemporary artists, some of whom sit at Formica workstations, creating new programs on their computers. These modern-day court painters, like puffed-up house cats, smugly profess to scratch the hand that feeds them. In exchange, they are paid off, pampered, and—while their backs are turned—declawed.

"Every one of you recognizes what I'm talking about. You're the ones who buy the work of these Ticketmaster artists. It's fine by me. It's your money, and if that's what you want, then hit the galleries and snatch it up. There'll be plenty more where that came from.

"Who knows if any good might come of it? If you truly desire to serve some purpose, all you have to do is think for yourself and begin to pay attention. You can start by writing your congressperson and telling them that the arts are going to the dogs in this country. New York is still the art center of the world. Putting aside that little jeremiad I just made regarding a few of my peers, there are still plenty of painters and sculptors of monumental talent working here in this city. There are also so-called outsider artists who struggle away, anonymously and without recognition, throughout America.

"Perhaps if young artists could find some affordable housing. If they could check off the box designating their occupation as 'artist' on a short form at Motor Vehicles, on the lease to an apartment, or a passport renewal, without others nearby snickering about how such a designation is an excuse for pretentious bums that have no talent and are too lazy to find real jobs that make money. If, in conversation at parties, they could introduce themselves as painters or poets with their heads held high, like in most European countries, on a level with doctors and lawyers, rather than having to deal with stares and denigrating remarks. That would be a more immediate method of serving the public good, rather than heaping praise on more established artists and their newly installed sculptures."

While the assembled aficionados sat gaping in silence, Billy stared . . . his eyes fixed in a fugue trance, his slender jaw quivering involuntarily. Denny stood and hugged him theatrically. He leaned over and spoke directly into Billy's ear. "Beautiful, man . . . I've never seen you go on like that. Apparently, going crazy agrees with you. I mean, they totally *bought* that bullshit."

"Hey, I was completely serious, Denny!" Billy insisted, sitting down. He was uncomfortable with his own didactic outburst and unnerved by Denny's assumption. The truth was, by the middle of his rant, Billy really hadn't known if he was making sense or tossing out pure gibberish.

"Well, no matter. You're learning," Denny insisted. Then, in his best impersonation of Max, he stage-whispered, loud enough for everyone around them to hear, "Well done, Billy Wolfram, well done."

Usually Billy was annoyed by Denny's impression of the late dealer, which was eerily on target. Billy was always susceptible to superstitions, particularly anything to do with death. He thought discussing such matters was unseemly. This time he smiled back at his friend. He knew Max would have had a similar response had his mentor been there, and Billy wished so badly that was the case.

Perspiration was trickling so heavily down Billy's forehead that he could barely see, so he dabbed his napkin lightly against his brow, then unfolded the starched linen and placed it in his lap. His eyes were still drenched, however, so he lowered his head and wiped his face once more.

He tried to focus on the woman across the table, but his sight kept getting weaker. Billy almost panicked, convinced he was going blind. He held the napkin underneath the table and examined it with his fingers, expecting it to be soaked. Instead, the linen wasn't even damp, and when he raised the other hand to feel his forehead, it was also bone-dry. Frantically, he began rubbing his eyes with the sleeve of his jacket, like a child with a runny nose. His vision returned immediately, just in time to catch perfect sight of the others, who were scrutinizing him uneasily. It wasn't sweat but tears that had caused his temporary blindness. He'd been weeping openly without being the least bit aware of it. He didn't want to waste time trying to find a rationale for crying. He'd save that for the doctor, along with the thousand other mysteries he needed solved. He excused himself from the table and made a beeline for the men's room.

Wealthy, powerful tongues wagged throughout the entire room, debating the merits of his tirade. It was so circuitous and obscure, none of them was able to say for certain if Billy was putting them down or offering a visionary plan for the future of art.

As he entered the elegant john, an overeager attendant handed him a towel, which Billy neglectfully flung into an adjoining sink. Staring into the mirror, utterly disoriented and lost in thought, he used his cupped hands to splash cold water over his face.

The watchful attendant became slightly nervous. He noted the way this fellow discarded the linen towel as if it were some dishrag. Billy's eyes were so vacant he looked hypnotized. Stepping backward, the attendant cautiously asked Billy how he felt.

Billy's hair, face, and shirt were thoroughly drenched. Reaching to retrieve the tossed towel, he recognized how upset the old attendant sounded. He smiled at the man and insisted he was fine.

"You know what they say about people having more fear of speaking in public than dying? Well, sir, believe me when I assure you it's quite true, and I was seriously worried I'd be doing both." The perplexed employee was won over by Billy's hasty joke, and handed him a fresh towel, returning to the mundane tasks of his profession, which normally did not entail subduing a madman.

Billy nodded his thanks, rubbed his red eyes, headed to the far urinal, and began relieving himself. Right above him to the left was a small window fitted with opaque glass, probably locked shut for decades. His attention was caught by a sound like a coin tapping gently against the pane. He turned to the towel man, but he was dozing off, sitting with a paperback in his lap. Billy then heard a weak yet familiar voice from the other side of the dense glass and focused on a diminutive figure moving about on the ledge. Though it was impossible to see any detail, Billy made out the dark silhouette of a bird. As it turned out, it wasn't a coin tapping the window but a curved beak furiously pecking against it.

Again the voice spoke from the window ledge outside. The actual words still remained inaudible, but this time Billy easily pinpointed those vocal characteristics. The raven had returned.

Billy hastily peeled off a $50 bill from a roll in his pocket and slipped it to the attendant, requesting he take a break for an hour or so. Stuffing it into a fake leather wallet, the weary worker left without a single question.

After staring down the corridor until the old bastard had shuffled out of sight, Billy locked the door and dragged the attendant's chair across the floor. Placing it beneath the window, he stood on the seat and worked desperately to pry open the frame, sealed shut by time and the changing weather. For 15 minutes, Billy used the attendant's shoehorn to chip away the dried paint, and then gave the sill one last shove. Though he nearly herniated himself, the damn window finally slid upward.

Though he'd wished it were all another delusion, he'd correctly identi-fied both the voice and silhouette. The raven had indeed arrived, and the figment of his imagination was hopping angrily back and forth across the outside ledge, immediately berating Billy for how long it took him to open the window.

"I don't even have human digits on my talons," the bird screeched, "but I can unfasten the lock to my cage at the zoo in under five seconds."

"That's great. I see you haven't changed." Billy assumed being bitter and recalcitrant was simply the nature of an immortal black bird capable of talking, mind-reading, and other gifts, which remained God-given and unrevealed.

He was wrong. Despite its initial harangue, the obstinate little wiseass was putting out a different vibe than during their previous encounters. Though difficult to perceive, the dynamics between the two were almost cordial. For a creature so ambiguous, the raven's moods were its most puz-zling characteristic.

Its tiny talons stepped to the inside ledge, where it cocked its head and relaxed. The bird was exhausted and could barely be heard. Its eyes pen-etrated directly into Billy's skull and Billy experienced an unprecedented calm. It was quite a feat. For the first time since he'd cracked, Billy felt a semblance of control.

As for the bird, its fatigue soon subsided. Despite its age, the raven had an immortal's stamina, and it quickly puffed out its breast and broke into Italian. The language's forceful, rolling intonation demanded complete attention, as Billy's imagination conjured up a landscape where the empty bathroom suddenly transformed into an open plaza, packed with receptive onlookers. The increasingly enigmatic avian immortal was taking on the inflated dictatorial appearance of a tiny Mussolini, perched on a stone balcony.

Once again, the analogy crumbled as the shiny creature sucked in its plump torso, ceased issuing demands, and dropped the "language of love."

"By the way, you have no idea how close that old attendant was to summoning the authorities and having you arrested." The raven had returned to one of its favorite dialects, that of an English aristocrat.

"You're showing off again," Billy replied, without comprehending how serious the raven was. "Convincing me that you're also capable of reading minds. Your continued reappearances have forced me to accept you're not a product of my dreams, so, unless I'm insane, I suppose I'm willing to concede you any powers. Why shouldn't I?"

"I wouldn't phrase it in exactly those terms, mate," said the raven, switching to a cockney idiom. "You've been questioning your sanity since she left."

"Quiet!" Billy should have seen it coming, but was again caught off guard, forgetting the extent of the raven's powers.

"I understand why you're losing your temper," the bird said, trying to calm Billy. It had undergone a complete transformation from the first night at the loft and now acted with genuine concern. "It's time you made some very personal choices. I'm quite aware you wish to evade the subject, but it's crucial that you pull yourself together."

"You are unrelenting, you know?" Billy was tired and in no rush to return to his table. He also figured from the way it was acting the bird might be able to offer some valid guidance. "That's fine with me, but you've got to cease with the bullshit. You must stop playing around, and stop evading the truth. Simply fill me in on whatever you know. If you are banned from some subject by some divine fiat, I will accept that, but just tell me up front that this is the case. Now, please answer me one specific question: do you know about the night that Marta and I made love?"

"*She* was making love!" The raven spoke in a deliberate monotone. "You didn't know what the hell you were doing!"

"Are you here to crack wise again, or offer practical advice?"

"With all the stress you've had to endure lately, I'm simply using a bit of levity to lighten the mood." Once more, the raven was acting out of its ordinary character, addressing Billy with an undeniable compassion. It then boldly raised its wings and flew around the bathroom, finally perching on the door of a toilet stall.

"And though I'm bending the rules slightly, I advise you to remain optimistic. You see, your company is more enjoyable than that of most of the other painters I've dealt with. Though the word has not been part of my vocabulary for over a millennium, I might even *like* you."

Billy was surprised by the compliment but knew it was only a pretext for the bird to change the subject and ramble interminably about some blast from his past. Since he'd acknowledged the vociferous predator was for real, Billy considered its endless penchant for dropping names was not only justifiable, but also inevitable. Apparently, the bird only associated with people of very high stature . . . all masters in their respective fields.

"I was speaking about other painters, right?" the raven queried.

"Yes, you were, and you better be quick about it." Billy checked the clock, worried the old guy was about to return to his domain and discover the door was locked and the window somehow forced open.

"Don't fret about the geezer," the raven reassured Billy. "That lush headed straight to the gin mill down the block to suck down that fifty dollars, and there's still forty-five left on the bar. Besides, I can fly out of this dump before he gets within fifty yards of that door, and—as I'm certain you'll agree—shutting the window will be far easier than prying it open. Just relax and sit on the sink. I assure you it will hold your weight while you listen.

"Gauguin was a challenge. For nearly two years, I urged him to get away from Europe and go somewhere else. As long as he remained in Paris, it was impossible for him to concentrate on his painting. I'm sorry to say it, but the man had problems.

"Every day, this nitwit was pursued by a mob of thugs threatening him because of money he owed from gambling. Aside from that fiasco, he wasted the remainder of his meager savings on whores.

"I suggested taking a long trip on some ship, but he insisted he was fine. Ultimately, I verbally portrayed the islands of the South Seas, describing their dark, docile women, the perpetually mild weather, and, naturally, the distinct light of the Pacific. He was attracted to the idea, yet remained hesitant. What was going on?

"Finally, he caught a schooner to Tahiti, and fell in love with everything about it. As the sails were being hoisted in the harbor, I flew out and alighted on a lower mast. When I inquire why he'd been so reluctant, the traveling painter bolts to the side and vomits, then wipes his face, and sheepishly confesses that he suffers from *maladie de mer*.

"I'd spent nearly a decade attempting to relocate this so-called genius, rescuing him from his squandering habits and protecting his bony ass from Basque ruffians, all because of seasickness! If he'd chosen to tell me this sooner, even in those days of crude medications, I could have flown east and procured some herbal substance that would have greatly eased his distress.

"*Merci!* An eternal bird's lot is never easy, but Gauguin was a piece of cake compared to Cézanne! He was the most impossible Impressionist of all! You think a scavenger like me takes any pleasure spending time looking at all that damn fruit in his studio? He also was so stubborn, patronizing, and without a shred of patience. You couldn't tell the buffoon anything.

"I was there under orders to interject his style with something that would distinguish him from the other Impressionists. I figured nobody else was delineating the figures in their paintings with a thick dark line, bringing the viewer's attention to them. I tried everything and then used a different approach.

"One afternoon I shed a feather, and it spiraled from the windowsill and onto the floor of his studio. He raised the feather up to the light and returned to the canvas he was working on. He placed the feather up against the work in progress, which involved some old men playing cards.

"It took awhile before it dawned on him, but finally he mixed the exact shade of black as my wing, and, before you could say 'ungrateful peon,' started outlining every figure in the painting in obsidian-black lines.

Later that night, he feverishly rushed through his older pictures and did the same.

"From that day on, this rip-off artist completely encapsulated each new piece in that black outline. All along, this was what I had desperately wanted to tell him, but I couldn't get his attention. He possessed no patience. The hack just ignored me, making no communication at all, verbal or otherwise. At that point, some quick salute would have satisfied me. I'd have settled for a lousy wink. It was as if I didn't exist!"

The raven was literally hopping mad, recalling Cézanne. Billy wondered if the painter had done something that the raven, for whatever reason, didn't want to admit. "Were you talking in the same manner you do now?" Billy had to bring it up. "I wouldn't admit you were real that night at my loft."

"The possibility of my being a dream was acceptable to you. That wasn't the case with Cézanne. I visited him in the middle of the day. I remember the heat, not to mention the smell that permeated everything in that century. For the first three afternoons, I calmly remained on his windowsill, which was rotting from termites, and addressed him politely, without any of the frivolous accents or hyperbole I employed on our previous encounters. On the fourth day I squawked so loud that a neighboring farmer's prize bull went berserk and charged a large scarecrow, held secure by an iron pipe, and knocked itself unconscious. I must admit being amused by the irony of a scarecrow knocking out a bull, especially since ravens have always been confused with crows."

"Sorry to ask," Billy again interjected, "but what exactly is the difference?"

"That's not the point!" The bird again flapped angrily, but remained perched above the door to the toilet stall. "Suffice to say the disparity is similar to that between midgets and dwarves.

"Also, because of your sly, provoking questions, I refuse to complete the final anecdote involving my encounter with Cézanne." However, as Billy suspected from the feigned tones of the raven's voice, it wasn't genuinely offended. The fact was, its little threat was a put-on, an attempt to amuse the young man, who was back at the sink, tossing handfuls of water on his face and neck. "Then again, your sarcasm does not affect me, and it would be ill-mannered not to finish my account of the swell-headed swine's character.

"Worse than all his other flaws, he was a stingy and tightfisted miser. After finishing his lunch, it wouldn't have hurt him to lay out a few of those leftover bread crumbs for a well-mannered raven at his window. Let him rot!"

The raven became disturbed and roused. Billy wondered how he might placate the dark bird, but he was in a men's room, for god's sake. It began flailing its wings.

"The old man is walking through the revolving doors as we speak." The bird looked down at Billy, his splotchy face, and the suit sliding from his thin frame. His tone then changed. "Billy, the solution to many of these recent problems can be traced back to your past. If you look back and contemplate with utter, harsh truth, you will find the source of your pain. Next, I implore you to remember this so-called zone is more important to an artist than the art itself. Recover it, and you'll rediscover God."

2

Billy wanted to believe in the raven, but he knew he was what clairvoyants called "susceptible." About a year after his meteoric rise, Billy fell victim to an art world scam of pre–World War Two origin. He never denied being fleeced, despite years of Denny ridiculing him as a "hapless sap." Billy took pride in his naïveté. He still held to his bizarre practice of offering anybody one shot with his trust. If he caught someone in a lie, Billy considered that person another asshole he'd never have to deal with again.

Unlike other schemes, this didn't involve any larcenous gallery owners, curators, or dealers connected to the art world. Postal agents traced the ruse to professional con men using the mails, and since they continuously moved about the country, changing addresses, none were ever convicted.

The most sophisticated of these operators had the savvy to spot young painters destined for success and would pounce on them when their reputations, along with the price of their work, had escalated to a suitable degree.

After the fact, the stunt seemed so preposterous that most victims were too embarrassed to admit being taken in, and denied it had ever happened. However, despite their protestations, many were indeed suckered in, especially if the perpetrator was among an elite coterie of very adroit old-timers who were as proficient at their work as the artists they were ripping off.

Basically, it was a variation on the age-old ploy of tugging on a person's heartstrings as a prelude to taking him in. Billy succumbed right after the Museum of Modern Art acquired its first canvas from him in 1974, and he never had any problem owning up to it. Whenever the anecdote came up at a party, he gladly recounted all aspects of the experience, particularly to talented young artists. The incident was mainly an embarrassing cautionary tale for them, and they couldn't understand the bizarre note of pride in Billy's voice.

It began when one morning, among the usual bills and invitations, Billy found a square purple envelope and opened it with a butter knife at the kitchen table. It contained a letter on cheap stationery that had a red lily embossed in the upper right corner. A small snapshot from a cheap camera spilled onto the table. The photograph showed a boy, probably about eight or nine years old, standing against a white wall in pajamas. His head was mostly bald, except for a few clumps of russet hair. The child's complexion was pale, with a slightly olive-green tinge. His red-rimmed eyes, filled with wonder and defeat, peered out from behind thick eyeglasses. The photo was so disturbing that Billy placed it facedown on a shelf and read the letter. As he unfolded it, he realized that it was also scented with cheap perfume.

> *Dear Mr. Wolfram,*
>
> *Enclosed you will find a photo of my son Timmy. Though I hope to God above that I am mistaken, it may well be the last picture taken of him. Timmy has an acute form of leukemia, which, I'm sure you know, is a cancer of the blood. I will spare you the wretched details, except to say that I am at the end of my rope. I had heard that a relative can donate marrow of the bone to replace the crippled cells of the poor boy, but they said that this is a different strain of lymphoma, which is particularly rare and virulent. I don't understand these medical terms, sir. Tomorrow he will have his third and final bone marrow transfusion. The specialists attending him are not optimistic.*
>
> *I am not, by any means, a wealthy man. My insurance does not cover this stage of the operation, but I am by no means soliciting money. I am sure artists like yourself are wary of letters like this*

from a total stranger. I hasten to assure you that this is not my intent. Instead, I would ask you for a gift greater than money. Though a workingman with little education, I have developed a great appreciation for contemporary art over the last ten years. The frayed prints of your recent work that line Tim's hospital room (I have basically been camped out beside the boy for the last month, sleeping in a cot that a night nurse generously provided) have afforded me the solace and strength necessary to get me through his wrenching ordeal. Tim appears to find pleasure in them himself, often recognizing images that I could never dream of finding. I am convinced the colors themselves provide a diversion that alleviates the pain, if only a little bit. I suppose we all find our support where we can . . . and while we can.

I feel obliged to say without any hesitation that your work is—in my insignificant opinion—the most powerful and moving of any young artist working today. You could provide Timmy (and myself) with the greatest of rewards if you might bring yourself to do a small drawing of my son from the photograph enclosed. I do not expect some photo-realist depiction, though I maintain that your abilities as a draftsman are without peer. Any manner in which you might choose to portray this courageous and long-suffering child would be beyond my most fervent hopes. I only ask that you sign the work. If you perchance hurry, perhaps Timmy might see it before he is wheeled into the operating room.

God bless you.

Richard Castrate

Later, Billy reexamined the note and recognized how the writer's use of certain anachronisms—particularly "perchance"—should have tipped him off. He didn't even notice the outlandishly cocky pseudonym the rip-off artist had used to sign the document. These clues were easy to find in hindsight, but Billy was caught up in the sentiment. There was no sense denying it: he had been hooked.

In a way, Mr. Castrate impressed Billy not only with his criminal skills, but also with his enormous acumen on the subject of art. Naturally, this sort of thing, no matter how skillfully contrived, only works the first time, which means the con man has to be a diligent aficionado of the arts. He was probably an avid reader of *Art in America* and *Art News*. If the guy had wanted to go straight, he could, no doubt, have made an excellent dealer or critic. Not only because he was a felon, but because he possessed a wickedly insightful knowledge of the contemporary art scene.

Simply put, this charlatan could distinguish the moneymakers before most critics, not to mention his flimflamming rivals. Aside from this cunning, his other gift was speed. In effect, he had to beat the competition to the mailbox.

Since that original letter, Billy had received dozens of similar, but inferior, solicitations. He had immediately tossed them out. When Marta took the job of organizing the studio, she would file them away in a large manila folder, believing that some of the letter writers would be caught and prosecuted someday, and the file would be essential evidence. She had a sense of American justice only an immigrant could maintain. Billy had tried to disabuse her of that notion, but he thought it a good idea to hang on to the letters because, despite their larcenous intent, the more polished ones had a bold finesse bordering on the poetic.

Wanting to believe, Billy had rushed to his drawing table and knocked out a pencil-and-charcoal sketch. He quickly executed a basic line drawing from the photo, accentuating the child's wide, startled eyes. However, he omitted the half-parted lips, with their wounded-doe expression of dread, and substituted a slight smile. Billy wanted to instill some sense of hope in the boy.

He incorporated a hummingbird hovering above each of the slumped, frail shoulders, even added some color to the wings with a nearby assortment of felt-tip pens. The remaining facial features were exactly the same as the picture. Billy then subtly shaded the portrait, trying to instill some semblance of light from above without seeming religious or maudlin. All in all, the hasty portrait was uncannily similar to the photograph. Billy was playing to the writer's flattery of his proficiency as a draftsman, but he saw it more as a challenge than an exercise in vanity. Satisfied with the finished product, he snapped a few Polaroids from various angles and placed them in a pile for Max. He then walked back into the kitchen and slid the piece into a large bubble-padded envelope. He printed the proper address, but didn't seal the flap, deciding to include a short letter in return.

> *Dear Tim,*
>
> *As you see, I have drawn a picture of you smiling. You can glance at it when you feel any pain or sadness, and see how happy you will look after the doctors make you all better. The main thing is to have hope, Tim. We must never give up our sense of hope. It is what makes the hummingbirds come and buzz right beside our ears, like little angels.*
>
> *I can feel you getting better as I write this. You're getting stronger and your dad is there to keep you safe and he'll get more nice pictures for you. Just be stronger than the pain, Tim, and keep your eyes on the hummingbirds.*
>
> *Your good friend,*
>
> *Billy Wolfram*

Billy sent out the package that same day, and it took three weeks before he told Max, who'd been in Europe on business, about it. The dealer came over to the loft and Billy showed him the snapshot of the boy, Richard Castrate's letter, and the Polaroids. He didn't mention including the letter he had written back.

Max explained the entire nature of the fraud to Billy but immediately added that there was no reason for him to feel foolish about it. He listed a number of Billy's fellow artists, some very famous and old, who had fallen for the same routine. He told Billy that this swindle had been used since he had arrived in America in the forties, and even mentioned the name of the man who was most likely responsible. Billy was astonished when Max told him that the guy was a painter himself, who had moved to Florida about ten years earlier.

"If it's the guy I'm thinking of, he's succeeded in cheating many of your peers with the same routine, and always gotten away with it," Max said. "He moves around and changes addresses so often neither federal nor state law enforcement have ever been able to make a case against him."

The dealer took out a magnifying device and studied the evidence, and finally dropped everything back onto the table. Billy watched in suppressed amusement, thinking Max made an unlikely Sherlock Holmes.

"Well, I'm certain now," Max said, delivering his conclusion with a wince. "There are too many similarities in your letter and the ones sent to painters from my previous gallery years ago. Mainly, I'm convinced by this photograph, which is a duplicate using the exact same child. This fellow has been using it as a trademark for at least a decade. I'll wager that, many years ago, the guilty party either found it on a sidewalk or stole it from some wallet, perhaps belonging to a relative. This child must be in his twenties by now.

"It's too bad, because it appears from these Polaroids that you gave up a sweet little drawing. Are those hummingbirds? Unfortunately, it's probably now in Miami Beach or Los Angeles, hanging beside other stolen works in some collector's private office. I'll bet it's in an unbearably tacky frame. I'd say he paid at least $10,000 for it. Don't feel bad, Billy, just chalk it up to experience."

When Billy told Denny about it the next day, his friend almost burst a bladder laughing. "You are the most gullible bastard I've ever known. You should have your certification as a New York City street kid revoked. Your name, and all images pertaining to you, should be struck from the obelisk behind the Met in Central Park."

Over the years, Denny never let up on his friend about his naïveté. While other artists vehemently denied ever having sent a drawing or even a signature to a fan, Billy never saw any harm in it. To him, it was a litmus test of one's skepticism in viewing the world. He had a different take on it than the others and made no apologies for that.

This was the way Billy always imagined he'd go through his life. Some of that optimism might have changed over time. Perhaps it was stolen from him, yet Billy had no regrets about sending that drawing. Nor did he give a damn about where it was now hanging, or how much money it had fetched for the thief.

3

After his ordeal with the raven, Billy sequestered himself in a small dressing room behind the ballroom's stage. The room was furnished with two leather couches and a wall of early Blane sketches for small sculptures. Between the two couches, a small table held a silver bowl with assorted fruits. On seeing this room, Billy had his first I-could-live-here moment in a very long time.

Naturally, Tippy had arranged for all this. He was hoping Billy might eventually appear at the podium to thank the assembled throng for attending and, possibly, say a few words about the new paintings. Billy suspected Tippy, who possessed a theatrical streak that rivaled his ambition, cared more about getting there himself and introducing him. Billy knew all about it. He'd noticed Tippy, holed up in another dressing room, working on his speech, scribbling changes in its margins. Seeming satisfied, the shrewd bastard had capped his Montblanc and quickly slipped the neatly folded manuscript into his suit pocket. The introduction must have been nine or ten pages long, single-spaced, and in type large enough for him to read without his glasses. Vanity was another of Tippy's endearing vices.

For all his shortcomings, however, there was no question that the tireless dealer took excellent care of his artists' needs. The sofa was so comfortable Billy could easily have spent the night sleeping on it. He stretched out on it and opened a bottle of mineral water. Drinking through a straw as he raised his feet onto the arm of the sofa, Billy recognized two barely audible voices from down the corridor. With the curtain lowered, Denny and Elsa were quietly conferring on the stage. He jumped up and, cautiously cracking the door, listened to their secretive whisperings, which sounded like radicals planning the last details of some intricate conspiracy.

He couldn't miss Elsa's thick East European accent questioning the wisdom of popping in on him without any warning.

"At the very least," Denny mumbled, "she definitely must go back and say hello. With the amount of people attending this shindig, someone is bound to tell him she was at the show. Everybody has a fucking motive. Either a grudging, bitter prick will throw it in his face out of spite, or an innocent fan, unaware of the true story, will just let it slip out."

"Either way, we have to handle the situation so he doesn't lose any progress with his shrink."

"That's a decent point, but I say we drop all the psychological crap and confront the inevitable. Billy has always been a master at concealing his true emotions."

"We'll let her make the decision. I think she's coming onto the stage."

Billy now recognized a third voice. Marta had arrived and was greeting the two conspirators. He stealthily closed the door and retreated back to the couch. Billy had anticipated this moment since the morning he'd awakened in an empty loft, and he now sat shuddering in fetal fear. Anxiety swept his mind blank. He'd forgotten all the apologies rehearsed while shaving before the bathroom mirror, and every expectation vanished as he listened to her voice, still defiantly clutching the last vestige of her Argentine accent. Within minutes, there came a faint knock on the door. Billy didn't answer. The second knock was accompanied by her voice.

"I know you're in there, Billy." Marta's tone was soft but insistent. "Elsa and Denny assured me. Please open the door?" Billy knew that if he didn't open it, she'd do it herself. He was amazed there was no lock on this backstage door. In the movies, actors are always locking their dressing rooms when drunk or suffering from stage fright. He decided that, if she was still angry, she wouldn't have come. Marta wasn't the type of person who latches on to anger or sustains a grudge beyond the course of a night.

She must have had another intention. By the time he swung open the door, his fear had shifted into guarded optimism.

One thing had not changed: Marta was as beautiful as ever. He stared at her and couldn't bear the tension. So much needed to be said that it all collapsed under its own weight. Billy fell into a reverie, as was his way. Unable to fly far away, he lowered his eyes and his mind lifted upward to the past.

Elsa had been the first to observe a peculiar phenomenon about Marta: "Are you aware that nearly all of Marta's features change at various times? Sometimes I have seen her appearance transform almost instantaneously. It's amazing!"

Though skeptical of Elsa's observations, Billy had witnessed these bizarre transformations himself, particularly in his assistant's eyes. He said to Elsa, "Marta and I were eating lunch, and one minute her eyes were clearly green, the color of jade before men overlooked its unrefined, primeval mystery for the emerald, which isn't appreciated for its clarity and brilliance, but its vulgarity and flash. Jade has permanence, with the subtlety and power of a panther's breath. As I glanced across the table, they shifted into an iridescent blue like the flame from one of those candles that float on oil. At first I attributed the cause to the angle of the sunlight entering the room through the window, but they returned back to green.

"Later, I thought I witnessed her skin color vary up at the loft. A shade of brown that never remained the same for more than 20 minutes . . . and in the middle of an NYC winter. One moment her face was the color of a concentric stain left on a sheet of typing paper by a mug of very light coffee, then it darkened . . . the tint of one of those thick manila envelopes. Perhaps her skin varies with her mood like one of those gimmicky rings from the seventies. Can she make her facial characteristics fluctuate according to the light, location, and time of day? It's one thing to use the metaphor 'like a chameleon' when describing a volatile or impulsive person, but imagine if she really could control it."

"Oh, I am seriously not believing she is aware of it," Elsa said. "I'm very much sure she's oblivious to these changes. I once pointed it out to her and she thought I was making a joke to her."

"I agree with your every word. Marta is not like some salamander, adapting to her surroundings. But her facial features definitely do transform. We've seen it."

Marta kissed Billy on both cheeks, breaking his reverie. "I've been wracking my brain over whether I should be here tonight, but all the while I knew I'd never miss your show."

"I was nervous too," Billy said, keeping his vow to remain candid. "When I finally saw your face and that little smirk, I almost lost it. Still . . . it's strange. Why didn't I see you in the gallery?"

"Oh, I was certain you would leave as soon as possible, so I waited across the street in a girlfriend's parked car. When you and Denny snuck out of the gallery's back door, and—with your heads down—rushed to this hotel, I quickly crossed the street and entered the gallery. They informed us that the dinner was about to begin at the ballroom here. I didn't care to eat with strangers at one of those tables, so I just squeezed into the corner of the bar, slumping low on a stool and nursing a margarita. The bartender and a few of the waitresses must have assumed I was hungry and kept slipping me plates of appetizers. Actually I've usually found the so-called side dishes to be far more delicious than the main course." Marta paused and looked around the room, then at Billy.

Billy sat down on one of the couches and gestured for Marta to do the same.

"I loved how you placed the middle panel of both triptychs diagonally on the rear corners of the main room," Marta said, still standing. "Since you had to fit them directly on the corner angles, the central panels protrude outward, and those pivotal canvases appear to bend as walls intersect behind them, randomly fluctuating from concave to convex."

"You don't need to say another word about the show," Billy immediately replied. "I knocked the paintings off to fulfill the deadline." She continued to ignore his suggestion to sit down, and he wondered if someone was waiting for her on the street outside.

"If you don't want to talk about the show, we won't. But I insist on giving you my opinion, which is my right. I liked it and I don't care how it was done. If nothing else, the one thing I could always trust that you truly cared about was my take on your work. Has that also changed?"

"No, you don't understand. I thought you were just placating me by talking about a safe subject. Please, just sit and talk to me. Of course I've always relied on your opinions, more than I ever really understood, and I still do. I'm just too confused and nervous at the moment to explain anything, but please, Marta, consider staying. Your presence will calm me. I've been waiting frantically for this opportunity. God, I'm glad you came." Billy started to cry.

Marta approached and wiped his face with a napkin she'd yanked from the fruit bowl.

"Blow your nose, now," she ordered him in a motherly tone. "Don't blow too hard, however. That can be bad for your ears."

When she'd finished cleaning Billy's clenched features, Marta sat across from him on the opposite sofa. She looked him squarely in the eyes, and Billy was so startled that his head tilted upward. She smiled and told him that she was probably more nervous than him.

In 38 years, Billy had never been with a woman who was both sexually and emotionally attracted to him. He had finally lost his virginity but was still grasping for what had caused him to blurt out those abusive words that drove her away. For some reason, despite finally surmounting the years of impotence in that timeless moment, he was caught so off guard that his own sensitivity had completely shut down. It had all gone blank as she straddled him with such tender dexterity, rocking him until he encountered the exquisite burst of physical release.

Given his limited experience he had no way of knowing, but Marta was clearly an experienced lover. The moment her green eyes had blasted straight through his, and the wind that followed them rushed through his brain, Billy had recognized how astonishingly oblivious he'd been to her unrequited love. When he unexpectedly got the chance to reciprocate that love, he had instead accused her of sleeping with Denny. It was one of those unforeseen paradoxes reserved for children and idiots.

For years she'd been harboring feelings for him in silence. All those nights when they sat on the sofa watching movies, she had desired him.

What a dimwit he had been, how blind to the unspoken gestures that transmitted her passion. Since Marta wasn't privy to his secret, he had been unable to explain himself or use his naïveté as an excuse. Why hadn't he told her? Probably because he feared she'd see him as pathetic, and he couldn't deal with such a thought.

He had often wondered if his genius was linked with his sexual absti-nence. He'd pondered this throughout his reclusion, and concluded it was nothing more than hubris and self-deception. But he couldn't shake off all those years of justification; whether the idea was spurious or not, part of him was still concerned that his sexual deprivation was the source of his creativity. He couldn't suppress the thought that Marta had shorn his locks like Delilah did to Samson. Was the seduction—or the gift, depending on how you looked at it—now going to rob him of his capacity to produce any-thing worthwhile? He was afraid the time had finally come to face up to his past work and recognize that all of it was nothing more than a ludicrous self-indulgent delusion.

Still, on this lunatic night of this umpteenth opening, he more than ever needed to check out all the suspicions. Was it possible to have both his lifelong commitment to art and an instant of ephemeral gratification? He'd never completely sublimated the idea that there was little separating a painter and a priest. Women would distract him from the devotion nec-essary to his vocation. At the moment, such evaluations and speculations were moot points. Billy had no means of comparing the two, especially since his abrupt transformation into manhood had transpired barely two months ago.

Billy finally began speaking and didn't breathe again until he was done.

"I'm so terribly sorry. You are the last person in the world I'd ever let anyone hurt, and I did it myself. Please forgive me. Please stay . . . I can tell you're already about to leave. How is that possible? We need to talk. There were certain circumstances that I could never reveal, even to you. When I was very young, certain traumatic events took place. They scarred me, but I'm getting help now, and I'll soon explain if you give me some time. I don't care at all what's taken place since you left, wherever you went. I appreciate now how much I need you."

After his confession, Billy immediately shut down, gazing forward in a stupor, confused and overwhelmed.

"Billy! You are slipping away from me, and I will not allow that. I want to hear everything, and the only thing that bothered me about what you just said was the last line." Marta was smiling as she continued. She seemed to be speaking English with less of an accent than a few moments earlier.

"Of course you *need* me. It goes without saying that I've always helped you. That was the problem . . . You treated me as another helper . . . a book-keeper and secretary. I know that I wrote of all this in the letter I left you. Nevertheless, certain things must be said face-to-face." She paused to make sure he was ready to listen.

"The man that I love must want and desire me, and be able to make love without any interference from foolish, paranoid intrigues. As we did, until you opened your mouth, sounding like a teenage boy from high school. I'm talking about love in all of its aspects, both the physical and the emotional. When two people are truly together, they need to trust in each other's love, that's the main thing."

Marta shifted forward on the sofa, intertwining her hands as if she were about to pray. The green of her eyes remained, but there was more intensity in them. Billy had no idea what was coming.

"Among other reasons, I think my main motive for coming tonight was to learn why you burst out at me so unexpectedly that morning, with such cruelty and immaturity. I'd never imagined you capable of asking such a startling question. Whatever happened, its effects have caused pain and resentment between us. I'm now beginning to see that you've had the harder time. I empathize with you, Billy, but now is not the right time for such a conversation. Let's just celebrate the success of your show, and we'll discuss everything else at a more suitable time."

Billy didn't know what to say. He agreed with Marta that they shouldn't get into anything heavy, yet he didn't want to go back to the party. He just wanted to be alone with her in the tiny room.

"Billy, do you remember how close we felt on that awful day Max was buried, consoling each other during the car ride, and holding hands during the service? Though I loved the man, I went along to commiserate with you, and you, in return, gave me a sense of safety and calm. That's what love is about, sharing in each other's triumphs, and comforting each other in misery . . . all with absolute trust and confidence. There is always the prospect of sadness and risk, but that's the price of all love's splendors. I always imagined that you, of all people, with your work so reliant on instinct, would agree with me."

Marta could see Billy's body tightening into a ball, looking tense and uneasy. She fell silent, aware that Billy was uncomfortable. He always attempted to become round in shape when he felt ill at ease.

"I'm sorry. We agreed there would be no more references to the past." She stood up and began massaging his neck with amazingly strong fingers. "My God, Billy, your muscles are taut as a trampoline! I want you to relax. I'm good at this."

Marta still had no idea of the enormous changes that Billy had gone through, and there was no reason she would. Being completely out of touch until tonight, she couldn't comprehend the effect her absence had had on the painter. Billy was unraveling to the core because he was finally being forced to deal with his awkward, contradictory behavior toward women. After slowly relaxing the pressure, she removed her fingers from his neck. Billy instantly longed for the return of her touch.

"Please don't leave. I'll try to explain what I can. First, as far as the new paintings are concerned: they're not connected to anything I've done before, and art is of little importance these days."

"Art is your life!" Marta was upset. "I can't listen to such talk. What are you saying?"

"I must tell you that from the moment I got up that morning realizing you'd left, my life has morphed into a miserable melodrama."

Billy's worst fear had been never seeing her again, because either she was unwilling to forgive his blunder or she had met someone else. There was another possibility, but Billy didn't want to consider it. During their time apart, Marta might have lost her feelings for him. Perhaps he was too passive in his lovemaking. Maybe she had determined that Billy's true devotion would always be to his art, something she could never compete with.

"My obsession to constantly create doesn't excuse my behavior," Billy said. "Oh, God, Marta . . . I'm lost without you. I need your heart beating beside me at night."

Marta asked Billy, who was the epitome of reticence, how he managed to bring himself to see a psychiatrist.

"It was your suggestion scribbled on that envelope," Billy said, his words traveling slowly across the room. "I'm not completely cured, but I've learned techniques to control my anxiety attacks, and I'm doing better with the racing thoughts. This shrink I'm seeing told me I was so lost and over-loaded inside my private reality that my mind simply needed to escape, so it ran off like a tethered dog that keeps pulling until its leash snaps. Thinking back, I realized I'd always felt this way throughout certain periods of my life. I assumed it was only a puzzle or curiosity, and, once it subsided— as it invariably did—could be dismissed as some momentary glitch. I'd be willing to bet there are a lot of people out there who have similar experi-ences but cannot articulate them and suffer silently in frustration, or self-medicate."

To Billy's consternation, the door suddenly flew open. Both of them were startled by the sudden infringement and Marta let out a quick man-gled shriek. Then the intruder broke into a loud guffaw and turned to Billy, who already recognized Tippy from his distinctive laugh.

"You two realize that the place is half empty, and no one is getting an opportunity to meet the man whose paintings they just bought for $800,000. Couldn't you make a quick walk through the ballroom?"

"You know where I stand on that crap, Tippy. Besides, according to the press, the mystery is half of my allure."

"Did my stealthlike entrance scare the two of you?"

"You almost got a chair over the head."

As his hand pulled the door halfway open, Tippy again broke into his infectious laugh, and Marta, despite pressing her fingers to her lips, couldn't suppress a tiny giggle.

"I could never imagine you resorting to violence, despite your ungrate-fulness. I'll make it easy, all right? I'll bring a few collectors back to you. If the mountain won't come to Muhammad . . . Well, I forget how that goes, but I promise to knock next time."

The frazzled dealer disappeared, finishing his last sentence exactly as he let the door shut behind him. This sense of timing was another of his little ploys, making it impossible for Billy to respond.

"I think he likes you and, underneath all his laughing, is a little hurt."
Marta looked at an indifferent Billy.

"People like Tippy don't allow themselves to get hurt. He's hardened
himself for so long that he's grown a shell . . . like an insect."

Marta raised an eyebrow at Billy, but he didn't seem to grasp how well
the simile applied to his own life.

"Marta," Billy said quietly. "Will you stay with me?"

Before Billy knew it, the party was over and the ballroom was nearly empty.
Billy's car was waiting, but he told the driver to leave and tipped him for
this trouble. Billy and Marta had decided to walk the barren streets and
soon passed the gallery where the paintings of Billy Wolfram hung in a dim
light. It was really the first time that night he had been able to face up to
his work. Without his usual instincts to rely on, the pieces had been fueled
by defiance and a fear of failure, for Max as much as himself. Twenty-five
paintings completed in three weeks' time, and without the usual help of
his assistants. In the low light, the paintings looked heavier, as if ready to
break loose from the walls. After all the pressure and demands that he had
endured while trying to claw them out, he thought that would make a fitting end.

Despite knowing the show had sold out in advance, Marta nevertheless commented on the number of red stickers beside the titles. She dearly
wanted to help him to break loose from the malaise that had him in its grip,
to see his eyes radiating with the former confidence and carefree resolve
that he'd invariably reach while working to uncover art's all-embracing
possibilities. She turned to Billy for his reaction but instantly detected that
his thoughts were a thousand miles from such matters. She wondered what
emotions were spinning, too rapidly to reach, within the disturbed features
of the man beside her. She expected him to press his face, childlike, against
the window glass, as he stood staring at the gallery walls, each containing rows of equally sized squares, and each square enclosing a series of
circles.

As they stood on the empty street at two in the morning, Billy didn't
have to deal with any of the distractions that had engulfed him earlier that

night. "Tell me something"—Billy had never spoken about religion with her before, and he felt odd talking about it now—"I know this is an imposing question, but what was your favorite prayer when you were young and still devoted to the church?"

"That's easy," Marta answered, as if she were expecting Billy's question. "The Hail Mary was always my most cherished prayer . . . and still is. It's probably because that prayer epitomized the feminine aspect of Catholicism. I loved the Cult of the Virgin in its various manifestations, and admired the church for the respect and veneration bestowed on her. All her apparitions, especially those at Lourdes and Fatima, fascinated me.

"When I was a teenager," Marta continued, "my mother told me a remarkable story about the Virgin Mother's involvement in my own birth. When she reached her late thirties, she had three sons and desperately wanted a girl, but her doctors assured her that having another child was impossible. With very dismissive attitudes, they told her to be content with her sons and forget the idea.

"She refused to accept their advice, however, and attended three novenas to Our Lady in the following year. Within a few months of the final novena, I was conceived. She swore it was the Blessed Mother's intervention. Every evening for two weeks, she'd take her rosary beads from a drawer beside the bed, tie a kerchief around her head, and walk the three long avenues to the church. She returned home within a couple of hours. After a few months passed, she would do it again.

"Women in my country have always considered novenas as the Christian equivalent of a fertility ritual. I've been told that American women use it for the same purpose. Everyone attending is either anxious to get pregnant or thankful because she already is. Women of faith need the hope found in rituals. After she has exhausted all avenues of modern medicine, a childless young wife's only alternative is to trust in the novena or plummet into despair."

"It apparently worked for your mother!" Billy couldn't understand why they hadn't talked about such things before. "She sounds like a woman with powerful faith, much like my own mother."

Billy and Marta continued discussing the obligatory prayers of their youth as they began walking down the wide avenue.

After a few blocks, Marta gripped Billy's arm and embraced him. He stood there, overwhelmed, unable to respond despite his painful longing. She broke away from his body, inhaling deeply as she stepped backward and raised her hands, palms facing outward.

At first Billy assumed the gesture was imploring him to keep away. However, the instant he saw her contorted facial expression, it was clear that Marta was signaling her own anguish and exasperation. She was so conflicted and overwhelmed that her hands remained extended outward, desperate to halt this emotional barrage and stand by the decision she'd already made. She faced Billy and bluntly informed him there was no way they could live together again, no matter the circumstances. Whatever the two had shared, she insisted its time had now passed, and they were both responsible.

Billy listened to her abrupt statement. He'd been anticipating this all night, but a part of him never truly believed she'd go through with it. More than anything else, he never expected she would speak to him with such harsh candor. His lean body doubled over with a sharp pain like he'd been kicked in the groin. He wrapped his arms around his stomach and tried to catch his breath.

Marta softened her tone, explaining, as if to a child, that there is a window of opportunity for two people who live together but fear to define their relationship. They never communicated their own feelings, nor dared to discuss matters of the heart, speaking only of art and the business of art.

She continued, "A few months after moving into the loft, I decided to open that window as widely as possible, and it stayed that way for years. I couldn't have made the opportunity more clear, but for whatever reason, you never even tried to enter. I sometimes think that I knew, before I came here tonight, that once you finally did pass through, it would slide shut. I don't know the reason, and I've tried my best to pry it back open, but I cannot." When she paused and looked at him for a reaction, Billy remained motionless, body bent and face blank. He appeared more and more disoriented, eyes searching with no signs of recognition.

She wanted to comfort him but was afraid he'd see it as an empty gesture or an act of pity. She also knew she couldn't hold out much longer before faltering and giving in to her emotions. "I spent years foolishly waiting with my futile hopes and passivity. I'm sorry to say that—though the window will always be left slightly open—there isn't enough room for me to remain. Our time has passed, Billy, and I can't endure that pain again.

"We have to finally face the reality of this situation, which we've created together. Yes, I wanted to go back to the loft with you tonight and make love powerful enough to erase all the damage, but my leaving isn't only about our past together. While I was away, I vowed to take that fearful step and go out on my own. If we remained living together, I'd continue subjugating myself, always burying my own instincts and feelings to shield yours. That's no good for either of us. Even if . . ."

Her remaining words were stolen by the city's windy darkness and her own mounting anguish. She ran into the street and rushed into a taxi, which peeled out so fast it seemed the driver had also sensed the tension.

An overwrought Billy walked the streets aimlessly, spurred on by the defiance found in exhaustion. After awhile, he recovered some semblance of focus and recognized the finality of Marta's decision. He understood what she meant by the window closing: he'd experienced it while creating his art, which was another love that he appeared to have lost. In the past, he'd conceived fantastic ideas for projects and let them slip away, never executing them because of prior commitments and a dozen other reasons. Eventually, he tried working on a few, but by then the passion he'd originally felt had vanished. At some undefined point, time had stolen concepts from him that initially had appeared filled with potential. Afterward, he could only imagine what might have been.

Had he lost Marta because of his procrastination, or bad judgment? Perhaps the reason was exactly what she'd claimed . . . a simple matter of not paying attention . . . or was it the fear of someone getting too close and learning too much? Billy knew that there were and always would be regrets. There would always be regrets.

4

Walking the few blocks back to his loft after that long night, Billy endlessly replayed scenes from the morning Marta walked out, when he had stood on the worn gray carpet at the end of the hallway, wearing black Japanese slippers and sipping mineral water from a bottle.

The two large doors leading to the working end of the studio had been only two or three feet ahead, but his inexplicable terror kept him from opening them. To Billy's left was the room where Marta had slept; without doubt the only tastefully decorated space on the floor. The room locked from the inside and had its own cramped toilet. He couldn't resist turning the knob of her door. As it opened, he faced the single large window and the cupola of Father Mishkin's church. The sun had barely risen and its soft light was already changing the dome's color. He hadn't been in this room since she'd moved in. If she'd left the door open, he'd glance in as he passed, but had never taken a step inside. Even at that moment, he felt like he was intruding on her privacy.

There were travel agency posters of her native country beside a large oak mirror that he'd bought for her at a nearby antique store. He recalled her rarely displayed exhilaration when she'd first noticed it in the window of the cluttered shop. He slowly reached down and touched the fabric of the striped blue sheets on her bed, then quickly withdrew his hand, as if he'd been shocked by static. It was an enormous brass bed. For some inexplicable reason, the bars above her pillows had dozens of thin silk scarves tied to them, and higher up that far wall there was a large black-and-white photograph of Marta when she was in her late teens. She was sunning herself, wearing a bikini, on the redwood dock of an Argentine lake, and her dazzling eyes were wide with conflicting emotions. He could perceive the peace she must have felt at that moment, maybe 15 years earlier, surrounded by the stillness of the water, which mirrored the maple trees from the opposite shore. Her shadow lay behind her, long and thin, so it must have been late afternoon when the photo was snapped. There was a distance and an intense anticipation in her facial expression, particularly her eyes, their lashes heavy with mascara. It was a yearning for some far-off city, filled with theaters, museums, and wild clubs, Billy surmised. He had stared so deeply that his fiery imagination zoomed in recklessly. Somewhere in one minuscule glint of light at the bottom of her pupils, he remembered when the two first met in the doorway of the gallery, on the day he offered her a job and took her back to this very room, where he now stood, his cheeks streaking with tears.

The sun had barely moved. He lowered himself onto the mattress. It was firm, but for some reason he worried it was about to collapse at any moment. The reason had nothing to do with his weight, but because, until the previous night, he'd been blind to her affections and subsequent passion for so many years that she'd evolved into a phantom, and phantoms have neither substance nor weight. He was furious with himself for acting so stupidly. Clearly, she'd held the entire operation together, yet he had treated her with no more significance than his assistants. She was just another cog in his well-oiled machine.

He had remained blind to the gorgeous and vivacious woman in that photograph. If he'd surmounted his masculine pride and divulged the so-called Memory to her, then all the passions the two had experienced the previous night might have occurred years earlier. With time to evaluate his secret, Marta might have empathized with Billy's juvenile suspicions and childish demonstrations of jealousy. Perhaps he'd been attracted to her all along, but even considering the possibility had been out of the question for a man so inexperienced.

A wayward flash of early sunlight, reflecting off the cupola and straying sharply into his eyes, had snapped him out of this useless speculation. He sat up, convinced he'd invaded her privacy by audaciously checking out the mementos on her bookcase shelves, then flopping around on her bed. Before long, he imagined himself rummaging through the dresser drawers, searching for her lingerie. At that moment, however, nothing would have pleased him more than if she had come through her door and found him caressing the layers of black and red lace on her most enticing panties.

Her scent was still buried in the sheets and pillows. Billy had breathed deeply as he stared at the ceiling, which she'd painted blue, with clusters of cold red stars, their perspective making the old plasterboard seem curved. Lying back, he had begun to experience heart palpitations and had trouble catching his breath. He had started sobbing so strenuously that his body heaved while the muscles strained against his gut.

Wobbling back down the corridor, he decided to call Elsa for information. Why hadn't he thought of her before? She and Marta were best friends, and the two might be commiserating together in her kitchen at that very moment. It was a slim possibility, but Billy had nothing to lose. Picking up the phone, he remembered she had always preferred speaking directly on the building's intercom, so he pressed the button and buzzed the third floor.

A woman answered, but it wasn't Elsa. In an icy British accent, she informed Billy that Elsa was at her gallery, overseeing her upcoming show's assemblages. Without even taking a name, she summarily removed her finger from the intercom. Billy buzzed again to identify himself and ask the bitch if she'd seen a woman named Marta down there.

"Absolutely not." Her voice's volume, fueled by jealousy, made the intercom feed back and squawk unbearably. "I am the only woman in Elsa's life. Now, I insist you leave me alone until she returns. It will be within an hour . . . maybe two."

It was a bad break, but the jealousy of the unexpected Brit woman was much too genuine for this to be a ruse. He'd give her another try later. Elsa might still have some answers, and, having experienced a similar episode herself about a year earlier, she could empathize with his worsening mental condition. As he'd finished eating at one of her dinner parties, she'd suddenly accused a petite female guest of attempting to poison her by slipping a packet of unidentified powder into her bowl of goulash. As a husband and wife restrained her, Billy had called the paramedics, who took her to Bellevue. The suspect powder was tested and turned out to be vitamins.

Billy sat on the kitchen floor, staring blankly . . . avoiding the clock. It seemed like hours, but only 40 minutes had passed when he relented. He spotted a magnetic "M" on the refrigerator door, holding in place an official-looking letter. He yanked the envelope from the "M" and undid the flap, using a stained fork as an opener. It was indeed a form letter, on Metropolitan Hospital's stationery, detailing the patient's name and address, as well as the dates and times of admission and release.

In the space reserved for the admitting psychiatrist to write his evaluation, Dr. Hui had referred to Billy's lack of cooperation:

The patient was lucid, but in complete denial through both conversations. In spite of obvious anxiety, he insisted on simply going through the motions and telling me what he imagined I wanted to hear. His only plausible comments were regarding his encounters with what he'd termed "racing thoughts."

Because of his previously mentioned reticence, I cannot give a definitive diagnosis, but I believe he suffers from a mid-range gradation of Bipolar Disorder, likely accompanied by Attention Deficit Disorder & Obsessive Compulsive Disorder.

I suggest that he receive further testing and seek immediate treatment for said afflictions. Under the circumstances, I see no reason for holding this patient for another two days, and recommend immediate release.

D. W. Hui, M.D

Holding the doctor's letter, Billy slumped over, forlorn and vapid. It was as if the wreckage of everything he'd ruined yesterday surrounded him. His panicky tears, the ensuing comfort of Marta's voice, and her tender but exacting touch were scattered like debris that needed to be gathered up and disposed.

Still dizzy, he clumsily lowered himself into a chair at the breakfast table and buried his face into his hands. Billy should have been celebrating, feeling a supreme jubilation after ending his long sexual drought, but Marta's hasty disappearance had wiped out even the slightest trace of physical or emotional satisfaction from his awkward lovemaking. An inexplicable attack of vertigo came over Billy, and his head smashed onto the Formica tabletop.

About a year earlier Billy had noticed the first pangs of mistrust, which had been quickly forgotten until this morning. These initial suspicions were so subtle he had dismissed them as a flare of paranoia. It was on a rare night when Billy had arrived late at the loft, walking in as Marta and Denny were watching a video together. The scene had seemed innocent enough. Denny often dropped by the loft and, if Billy wasn't there, spent the time with Marta, drinking coffee, talking about music, and watching TV, or mainly dozing off, exhausted, in an overstuffed armchair which Denny himself had bought. As Billy had opened the door, the two were lounging together on the sofa like two longtime friends, watching a movie they'd both seen many times before. A few minutes later, changing his shirt in his bedroom, Billy couldn't resist checking them out again through a crack in the door.

Billy had thought nothing more about it until later that evening, when he was on the phone to a West Coast gallery owner, an attractive young woman who had grown tired of the New York art scene and its mandate to constantly network. She had moved back to her native L.A. Billy had mentioned that Denny and Marta were watching a movie in the other room, and the woman then spoke of her personal experience with Denny's womanizing, calling him "charming, but lacking feelings." None of this was news to Billy. She then casually added that there was always the possibility he was hitting on Marta, and that Billy should not discount this simply on the basis of their friendship. "He's not beyond that, you know."

Billy had taken it for granted that Denny had hit on Marta the first time he laid eyes on her, as he did with every woman he met. When the gallery owner hung up, seemingly satisfied with Billy's feigned indifference,

Billy was relieved that she'd ended the conversation unaware of his naïveté and pain.

In time, however, this troublemaker's divisive words had their desired effect. From the moment he foolishly believed her innuendo might possibly contain an iota of truth, he allowed her spiteful comments to snowball. At any rate, Billy got the message. For a long while he'd just sat, baffled in doubt and locked within his cage of sexual naïveté. Eventually, he had to ask himself, what was the point? Years before, he'd decided that bothering to gain information on the subject was clearly a waste of time. Although he wouldn't acknowledge it, just thinking about sex and women was too painful an experience. Was there any purpose in staring at men's magazines, or studying the 8,000 therapeutic paperbacks available? While still a teenager, he'd concluded these matters were academic and no longer applied to him. Sex could only bring him ruin.

He took another glimpse at the envelope he'd tossed onto the table and quickly snatched it up. Earlier, when his weary peripheral vision had first spotted it under the magnet, he'd assumed the handwriting was from some postal agent. Now, on closer examination, he recognized Marta's unique penmanship, scribbled hastily with her pink felt-tip pen. Only she used that pen. He struggled to make out the rapidly scrawled note.

Billy,

I put this on the refrigerator under my initial, hoping you'll find it. I suggest that you read it very carefully, giving it your full attention. I hope with all my wounded heart that you do something about this. I don't understand all the medical terms this doctor uses, but it sounds very serious and it's urgent that you call someone as quickly as possible. I pray you follow through on his recommendations.

P.S.—I just realized that you might not have found the letter that I wrote you. It's underneath the pillow where I laid my head last night.

Billy dashed into his room and tossed the pillow on the floor. The letter was written on lavender stationery. Picking it up, Billy was surprised to find it was scented. He breathed through his mouth rather than his nose, gulping down the air as if it were water in a canteen, and he were a movie cowboy, dying of thirst in a desert.

He held the letter up to the light and read, his hands trembling.

> *Dear Billy,*
>
> *I cannot comprehend you. I have loved you since the first time I saw you in the doorway to that gallery. Did you ever notice the happiness in my face when you greet me in the morning, and the sadness when we say good night? The nights were the worst, when we'd each turn in opposite directions to our bedrooms, where I would cry myself to sleep. It was always (and only) you, Billy Wolfram!*
>
> *Though I am not capable of understanding you, I always suspected you also had feelings for me, but were unable to express them. I've done my best attempting to figure out the reason, but it remains a mystery.*
>
> *Last night changed everything, and proved how wrong I was. It is impossible that you ever had any feelings for me when you accuse me of betrayal the instant after we first made love. Why would you go off on me when our arms were finally wrapped around each other? I might have forgiven anything else, but I must go now. I cannot bear the idea of being in the same space, with you looking at me and thinking I would do such a thing. We would both be uncomfortable, and I might learn to hate you.*
>
> *I loved you and had so much to give you, but I must leave. I'll probably continue to love you wherever I go. Will I be able to forget about you? I already know that I won't, and once more I will cry myself to sleep tonight. It seems there is no way either of us can be happy about my decision. Still, I must try it.*
>
> *I love you and I'm so sorry.*
>
> *Marta*

Billy approached the intercom and gave the button one last press, holding it down about ten seconds. The moment he recognized Elsa's voice, he didn't even speak, but rushed downstairs and pounded on the door. If anyone knew where Marta was, it would be Elsa. He wasn't in very good shape for analyzing people, but Billy prepared himself to read Elsa's affect, knowing that, if she had seen her, it wasn't beyond her to lie for Marta's sake. Billy knew she had nothing against him, but he was also certain whose side she would take between the two.

As it turned out, his blond neighbor was so genuinely bewildered and distressed by Billy's rambling report that it was obvious she clearly hadn't heard a word from her missing friend and didn't have a clue where she might be. Elsa assured him that if, by any chance, Marta did call there, she'd inform him immediately. Of course, she wanted to know what happened and was indefatigable in her attempts to find out.

In a roundabout way, Billy acknowledged that something had gone down after sex, but didn't go into details. He wouldn't know how to go about explaining anything involving the previous night. Billy had no intention of staying and talking with the artist, but she took his hand as he stood in the doorway and insisted on sitting him down and making some tea. She stared at Billy. He wondered if she could sense she was speaking to a man who had lost part of his mind.

"You look terrible." Elsa was blunt. Billy appreciated her candor. "Pardon me for saying this, but your skin is green."

"I do feel a little funny." Billy was in full prevarication mode. If he began to open up to Elsa, he'd likely be there for days. "I'm probably just stressed out. My belly aches a little."

"Your belly?" She tittered and raised her hand to her lips. Billy realized how flirtatious she was. "Excuse me, but *belly* is a funny word. I will make you a cup of ginger tea. It is good for the stomach pain . . . for the belly. Would you like some stronger medicine? I have the Pepto-Bismol."

"Oh . . . no. No." Billy was emphatic. He suddenly felt even stranger. "No, really. I can't even stay for the tea. I feel like I'm imposing."

The kettle, however, was already whistling. Elsa poured the tea and sat across from Billy. She was curled up on the seat and her hair was spread across her shoulders. Billy sipped the tea. It tasted good. He needed heat in his stomach, but he wished it were mate.

Billy didn't even know Elsa that well, but he needed human contact on any level. He'd rather be here than in his loft upstairs, where he'd be alone with his many regrets, waiting for Denny to call.

Still, he was confused and uneasy. He tried to avoid eye contact with Elsa, but it was difficult. Her entire attraction radiated from her eyes. They were thickly framed in dark liner. Her lashes seemed almost wet with mascara. It was amazingly alluring. She knew this, and used it. It was the last thing that Billy wanted to hear, but she launched into a monologue about the sexual side of the downtown scene. Billy listened, thinking how enormously she had changed since she had arrived from the Romanian countryside.

"Sex is not any longer a *beautiful thing*," she said. "It has become an entirely separate entity from what was quaintly known as *making love*. It's been transformed into a game between the sexes. It is as deceptive as chess and anonymous as those men in helmets, racing cars on the TV. This generation of men and women has turned it into a frenetically overenergetic contest and a performance. The more outlandish the game, the more popular it becomes. Also, sex is like a drug with an ever-increasing tolerance, which, as it increases, demands that every freaky requirement be fulfilled. Achieving any true intimacy is usually accidental, and often goes unrecognized.

"Everyone has their own agenda and their own needs. The perfect people—and it doesn't matter if they're men or women—put in their appearance at all the trendy bars on the weekend. Their minds are like purses, containing only a checklist of criteria, and they expect each item to be met. It all gets rather played out after awhile, you know? I've moved beyond that type of thing, and you know who was responsible for showing me the foolishness of my ways? It was Marta, naturally. She wasn't wired to play games, and couldn't abide that crowd by the second weekend. When she came down and explained her reasons, I was so convinced that I followed her lead. God, she had those types pegged. I admired her so much, but her insight was her greatest gift. Still, I'm really surprised that she took off like that. You must have known how devoted she was to you, right? I used to tease her about what a hopeless romantic she was. Still, I respected her feelings. No other man meant a thing to her."

"So she did see other guys?" Billy asked. "I suppose I'm a little obsessed about it." He couldn't gauge how much he cared. It was as if some portion of his brain had utterly failed to evolve.

"She definitely didn't lack the opportunity, back then or lately," Elsa replied. "Men were all over her wherever we went, which is understandable. She's smart, funny, and fantastically attractive, as even you have now finally acknowledged. We went out on weekend nights together. But as I've already mentioned, she had no interest in playing games.

"Even on those rare occasions, she always ended the night upstairs in her bed. She always returned to her love. I should not tell you these things. Many nights she would sit at this same table and cry, attempting to figure out why you did not want her. Always she vowed that she would wait and wear you down. At first she joked about that, but she began to speak very sadly about her obsession within the past year.

"I should be mad at you if she has left. She is a good friend to me. I care very much for her, as I know you do too. I think she will be back, and I do not say this to make you feel better. You men always need something drastic and painful to take place before you appreciate what you have."

"I'm sorry, Elsa, but I really have to split." Billy pushed away the chair. He was profoundly dejected and detested having to climb back upstairs, but he couldn't stay. He was not exactly enthusiastic about being alone, but if he stayed with Elsa in this disorientated, flustered condition, there was too much possibility he'd say or do something impulsive, and severely regret it later. He didn't know what—this was all too completely new to him—but it would result in an embarrassment he couldn't handle, and he had no idea how to manage it.

"Well, I really should leave," he muttered. "Sorry about laying all this on you. All I ask is that you keep our talk confidential. I can't stand bothering other people with my problems. It goes without saying that if you hear from her, you'll fill me in, all right? Thanks a lot for the tea."

"I will, but you must try to calm yourself down. Call me if you feel worse, eh? I'll probably be in all night."

Billy could barely make it up the stairs. He collapsed halfway and lay on the landing, balled up in a fetal position and mumbling. He wanted to scream but was having trouble getting his breath. Breathing was again the problem. He had still not learned to breathe, even in his wasted reclusion, and it brought to mind the Indian driver who'd picked him up at the hospital. Three weeks had passed, and he was now worse off than when he began.

There was a perverse symmetry in the complete circle he'd made during his isolation. Exhausted on his own stairs, he was wondering if it was too late to go next door to the rectory and speak with Father Mishkin. Any priest, even Eastern Orthodox, would serve the purpose. In fact, he'd likely be preferable.

5

It could have been an hour or a day after Marta's abrupt departure, but eventually Billy called to set up the appointment she'd been urging him to make as follow-up to his brief stint in the locked wing. A few days later, he headed to the doctor's office on the West Side, not far from Central Park. This area was a bastion for the psychiatric profession. Walking in the park, he passed by the softball fields near the Columbus Circle entrance; they still had a few white clumps from the snowfall last week, which would soon vanish in the strong afternoon sun. He veered off to a side path, walking with the tentative stride of a man who is nervous and about to be analyzed. He turned a corner at a perennial bush and saw a black man, in his late teens or early 20s, approaching him with a girl's bicycle. He'd most likely been taking a leak behind the shrubs. Billy stepped to the side of the path near a bench to let the guy pass, but the man stopped.

"You interested in buying a bike, my man? You'd be doing me a favor."

"Sorry, I don't need one," Billy said. "I was just making for an exit. I have an appointment."

"Well, buy it from me and park it outside your appointment." The guy was jittery and pressing Billy with his eyes. Still, he maintained a smile. "This area is safe. Nobody's going to steal anything around here."

"How come it's a girl's bike?" Billy might have been crazy and secluded for nearly a month, but he still knew a wrong situation when it appeared to him from behind a bush. "Besides, a twelve-year-old could barely fit on that thing."

"It's my sister's, man! Come on . . . I need the money bad. I'll be honest with you. I need it for drugs." The fellow nervously bit down on a strip of laminated plastic held in his fingers. It looked like a series of photo negatives. "I stopped you 'cause you look like you've used yourself."

"Why do you say that?" Billy was amazed.

"I don't know, man." The guy whined like he wasn't used to answering questions. "You be thin, pale, and you got that thing where you roll your shoulders when you walk."

Billy didn't fathom that logic at all, but he felt a sudden compassion for the guy, who, at least, told the truth. The bike had to be stolen, but Billy reached in his pocket and laid two five-dollar bills on the bench between them. The guy snatched up the money and rolled the bike toward his benefactor.

"Hey, I don't think I'll need this," Billy said, and rolled it back. The last thing he needed was to show up for his first shrink's appointment with a girl's bike in tow.

The guy snagged the wobbling bike and hopped onto it. He was short, but he still looked ridiculous as he turned and began pedaling furiously. The mini-cycle made him seem like a circus performer. "Well, if you don't want it, then I'm out of here." His voice was less shaky since he'd stuffed some money in his pocket. "Good looking out, my man."

After entering the building's lobby, Billy was buzzed into the office and took a seat. He needed a minute to recuperate from the incident with the bicycle thief.

After some general palaver concerning referrals and finances, the doting receptionist handed him a form attached to a clipboard. It was a standard medical form, which immediately caused Billy's anxiety to soar. He loathed forms on a good day. As it was, sitting there with his sneakers dotted with red paint, Billy felt susceptible to suggestion and was afraid that, by answering these sorts of questions, he would cause some irreversible process to begin.

A teenage boy emerged from the doctor's inner sanctum and tried to leave by walking into a large closet. He fumbled around in the coats before the receptionist called out his name. The boy was red as he materialized from the closet. *He can't be doing well*, Billy thought. The painter scrutinized the young man as he passed by. He felt an unlikely empathy for the boy, who had the insouciance and spaced-out demeanor of old money, dressed in khakis and a button-down shirt, leaving the doctor's office with vacant eyes. Billy realized he had felt a surge of compassion for every hard-luck case he'd encountered since leaving the seclusion of the loft and wondered if either heartbreak or losing one's mind might somehow make one a better person.

Of course, everyone in the waiting area must be crazy to some degree or another. That's what a person assumes, after all, while sitting in a psychiatrist's office. In the other patients' eyes, Billy was probably no different than that boy who'd walked into the closet. He was also searching for a way out.

When informed the doctor would see him momentarily, Billy paced hastily around the office, scrutinizing a wall filled with Joseph Cornell imitations. Billy wondered if the doctor's patients had done these varied collages and assemblages, possibly as a form of therapy. In any case, this might as well have been the first time he had ever seen such work, which discarded all fundamentals of style. Whoever created them, their minds were intent only on expressing their psychological trouble as quickly as possible, unimpeded by the restrictions of form and technique.

He also scanned a large reproduction of a Flemish master, hanging on a wall to the left. The "canvas" was processed, burnished too dark to look genuine, appearing textured from thick layers of paint, which only made it seem tackier, diminishing the other works in the room. An old schoolmate of Billy's employed a similar technique as a means of making money. The same fellow also designed mausoleums and statuary for cemeteries.

Billy hadn't stopped crying since reading Marta's letter. All the damaged mental baggage he needed to rummage through with the doctor was overwhelming him. Only now in the waiting room did Billy understand the extent of the injuries he'd suffered. Closing his eyes, he began to envisage his past like a drive through the twilight on a straight, empty highway, one hand gripping the wheel as the other maneuvered the stick. After exceeding a certain distance, however, his attention would invariably crumble from its original clear-cut focus to disregard and neglect. Billy later admitted that this vehicular metaphor finally helped him acknowledge his enormous lack of patience, with its possibly serious consequences. Continuing his imaginary drive, the sky grew darker, with a heavy fog rolling in. Once again, Billy grew tired and ignored the messages from electric lights in large signposts, which flickered warnings regarding the highway's hazardous conditions. He'd been ignoring similar alerts since he first began this drive many years ago. Billy now sat in the waiting room, unsure whether to keep his eyes fixed on two yellow lines in the darkness ahead, or to scan the rapidly flashing signs. His eyes remained straight before him and he gunned the car into the fog.

He was about to find out that when you open a door with a psychiatrist's name on it, you'd better be prepared to witness exactly how fucked up your life has become.

The scene at the Met had only been a prelude, Billy realized; his entire way of life had now departed for places unknown. Since his brief experience with sex, Billy had found himself trapped in a place where time was either frozen or out of phase. His organic creative process, with its heightened intuition, wasn't the only certainty that had abandoned him. He had also misplaced—to varying degrees—many of its related attributes, including his spontaneity, persistence, drive, and confidence. There were many essential aspects of his work that he never fully realized had ensued from that initial gift.

Billy was questioning every molecule of his being when the doctor emerged from his office clutching a folder containing his new patient's forms and a few letters. Dr. Mastro was shorter than Billy had imagined, and had lost most of the thick accent of his native French tongue. However, the man still spoke with quirky syntax, sounding like a parody of Charles Boyer. He smiled, extended his hand, and asked Billy to step inside.

Billy slumped into a thick armchair. It quickly became clear that none of the concatenation of complaints that he'd prepared in the waiting room, even scribbling a crib sheet on his forearm, was going to be resolved in one session.

Billy lay out on the divan for the official start of his psychotherapy.

"If you can, would you please tell me about the first time you recall feeling truly afraid?" the doctor began. He was using a pencil that had no eraser on it, which was the one thing that grabbed Billy's attention. *If your pencil doesn't have an eraser,* he thought, *then use a damn pen.*

"Yes, I can. I'd just turned five years old," Billy said without hesitation, his voice about half an octave higher. It made him sound a bit childlike. "Fear must play a large part in imprinting memory, because this was the first event in my life that I recall from beginning to end in vivid detail. It's different than those earlier fragments of recollection when only a few seconds embedded themselves abstractly in my brain, like something involving the pattern of my aunt's bedspread, or the big crucifix hanging over my grandfather's deathbed.

"I was in the back of a truck, half standing . . . with one leg kneeling on a seat wide enough for two people. I was high up in the air, trapped inside an iron cage."

Dr. Mastro stopped Billy. "A moment . . . please describe this truck with a cage. What was it for? Where were you?"

"I was about a block from my building, across from the Catholic school. Every school day, right before three in the afternoon, I'd sit on a bench with my mother, waiting for school to let out so we could walk my brother, Brian, home. He was in the first grade, which I'd start in another year.

"We'd sit on this long row of wooden benches, directly across from the gray three-story schoolhouse, along with a lot of other women. The benches and the school building were separated by a 'play street,' which is a regular street where no traffic is permitted on weekdays. So kids could run around during recess, and play roller hockey after school, without having to worry about getting hit by a car. The only other vehicles allowed on the street were the flat-bedded trucks that came three days a week."

"Trucks?" the doctor prompted Billy.

"They were just plain trucks, but they pulled these wooden beds, about 20 feet long. They were only about eight feet wide, I guess. Everything seems bigger when you're so young and small. There were three of them, and a different truck came every Monday, Wednesday, and Friday, always at 2:30 in the afternoon. The first was pulling a small merry-go-round, a miniature version of the ones you see on boardwalks and at amusement parks. On Wednesday, the truck had a ride where you sat in cars that were round and painted to look like teacups. The third truck was by far the best, especially for the boys. That was the one with the Ferris wheel on the back.

"There was always a long line that formed the moment a truck came over the top of the hill into view. Sometimes fights would break out when someone tried to cut ahead of another guy in the line, but the mothers would quickly break it up. Actually, the moms didn't like the Ferris wheel, and some of them wouldn't let their children get on. Some days it made a sort of metallic groan as it was moving.

"The same guy drove all the trucks, and he was scary-looking. He also never spoke, but made signals with his arms and hands like a cop directing traffic. Everyone assumed he came from some foreign country and didn't know English. Some of the mothers began a rumor that he was from a place behind the Iron Curtain and a communist. His face was clean and smooth on Monday, but then the guy wouldn't shave for the rest of the week. By Friday, people would say he had a full beard, but in fact it was just sort of grizzled-looking. It was a bit frightening. In those days, men never wore beards, except guys in the circus, or the beatniks I'd see in *Life*."

Billy described how at each stop the man would lower a gray wooden stairway onto the street. Once the portable steps were in place, everyone in line moved as quickly as possible, but they remained orderly, mainly because the kids were more afraid of the ride's silent operator than of their own moms. After ascending the four or five steps, the kids walked sheepishly onto the truck's bed, and gave the scruffy guy, who was less than five feet tall, a dime. He'd open the door to the bottom car of the Ferris wheel, and once four kids were inside, he'd push a button and the wheel would move, making that funny noise, like a metallic yawn, as the next car would move down to the bottom. Each of them had different colors . . . red, green, blue, and yellow. Once it began, the entire ride lasted about four minutes, but seemed much longer.

"There was one day," Billy continued, growing more animated, "when, for some reason, only four kids were waiting to ride it. We were so happy, because all of us, if we wanted to, could have a car all to ourselves. When it was my turn, this girl asked if she could sit beside me, but her mom wanted her to be in a car with her girlfriend, so I got in the blue car by myself. Each of the four cars was totally enveloped by this sharp metal grid, from the floor to the ceiling, which was also covered. It was like sitting in a wire cage. The thing was made of a kind of iron mesh, with some filigree design. I don't recall the exact dimensions or shape, but it was basically square. And a kid could reach the ceiling when he stood up.

"You didn't feel trapped because you could see out so easily, but once you got in one of those things, there was no way out, except when the operator opened that door by lifting a latch. Also, the latch could only be lifted from the outside. I don't know where it was located, but some-place that no kid could reach. The cage was accident-proof, but safety wasn't the problem that day."

"What did happen?" the shrink asked.

"The wheel began turning, and I waved at my mom, showing her I was alone. She looked a little funny for a second, but then waved back, and continued talking to the lady beside her, who was holding a dog. She lived in the same building as us, and her children were all married and had moved somewhere out west. Sometimes I'd play with her pooch, a brown and white beagle, in the lobby.

"The ride itself was great. Since I didn't have any wimpy companions, I could use my body to make the car sway back and forth. 'Rocking,' as they called it, was against the rules, and the guy usually kicked off anyone who did it, but I saw that the driver was busy reading a *TV Guide* and didn't care, since he had so few kids aboard. He never ran his hand across his throat, which is the signal to stop. The school bell rang and all these kids came bursting out. I thought it was terrific that I'd be rocking on the ride when my brother stepped through the door.

"I saw him just as the four-minute ride ended. The scary operator pushed the button and the red car stopped flush on the flatbed. Two gig-gling girls got out and went down the stairs, where their mothers stood waiting. The wheel moved again, and when it stopped, the next kid got out. I was at the very top, rocking back and forth while I waited for him to push the button and lower me down. Instead, the guy checks the next car and sees that nobody's in it. I kept rocking, but then watched as he lifted up the portable stairway and wiped off his hands with a rag. Next thing I know, he's leaping off the back of the truck and opening the cab door. I quit rocking and sat very still, realizing that my presence at the top of this thing had gone completely unnoticed as he started the engine and drove off. I'm stranded in a blue cage, and my mom is busy greeting my brother while continuing her conversation with the beagle lady.

"As we're about ten yards down the street, however, another woman taps my mom on the shoulder and asks if that's her son, waving frantically from the top of the truck. She immediately grabbed one of the nuns, who was supervising the students in the middle of the play street, and they began running after the truck. The nun was dragging along my brother, who was looking at me and laughing as I screamed futilely over all the noise.

"Suddenly every woman remaining on the benches stood and pointed at the truck, grabbing their children and joining in the pursuit. By the time the truck made a right turn at the bottom of the play street, a phalanx of perambulator-pushing mothers, moving like an angry wave, was trailing my mother, brother, and the nun.

"The flatbed was speeding up and the crowd receded farther behind us, but at least they were still in view. The idea of losing sight of my mom terrified me. I had a terrible separation anxiety. All the while I was imagining he was taking me to New Jersey, which to me was, for some unexplained reason, the most terrifying place on earth.

"When the truck veered to the left down a short hill, I could no longer see my mother and her little army anymore. That was as frightening as I'd thought it would be. Suddenly I no longer thought this whole mess was an accident; I was certain that the driver *knew* I was in the blue cage. Everything had been carefully planned out. He was on his way to the West Side Highway, which led to the George Washington Bridge. When he got across the bridge, the communist would lower my cage while he stood waiting on the flatbed, grinning with his tiny black teeth, then drag me out and toss me off the platform. I'd land in the reeds and turgid water of New Jersey, while the man, without ever saying a word, would drive away."

"You developed paranoia in your shock!" said the doctor, stating the obvious. "That's unusual in one so young."

"I guess so. I didn't understand the meaning of paranoia, but there was no doubt that I had it badly. When the truck reached the bottom of this hill, however, it slowed down, turned, and stopped. Looking around from the top, I could tell where we were. It was the little playground at the edge of Highbridge Park, only about five long blocks from the school. I suppose the guy had a regular route and this was his next stop. Everyone ran out of the playground to get in line. Some jumped off swings in midair. I was so relieved we'd stopped moving, I just slumped back onto the seat, finally releasing my two bloody hands from the metal.

"By then my mother's mob, which appeared to have doubled in size, was swarming down the hill. It was as if they were all in a race, and the first one to reach the truck would be the winner.

"Too much was happening at once. I lay down on the floor of the cage. Some girl from the playground was pointing out something to her friend while running toward the ride. I recognized her finger was directed right at me. She then asked the driver, who was obliviously exiting the cab, why there was a young boy alone in the car at the top of the wheel.

"The operator jumped up on the bed and frantically pushed the 'start' button, but nothing happened. He slapped it, as if he were trying to wake a drunk, then ran about like a frightened terrier, lifting levers and finally, after opening a hidden locked box with a big key, pulled a red switch. The wheel started moving and my cage went from the top to the bottom in one motion, where the man stood waiting, shaking so badly that he fumbled his first two attempts at undoing the latch. Finally, he swung open the door and extended a hand toward me, but I ran past him, leaping five feet off the back of the truck. I would have broken a leg if one really tall guy, looking on, hadn't caught me like a football and carried me over to a high curb.

"The nun crossed the finish line, followed by the rest of the play-street brigade, just as I sat slumped on the curb, sobbing. Waiting in line at Highbridge, the younger kids ran in fear, believing this arriving pack of crazy ladies had a compulsive need to ride on a Ferris wheel."

Billy suddenly fell silent. Momentarily overwhelmed by the clarity of his recollection, he drank some water and searched for the words to continue.

Mastro made a note and asked a number of short questions, hoping to prompt him back into his detailed recollection. "So . . . you finally managed to be freed from your confinement, eh?"

"Yes, that's where it ends, I guess." Billy's tone had changed. He sat with a quizzical gaze on his face . . . stunned and silent.

"Did the man drive off with the truck?" Mastro persisted. "What happened with your mother?"

"My mom sat with me." Billy again paused, then continued, lucid one moment and muttering awkwardly the next.

"And what did you do?"

"I was still sobbing, with my mother consoling me."

"And then?"

"The man jumped off the truck and approached me. In a lame attempt at consolation, he handed me a batch of pencils secured by a rubber band. Even the driver recognized that pencils weren't much compensation for his inadvertent actions, but they were the only thing he was able to find while rummaging frantically through the glove compartment of the truck.

"Rising slowly from the curb, I snatched the pencils and tossed them down the street.

"The driver slumped away, alone and distraught. My mother said he could lose his job if we filed a complaint. The nun, who had already admonished him for his reckless actions, was now commenting to my mother about his shockingly paltry salary. 'With what this poor soul takes home every week, I pray he doesn't have a family to feed. He gets less than $180 a month!'

"The driver stumbled and my mother grabbed his arm and offered support, fearing he might faint.

"When I peeked up and saw her comforting my kidnapper, his grizzled face streaked with lines of sorrow and humiliation, I wondered if my anger was justified and immediately regretted flinging down the pencils."

"I would like to know what made you suddenly feel such strong regret," Mastro said. "What gave you the power to forgive this man, despite all the anguish and fear he caused you? It was his fault, after all. Everything that happened was created by his lack of attention."

"Well, I saw the way my mother was acting toward him, and there was something about the guy's frantic gestures, and the look of disgrace and worry in his eyes, that reminded me of something I'd heard at church a few Sundays earlier, during the priest's sermon on one of my favorite parts of the Gospels, the story of 'The Widow's Mite.'

"The priest had described Christ's parable about an old woman in black tattered clothing, who entered the temple to make an offering. She was followed by the wives of rich merchants, dressed in well-woven, bejeweled robes, their hands full of silver and gold coins. When the elderly woman approached the donation basket, she dropped in a single mite. The wealthy wives snickered, ridiculing her for such a pathetic lack of charity.

"On seeing this, Christ instructed his followers that she was a poor widow, and the Lord would bless her far more than the others who had given much larger donations. One of the apostles asked his master why.

"'Since they are wealthy, those women contribute a great deal, but withhold much more,' Jesus explained. 'By offering that single mite, however, the widow gave away the only thing that she possessed. The others donated little, and she contributed all.'

"I knew there was a connection between Christ's teaching and my situation and I felt a deep shame. Those pencils were the only things that the distressed worker could find to make amends, I thought, and he gave all of them to me, like the widow with her mite."

The doctor scrawled speedily on a small pad while he spoke, telling Billy that his recollection was very thorough, and he would examine his notes over the next few nights, seeing the story provided some insight he had been searching for. He also encouraged Billy to review this memory. "You might have forgotten some small detail that seems insignificant"— the doctor made direct eye contact for what seemed the first time—"but details sometimes provide a perception that will give us a valuable understanding of your difficulties."

Their time was up and, as they shook hands, the doctor handed the painter a prescription. He shoved it into his pocket and booked the next appointment with the receptionist.

Billy bought a paper at a kiosk off Columbus Circle. The owner, who sounded like he'd just gotten off the boat from some Iron Curtain country, was standing inside his cramped quarters, listening to a country-western station. Billy sat on a bench and tossed the paper aside, thinking about his . . . well . . . so-called reclusion.

6

D enny, sick of Chinese take-out food and stuck for another night accompanying Billy in the isolation of his loft, suggested they take a walk and eat food from a different continent. The pair were soon entering the Vertigo restaurant in the Meatpacking District of the West Village.

The Vertigo was open 24 hours a day, a popular late-night breakfast spot for painters, musicians, and drag queens. Since the enigmatic artist hadn't been seen in public for quite a while, their trip down the narrow aisle to a back booth provoked all sorts of whispered rumors. Denny, however, had noticed a marked improvement since Billy started seeing the shrink.

"Look at these twits, staring at me like I'm a mummy. I've been out walking at sunrise . . . you know? Don't worry about me sitting around the apartment all day and brooding." Billy ordered ginger tea and a bowl of figs, nuts, and raisins in cream. "I like the breeze from the Hudson, and checking out the old High Line. I don't care about the 'No Trespassing' signs. I looked at the other side of those signs, and none of them said a damn thing. That's the side I pay attention to. One day I climbed the fence and walked along the defunct railroad tracks, with their rusting rails and rotting wood ties. The place is a monument to decay and entropy. I was moving along slowly that day and, under the weight of my step, a block of lumber, which once supported tons of weight on wheels, crumbled into a pile of sawdust and termite larvae. I almost broke my ankle.

"An amazing variety of wildflowers was blossoming up there last summer . . . out of tufts of tenacious grass, growing through the dead wood and cracks in the asphalt. I saw some gorgeous posies and purple heather spread alongside ancient garbage, mainly piles of corroded beer cans. The few times their labels were legible, I realized the brands went out of business 40 years ago.

"I've even ventured down to Soho and checked out a few shows. I was shocked by how much the art world has changed in recent months. For example, there appeared to be an astonishing number of 'graffiti art' exhibitions.

"Apparently, this movement has escalated from a few kids with Magic Markers scribbling their street names, along with some cryptic numbers, all over the inside of subway cars. They called themselves taggers, and indulged that teenage compulsion to make your street rep by screwing the man . . . the same juvenile bullshit every generation of city kids does out of boredom.

"I suppose it is sort of clever, figuring out a way for your name to travel, day and night, beneath the city. You tag a car on the A train at the 125th Street stop and, within an hour, both your reputation as an outlaw and your lousy penmanship are pulling into the Rockaway Beach station."

"It's like your own private exhibition," Denny added. "Constantly on tour."

"Exactly." Billy acknowledged the remark and scurried back into his own thoughts. "I suppose you might call that the movement's minimal, black-and-white period, and it faded in a couple of years. Slightly older guys, with more ambition and talent, followed the taggers. They'd sneak into those huge transit system yards where the city stores unused trains, and spray-paint the entire outer sides of subway cars with elaborate motifs in bright DayGlo colors.

"After the newspapers started covering the story, some clever dealer sought out the more interesting of the bunch. He gave them canvas and space, and arranged for them to do murals on buildings. These street kids are suddenly legitimate artists, and their huge paintings dominate a bunch of fairly prestigious galleries. I liked some of their stuff.

"The problem is the effect on the young critics who were supporting this movement before all the surprising attention. These pretentious mothers have their own criteria for this new art, based on apathy and defiant posturing, and they've persuaded these young artists that the greatest crime they can commit is embarrassing themselves." Billy looked intensely at Denny, who listened while continuing to rearrange the condiments. "With all the constant nudging from the critics, they'd rather confine themselves in a comfortable, secure box, which has been labeled and sealed. These graffiti artists' main concern is maintaining a contrived attitude, which only limits their parameters, restricting both their art and themselves."

"It's lame to confine yourself by any rigid standards. It reminds me of artists in the Soviet Union who are strongly urged to paint tractors," Denny said. He was adding some drops of cream onto a pile of sugar that he'd poured on the tabletop. He then proceeded to stick his fingertip into the sticky mess, which he raised to his tongue and licked. It was an old habit, caused by a sweet tooth and slow waiters. "Especially if everyone puts you down for being a lame jerk. That's not the way it is with punk rock. Anything goes, and later you separate the wheat from the chaff. It's a force that's given rock and roll a required kick in the ass. These painters just seem to know what they *don't* want. That's like driving defensively. You get there safely, but it's not where you want to go."

"Well said, my brother," Billy replied, inserting his pinky into the free confection. "I couldn't abide some idiot judging the merits of my work on the basis of his damn *attitude*. Also, can you imagine having the presumption to speculate on any artists' motive? These jack-offs aren't legitimately evaluating the art on its substance. They're just indulging in some form of soothsaying! They must be driven out."

"When you use phrases like 'driven out,'" Denny said, still paying attention despite maneuvering the condiments, "it almost sounds like some of these backbiting idiots were inhabited by demons that need to be exorcised."

"That's a truer statement than you'll ever know." Billy hadn't expected Denny to pick up on an unintended reference. "The whole thing is outrageous. I may be turning into a cranky bastard, but I don't need one of these little snots to divine my inspiration! Fortunately . . . well, I think it's fortunate . . . my reputation is fairly intact, and, as always, I don't concern myself with any movement's opinions or standards. Though I think it's exactly what some very gifted artists need to nurture their talent, I've never been a joiner. I've always measured my work according to my personal point of reference, taking in as much as possible of what others are thinking or doing, without being dependent on it."

"First of all, your suspiciously noble discourse sounded like the aesthetic equivalent of an insatiable lady's man, always avoiding getting too attached to one woman," Denny quipped, blowing a fistful of pepper into the fan directly above. His tone of voice turned serious. "What's going to happen if this young crowd's critical paradigm expands and becomes the rule? Will it eventually affect established artists like yourself?"

"I don't think it will," Billy continued, after sneezing and giving his companion a look.

"When it comes to art—as in the traditional sense of paint applied to a canvas—too many barriers were broken down in this past century. Fads come and go, but, again, the wheat is always separated from the chaff. There are even a few worthwhile graffiti artists whose reputations will survive, and the rest will disintegrate like that wood up on the High Line. No artist or critic defines the norm. The norm defines itself. It's like a worm after being cut in half. It regenerates, slowly returning to what is meant to be. It's a form of homeostasis.

"One of the benefits of my past success is being able to take the big risk, going for broke on that elusive masterpiece. You see, at some point in their careers, almost all contemporary artists have an overwhelming urge—something irresistible built into their aesthetic drive, causing them to throw caution to the wind and take a shot at exceeding all expectations. You need to find out if there is that grain of a Picasso or Matisse in you . . . even for one work. This drive seems to activate itself, almost mechanically, when the time is right.

"Any artist worth his salt needs to spend many years of exhaustive preparation waiting for that propitious moment, and the chances of succeeding are still very slim.

"I can't overemphasize the dangers of some cocky kid, out of greed or lust for celebrity, forcing open the triggering device on this mysterious apparatus too soon. They're simply not ready to follow through."

"You always hated theory," Denny commented, clutching the phallic saltshaker. "As I think about it, you never liked discussing anything about art or artists, yourself included, until the day of your freak-out. After that, you just whined about your inability to work and then about losing Marta. Tonight, I suggest we eat out, and you unexpectedly break into this tirade about young painters and wanting to be Picasso? What's up?"

"You know me well, don't you? True, I've never been into this theoretical crap, but my gallery trip, and all the ridiculous affectations of these poseurs, did have an impact on me," Billy said. "Besides, while I can't paint, what else can I do but talk about it? I know how I brooded for a while, and I still wish time would just freeze while you're incapacitated and unable to produce, but that is not going to happen soon.

"On the night of the fiasco at the Velázquez retrospective, when the links of the chain that holds my brain together snapped and scattered across the marble steps of the Metropolitan, I had just finished constructing a two-tiered scaffold in my studio. The following morning I'd planned to begin on the most decisive and momentous piece of my career. One of my assistants and I had already stretched three nine-by-twelve-foot canvases, which would align with each other like a triptych. I'm considering adding another dome-shaped canvas that will go on top of the other three, but I have to have that specially assembled from this guy on Tenth Street who shapes wood.

"I'd been planning this project for years, and I must have two dozen notebooks filled with sketches and notations. I wanted to tackle something that was both innovative and old as an antelope on the wall of some French cave. I even, for the first time, designed the dimensions in scale. It would obviously be quite large, but never intrusive or overbearing. In fact, the desired effect on the viewer would be a sense of comfort on entering, leading to paths of a gradual intensity and uncertainty. Of course, once I had begun, all those notes and preconceptions would probably be discarded as the flow entered and took control. You know, in that sense, it's like you're flying a plane on automatic pilot.

"I don't have any idea if I could have succeeded with such an elaborate task, but I needed to satiate that driving force. I had to test myself, and define my limitations.

"It's now become academic because of my current inability to create . . . and so be it. However, I simply refuse to abandon hope. Once you give in to despair, there's no coming back. I need to, at least, consider future possibilities. Who can tell? Someday I may get my chops back, and if I do, then I will know."

"As even now, you have been known?" Denny said, smiling sweetly, with no sarcasm.

"We'll see." Billy lowered his head and almost wept. "Anyway, it really is ironic that this endeavor happened to be my main priority right before the incident at the museum, which seems so long ago. Nonetheless, nothing's stopping me from dreaming, musing, and even theorizing about art, and I'll guarantee you one thing right now. If I do, by some far-fetched chance, manage to chisel away at the bars until there's enough space to shimmy back into the zone, I now make this vow. I will toss my entire being into that major project, without an iota of hesitation or procrastination, and deliver. You can take that to the bank."

"What are you talking about?" Denny asked, moving the salt and pepper shakers about like they were chess pieces. "You never procrastinated a day in your life. You're starting to turn back into the eternal optimist, Wolfram . . . and I like it."

7

B ack at his loft, Billy became convinced of one thing. If Marta was not going to be a part of his life, he still had to make art, despite the difficulties that would involve. He needed to reverse the direction of his work process 180 degrees, no longer able to rely on his intuition to pilot him into the so-called zone, that ineffable state where his art flowed without time or effort. For his entire career, Billy had "locked in" and allowed this instinct to take control. He would attack a canvas relentlessly, persisting with abandon until the piece was complete. Within the first hour, Billy would have envisioned the entire finished painting. Of course, he'd return later and do some fine-tuning, but that invariably meant reducing rather than adding to the canvas.

Throughout that seemingly charmed period, Billy had simultaneously been honing his craft and testing the depths of his judgment. He still controlled those basic skills, which came from years of experience at the canvas and now provided Billy with his only hope for completing his show. For a mostly self-taught painter, he possessed remarkable mechanical skills as well as a distinctive palette and a unique system of color-coding. His abilities as a draftsman were unrivaled and the source of envy among certain critics and peers. Billy Wolfram knew every trick in the book.

Billy determined to call on these assets and try a different system of working, wandering as far as possible across the tracks. The biggest obstacle now was simply getting started. Billy was lost without his internal guides.

He didn't have the slightest idea where to place his first brushstroke, and would constantly overthink his color choices. Billy knew that even if he managed to swipe some acrylic onto the canvas, enhancing that single stroke would take hours. With these incessant deliberations, it seemed his stylistic expertise was more of a hindrance than a help. He paced the studio in exasperation, lost within his crippled instincts.

Hours passed; the canvas remained untouched. Billy had to laugh at the irony. He had been painting for over 20 years and never before experienced the passage of time. He now ached through every instant, feeling like fire ants were crawling across his body. Billy Wolfram had been spoiled and never had to confront the tedium and physical exertion involved in creating art. He took a large book on Eastern art from the shelves in the living area and flipped through it for another hour while eating a bowl of Cheerios.

While scanning the reproductions in this book, Billy came across a particularly striking mandala and tried a little exercise. With his keen pictorial imagination, he focused his eyes on the brightly colored painting while simultaneously visualizing the sound of the Hail Mary. He began to silently recite the words, following their spiraling movement as they rotated through his mind. From its repetitively circular rhythm, Billy now knew, without a doubt, that the terse Western prayer had been written in the form of a mantra, and was, like any mantra, the verbal correspondent to a mandala.

The use of symmetry in these Eastern paintings was astonishing. Apparently, these geometric figures represented the universe in Hindu and Buddhist symbolism. Carl Jung, who collected mandalas and later integrated them with psychoanalysis, had written in the book's foreword that they represented a dreamer's pursuit of completeness and self-unity.

Billy had finally found the catalyst for his show. It happened on a day that he was honestly on the verge of giving up . . . his inner voice had gone hoarse from repeating incentives to remain focused. As a desperate means of getting under way, Billy reverted to the most fundamental geometric forms. Those basic shapes, like squares, triangles, and curves, Galileo wrote, had been used in the creation of the universe. Reaching to the top of a supply cabinet, Billy randomly grabbed a previously unused brush and dipped its virgin bristles into an unfinished pigment.

After a long minute, he stepped up and thoughtlessly dabbed a single red circle onto the center of the canvas. Frustrated and expecting the worst, he moved back about ten feet. Billy slowly scrutinized it, and finally marveled at the perfection of the red sphere and its sublime coherence on the flat white field. By now Billy had learned not to question the rare offerings of chance, and, however small, he considered this a significant start. Dropping the brush into a can of cleanser, he walked out of the studio.

Billy had a light meal, wondering, as he ate, about the significance of that spontaneous red circle he had left on the canvas. Shaped like a dome, or a blood blister that had risen over time, the circle was beyond all his expectations. Despite his shackled instincts, Billy had already started to envision a few sequential brushstrokes to supplement the round shape, but he knew from experience that it was best to stifle further conjecture on his work in progress until returning to the studio in the morning. For now Billy needed some diversion to help him relax.

He rose and dropped his plate into the sink, then walked over and slowly pulled the cover off of the mahogany billiard table, folding the cloth sensuously like a satin sheet, as if he were preparing a bed for a night of love. He grabbed a tray of vibrantly colored pool balls from a cabinet and cautiously emptied them across the playing surface. The gleaming colors silently rolled in steady alignment across the green felt.

Billy was bending over the table, about to take his first shot, when his legs began shaking uncontrollably. Stunned and acting reflexively, he leaned against the table until regaining enough balance to straighten up. Billy hesitantly scanned the green surface, seeing the minute red dot on the new cue ball, which had arrived by messenger only three days earlier. The Monarch Billiards Company, typically so reliable, had mistakenly sent him a cue ball from an old—and seldom played—form of English snooker, rather than the usual cue that he'd ordered. Billy braced himself against the mahogany rails, all color draining from his face.

Billy slowly came to terms with the connection between the dot on the ball and in the painting he'd just begun, and speculated on the nature of these corresponding images. In the end, he concluded that it didn't matter if the spotted snooker ball had influenced his starting brushstroke or was merely a coincidence. Billy had found a nexus, and the fact that there was a definite correlation didn't diminish his sense of satisfaction. If anything, he had found another facet to the game of pool . . . a harmony between one passion lost and another found.

He continued to study the table as if it were a canvas. All these possibilities seemed logical gifts of chance, which he would have jumped at without question in the past, but he still hadn't regained the confidence he'd lost at the Met.

After doing nothing but play pool for the next two days, Billy heard a familiar sound coming from the windows overlooking the courtyard. Lying in bed with a reading light on, he saw the raven battering the glass with its beak. It was loudly and rapidly pecking with immortal stamina. Billy got out of bed and opened the window, hitting the switch for the seldom-used track lights.

"I only have a short time, so listen carefully." The raven, in fact, spoke without any of its usual self-amusing accents or airs, and the tone of its voice had a single function. "Are you an idiot? Haven't you learned anything from your recent obsession with this game? Doesn't your loss of time parallel events from your past, when hours simply evaporated without your awareness? I am, of course, referring to those long days in the studio when you painted, obliviously and nonstop, straight through the night. It wasn't that long ago.

"Also, I am taking a liberty by informing you that your intuition is about to return, and you must be ready to follow its pent-up demands. You've already had fleeting moments, I suspect, when you've recognized this renewal. However, since your trauma, you've become overvigilant about such things, and feared to even consider the possibilities. Don't you understand that, by no longer trusting your instincts, you have sabotaged your greatest assets?

"Listen to an old bird. Your renewed lapses in time—no matter what the reason—signal that you are on the verge of some resolution, and you must appreciate its significance. I cannot say if it will lead to a return of your art, but recovering this harmonic flow is far more important than the painting itself.

"I can offer you this advice. You should open your mind to something beyond the lovely sounds of pretty balls clicking and rolling. Lately, I've watched you slowly adopting an unremitting state of repose, passively observing your surroundings. This can be comforting and informative, but some very substantial changes are coming, and you simply must prepare yourself to take action at any moment.

"Be well, Billy . . . when you see it, you'll know what you must do. I won't return again until you truly need me."

It was the briefest appearance by the raven, and as it flew off, Billy had a feeling that he should take very seriously every word just spoken by the disheveled immortal.

Most cultures have possessed systems to foretell fate. Originally, the *Sortes Virgilianae* was a Roman method of divination. The practitioner would arbitrarily open Virgil's poem *The Aeniad*, and the first verse haphazardly touched by his fingertip contained the prophetic response. It might have been a warning, a prediction, or some message from a relative in the legions, far off at war in a Germanic province.

At the height of their power, Romans were obsessed with any practice that could portend the future, whether by flipping indiscriminately through Virgil or examining the intestines of sacrificed calves and goats. Based on the oracular results, they made both serious and superfluous decisions. Citizens used these systems to guide their love lives and business affairs, and generals devised military strategies for the protection of the empire. They would consult the poem, for example, when deciding the most propitious time for an invasion.

When the Catholic Church became the empire's official religion, the Bible supplanted Virgil as the authorized text. Although the Church renamed the divination process the *Sortes Biblicae*, Romans, including educated Christians, continued to use the original title. These visionary rites grew over time and were eventually accompanied by books that contained strict rules and instructions for the interpretation of these random verses. Over the centuries, however, the attitudes of those men in power changed, and they covered up the secret, abstruse knowledge within these ancient disciplines, at first slowly and cautiously, by filling the books with extrapolations and interpolations, and later either hiding them away or destroying them by fire. The true wisdom, for the most part, has completely vanished.

As for the *Sortes*, believers had little trouble extracting endless implications in Virgil's fragmentary verses, or the prophetic chapters of the Bible. This was particularly true with the Bible, a book consisting mainly of signs and symbols. With endless interpretations, the Scriptures can be manipulated to suit any desired outcome. The written word can delight with its connotations, innuendo, and rhythms, and be treacherous in its ability to deceive.

Volumes have been written about decoding runes and deciphering the hexagrams of the *I Ching*. No one had ever considered looking into the random formations of multicolored balls. But Billy had his painter's eye to anticipate shape, and his vision was filled with profound wonders.

Billy saw a surprising amount in the chance structure of balls settling to a stop after each shot. Interpreting these abstract configurations was different than using books or proscribed systems, despite their complexity. It also saved so much valuable time and energy when his purpose was to simply crack the balls as hard as possible, intending to disperse the pack as widely as possible, ignoring the game's customary objective of knocking each ball into a designated pocket. He could overlook other superfluous details, as well—such as accuracy, finesse, and precision. Scanning the bank shots, caroms, and combinations, then making sense of the remaining abstract structures, was also entirely unlike thumbing through the index of a book. There were no illustrations in any reference book where Billy could find any resemblance to a clump of 11 balls shaped precisely like a torn beehive. By constantly examining the radiant spheres' formations after each shot on his large emerald tablet, Billy had invented a kinetic version of the *Sortes*.

If the old bird continued to be accurate in his predictions, Billy didn't mind moving in stages. He'd already accepted the amount of time and difficulty involved in a return to painting. By now he had surrendered all doubts and took the immortal creature very seriously, and the raven's confirmation had provided the frustrated artist with a long-sought sense of optimism.

Billy had reached that fortuitous moment with pool when he found himself in the same place he'd once been while painting, becoming one with the cue as he had with the brush, and not aiming but relying on pure intuition. He was convinced that from this point, it would be a matter of weeks before he could take this precious state and transfer it from the pool table back to his art. His mind was so crammed with optimistic plans and speeding ideas that there was neither time nor space remaining for reason. Billy thought this so-called switch would be as simple as carrying rolls of new canvas into the studio.

Only now had Billy begun to feel discouraged and upset about this entire fiasco. He had no idea what he was supposed to do next. He hated being stuck in uncertainty, wasting his time with nothing to show for it. He realized how out of control this had become, diving into complete recklessness. The painter, of all people, had forgotten to take those few steps backward and pause, until he'd seen its progression from each diverse perspective. He made the mistake of indulging himself in continuous, thoughtless action without a moment's rest, and this fatigue quashed his ability to trust his own insights.

Despite the realizations and frustrations in his moment of clarity, Billy had a literal aching in his gut to pounce at the table and continue to mindlessly blast away until escaping into a complete illusion. He understood that the sensation was bogus, of course, and entirely unconnected to his original intent, but he didn't care. The mesmerizing green landscape yanked on him seductively. For more than two weeks, the desperate artist had relied on it like a powerful drug.

Billy couldn't focus and his thoughts were vague and dim. His mind was like an old, handmade map that had lain neglected for years in bright sunlight and was now too torn and faded to indicate the thieving crossroads, sharp turns, and dead ends. He sat about half an hour, antsy . . . sipping from a glass that was already drained, and replaying the past week . . . fast-forwarding like a tape recorder . . . stopping when he was coming up on . . . Saturday morning. That was it. He was so sure that he forgot to press "stop" and, instead, went right to "play." That can break a tape recorder, he thought.

It was the day a loud, terrible fight broke out between two parking lot attendants down on the street, just as Billy had anxiously grabbed his cue stick and headed for the table. He always left the balls in the rack after finishing; it was a superstition and courtesy to both himself and the game. Bending over the table, he was tempted to go to the window and check out the fight below. The sound from the street kept getting louder. Some coworkers yelled encouragement; others tried to separate the two men. Billy stood firm and rammed the cue ball into the pack. A woman next door screamed from her window, threatening to call the police if the brawl continued.

Billy now calmly approached the table and walked himself once more through that moment. He wanted to recreate the exact progression, hoping it would validate every factor of the memory. Saturday morning, despite the ruckus in the street and a woman's strident threats, he circled the table, chalking his stick for his second shot. Hunching above the cue ball, Billy noticed a lone 12 ball, lying apart from the pack and perfectly aligned for a successful bank shot. He yielded to temptation and reverted to the game's true objective. He tapped the cue ball into the 12. The lavender-striped globe caromed off the rail and rolled softly across the lawn of green felt, dropping quietly into a burnished leather pocket.

His thin body trembled. He suddenly understood how much he'd forgotten during his obsessive rampage. He had entirely overlooked essential attributes like grace, fluidity, and precision, which are by-products of that elusive trait called "touch."

The course now seemed remarkably clear as he grabbed a stick and tossed a few balls around the table. The answer was in the most fundamental change possible, and Billy was anxious to get under way.

This task couldn't only be about the chaos theory or esoteric analogies to Roman rituals. It was time to stop bruising balls with excessive force and expounding on their mysterious random arrangements. He might as well be deciphering the shapes of passing clouds. Billy desperately needed participation and interaction, and he wanted to line up a shot, gently stroke his stick, and sink the ball in the thick leather pocket. This was the game's purpose, after all. He wanted to aim, which was creative, and if he succeeded, that was a goal.

Since Marta had left the loft, while aimlessly wandering and wasting time Billy longed for a goal to meet . . . any sense of purpose leading to something productive. He fully appreciated every aspect in the act of creating, from beginning to end. It wasn't solely through intuition either, but through the wisdom of his experience and overcoming previous failures. Billy needed a more competent universe around him, giving him the opportunity to compensate for everything he'd screwed up and tossed away.

Besides, he'd grown sick of keeping constant vigil over the capricious arrangements of spheres. A crucial step in that last plan wound up being unbearably passive, without any objective or aspiration. Art involved precision and finesse. It had nothing to do with obliterating balls with brute force and accessing the results, as if the best artist of his generation were an accountant calculating an actuary table. Once he discovered the proper way to proceed, the change occurred rapidly. While still thinking clearly, he concluded that the universe demands a return to order and exactitude, even in the most chaotic situations.

Billy Wolfram started to paint.

8

Producing 25 paintings in three weeks, Billy had come out of
his self-imposed desert. Like Moses, he had seen the Promised
Land, though he would not enter, not in his lifetime.

The day after the opening, Tippy had sent a magnum
of Mumm's and a box of Cuban cigars. There were over 40 messages on
his answering machine. The newspapers were unanimous: *Wolfram has
attained a new depth of spirituality, merging Eastern and Western disciplines
into a unique third. His colors' texture fits the subject perfectly, appearing primitive from one angle and brilliant from another.*

Billy's only interest was returning to the pool table. After the tension
of the show and the debacle with Marta, he just wanted to find a way to get
back into the flow as quickly as possible . . . whether it was through the precision he'd just rediscovered or slamming billiard balls into chaos in search
of a half-cocked divination. What had at first been a gift had now become
a curse. Billy needed only to follow the certainty of his intuitions, allowing
him the confidence to infuse each painting with his own insight and stunning technique, but the powerful and pure flow had been transformed by
his obsession for shooting pool. Billy had hoped it would lead him back to
his art, but he discovered that gaining access through these superficial and
abusive means was more like the actions of a drug addict than those of a
true artist with such enormous potential.

Billy's complete absorption was partially snapped when thick globs of sweat began flowing from his forehead onto the precious green felt. Somewhat dazed, he pulled away from the table long enough to splash cold water onto his face and throw open every window in the loft. He then returned to the game in a complete stupor.

Unbeknownst to Billy, the building's boiler had unexpectedly gone into overdrive, sending up unnecessary heat. The entire building was sweltering hot. The boiler was new and supposedly required little maintenance. The superintendent made a futile attempt to fix the thermostat but decided the best course of action was to shut the boiler down until a plumber could come in the morning. The tenants were moving onto the sidewalk.

"God forbid this should happen in August!" a silver-haired fellow said. "A person could die of heat prostration. As I was evacuating my place, the radio said the temperature was 48 degrees. We're all fortunate that the weather is so warm for January."

The tenants were gathered on the sidewalk out front, drinking water and talking in small groups. A young woman was sitting huddled on the stoop barefoot, wearing nothing but a tightly cinched terrycloth robe. She had just gotten out of the shower and, hearing the shouting and continuous stomping of feet on the stairway, assumed the place was on fire. A woman noticed her predicament and sent her husband back to their studio to grab some slippers for her to wear. He returned quickly and handed her some rubber slippers and a trench coat. The neighbors applauded, treating him like some sort of hero but, aside from a flushed face and drenched shirt, he was fine.

Three teenage brothers who lived on the top floor tossed around a football on the street, and some of the men joined in. Somebody bought a large tray of coffees and a sack of powdered donuts from the bodega around the corner. The gathering of sweltering tenants had turned festive, resembling a block party.

The young woman in the borrowed slippers was the only one at the impromptu gathering to mention Billy's absence, adding he was probably away at some exhibition. Many of those present immediately turned indignant, making embittered remarks about the prestigious Wolfram. Over the years, they had grown to mistake his solitude as aloofness and superiority. An elderly couple that had never met him announced they no longer considered him a neighbor.

Despite this increasing vitriol, a few of the younger tenants jumped to his defense. Whenever they inadvertently ran into him on the stairs, he had always stopped to greet them and chat, cordially and sincerely. They argued that the same hypocrites now ranting against him had previously been intrigued by Wolfram's image as a loner but refused to accept him now that these quirks affected them personally. Elsa, now the only tenant in the building who actually knew Billy, had rushed to Bucharest to see her hospitalized mother three days earlier. Unfortunately, she was the only resident who might have had either the ability or willingness to contact Billy.

All the while Billy remained upstairs, oblivious to the tenants gathered outside, as he persisted with a game he'd been playing nonstop for the past 18 hours. He couldn't miss, moving around the table with a flawless rhythm until the cue stick appeared to fuse with his arm as he continued knocking in ball after ball with the same steady speed and precision.

He didn't actually feel the stifling heat, but eventually he observed expanding pools of water forming on the new green felt of his precious table. The sweat was flowing from his forehead, chest, and forearms. In some sort of trance, Billy made one more unconscious concession to the heat before returning to the game. He grabbed a large towel from the bathroom and soaked it under the cold-water faucet before wrapping it around his neck. Though it cooled him for a short time, the towel soon dried out and he could only use it to wipe perspiration from his forehead. The windows remained wide open, and Billy never looked toward them to see the fierce array of clouds, the blue and black color of dead blood to the north. He was girded in towels, his eyes focused on a green field covered with large boulders shaped like globes. By early evening, a ferocious blizzard attacked New York with tremendous speed and force.

By midnight the temperature had plummeted to 11°F, abetted by 45-mile-per-hour winds. The freak cold front caught the local weathermen off guard and bulletins immediately filled all media airways. They explained that the storm was due to a meteorological phenomenon called an "Arctic Express," and by morning the storm would dump 25 inches of snow on the city, with drifts that reached eight feet.

The other people in the building had sealed their windows shut hours earlier. Some had electric space heaters and huddled around them. Billy, still in a T-shirt and jeans, felt nothing. At this point, the billiard oracle kept him free-falling deeper into the flow, completely sealed off from the material world, including all physical sensation of the elements. Cold is a more devious condition than heat. It left no drops of sweat on the spotless green felt as a warning to the oblivious Billy Wolfram, who finally dropped to the floor, dreamily and heedlessly beginning to freeze to death.

Billy lay on the floor, curled and facedown like a fallen leaf, trying to hear the familiar voice behind him. It was barely audible, as if the words were trapped in the shrill, ferocious wind. Still, in his semi-delirious state, he strained to rotate his head toward the window.

"Oh, please, I implore you, do not move," the raven pleaded somberly. "Please . . . rest yourself."

Billy had already turned enough to give the raven a quizzical look . . . as if to ask, *Why are you here?*

"You still don't fully understand, do you, Billy? I constantly keep watch over you. Whether I'm in your sight on a window ledge, caged in that regrettable petting zoo, or flying through a parched valley in the Ukraine, I follow the course of your day.

"I also remember it all, particularly a recent morning. In a rare lucid moment, you realized how you foolishly sped through your task, virtually inviting it to fail. That kind of reckless, blind haste is a form of hubris, you know?

"But you vowed to amend that error and also discovered an effective way to maneuver through the next step. Suddenly you appeared to have control again.

"Unfortunately, you quickly reverted to behavior that was frighteningly similar to your earlier malaise. Within four or five hours, you were moving thoughtlessly around the table at a progressively faster pace. I'm sure you've heard that the textbook definition of *insanity* is repeatedly making the same mistake.

"At that point, I was flying over a very distant shoreline, but I suspected you'd passed the point of no return. I have just completed an arduous trip to verify this fear and, to my great regret, found I was correct.

"Billy, this erratic behavior during the storm epitomizes your problem over the last year. As a result of your arrested development, and other psychological damage from your childhood, you were overwhelmed by a sequence of misconstructions and conflicts. When you've stripped yourself of hope and discipline, this is the consequence. Over the past year, this desperation has driven you from your old productive seclusion to this restless, impenetrable isolation.

"In the face of this dilemma, your solution worsened the problem. I think that doctor was correct in his diagnosis. Your moods lately have swung with alarming speed. You flipped from irritability and depression into this compulsion as quickly as an acrobat doing a somersault. These reckless, disproportionate responses grew with each new crisis like the links of a chain. Finally, you were dragging around this chain of obsessions, and the weight increased with time.

"It consumed all your patience, prohibiting you from understanding and attending to your place in the world. When you surrendered all your focus to this extravagant game, you lost contact with your greatest inspirations, the common joys. You no longer walked each morning to watch the freshly cleansed sun ascending from the East River. For months now, you haven't glimpsed at a row of your beloved old brownstones. You once stared at them for hours, entranced by the lines of unresolved space as the surface of their façades met the palatial sky.

"Tonight, as those ominous clouds approached, you were too consumed by those unrelenting pool shots to raise up your eyes and heed the warning. You ignored the elements themselves, Billy. A year ago, you would have proceeded cautiously, through action and repose, instead of accelerating into a frenzy of oblivion."

Billy had twisted his body, colored dark blue like an avenging Hindu god, into a fetal profile. From this position, he muttered a few defiant words to the harbinger at the window.

He thought he had grown close with the bird, but he couldn't deal with its prolix badgering . . . all this recapping of his mistakes. Billy had typically found its rants entertaining, even on that first night when he thought the raven was a figment of his anxious dreams, but right now he lost his patience.

"Please, stop! I have already numbered my mistakes. Why do you reprimand me like this? I am aware of my awful decisions. If you insist on rambling on, can you at least tell me who sent you to me? Why me?"

"Please, Billy . . . even now I cannot speak of those things. I have already revealed more than I should have. You can't question me about these larger matters any longer.

"I can tell you why I was recapitulating the events leading to your demise. It is partly a result of my frustration, perching here, unable to offer any aid. I hope you haven't thought I've come to judge or place blame on you or anyone else. Such issues are pointless and completely insignificant right now. Mainly, it is my duty to detail certain matters, despite this regrettable moment. Believe me . . . I am well aware how difficult this must be for you but, as a messenger, this is what I do.

"I must inform you on some particular issues and reassure you on others. Excuse me for saying this, but there is not much time. You see, one of my most important functions is being there at your end, escorting you, as it were, into your next stage. Ironically, that marks the final instant of both our tasks.

"There are several subjects to touch on, including why . . . Oh, Billy! I now see you've decided to stop listening, haven't you? You're convinced that the sole purpose of my jabbering is to torment you. I sympathize, but despite that scowl of exasperation on your face, I'm afraid I must continue. Yes, my friend, I've seen that smirk on your lips since alighting here and even detected a momentary glint of rage in your eyes.

"Don't you trust me by now, Billy? I've already made clear that these affairs are beyond my control. I'll explain another underlying motive. Though your body remains motionless, I fear that vestiges of your mind and spirit are quite active but confused, and are clouding your full perception. I drone on this way to capture your attention. Anger and frustration can force a person in your state to slow down and focus. In that sense,

I believe I have succeeded, and if this small victory required being the target of your acrimony, I don't mind. But I've come a long way, Billy, and this is the culmination of my assignment. Actually, *both* of us have come a long way together, and I beg that we continue.

"I fear I've used that phrase about being only a bird and mimic too often, usually to deflect questions I was forbidden from answering. But the fact remains that, aside from my age and history, I *am* nothing more than a raven, and language is my one enduring strength. I manipulate others by using every language extant in this modern world. I've witnessed so many more tongues vanish over these past millennia.

"If I could make you listen some other way, I would. I recall a fellow raven and I attending drive-in movies, probably during the fifth decade of this century. We watched from the same lower branch of a leafy aspen on a hillside that overlooked the cars and gigantic screen.

"Unlike an effective gesture used by the characters in those films, I'm not able to shock you out of your hysterics with a slap to the face. I suppose the reason is fairly obvious, since I have no hands, only talons.

"Dousing you with cold water is also out of the question, for the exact same reason . . . no hands. You must see that I have only my voice to bring you to your senses.

"You must recognize that, under the current circumstances, I'm your only connection to the rest of the world. You've never felt comfortable giving others too much of yourself. This probably goes back to the damage caused by your father and brother abandoning you. There are also the many friends that you've cut off from your life. As I've said, the reasons such things happened are meaningless. What matters is reuniting you with the assembly.

"Do you know this *assembly* I'm referring to? Well, that was the precocious word that *you* yourself used as a child. It was far beyond the vocabulary of a six- or seven-year-old boy, but on one night when he took your mother and you out for her birthday to her favorite restaurant, you heard your favorite young priest evoke the term three times during a single dinner, and for the rest of the night you kept repeating the word.

"I am certain you'd give up your money and success simply to return to that childhood and your fellow parishioners. You needed to be a part of that resolute gathering for an hour each week. It was the only time in your life that you experienced a genuine sense of belonging and, through that belonging, could accept the embrace of peace and protection. Think back to how engrossed you felt, awaiting your beloved mystery language, '*Dominus vobiscum.*' "

The bird spoke and then paused, as if actually receiving the blessing, and responded, " '*Et cum spiritu tuo.*'

"In your precocious teens, you lost your faith and sealed yourself off from the church. I can concur with much of your frustration in dealing with organized religion. If I told you how the leaders of various Christian sects— from the beginning to this present day—have indiscriminately altered and misused His true teachings, it would further confirm your doubts.

"But the failings of men cannot diminish the goodness and truth of Jesus and other wise and holy men like Him. I don't care what religion you subscribe to, Billy, but all humans need hope in order to survive and live with an objective. They must aspire to some goal. That goal, in turn, will inspire them.

"And you confirmed my contention when you realized that the simplest solution to your task was a return to the game's customary rules and purpose. It's a bit like Occam's razor, isn't it?

"No matter, Billy. The point is you were tired of the vigilant passivity and required a goal that would attain a worthwhile purpose. You again valued precision and finesse, rather than all that vulgar force and brute strength, which accomplish nothing.

"Don't you see that faith is a form of finesse? It is the natural consequence of this sense of 'touch' you've spoken of, when everything comes together in an effortless, fluid harmony. Belief in a higher power is the first and final link in your exalted *flow*. I could waste time, using arcane theological terms, clarifying that statement, but let's call it a chain of binding energy, connecting everything in the universe. You know, one cause leads to another, and that to another . . . on and on."

Billy rattled on the splintery old wood floor, and the raven spoke faster, its cadence somehow producing a soothing effect.

"When you keep moving without any purpose or restraint, you'll eventually accelerate into the hollow flux of madness, caused by all the long-suppressed fears opening in a single moment.

"If I had the ability, I would have come and somehow pulled you completely out of this tainted, fallacious *zone*, which was like an abandoned mine shaft where you had been descending increasingly deeper. As soon as you returned to the *flow*, you again lost all control and recklessly ventured too far into that mine, unaware of the distance you'd strayed. Eventually, you took a misstep in that primordial darkness and began falling, plummeting, downward.

"There are many levels to the shaft, and each is filled with illusory paths that lead nowhere. They are crammed with all those negative traits you've realized you must escape. When you saw the flaw of blasting the pool balls around without aiming and without any goal, you needed to return to poise and skill, accepting your life was bereft of any purpose.

"Well, this mine resonates with a horrifying lack of purpose or end point. There is no light—and I mean darkness where even I would be unable to maneuver. Even if your mind maintained its former clarity, you aren't authorized to explore this environment. Whatever is concealed in that complex of shafts and tunnels is reserved for those firmly anchored by the strength of their belief. Their faith guides them and shields them from danger.

"This is how you debased the *zone*. Even if I were capable, there isn't time to reveal the true cosmological meaning of this condition, or explain the extent of its sublime magnitude. Do you recall my last visit at your loft? I concluded by assuring you that your return to the zone was more significant than your return to painting. Of course, since you'd always accessed it with such ease, as an extension of your powerful intuition, I assumed you'd continue to use it wisely, and with clear intentions. It is a form of spiritual gluttony to exploit this gift in such a manner. You know now that your lack of discipline tainted its truth, and what you sought so badly became your death sentence.

"If only you had developed some modicum of faith. I'm aware, of course, of your experience while examining the stained glass in that nearby church, and mentioning it later to Marta during your conversation. It might have helped to stop your fatal backslide and supplied you with the finesse of grace and the necessary discipline.

"Still, despite your continuous falls, your original intentions always persisted righteously. As I've told you, Billy, by that time you were out of your mind—in every sense of the phrase. You bear no responsibility. Throughout your life you remained true to the man you were, and in the past weeks you remained true to the man you'd become.

"I can feel a difference in you as you lay there. You've settled down, your fear subsiding. It always happens at this moment.

"Now we can communicate, and I will do what I can to prepare you for what lies before you. Sometimes the greatest gift you get is to have it all stripped away from you. You'll be staring into a deep abyss, and be given the opportunity to discover what birds, since they fly with impunity, have always known.

"We'd gather near some precipice. It was either a man-made bridge or some jagged stone cliff, carved over millennia by nature's elements . . . the air . . . water, or some volcanic eruption.

"Anyway, we would watch from our vantage point, and observe the hopeless and lost beings, who developed immunity to all consequence, and finally chose suicide. Mainly, they've cut themselves off from that persistent intangible voice within, the voice that reassured them they were exactly where they were meant to be at that instant in their lives. It is another aspect of human nature that's never changed, and persists to these times.

"As they stand at that irreversible juncture, their authentic intuition whispers a sincere and explicit warning to their soul.

"Wait! Excuse me! Maybe it's 'an explicit warning *from* their soul *to* their soul,' since the soul both gives and receives.

" 'Stay put . . . don't dare move a muscle,' the voice tenderly cries out. 'Stand still with your two feet firmly planted on terra firma. If you twitch a finger, disaster will follow.'

"Of course, when faith is lost, all trust is vanquished, and they reject this one indisputable language . . . persisting with their final ritual. We've seen it time and time again. They suck one final breath from the swirling winds, and casually step off the edge.

"Some have many to blame, while others struggle until they lose, cultivating more and more reasons to justify their actions. Dante did a good job, but omitted a few vices from the list. I know them all, but I'll name just a few. There is insecurity, fear, bitterness, grief, hubris, and greed . . . always so much greed. In these times, many offer their deficiencies as an excuse . . .

like loss of power, loss of love, or loss of hope. I suppose it is understandable to pity some of these explanations, but the enlightened regard all as pretexts, resulting from lack of courage, and consider all defenses completely inconsequential.

"Once that irreversible action occurs, they invariably reach the same conclusion."

"What?" Billy begged in a parched burst.

"When you leap or fall from a very high place, the landing is dreadfully painful, but as you soar down, seeming to defy entropy and gravity, and all other rules and laws that this expanding cosmos utilizes to restrict and hold us in check, you quickly learn two very important lessons."

"What?" Billy looked upward, barely able to speak, his body, mind, and spirit cramped and bent by pain. "I thought you were giving me the lesson."

"It's a big lesson, a message of advice within a lesson . . . a tutorial." The raven seemed to enjoy Billy's frustration. "First, that the action you took was quite foolish. Second, the plunge downward, though glorious, is astonishingly quicker than the ascent to the top."

"That's a contradiction," Billy whispered. "Get away. You've just slipped and proven yourself as diabolical. I always knew it."

"Yes, Billy, it is a contradiction. It most surely is." The raven flew to the floor beside Billy and offered him a piece of bread that was suddenly in his beak. He ran his sharp talons softly across Billy's numb, bluish hand as a gesture of comfort. "By the way, I have no truck with the adversary, my poor misguided Billy Wolfram. It is important you be assured of that one thing."

"What should I have done?"

"Exactly what you did. Marta came into the dressing room and forgave you for the years you treated her like another hired hand, ignoring her womanly charms and sexual desirability, as well as the boneheaded remarks made in your seizure of jealousy. She suspected your behavior was due to some suppressed trauma from your past.

"You could have taken her to your place, determined to patch up things, trying to resume a relationship that never really existed. It might have meant spending weeks confirming her assumption, revealing that this trauma was never suppressed, but continued as an ongoing ordeal.

"You could have revealed everything, shedding a spotlight on the true cause of her misconceptions and your sexual immaturity and omissions.

"However, no matter how many times you clarified her questions and made love, in the end it would have been a patch-up job.

"I will tell you this much. By that opening-night reunion, you had an inkling your sadness was only partly due to the inability to paint. The greater cause of this sorrow was a change that was crucial to your future and had been growing, imperceptibly, for a long time within you.

"All change is disruptive, confusing, and difficult, especially at such a propitious point in one's career. You somehow realized that solitude was critical in bringing this transformation to fruition, and such solitude required patience and silence.

"Humans are in a continual process of becoming something else. The world changes us from the outside and we change the world from inside ourselves. We create the future that we inhabit through a series of fluctuations, constantly altering one thing and adjusting another. It is a tiring procedure.

"Every internal modification must be allowed to develop in serenity and quiet, whether it is the gestation of a child or a change in our future being. I tell you this not only because, afterward, the sadness will dissipate, but also because the changes within are invariably superior to those that are constantly forced upon us by external events. These are not really changes, but adjustments to situations.

"You also knew, by the return of your intuition, that a period of seclusion was indispensable in recovering the intersection of all consciousness, which you had most recently referred to as 'locking in.' Learning this condition is as important as painting itself. You have only the slightest hint of its implications. Nonetheless, painting was always your means of getting to that place. Now your only chance of bringing about this growth and revitalization was continuing to live and work alone."

"Can't you have both?" Billy's words were now creeping out through sheer adrenaline, sometimes difficult to understand. "Do work and find love . . . cannot together?"

"Yes, some have done both, but their sacrifices were different than yours. Some don't need the solitude, which you have always carried around inside yourself. You love people, but not mankind in general. It's a trade-off in a life filled with all kinds of trade-offs and sorrow. One can't expect either happiness or genius to last. At first the light burns brightly, then begins to flicker, and eventually sputters out like those candles that float on oil."

"Changes from green to blue I glimpsed a moment that night?"

"Yes . . . like that. I have made this final visit to assure you that you can soar with the impunity of my fellow birds. I love you, Billy Wolfram, and soon you will fly."

The bird turned and glided silently back to the window. It was as if it were keeping a vigil. It didn't want to leave Billy and would continue talking until the painter had taken his final breath.

Billy was nearing death from exposure in his own home. The body had curled in a fetal position, thin and crooked like a dog's leg, no longer able to bend its neck and watch the raven's final speech.

"Let me assure you of one thing," the raven said from the windowsill, now completely white from the rush of snow, speaking so loudly the words echoed through the room. "Among the countless men and women I've been sent to visit over these past millennia, I have observed one abiding truism.

"Those artists possessing the greatest genius invariably confront the greatest hardships and obstacles throughout their lives. I have seen it time and time again.

"You may call them the fates, or the Lords of Karma, though names for such entities are meaningless. They have driven these remarkable painters and sculptors to face every conceivable deterrent. Each bit of torment, pain, and grief was a preparation for what lay ahead. The few that succeeded are counted as giants of art. You are familiar with most of them, though some remain unknown in the history of art. Billy?" The old black bird raised his voice. "Billy, listen to me! Do you know that? Can you hear me, Billy Wolfram?"

The old black bird paused a moment, then raised its voice. "Billy, listen to me! It is important. Do you know the *only* virtue that each of these diverse and gifted individuals had in common? They all possessed the courage to meet this life of adversity without ever giving in to despair. They would reach the very edge of that abyss, but never succumb to it."

The figure lay motionless on the floor, but his mind still flickered in dim delirium. This connoisseur of building material had never even noticed the unique floorboards made from old planks, thick as the beams of a ship.

Finally, a last sigh of consciousness rocked him gently on the deck of an old schooner ship. Billy's body, dark blue like the storm clouds, shuddered, and his dull eyes closed. Sensing young Wolfram had given up the ghost, the raven glided back down beside the dead artist, whispering a last demand.

"It's time your eyes remain shut, Billy Wolfram. Now is the time, so get on with it. Take that single step and fly."

Now that its vigil was over, the raven rose from the floor and through the window, disappearing north into the whiteout night of the great blizzard. Soon another bird soared down from the huge Port Authority building. It was a dove, gliding directly beside the long black wings, barely visible in the pale, frigid air.

Also available from Penguin

Void of Course
In these seventy-seven poems, Caroll's major themes—love, friendship, desire, time, memory, and, above all, the ever-present city—emerge in an atmosphere where dream and reality mingle on equal terms.
ISBN 978-0-14-058909-2

Fear of Dreaming
The Selected Poems of Jim Carroll
This volume collects selections from Carroll's first two works of poetry, *Living at the Movies*, published in 1973 when he was twenty-two, and *The Book of Nods*, released in 1986.   *ISBN 978-0-14-058695-4*

Forced Entries
The Downtown Diaries: 1971–1973
Intimate and revealing, *Forced Entries* chronicles Carroll's experiences during the early 1970s when he was a young and rising star in the creative and crazy downtown scene in New York City, providing a sometimes hilarious, sometimes frightening glimpse of people who tested the limits of life and sanity.   *ISBN 978-0-14-008502-0*

The Basketball Diaries
New York Times Bestseller
A diary of unparalleled candor that conveys Carroll's coming-of-age in the mid-1960s on the unforgiving streets of New York City—playing basketball, hustling, stealing, getting high, getting hooked, and searching for something pure.   *ISBN 978-0-14-010018-1*

Living at the Movies
In this, his first collection of poetry, Carroll transforms the everyday details of city life into poetry with language at once delicate, hallucinatory, and menacing.   *ISBN 978-0-14-042290-0*